LIFE IN THE TOMB

The publisher wishes to express his sincere thanks and gratitude to Mrs Aliki Vakirtzi for her kind permission to use George Vakirtzis' painting on the cover.

Originally published in Greek under the title Ἡ ζωή ἐν τάφῳ

Library of Congress Cataloging-in-Publication Data

Myriveles, Strates, 1892-1969.
    [Zoe en tapho. English]
    Life in the tomb / Stratis Myrivilis ; translated by Peter Bien, with an introduction by Speros Vryonis, Jr. and a foreword by Vangelis Calotychos.
        p. cm.
Translation of: He zoe en tapho.
    ISBN 1-932455-05-1 (pbk. : alk. paper)
    1. World War, 1914-1918—Fiction. I. Bien, Peter. II. Title.
PA5610.M9Z413 2003
889'.332—dc22

2003026291

First published in 2004 by:
Cosmos Publishing Co., Inc.
P.O. Box 2252
River Vale, NJ 07675
Phone: 201-664-3494
Fax: 201-664-3402
E-mail: info@greeceinprint.com
Website: www.greeceinprint.com

THE GREEK EXPERIENCE
Books, Music, Video, Art
www.GreeceInPrint.com
262 Rivervale Rd, River Vale, N.J. 07675
Tel 201-664-3494 Email info@GreeceInPrint.com

Printed in Greece

STRATIS MYRIVILIS

LIFE IN THE TOMB

Translated by
PETER BIEN

With an Introduction by
SPEROS VRYONIS, JR.

And a Foreword by
VANGELIS CALOTYCHOS

COSMOS PUBLISHING

LIFE IN THE TOMB

Life in the Tomb, a war novel written in journal form by a sergeant in the trenches, has been the single most successful and widely read serious work of fiction in Greece since its publication in serial form in 1923–1924, having sold more than 80,000 copies in book form despite its inclusion on the list of censored novels under both the Metaxas rigime and the German occupation. Published in nearly a dozen translations, it is the first volume of a trilogy containing *The Mermaid Madonna* and *The Schoolmistress with the Golden Eyes*, both of which have been available in a variety of languages.

Generally regarded as one of the most important works of modern Greek literature as well as one of the most sensitive novels to come out of the first world war, *Life in the Tomb* covers a wide range of human emotions in environments of both peace and war. Myrivilis has written a meditative, lyrical, yet harshly realistic account of trench warfare on the Macedonian front in 1917–1918. A young intellectual volunteers in a spirit of ardent patriotism and revolutionary idealism to serve on the side of Prime Minister Venizelos and the Allies. His letters to his girlfriend in Lesvos reveal an educated, sensitive man who soon learns how different reality is from dream as he confronts the boredom, mud, incompetence—and finally the brutality—of life in the tomb.

STRATIS MYRIVILIS

Stratis Myrivilis was a member of the Academy of Athens, and was nominated by the Greek Society of Authors for the Nobel Prize in 1960. A prolific writer, he was also an active journalist and broadcaster, being General Program Director for the Greek National Broadcasting Institute from 1936 to 1951 (excluding the period of German occupation, when he was dismissed because of a broadcast he gave calling on Greeks to resist). After the war he was elected president of the National Society of Greek Writers.

CONTENTS

Introduction by Speros Vryonis, Jr.   xi

Foreword by Vangelis Calotychos   xv

Historical Note   xxii

Translator's Preface   xxiii

Terms & References   xxvii

LIFE IN THE TOMB

1. In Front of an Old Chest (by Way of Prologue)   1
2. An End that Is a Beginning   5
3. The Deceased Die: End of Anointed Majesty   12
4. Balafaras   16
5. The Ships   20
6. Salonika   24
7. Marching   27
8. Blinded …   31
9. Constantine Palaiologos   33
10. Poppies on a Hillside   39
11. M'chaghilous   42
12. The Ghost Town   60
13. The Cyclops' Eye   65
14. Carrion   71
15. Digging   76
16. Animals   82
17. In the Woods   85
18. The Hour Glass   109
19. Anchorites of Lust   117
20. War's Bindweed   119
21. "… this lethargy anticipating death …"   122
22. Twelve Thousand Souls   133
23. Artillery Duel   137
24. Out of the Depths   142

25. Uncle Stylianos the Hunter   149
26. Moonlight in the Trench   153
27. The Concealed Poppy   157
28. Jacob   162
29. Balafaras at the Front   166
30. Three Nights   170
31. The Song of Life   178
32. In the House of Kindness   184
33. The Judgment of the Lord   190
34. Zavali Maiko   194
35. A Letter from Home   198
36. Longing for the Aegean   202
37. Face to Face   206
38. Court-Martial   209
39. The Condemned   217
40. The "Hellene"   225
41. Autumn Rains   228
42. Asimakis Garufalis the "Good-Looking Young Man"   231
43. How Zafiriou Died   236
44. The Parade   239
45. Mothers in Wartime   249
46. In the Mud   256
47. "A Voice has been Silenced"   262
48. The Two Heroes   268
49. Sacrifices to the Sun   280
50. *Coup de Main*   298
51. The Deserters   306
52. Alimberis Conquers His Fear of Shells   311
53. The Jack-of-all-Trades   318
54. Gas   321
55. Waiting for a Quarter Past Two—I   325
56. Waiting for a Quarter Past Two—II   333
57. Waiting for a Quarter Past Two—III   339

MAPS
    Greece and Environs   351
    Mytilene (detail)   352
    The Front (detail)   353

Introduction

*A*s is well known in the realm of modern Greek literature, *Life in the Tomb*, the semi-autobiographical novel by Stratis Myrivilis, was one of those rare literary events, achieving immediate success when it first appeared as a book in 1924. Furthermore, it has retained its freshness and its success has been, and will very likely continue to be, continuous. For the Greek reading public from the 1920s to the 1950s its historical background was a vital and living memory since many Greeks of the time had fought, or had sons who had fought, in the war that Myrivilis so skillfully describes. With the eruptions of violence in recent years in the Balkans, in the wake of the collapse of the Soviet Union, a reprinting of the English translation of *Life in the Tomb* seems most timely. The dissolution of Yugoslavia brought Slovenes, Croats, Serbs, Bosnian Muslims, Albanians, Montenegrans, and Slavo-Macedonians into violent confrontation. On the sidelines, Bulgars, Greeks, and Turks began to feel repercussions from this violence and to prepare themselves for the possible spread of conflict into their own lands. These recent events have vigorously stoked the still glowing embers of long-smoldering political and cultural conflict.

Historical memory and recent events surely have contributed to the current interest in Myrivilis' novel. However, two other factors have also contributed to its continued success. The first is the narrative perspective that Myrivilis chose from which to present his own experiences of World War I fought in the trenches of the Balkan front. This long ago attracted the notice of translators and students. His perspective is that of a soldier looking up from within the stinking, damp, slimy trenches. The view from the army mess was, monotonously, always the same. The constant companions in each trench were lice and worms. Indeed the dust jacket of the 1977 Bien translation features a soldier who in place of eyes has two cannon barrels that prevent him from seeing the countless long-bodied worms swimming in the tiny space before him.

In telling his tale, Myrivilis sketches in, one by one, recognizable social types whose features are exaggerated by the cruelty of war: the braggart, the coward, the opportunist, the peasant, the musician, the intellectual, the homesick boy-soldier. Some of his characters are sketched in bold colors: the general, all spit and polish, calculating advances and losses in terms of glory and power; the nascent village capitalist looking to turn everything to gold; the good-natured captain who sympathizes with the pain and suffering of his men; the brave, patriotic sergeant who in a fevered state arises in the night to relieve himself and accidentally falls into a deep abandoned cesspool and drowns in its fecal sea.

As the narrative slowly unfolds, these recognizable stereotypes crystallize into complex individuals with distinctive physical, psychological, and moral features, all responding in their own ways to exploding enemy shells, foiled reconnaissance sorties, and their own firing squads. The narrative pace is even, never rushed, and yet never unnecessarily prolonged, as Myrivilis prefers short vignettes to long chapters, *multum in parvo*.

The second factor contributing to the current interest in Myrivilis's book is its message, so resonant in our times, that there is little heroism in the impersonal killing and misguided patriotism of war. The real heroes in Myrivilis's war are the narrator, Sergeant Kostoulas, and the Slavo-Macedonian villagers of Velušino where he is sent to rest after having served strenuously in the front line trenches. Readers first meet these villagers in Chapter 32, "In the House of Kindness." The chapter's very title suggests the generosity and concern of the people of Velušino. The two principal characters there are the strong matriarch whose two sons were taken away and conscripted into the Bulgarian army, and her young daughter, who begins to fall in love with the narrator. They belong to a typically extended Slavic household whose members extend warm hospitality and understanding to the fatigued, lonely, and unhappy Greek sergeant. He exclaims:

But truly, at this point I am neither a Christian nor a Greek nor a

Serb, but simply a human being filled with expectations, nostalgia, and fatigue: an exhausted, contented human being who admires these people—envies them—for being the lovely, openhearted creatures of a beneficent God.

I wish to express gratitude to Peter Bien for first translating *Life in the Tomb* into English in 1977, and for seeing this new edition to press. Professor Bien is extremely well known within the small circle of Neohellenists. For those who have not had the pleasure of knowing him or his work, it suffices to say that Professor Bien, long the holder of an endowed chair in literature at Dartmouth College, is one of the founders of modern Greek studies in the New World, and that his scholarly, teaching, and organizational activities have been energetic, rich, and often influential. His colleagues honored him in 1997 with a Festschrift entitled *Greek Modernism and Beyond* in which, calmly but firmly, he defined his place in the scholarly landscape and the battles going on in the field of Modern Greek literary studies today. Speaking of three modes of literary discourse—premodernism, modernism, and postmodernism—he places his preference squarely between the old and the new, between premodernism and postmodernism, on the grounds that "postmodernism, unlike modernism . . . is now an entrée to Nothing." Besides his work as a translator, he developed, with the assistance of colleagues, one of the leading teaching manuals for Modern Greek. He was also one of those instrumental in founding the Modern Greek Studies Association and the *Journal of Modern Greek Studies*. His scholarly works remain seminal and have become classics within this field.

I must now confess a particular weakness for Myrivilis's *Life in the Tomb*, as it was my first exposure to the richness of modern Greek literature.

After graduating from college, I was fortunate to receive a Fulbright Fellowship to the American School of Classical Studies in Athens in 1950–51, and although the curriculum there was strictly classical (we read most of the ancient Greek text of Herodotus that year), many of the students took modern Greek lessons from Madame Zikou, a dynamic teacher who conveyed her enthusiasm for literature to us. I asked if she had an hour a week for me; she kindly consented, and after suggesting I read a volume of articles by a modern Greek journalist, she gave me the Greek text of *Life in the Tomb*. I had never heard of either the author or the work, but was immediately mesmerized by the text. I had never read literature in Modern Greek, only classical texts, and my learning of modern Greek in the family had come to a premature end when I turned ten and was shipped off to a military school. Thus the lexical richness of Myrivilis was something of a challenge, but an enchanting one. I slowly mastered the new words, many of them Turkish, Italian, and French. *Life in the Tomb* remains, even at this late date, my yardstick for all modern Greek literature, both because it exemplifies literary art at its best and because it proves, over and over again, that in war, as the Bible says, there is nothing new under the sun. Thus my life in Athens offered me two ultimate exercises in pleasure: the reading of the "exotic" Myrivilis, and active participation in Greek basketball as a member of the Athlitiki Enosis Ambelokipon team, which had a remarkably successful year.

Speros Vryonis, Jr.

Foreword

*I*t has always been my impression that Greeks are not avid letter writers. And I believe I am not alone in thinking this. Even at a time when
letter-writing was more in vogue than it is today, Greeks seemed too absorbed in their vital public culture and family affairs to care about corresponding. They preferred to exchange news regularly by word of mouth in
the village, in the neighborhood or *mahalás* of the small town, in the coffee
shop and, eventually, on the phone. It is surprising then that the first novel
of the modern Greek state, Panayiotis Soutsos's *Leandros* (1834), was an
epistolary novel. While it has much to commend it, its epistolary form
disappoints. It is chiefly comprised of letters from one central protagonist,
and the interplay of viewpoint is limited. The genre did not really take
hold in modern Greece. And the fictional diary, too, with its introspective
soul-searching, fared only marginally better. Despite the appeal of Goethe's
Werther in the nineteenth century and André Gide's techniques in the
twentieth, the epistolary form seems more suited to the isolating frigid
winters of New England than to the mild climate of the Aegean.

However, Greek literature can boast a healthy tradition of letter-writing in the shadow of death. Death does seem to focus the mind; after all,
one ultimately faces death alone even when surrounded by friends and
family. One of the most unique suicide notes in any literature is the poet
Kostas Karyotakis's of 1928. It includes a postscript written after a failed
suicide attempt, advising prospective suicides to avoid drowning by sea,

for "every so often, without comprehending how, my body would rise to the surface." In the Greek mythological and folk tradition, in particular, letters are forever anticipated from those exiled or from the dead. Indeed, one of the most prevalent and evocative exchanges of letters occurs in the return of birds from Hades. The birds bring back letters from the Underworld that the beloved has inscribed on the birds' wings. They dutifully carry the message to show the kinfolk:

> *Μά ἄν εἶσαι ἀπό τόν τόπο μου κι ἀπό τή γειτονιά μου,*
> *χαμήλωσε τίς φτερούγες σου τρία λόγια νά σοῦ γράψω,*
> *τό 'να νά πάς τῆς μάνας μου, τ' ἄλλο τῆς ἀδερφῆς μου,*
> *τό τρίτο τό φαρμακερό νά πάς τῆς ποθητῆς μου.*

> *But if you are from my homeland and from my neighborhood,*
> *Lower your wings so that I might write three words,*
> *Take one to my mother, and a second to my sister,*
> *And the third and most poisonous, take it to my beloved.[1]*

Stratis Myrivilis, the nom-de-plume of Stratis Stamatopoulos (1892-1969), confronted death far from his home very early in his life on several occasions. Indeed, no sooner had he left Mytilene (Lesbos), his home island, for Athens in 1911 to study and try out a career as a journalist than events led him to volunteer for the Macedonian front to fight in the First Balkan War. It would not be the last time. In the space of only a decade, he would leave time and time again, each time unsure that he would ever return home. In 1915, during World War I, Myrivilis was conscripted and sent again to Macedonia at the time of the schism between the Cretan politician Eleftherios Venizelos and forces loyal to the Germanophile king. In 1917, with Greece's eventual entry into the Great War on the side of the Allies, Myrivilis was mobilized with the Archipelago Battalion to Florina and Monastir. In 1919, as the rest of Europe was at peace after the war that was meant to end all wars, Myrivilis was being shipped off again, eastwards

---

[1] "A Song of Exile," from Nikolaos G. Politis, *Selections from the Songs of the Greek People*, No. 165.

this time, to join the ill-fated campaign for the liberation of the Greeks of Asia Minor. Hellenism's Catastrophe in 1922 bankrupted any visions of incorporating all Greek peoples of the Ottoman Empire within the borders of the Greek nation-state. Only in October 1922 was Myrivilis finally able to return home and slip quietly into a civilian way of life.

It is hard to imagine how such experiences play themselves out in the heart and mind of a young man. Of course, many of the writers who lived through these events, particularly in Asia Minor, wold make their mark on Greek literature in the following decades. Stratis Doukas, Elias Venezis, and Dido Soteriou placed oral testimony at the center of their fictionalized narratives. In Myrivilis's case, the material drawn from these experiences informed his novels *The Schoolmistress with The Golden Eyes* (1933) and *The Mermaid Madonna* (1949). As for *Life in the Tomb*, when he was away from the front writing as a journalist, he maintained a correspondence with two women: his future wife, Eleni Demetriou, and a reader, Eleni Mangana, whose letters from the Macedonian front in 1915–1916 have since been published. This correspondence anticipates the rhetorical strategy at the core of Myrivilis's more famous novel, Ἡ ζωή ἐν τάφῳ (*Life In The Tomb*). Originally written after Myrivilis's return to Mytilene in the journal Καμπάνα (*The Bell*), in forty-two installments from April 10, 1923 to January 29, 1924, the novel consists of letters written by a sergeant at the Macedonian Front in 1917 to his beloved back home. Sadly, we are informed very early on in the novel that "Sergeant Kostoulas was incinerated (by mistake) in the Bulgarian trenches soon after we overran them." Killed by his own men, our protagonist is stripped down to the bone by this "mistake":

> We found him burned to death, his face completely devoured by the flames, the entire front portion of his head a black and red mutilation recognizable only by three white marks engraved upon it—a row of teeth between tightly clenched jaws entirely stripped of flesh, and two globular eyeballs puffed out like a pair of ivory billiard balls. The lower right canine was covered by a golden crown, which glistened.

This stark description of our narrator in the first pages of the novel alerts us to the fact that neither the letters nor their writer will ever make it home. His addressee, his beloved, "whose name nowhere appears," will never hear from him or see him again. And these undelivered letters will assume the form of a diary entry by default as their exchange is left suspended in the space between self and projected addressee.

But the letters do in fact reach a wide readership thanks to the intervention of a young N.C.O. who discovers the wizened papers in a recovered pack belonging to Kostoulas. In the letters, the N.C.O. meets "a real man, but as quiet, sensible and reserved as a girl." And, in the episodes that follow, this peculiarly gendered voice brings private life, emotions, and musings to the fore in an analysis of the thoughts and actions of men thrown together in desperate circumstances. Like some of the canonical western women writers who made the letter or the diary their own, Myrivilis writes in the liberating space of interiority and beyond the confines of gendered hierarchies. In so doing, he changes the status of writing that speaks about war to propose a pacifist and anti-heroic alternative from the trenches. From "rats alley / Where the dead men lost their bones," as T. S. Eliot famously wrote in *The Waste Land*, the N.C.O. resolves to share the letters of this placid, feminine sensibility with "every woman touched by carnage, and beyond that, with every human being made destitute by war and standing now with outstretched hands, begging for love among all peoples of the world." The now redirected letters forsake their private dimension while retaining the sincerity and intimacy of a cherished, personal correspondence. The probing insights of one individual who experienced war in a specific place and time, far from home, unfold alongside the gradual stripping down of everything that that individual believes: who he is, why he is there, right down to the glistening canine tooth of his animalism. The effect is to lead us through nihilism and on to a greater humanity:

> In trench warfare, as you can see, a soldier is granted ample time to think. This is not good, because the more a soldier thinks the more his faith deserts him. The truly horrible thing is to wage war without believing in it, and in addition to lack an "unbelief" sufficiently strong to push you to the other extreme of denying war completely, come what may.

This "come what may" reinforces the book's anti-war sentiment, and is catholic in its condemnation. The protagonist knows that when those who fall for Faith and Fatherland seek their recompense from the Lord Almighty, God "will expectorate smartly in our eye with his holy spit."

To publish the sergeant's letters is like "resurrecting this gallant lad." And although the novel digs deep to claim the mythic and religious underlay of Christ's resurrection, the glint of the protagonist's lower right canine in death prevents us from seeing His kingdom. For it is difficult to achieve transcendence when the flesh is tortured so mercilessly. Perhaps it is better to think of *Life in the Tomb* as a reflection more on exhumation than on resurrection. In exhumation, the deceased are raised from the black earth and women who mourn them can throw off their clothes of mourning. In the words of the anthropologist Loring Danforth, exhumation is "associated with images of departure," since it marks a complete and final separation of the dead from the living and brings their relationship to an end. Paradoxically, however, exhumation also serves as a rite of incorporation and return, for the deceased are "not only leaving the world of the living," they are "coming back to it as well." The dead—who, at exhumation, are decomposed and are marked by their terrifying transformation—offer themselves to be reclaimed. Exhumation promises to return that which it cannot; Kostoulas's papers promise to bring our hero back to life in the hands of his beloved. Women have the last word. They control the gestures and symbols of interment and mediate the space between the living and the dead.

The task resurrection sets itself in the novel is reminiscent of the modernist novel's self-conscious anxiety about its ability to relive, revivfy, or to do anything from language's prison house. This anxiety is shared by another Greek modernist contemporary of Myrivilis's, Nikos Kazantzakis. In *The Life and Times of Alexis Zorbas* (in English translation, *Zorba the Greek*), Kazantzakis seeks to resurrect Alexis Zorbas and his philosophy by writing a novel about him. Throughout this novel, Zorbas's boss is unable to animate himself or the life around him. He has writer's block. But in the book's prologue, Kazantzakis sets himself this very task: "It is as if I wanted to exorcise [Zorbas's] death. I fear that this is not a book I'm writing; it is a memorial service." True to the tradition of hagiography alluded to in the work's Greek title, the presentation of the life and times of an improbable saint offers inspiration and moral instruction. It asks us to convert to its protagonist's philosophy.

Like Kazantzakis, Myrivilis shares a passion for the fate of the body in the hereafter. Orthodox doctrine distinguishes itself from other Christian teaching by asserting the fact that rebirth in the afterlife will also glorify and redeem the body. The righteous will rise from the tomb and be united again, transfigured, with the body. At many points in the novel, Myrivilis bemoans the impossibility of this transfiguration. Like Kazantzakis's evocation of a "gorgeous green stone," Myrivilis's protagonist comes across "a tiny red pennant of flaming life . . . , a red poppy" amid rotting sandbags and debris. The poppy becomes a symbol for the soul. In a state of rapture reminiscent of the poet Solomos's moments of epiphany, Kostoulas experiences a sublime sensation of "sorrow or joy" that vibrates within him in the poppy's presence. This heightened awareness suggests to him a communion with "the lovely fairytale of Divine Providence." Unfortunately, it is also a realization that cannot revel in self-delusion for it knows transcendence to be precisely a fairytale: "my soul is frisking tonight; it is an abundant and joyous spring even though it lacks anywhere to send its water or its songs. Once more, however, I find it impossible to speak to God, despite my feeling that he is close to me, so very, very close . . ."

God and the beloved are present in their absence. In the darkest hour of this existentialist paradox, Kostoulas dreams of being close to someone dear, another human being who understands and offers communion. This beloved, like the novel's addressee, need not speak, need not even be there in reality. Kostoulas wills into being a loving couple who sit next to each other in peaceful surroundings. They sit in silence, each the unsuspecting auditor of the other's inner soliloquy: "That is the golden moment, because their souls, as free now as two swallows, escape, meet the boundless Oversoul of the cosmos, and disappear fraternally absorbed in it." In their flight, "many truths have grazed them gently with their wings, like rosy butterflies."

Peter Bien's translation of Myrivilis's *Life in The Tomb* was first published in 1977. The work was reprinted in 1987 and now happily receives a further reprinting. It is perfectly understandable to me that Bien also happens to be a celebrated translator and the foremost critic of Nikos Kazantzakis's work. In fact, he has spent much of his academic life bringing both writers' worlds to life in a series of acclaimed translations and books.

This new edition resurrects this important anti-war novel after the end of a decade of renewed hostility and killing in the Balkans as well as at the beginning of an era of terrorism and frightening talk of preemptive war. Myrivilis's novel will once again reaffirm the value of life in the shadow of violent death. It is a message most compellingly delivered in Bien's evocation of Myrivilis's language. The episodic structure, the architecture of *Life in the Tomb*, may not appeal to all modern readers; nor might the cut of some of the larger-than-life figures. But there is a thrill still in being swept up by the vigor and rush of Myrivilis's prose in the way that Pynchon describes the flight of a German rocket: "a screaming comes across the sky." We feel the effects of a muscular idiom, words exploding in the mouth. For the novel bears the marks of a specific moment in the Greek language. The other war that raged while Myrivilis was at the front, the spirited struggle between the purists and demoticists over the preferred form of the Greek language, had been largely won by the demoticists in the literary sphere by the time of this novel in 1930. They had championed the use of the vernacular idiom in all forms of social, political, and cultural life. Myrivilis's passionate advocacy of the demotic language in the novel revels in this victory as he rides the tiger of a zestful yet still-untested vernacular. With compound epithets and long, bounding sentences, Myrivilis throws himself confidently into his medium, full of faith and hope in its untried potentialities. An analogy to the perspective of Greek men in the trenches is not far out of reach. Terrified, although concealing that terror, they enjoy confidence drawn not from their officers, their plans, their tactics, their political reason for being there, or from the Divine, but only from their *filótimo*—self respect—,which, like language, "transubstantiates baser metals into gold. It alchemizes soul, spurring men to perform signs and wonders."

Vangelis Calotychos

Historical Note

The island of Lesvos (the ancient Lesbos—also called Mytilene, after the name of its chief town) was ruled by Turkey from the fifteenth century until shortly before the first world war, when it was restored to Greece. During this war the whole of Greece was divided in allegiance, with King Constantine favoring Germany and Prime Minister Venizelos the Entente. Lesvos supported Venizelos when he set up an antimonarchical Provisional Government in Salonika and sent troops to fight side by side with the French and English in the Serbian campaign.

Translator's Preface

*M*yrivilis participated in the events described in this novel, and it is therefore not surprising that the geographical locations indicated in the book, the troop movements, and the nature of the fighting are all very close to descriptions given in historical accounts of the Salonika campaign. The Peristeri ridges are easily located on a detailed map of the area between Monastir and Lake Prespa in (what is now) the Former Yugoslav Republic of Macedonia (FYROM). The time seems to be the spring of 1917, when General Sarrail was conducting an offensive and when "around Monastir each side threw hundreds of rounds of high explosives across the valleys, but, apart from patrol activity, the infantry remained in their trenches."[1] The location of the Turtle is more difficult to determine. Various bits of evidence in the book seem, however, to suggest that it is the famous Skra di Legen further along the front about ten miles west of the Vardar River—a rocky massif whose defenses "determined the fate of any attack launched along . . . the right bank of the Vardar. If ever a general assault were to be made on the Bulgarian front, the Skra di Legen . . . had to be captured."[2] The supreme commander of the Army of the Orient, General Marie Louis Adolphe Guillaumat, who had replaced Sarrail in Decem-

---

[1] Alan Palmer, *The Gardeners of Salonika* (New York: Simon and Schuster, 1965), pp. 126–127.

[2] Palmer, p. 178.

ber 1917, entrusted this task to the Greek Army of National Defense, reinforced by French troops and allied artillery. The central attack was the
responsibility of the Archipelago Division, which was supported on the
western flank by the Seres Division and on the eastern by the Crete Division. The attack took place at dawn on May 30, 1918, after thirteen hours
of continuous artillery barrage, and was immediately successful. "The Skra
di Legen . . . became famous overnight in Athens . . . . The Greeks had
captured more than 1,600 Bulgars and even 200 Germans (mostly
signalers), and fewer than 500 of the attackers had been killed . . . .
Guillaumat was well pleased with the action."[3] Indeed, it was this victory
that made the High Command determine that a general offensive could
and should be undertaken as soon as possible. (This final—victorious—
offensive began on September 15, 1918, under Guillaumat's successor,
Franchet d'Esperey. The Archipelago Division was now on the Moglena
Front slightly to the west of Skra di Legen, attached to the French army of
General d'Anselme and supporting the Serbians' eastern flank in the crucial assault upon Dobropolje and the Vetrenik, an operation that broke the
center of the enemy line and made possible the rapid advance northward
to Belgrade. But all this takes us beyond the death of Myrivilis's hero.)

The commander of the Greek Army of National Defense was Emmanuel
Zymbrakakis (1858–1928). The organizer and commander of the Archipelago Division was Dimitrios Ioannou (1861–1927).

Although the Balkan Front was often considered a sideshow during
the war, its strategic importance is now increasingly recognized. The continuing interest in this sector is evidenced by Alan Palmer's excellent account in *The Gardeners of Salonika*, which lists more than 100 (non-Greek)
volumes in its bibliography. Among the many books that appeared during
and soon after the conflict are George Ward Price's *The Story of the Salonica
Army* (London: Hodder and Stoughton, 1917); Harry Collinson Owen's
Salonica and After: the Sideshow that Ended the War (London: Hodder
and Stoughton, 1919); Gordon Gordon-Smith's *From Serbia to Jugosla-
via: Serbia's Victories, Reverses and Final Triumph, 1914-1918* (New York
and London: G. P. Putnam's Sons, 1920); General Maurice Paul Emmanuel

---

[3] Palmer, pp. 179–180.

Sarrail's *Mon Commandement en Orient, 1916-1918* (Paris, 1920); Luigi Villari's *La Campagna di Macedonia* (Bologna, 1922), translated as *The Macedonian Campaign* (London: T. Fisher Unwin, 1922); Lieutenant Colonel Henry Dundas Napier's *The Experiences of a Military Attaché in the Balkans* (London: Drane's, 1924); and A. J. Mann's and William T. Wood's, *The Salonika Front* (London: A. C. Black, 1920).

To these we must add Myrivilis's *Life in the Tomb*, a fictionalized account, to be sure, but nevertheless one that is true not only to the places and circumstances of the campaign but to the human feelings of those engaged in it. Myrivilis composed the first sketches in the trenches on the Monastir front in 1917; one chapter was published in the newspaper *Néa Elladha* (Thessaloniki) in the same year. After he returned from the Asia Minor campaign, he published the novel in installments in the Mytilenian newspaper *Kambana*. The offprint from these installments constituted the first edition (1924). In 1930 the book was reissued by the firm of Theophanidis and Lambadaridis, but its circulation was forbidden during the Metaxas dictatorship and the German occupation (1936-1944). A new and slightly revised edition appeared in 1955, published by Kollaros. This has enjoyed successive reprintings; indeed *Life in the Tomb* has been the single most successful and most widely read serious novel in Greece in the period since the Great War, having sold more than 80,000 copies—an astonishing figure for such a small country. An abridged version entitled *De Profundis* appeared in French in 1933, and the complete text has been translated into Polish, Serbo-Croatian, Italian, Czech, Rumanian, Hungarian, Bulgarian, and Turkish. To these translations we now add a reprint of the English version, hoping that it will make the book better known in the Anglophone world. The present translation is based on the 1955 text collated with that of 1930; phrases from the earlier version have been included in a few instances.

Stratis Myrivilis (pseudonymn of Efstratios Stamatopoulos) was born in 1892 on the island of Lesvos. He spent the decade 1912–1922 fighting, first in the Balkan Wars, then in the Great War, and finally in the disastrous Asia Minor campaign—experiences that provided material not only for *Life in the Tomb* but for the novels *The Schoolmistress with the Golden Eyes* (1933; English translation 1964) and *The Mermaid Madonna* (1949;

English translation 1959). Among his many short stories and novellas, *Vasilis Arvanitis* (1939) is the best known and is considered a classic of modern Greek prose. An active journalist and broadcaster, Myrivilis became general program director for the Greek National Broadcasting Institute, president of the National Society of Greek Writers and, in 1958, a member of the Academy of Athens. He died in Athens on July 19, 1969.

The translator wishes to acknowledge the assistance he received from many friends and colleagues, without whom this work could never have been completed. Especial thanks go to Chrysanthi Yiannakou Bien for her patient responses to six years of queries; Dimitrios Yiannakos, quartermaster in Venizelos's army, for remembering the truth; Christos Alexiou, Constantine Tomazinos, Yorgos Yiannakos, and Mario Vitti for tracking down unknown words; Mito Lambeski, Aleksander Zebich, and Dr. Themistocles Altas for information on Macedonian dialect; Talat Halman, Speros Vryonis, and Walter Arndt for help with Turkish; John Tallmadge for stylistic suggestions; Robert Liddell for permission to use his rendering of Athanasios Diakos's poem[4]; Irvin Ziemann for his provisional translation, which solved many cruxes; Thomas Doulis for alerting me to textual inconsistencies; Yannis Lappas, Peter and Eva Topping, Lily Macrakis, and Niki Stavrolakes for advice; Mr. and Mrs. Lambis Myrivilis for hospitality in London and Athens and for superhuman patience; Rixford Owen Jennings for making the maps; Myril Adler, Harry Mark Petrakis, David Horne, Petros Haris, Peter Mackridge, Philip Sherrard, Eleni Vlachou, Andonis Decavalles, Gene Lyons, Richard Sheldon, and Leonard Rieser for general encouragement; and Edmund Keeley for initiating the entire enterprise.

Peter Bien

Ai Yanni (Pelion), Kallithea (Kassandra), Riparius (New York), Hanover (New Hampshire), June 1970, June 1976-September 2001, March 2003.

---

[4] Published in Linos Politis, *A History of Modern Greek Literature* (Oxford: Clarendon Press, 1973), p. 86.

Terms & References

The translation employs certain terms and references that may mystify non-Greek readers. They are listed here in alphabetical order.

Adramyttion. A city in Asia Minor, northeast of Lesvos. Now called Edremit.

Agathangelos. Supposed author of a prophetic book that encouraged the Greeks during the years of Turkish rule. The book records Agathangelos's revelation that Constantine will come again and restore Byzantium. Written in 1279, the text was published in Italian translation in 1555 and then in Greek in 1751.

Aivaly. A city in Asia Minor, directly across from Mytilene. Now called Aivalyk.

arapades. The word *arapis* (plural: arapades), although literally meaning "Arab," is also commonly used in Greece to mean "negro." M'chaghilous, in Chapter 11, is of course trying to say "arabades," the plural of "arabas," a kind of wagon.

Ayiassos. A town in Lesvos, southwest of Mytilene.

Baba. Cape Baba is on the mainland north of Lesvos.

baclava. A sweet consisting of crushed nuts between layers of paper-thin phylo dough, bathed in syrup or honey.

Balkan Wars. In the first Balkan War, Greece fought against Turkey over Macedonia. The great events were the occupation by Greece of Thessaloniki (Salonika) in October 1912 and of Janina in February 1913 (see "Bizani," below). The war ended favorably for Greece (Treaty of London, May 1913) but Bulgaria, unwilling to have Greece control Thessaloniki, began the second Balkan War in June. This, too, ended favorably for Greece, after bitter fighting (see "Kilkish," below).

Bizani. A village and strategic hill about ten kilometers southeast of Janina, along the supply road to that city. It was fortified by the Turks and was captured by the Greeks during the first Balkan War in the offensive (February 18-20, 1913) that resulted in the occupation of Janina by Greece.

bonbonnières. There is great bitterness hidden behind this word, because in Greek custom the *bonbonnières* are almond candies wrapped in toile and distributed to wedding guests as symbols of fertility—whereas in *Life in the Tomb* the *bonbonnières* are scattering death.

briki. A special pot with a long handle, used chiefly for boiling Turkish coffee, but also put to other uses.

caique. A small sailing vessel for commercial use.

Constantine Palaiologos turned to marble. Constantine Palaiologos was the last Byzantine emperor; he died on the battlements defending his city on May 29, 1453. The legend of the "enmarbled king" occurs in various forms, one of which is as follows: Just as Constantine was about to be slaughtered by a Turk, an angel snatched him away and brought him to a cave (in other versions: to the vaults of Hagia Sophia) where he was turned to marble. He—and all of Hellenism with him—now waits for the angel to return and revivify him when the time comes for the Greeks to win back Constantinople and reestablish the Byzantine Empire.

eleleu. A "cry of joy" uttered by ancient Greek soldiers at the start of battle.

Eressos. A town in western Lesvos, northwest of Mytilene.

evzone. An infantryman in a special part of the Greek army that retains as its uniform the skirt *(foustanela)* worn by soldiers in the Greek Revolution.

Forward, sons of Greece. This is from Aeschylus's *Persians* (line 402) with the word order slightly changed. A literal translation would be: "O children of Greece, go save the fatherland, save children, wives, the seats of the country's gods, the tombs of ancestors . . ."

Fykiotrypa Rock. A large rock formation jutting into the sea to the north of Mytilene-town; site of a lighthouse.

Gateluzzi. The Genoese family that ruled Lesvos from 1355 until 1462, when the island fell to the Turks.

Golden Horn. A horn-shaped gulf dividing Constantinople in two.

Great Idea. The driving force of Greek nationalism from the end of the nineteenth century until the (temporary?) destruction of the Idea in 1922, when the Greeks were forced out of Anatolia. The Great Idea was that Greece would recapture Constantinople, reestablish the Byzantine Empire, and become the dominant nation in the eastern Mediterranean.

homoousian. A theological term meaning "of the same substance" and opposed to homoiousian, which means "of similar substance." These issues were at the center of the Arian controversy in the fourth century, when the question was whether Christ's nature was identical to that of the Father, or only similar.

Hymn to the Virgin, the Protecting General. One of the favorite hymns of the Greek Orthodox Church, prescribed for the Sundays in Lent. It invokes the Virgin as the Champion or Defender, and as the victorious General of Hellenic Christendom.

"I shall fight both alone and with many." This oath taken by the young men of Athens is preserved in an anthology of excerpts compiled about A.D. 500, Johannes Stobaeus's *Florilegium.*

Iota subscript next to a capital omega. Looks like this: Ω_ι

Islands of the Blest. In Greek mythology, the place where those favored by the gods (in later conception: heroes and patriots) enjoy a pleasant life after they have died. The islands were located in the stream Oceanus, far away in the west. Another name for the Elysian Fields.

Karaghiozis. The chief character of the Greek shadow-theater. He is a complete rogue and speaks with a ridiculous twang. His hut is always included in the scenery.

katharevousa. An artificial language constructed by nationalists in the late eighteenth and early nineteenth centuries as a compromise between ancient Greek and the so-called "demotic," the spoken language that evolved naturally during the Hellenistic and Byzantine periods and the 400 years of Turkish rule. The linguistic nationalists attempted to "purify" demotic of foreign words and to return as much as possible to the vocabulary, syntax, and grammar of the ancient Attic dialect. In 1917 Venizelos introduced educational reforms meant to deemphasize katharevousa, but the "official language continued to be employed for documents, scholarly books, pompous oratory, university lectures, etc., especially under the more conservative regimes that followed. It was not until 1975 that the linguistic clause specifying katharevousa as Greece's official language was removed from the Constitution.

Kilkish. A town in the nomarchy of Thessaloniki. From June 19 to 22,

1913, one of the fiercest and most decisive battles of the second Balkan War took place here, with the Greeks defeating the Bulgarians.

Kioski. A neighborhood in Mytilene-town on the slope leading up to the Castle.

koumbaros. An untranslatable word applied to someone having a very special relationship to someone else, yet a relationship neither of blood nor of marriage. It is much stronger than "best friend."

Koupa. Village directly south of Skra, southwest of Gjevgjeli, near the present border between Greece and FYROM.

Lepetymnos. A mountain range in northern Lesvos, near the city of Mithimna.

loukoumadhes. Delicious dumpling-like sweets consisting of blobs of dough quick-fried in oil and served liberally bathed in honey.

Magarova. A village directly west of Monastir.

Marathon. In Greek political oratory, a touchstone of patriotism. There, in 490 B.C., a force of heavily outnumbered Greeks defeated the Persians.

"March threads." This refers to the custom whereby children, on March 1, wind multicolored threads around their fingers as a charm against sunburn.

Mesotopos. A town in western Lesvos, directly west of Mytilene.

Monastir. City in southern FYROM, east of the northern tip of Lake Prespa. Now called Bitola.

Olympus. A mountain in southern Lesvos, near the town of Agiassos.

ouzo. An extremely potent Greek apéritif distilled from the skins of pressed grapes.

Peristeri. A mountain range running north and south about halfway between Monastir and Lake Prespa. The peak is 2359 meters high. The word "peristeri" in Greek means "dove" or "pigeon."

Plomarion. A city on the south coast of Lesvos.

purist; puristic. See "katharevousa," above.

Rizarios School. A famous seminary in Athens founded by George Rizaris in 1843.

sela. The old-fashioned baggy trousers worn on the Greek islands have ample folds of cloth hanging down in front and in back. Each of these is called a *sela.*

Seven Hills. Rome was built on seven hills. Constantinople was called the city of seven hills because it was meant to be New Rome.

syrtos. A circle dance very popular in Greece.

Theodora. A bugle call in the Greek army.

Three Hundred of Thermopylae. Like "Marathon," a touchstone of patriotism in Greek nationalistic oratory. The reference is to the three hundred valiant Spartans under Leonidas who faced a superior force of Persians at Thermopylae in 480 B.C., and died for their country.

Tsesmelian. An inhabitant of Tsesmes, a town in Asia Minor, directly across from the island of Chios. Now called Çeşme.

Valaoritis. A nineteenth-century poet who wrote, in demotic, about the heroes of the Revolutionary War.

Velušino. Village directly south of Monastir, about halfway between Monastir and Florina.

"What a season Charon chose . . ." These verses were reputed to have been recited by the revolutionary hero Athanasios Diakos on April 23, 1821, as he was being led to execution after he had been captured by the Turks.

Zalongo. A cliff in Epirus, famous in modern Greek history because here, on December 18, 1803, fifty-seven Greek women chose death rather than capture by the Turks. After hurling their babies over the cliff, they began a circle dance, and each, as she approached the brink, jumped to her doom. The usual phrase is "women of Zalongo"; Balafaras changes it to "men of Zalongo."

Η ΖΩΗ ΕΝ ΤΑΦΩ₁

Ἡ ζωή ἐν τάφῳ, κατετέθης,
Χριστέ, καὶ ἀγγέλων στρατιαὶ
ἐξεπλήττοντο, συγκατάβασιν
δοξάζουσαι τὴν σήν.

Thou, Christ, the Life, in the tomb was laid,
and armies of angels were amazed, and they
glorified thy humiliation.

From: the Lamentations
sung in Greek Orthodox churches
on Good Friday

1

In Front of an Old Chest
(by Way of Prologue)

*T*oday I rummaged through my little gray field-chest. I was searching for a certain official document pertaining to my military service, a document that I needed once more, although many many years had gone by. At the end of the war I had deposited a pile of mementos in this old army-chest, a wooden one of German manufacture, very solid and antique. Now, when I released its rusty clasp, the cover creaked so loudly that I imagined I was prying open the lid of an ancient and forgotten reliquary. Inside I found a bronze half moon biting a tarnished star (torn off some Turkish flag-staff), my sword, a steel helmet, a German gas-mask shaped like a pig's snout, my faded, typewritten discharge papers, some photographs, a leather port-folio, two or three hand grenades, and a whole collection of other odds and ends. I also discovered a large packet done up in brown paper and tied cross-wise with twine. By this time I had completely forgotten what was inside. I snipped the knots with some scissors and undid the wrapping, exposing a sheaf of copybooks and loose sheets of various sizes, all of which poured out with a mournful rustle. The pages were densely covered with writing in a uniform but extremely cramped hand. Then I suddenly remembered the note I had once placed on the wrapping paper in blue pencil. Finding it— the letters were nearly obliterated—I read it once more:

THE MANUSCRIPTS OF
SERGEANT ANTHONY KOSTOULAS

I drew out all the papers and allowed the cover of the oblong chest to fall shut again. Truly, this little case was a reliquary, a genuine casket, and these sheets so yellowed with age and bearing the marks of the twine on all four edges were a lamentable cadaver: a body yearning to speak and be heard.

Spreading the papers out on my desk, I arranged them in sequence according to their pagination, and began to read. Without realizing what was happening, I gradually found myself transported years back into the past. I had first discovered the copybooks after the horrible battle of Hill 908 in a pack belonging to a soldier of the Fourth Regiment of the Archipelago Division. I was still an N.C.O. at the time, and we were sorting out government property, separating what belonged to the dead and wounded from what belonged to uninjured survivors. The notebooks in question—with their cheap paper densely covered with cramped, penciled script—were discovered in the pack of Sergeant Anthony Kostoulas, a volunteer. He had been leader of the third platoon of the Seventh Company. I recalled him vividly and clearly—a university student, tall and olive-complexioned, with a long face and abundant bushy hair. He was a real man, but as quiet, sensible, and reserved as a girl.

Sergeant Kostoulas was incinerated (by mistake) in the Bulgarian trenches soon after we overran them, while the flame-throwers and the mopping-up detail, the latter with trench knives in their fists, were exterminating the last remnants of the enemy: those who, whether from fear or treachery, had remained hidden in the dugouts of the conquered line. The man who incinerated him was a French lance corporal, a member of a squad of "specialists in liquid fire." This squad had joined our regiment on that terrible and extraordinary day because at that time our Balkan forces had not yet added such West-European "specialties" to our store of weapons. It so happened that as the Frenchman in question was spraying a tongue of streaming fire into an enemy dugout a Bulgarian who had been crouching in the trenches sprang forward and slashed him in the abdomen. In the moments before the Frenchman gave up the ghost—flopping about as he was like a fish, his guts hanging out and his fingers clawing at the discharge tube—he continued to shoot the stream of fire haphazardly

2

in all directions. This was the moment when Sergeant Kostoulas happened to leap into the trench. We found him burned to death, his face devoured by the flames, a black and red mutilation recognizable only by three white marks engraved upon it—a row of teeth between tightly-clenched jaws entirely stripped of flesh, and two globular eyeballs puffed out like a pair of ivory billiard balls. The lower right canine was covered by a golden crown, which glistened.

We dug a pit and buried him on the spot together with the Frenchman and three Bulgarians. Many days later I experienced a cold chill reaching deep into my marrow as I traversed the area and felt the hollow earth give way beneath my careful tread. But it couldn't have been arranged otherwise, because to bury them anywhere else was absolutely out of the question. The enemy, you understand, continued ploughing up their former stronghold with shells from the moment they had abandoned it into our hands. They continued this for many days in the hope of preventing us from "organizing" it.

One might even hazard that those who chanced to be killed in the trenches or in a vicinity close to the parapets were actually fortunate, because the others—the ones who fell out in the open—rotted away beyond the barbed-wire entanglements, unburied, with bursting shells tearing open their bellies every few minutes and bouncing their carcasses off the ground. This is not to mention the rain that followed, beating down into their black gaping mouths for days on end and drumming their transfixed eyes; nor the shells that then lunged once more over those wretched corpses with incomprehensible fury and dove like hogs into the mud, splattering the bodies deplorably and sometimes, because of the jolt, making them sit up (as though momentarily resuscitated), shift their limbs about with abrupt kicks, and spread their thighs obscenely.

All these memories have assaulted me again like a swarm of repulsive mice now that I have sat down and begun, with fingers as well as eyes, to grope my way through these old wizened papers that I had completely forgotten for so many years. Today, the same day they reëmerged into the light, I resolved to have them published. The form they take is epistolary: they are a series of letters to a girl whose name nowhere appears. If this girl is real, not imaginary, and if she is still alive, I must ask her to forgive my

3

audacity. In my opinion, however, I am actually fulfilling an obligation by publishing the letters, because murmuring within them is a tormented soul forming part of the cosmic Oversoul. I feel that these utterances, which Fortune prevented from reaching the woman for whom they were intended, somehow belong to every woman directly touched by carnage, and, beyond that, to every human being made destitute by war and standing now with outstretched hands, begging for love among all peoples of the world.

In addition (why should I hide the tormenting superstition that has taken hold of me?) I feel that in making these papers available I shall be resurrecting this gallant lad who was killed, shall be clasping him by the hand and drawing him out of his unmarked grave, giving him back the speech and share of intellect that decomposed along with his brains. It is a heavy thing to have a corpse inside you yearning to be heard, and to seal his lips with your palm. He signals you from the Beyond, beckons you with supplicating gestures directed at your heart—because he wishes to express himself.

For me, publishing this book is a personal redemption. That is why I ask forgiveness for doing so.

STRATIS MYRIVILIS

P.S. The title of the book itself has of course been supplied by me, as have the headings for the individual chapters. They are meant to help readers orient themselves, since the original manuscript contains nothing but the pagination of the copybooks.

But why do I sit here delving into such things? What difference do they make, any of them?

2

An End that Is a Beginning

*H*urrah! We've finally stopped, thank God. We've reached the trench. That means an end and at the same time a beginning—an end to that agonized, wretched life of incessant marches, a beginning to trench-life, something we are tasting for the very first time. There were days when I said to myself, "Good God, this walking will never cease. I'll grow old, always walking, and will stop only when it's time for me to die."

Tired of being separated from you, I have decided to send you my impressions of this new life. I shall write every now and then, whenever I have the time (and the heart), as a way of conversing with you. To know that someone dear is nearby—a person who understands and who offers communion—is so very comforting, especially when one is participating in life's most critical moments. Such a person hears your thoughts, inwardly, even though he may imagine he is not listening to them at all. You must have observed this from time to time: a woman sits with her beloved in a cozy little room, only the two of them present, with nothing but a few good books, one or two paintings on the walls, a lamp awaiting the night with thumping heart, an inkstand (what an important object that is!), and the chairs arranged in a circle, filled with patience. Neither of them speaks. Each is engrossed in his or her own thoughts or perhaps is not thinking any conscious thoughts at all. That is the golden moment, because their souls, as free now as two swallows, escape, meet the boundless Oversoul of the cosmos, and disappear, fraternally absorbed inside it. Most often, however, each of the souls converses with its own silence. Yet notice how indispensable to this "conversation" is the very special companion who sits close at hand without speaking, or who now and then utters a few words about current events, words that constitute his rationality's paltry attempt to justify the sweet-voiced silence. As he sits there tacitly, he is an unsuspecting auditor of the other's unvoiced soliloquy. But as soon as he decides to rise and leave his lady's side, everything is finished—ended. She finds it beyond the limits of possibility to continue her silent, inward communing with the depths of her being. Sometimes the lady is the first to rise after one of these joint silences. Not a word has been exchanged the entire time, yet when she gets up to leave, smiling at her companion, at that same moment both feel their souls fuller and riper, brimming with strength and freedom—because many many truths have grazed them gently with their wings, like rosy butterflies.

Something similar is happening to me, making me wish to address my thoughts to you. Despite your silence, I assume that you are here, somewhere close to me. At such times I devote myself body and soul to my soliloquy, which your absence fills with presence.

When God sees fit to end this war, some day we shall sit down together, side by side, and leaf through these unworthy pages. The long winter nights will have already begun, and the passers-by will be walking with hurried steps. We shall only hear their tread on the cobblestones, but we shall know nevertheless that their hands are thrust deep into their overcoat pockets, their hats pulled down ridiculously over their skulls, reaching down to their eyebrows, and their shoulders hunched up to their ears. Your green shutters will be firmly latched, the fragrance of ripe fruit will saturate the room, and I shall be lounging lazily in the armchair in front of that gigantic copper brazier from Constantinople. I'll fill my pipe and light it; I'll stir up the coals, poking the bronze tongs into their burning core that resembles cherry-colored velvet; and I'll watch you as you sit at the walnut table beneath the circle of light thrown by the green lampshade, reading from these copybooks in your full, clear voice. I shall hear its boyish timbre and imagine that I am listening to a gurgling stream of water flowing exclusively for me in the depths of the earth. Exclusively for me— and not a soul shall divine my secret bliss.

We shall be married then, and shall have a home of our own. We'll choose our furniture together, making certain that it is simple and sturdy, so that we can love it. (You cannot imagine, dearest, how unpleasant it is to be companioned by the kind of furniture that stands there putting on such airs that you cannot get along with it.) You will love our furniture, and you will also love this notebook, because as I write in it I am thinking of you constantly.

* * *

Dearest, during this very unusual time when my life is so near to death and my hands are so far from yours . . .

* * *

You must not expect to learn anything about my true existence from the postcards that the mailman brings you. No letters may be sent from the trenches, only those blue cards with their evzone and their imprinted message: "Postal Zone 999. I am fine. With best wishes. . . ." Even these, before they reach your eyes (which I love so very dearly) will pass before a thousand and one bespectacled bleary-eyed censors. In short, it is only in these manuscripts that I shall record life's significant moments as I encounter them in my inner world or in the world without. I shall not bother you with dates and locations, because such things no longer exist for us. All the days here are identical, all equally ugly, with no trait to distinguish the features or significance of one from the other. Unbearably the same, identically empty, the days and nights pass in an endless procession, dragging their feet. Imagine a chaplet with alternate white and black beads, one white, one black changing places ever so slowly for all eternity, and devoid of any meaning whatsoever. Oh, the tedium of it! And what applies to time applies equally as well to place. Nothing but foreign words, symbols, numbers, letters of the alphabet—code-signs that become comprehensible only on the maps of the General Staff.

When I was near you, however, it was not like this, not at all. Each day there—each hour and minute—displayed its own personality. Each was

7

so richly colored, so ardent with expressiveness and palpitating life. Even now I could summon every one of those days individually by name and by virtue of certain distinctive details.

The rose-tinted mornings, when your diminutive steps took you down to the girls' academy and your sweet little pupils greeted you with bouquets of freshly picked violets. . . . The white forenoons ablaze with light, when the schoolbell rang and you emerged with your cherry-colored parasol opened like some exotic flower, dripping red splendor all over your face. I would be waiting for you then, and how your chestnut eyes did smile! . . . Early evenings, golden and blue, when the sun began to sink and I would be so impatient for us to leave for the sea in time, so that we could observe the sunset from the Fykiotrypa Rock. . . . Wednesday afternoons when you brought your children to the pine grove and they danced with such mad vigor, linking hands and forming a circle around you. . . . Sundays with their picnics, Marianna's huge wicker baskets, the stylish affectations of our fine friend Angelica. . . . Cleanth's violin on midnight boat rides in dark waters, with the fortress and its sea-rooted battlements looming above us. . . . Saturday evenings at Apellis's café when we carried our chairs down to his waterfront and placed them in the shallows. What a Robinson Crusoe he was, that refugee who built his cottage and café on the inhospitable crags by the sea—everything with his own two hands, his wife forever whining at him and bearing him a new child every year; and the countless little Apellises of every age and height who used to welcome us with joyful screeches:

"Papa, papa, come out, the friendth 're here!"

"Papa, the friendth 're finithed."

One day you were wearing an attractive little hat, black with a red brim, and were walking with those short hurried steps of yours. (They resemble a bird's, when it tries to hop on the ground.) It was Easter Sunday; resurrection and brightness filled the air on all sides. With laughing eyes you were bringing me a huge bunch of lilacs. Easter Sunday, three in the afternoon, and you were bringing me lilacs. . . .

Ah, those lovely hours we passed together, those beloved times. . . .

Out here everything is the same: fatiguing, silent, unchanging, terrible. Time stands still; the earth rotates no longer. One month is just

like any other; the days are nameless; festivals and holidays do not exist.
Night is indistinguishable from day.

* * *

Here at the summit of this Macedonian mountain composed of fiery flint,
I am reexamining the events that catapulted me so far from Lesvos. Revolution! Some revolution or other must beat its wings inside the breast of
every twenty-year-old. This term *revolution* has a powerful effect on me,
and will always have such an effect. Certain words like this throb in one's
temples like strong whisky. Youth is credulous. Words, in one's youth,
are filled with pith, sap and fire; only afterwards do they drain, little by
little, until nothing is left but hollow shells. (The only trouble is that more
often than not those who serve potent drinks to the young keep filling
their own glasses with pure unadulterated water until they see their victims roll on the floor, hopelessly drunk.) *Revolution* is one such word. I
first felt its power when I was a mere schoolboy. I smiled at it then, fasci-
nated by its immeasurable and never-ceasing excitement. Even now I keep
repeating this word to myself, articulating its syllables in an undertone,
pronouncing it secretly for my inner ear, like a prayer. I squeeze my eyes
closed and see it inscribed upon night's black page in phosphorescent letters so vibrant that they resemble serpentine thunderbolts. Then, all of a
sudden, something strange happens inside me. Flags smack the air; their
goad-like staffs prick the majestic heavens (which are resplendently draped
in the national colors like some public edifice). Rockets whistle upward
into the azure void, then burst with frenzied and triumphant clamor. And
the snare drums, thousands of them, convert one's soul into a vibrating
drumhead as they rattle like a distant thunderclap rolling along heaven's
ceiling. At such times you clench your fists (although you are completely
unaware of this reaction) and your spine arches backward like a flexed
bow ready to release its arrow.

Revolution!

Fight for freedom, we were told. Fight for the enslaved Greeks of
Anatolia and Thrace, for all enslaved peoples everywhere. Fine! To fight
for freedom and to liberate slaves is always a splendid enterprise. Inside

9

every slave lies a portion of our own enslavement. But we must kick out the king in the process! The people are a robust bull, and nothing infuriates them more readily than the royal purple. If someone knows how to wave this cape in front of their enflamed eyes, nothing else is needed. . . . So, the torrent swept me along, body and soul. I was clamped like a sliver of wood to the frothy crest of a blind, all-powerful wave, and now here I am, a shipwreck cast up on the summit of some craggy hill in Serbian Macedonia, terribly surprised, and also sufficiently frightened. Yes, here I am, rendered up to war, irrevocably bound to its monstrous wheel. At this point the situation has no remedy, a fact that I have accepted with a peculiar kind of romanticism, but, also begrudgingly (as though the whole thing were not of my own doing in the first place). I shall endure with patient resignation, however, for I have no lack of perseverance. In addition, boring into me continually is an indomitable thirst to lead a vigorous life of intensity and struggle, also a thirst to feel the bitter pleasure of misery, to feel it drive its tooth cruelly into my flesh and make me more vibrantly aware of my existence. Misery can do this better than joy. So I have abandoned myself to the vertigo of the fearsome wheel. Bound upon it, I am experiencing the bitter and cunning satisfaction of the early Christians who viewed their tormentors as unwittingly distributing entrance-passes to Paradise. After all, I am very young.

The wheel! Warfare's wheel!

We see it, millions of us, as it emerges from the moldy abyss, creaking stridently like a huge capstan as it revolves. The horizon is reddish black, the soil exhales scarlet vapors. The huge wheel turns and turns, rotates for eons together with the earth, and howls through space with heart-rending moans. Bound hand and foot upon it, I have little choice but to follow its deadly revolutions. They are sluggish, for the wheel turns without the slightest haste. Hopelessly slow, it exhibits the sure and inexorable motion of natural law. It is an enormous iron-toothed beast that impassively champs writhing human meat: human bodies freshly caught in full flower.

The laden sky hangs low, pressing down upon us like a gigantic helmet. The immobile clouds have surrounded us with their ashen rags— dirty laundry hung out to dry and then forgotten. Far in the distance, the great seas of the world hold their breath and prick up their ears in order to hear the ordeal because audible in the distance, if one listens carefully, audible amid this immobile silence and the sudden howls of the titanic wheel, is a remote and strangulated rattle, the same that is emitted by the soul as it lunges to slip between the lips of a knife-wound, together with the fresh gurgling blood. If you listen intently, you will hear in addition, far away, a mild, hollow clatter suggesting bodies being crushed and shattered, or skulls grating as they are pulverized beneath a slowly lowered press. What you hear is trench warfare; that is what operates in such a leisurely, assured fashion. What you hear is war, which, prior to shattering the body, first decomposes the spirit, gradually, mercilessly, in the isolation of life underground. You hear the relentless terror that shares a soldier's dugout. The walls are dotted with promenading slugs, those children of horror. The soldier reaches into his pack to draw out a mouthful of bread, and clasps instead the soft, slimy back of a mouse that then escapes in a fright between fingers paralyzed with queasy abhorrence.

The incidents that brought me here, so far from our island and from you, are returning vividly to my memory, one by one.

3

The Deceased Die:
End of Anointed Majesty

I remember what a great commotion the revolution caused. The people—thousands strong—were in a state of emotional fervor, filled with an anxious and uneasy joy. At such times one's condition may be described as follows: coursing dizzily through your arteries is something fiery and unrestrainable, rather like a blast of the *flatus divinus*. You have to do something—anything—but you don't know what. Should you utter a victory-roar so fierce that your voice reverberates like the trumpets of Jericho against the walls of the Gateluzzi fortress and the city's major public edifices, then echoes as well among the hoisted sails of the caiques in the harbor? Or should you weep gently, shedding warm syrupy tears while your head remains softly cushioned upon the chubby knees of the woman you love? In times like these, as soon as the Man of the Hour appears—someone who says, "Do this!"—you do it with a boundless sense of deliverance; and you deify this man into the bargain with your tear-filled gratitude, even if he tells you, "Jump into the fire!"

Commotion everywhere: waves of intoxicating uproar formed from a thousand disparate voices. The city's church bells had gone insane. They cried in exultation above our heads, over the red-tiled roofs, like a flock of frenzied, hooting archangels beating lances against brass shields and filling the air with a horrifying reveille. With their brazen voices and frightening wings they made the atmosphere as turbulent as a storm-lashed sea. (Church bells are remarkable things when their thick lips begin to proclaim the reckless knight-errantry of the world's peoples.) Their clangs entered our bloodstream, coalescing there as warm vapor. Their cotton-tipped fingers prodded the masses. Turning into ropes, they captured the populace—men, women and children, the very young and the very old—and bound their souls one by one to the frenetic clappers high above in the bell towers. Rivers of people kept pouring out of the lanes that descended to the harbor. Various lost and confused animals darted between their legs. Flags, and silken banners depicting the saints, cavorted mirthfully in the air. Their golden fringes dripped with sunlight, the blue and white tassels on the banners sent shivers down the spine when they grazed your hair. With every breath you swallowed a dram of precious liquor. Invisible electric currents flowing through the sunlight above the dense sea of swarming human heads made every soul tremble like a reed, every finger curl inward spasmodically.

I do not know how it happened, but suddenly in the midst of this outlandish and spooky gathering (which assuredly must have been engendered in the dreams of some febrile child) the thunderclap broke—a thunderclap never heard before, one pregnant with terror and hatred combined.

"Down with the king! We want war!"

The speaker on the platform had not shouted this. With his fervid voice and premeditated, operatic gestures, he had acted only as a midwife, delivering it expertly from the throats of the populace. This orator was tall and slim, and had pleasing (if theatrical) features. His blazing eyes seemed those of a man bed-ridden with fever. His wavy hair received repeated furrowings from long consumptive fingers. The pronounced nose seemed sincerely affected by his speech, judging from the way it inclined so attentively toward the orating mouth, afraid lest it miss even a single word of the exhortation that was being emitted directly beneath it. . . . And then, at a moment when his long arms had stretched out toward the populace like wings, like supplication (yet all done with the utmost delicacy and finesse), it was then that the thunder crashed:

"Down with the king!"

It reminded me of one of our teachers, a man so scrawny and emaciated that if you so much as blew on him—puff!—he would have collapsed to the ground. But this man, when he stood behind his electric generator in the classroom, produced terrifying sparks potent enough to slaughter buffaloes. And he did this with the same elegant gesture:

"Down with the king!"

After we shouted it in this way for the first time, fists clenched at our thighs, teeth locked over each syllable as though biting each in turn, we all stood still for a moment. Holding our breath, we listened to this unheard-of cry of ours as it echoed against the waters of the harbor and the walls of our flag-adorned homes, clacking somewhat peculiarly. An equally peculiar sensation had invaded us. Something was disintegrating; something had vanished in our hearts, leaving a sudden and disagreeable vacuum. Was it the vacant pedestal? The pedestal whose age-old idol we had toppled with the first vigorous kick?

At such times, when an entire people becomes a gigantic, robust beast with a single soul and a single head, when every person's action seems to arise from drives as deep and obscure as instinct itself, when all breasts amalgamate into a single great breast as broad as a church dome, and this composite breast gasps in a single rhythm, heaving like an undulating sea, one begins to wonder what has happened.

I would hazard that a long line of venerable fathers, great-grandfathers and other ancestors had come to a momentary halt within the mysterious passageways of the huge monster's bloodstream. These ancestors—these myriad souls, myriad corpuscles—had been living in our blood for centuries; they were our Byzantine heritage. My conjecture is that in the midst of their never-ending march they halted out of bewilderment and fright the moment they registered that unheard-of blasphemy. Amazed, they knotted their hoary brows, banged their crutches down upon the paving-stones, and shouted:

"What? . . . And the Great Idea, have you forgotten that? And our Emperor Constantine Palaiologos, turned to marble in the sanctuary of Hagia Sophia—will he not emerge again to finish the Divine Liturgy? And our great hymn to the Virgin, the Protecting General? And the double-headed eagle stamped on your New Year's pie? And the saying 'One Constantine gave, another Constantine shall take'? And the prophecies of Agathangelos? . . . Anathema! Anathema! Anathema!"

But we—intoxicated with our own unbounded audacity, stirred to our emotional depths by uneradicable love for our nation, ready to lay down our lives for Greece "all together, arm-in-arm"—we shouted again, and then again, repeatedly, with obstinate, rabid fury:

"Down! No more kings! Away with the whole filthy lot of them!"

Though our lips were quivering slightly, our voices managed to cover the ancestral curse.

"We are the nation's youth," we told ourselves. "Its youth! The freest of the free! Our Greek blood is redder than any royal purple. The time has come for sweet fairy tales to doff their golden cloaks and heavy velvets, and be supplanted by reality."

The royalist bias, whose anemic fingers had closed the eyes of all our forebears from Byzantine times to the present, was fluttering now in a daze all around us, a bewildered bat that had lost its bearings and was darting crazily back and forth in the light, striking against walls and lampposts, crashing into treetrunks, the breakwater, ships' masts—a poor blind creature as ugly as it was wretched. And our victorious wrath pursued this bat for hours, lunging at it pitilessly, like a child with a broomstick. Iconoclasm Triumphant pursued the Great Idea.

"Down, down with the king!" ("king" pronounced with the smallest possible k).

That night, when each of us lay in his own bed, separated from the crowd, we repeated the audacious phrase gallantly to ourselves, over and over, in the hope of growing accustomed to it. Perhaps something comparable happens when a person keeps an all-night vigil over a corpse. He knows full well that the cadaver cannot budge, cannot do him the slightest harm, cannot even wink its eye at him. His reason assures him that the deceased is just a thing, no different from any table, bedroom slipper, or cushion underfoot. Yet despite all this, he dares not touch it, not even with his shoe, nor can he bring himself even to look at it for any length of time. The new situation is something he cannot grow accustomed to. Trembling deep down in his heart, he has an impulse to plead with the corpse lest by some quirk it decide—heaven forbid!—to play some kind of a trick on him, sticking out its tongue for example, because in that case he might find himself riveted to the spot by fear and consequently unable to take to his heels in time.

Imagination is invincible, and so is the soul. Reason is the weakest of all bulwarks against their frenzied action.

4

Balafaras

*F*estivities. Parades. Manoeuvres.

We donned the colors, placed the blue cap of the revolution on our heads (rakishly cocked toward the ear), and formed companies, regiments, and eventually an entire division, the Archipelago Division. They sent us a shipload of officers—from the mainland, naturally!—with the general leading the lot. Our recruits nicknamed him Balafaras the moment they laid eyes on him.

Balafaras!

Why they gave him this particular name God only knows; no one can say even if it means anything. Yet everyone called him this; it was applied *en masse*. The name fits him like a glove. There are certain people who seem to be born for one purpose only: to act as stuffing for some preëxistent name that is precisely right for them, and that patiently waits for them to appear. An unknown gentleman is striding along the sidewalk across the street from you. You've never seen him before in your life and don't know him from Adam, yet a sudden impulse tells you to quicken your pace, cross the street, catch up with him, and then, as you pass, to move close and give him a push with your elbow, whereupon you say right into his face: "Excuse me, Manny." This of course may not be the poor fellow's Christian name. Nevertheless, he has all the attributes of an Emmanuel, and if he turns out to be called by some other name, it is simply because his godfather did not know any better. In short, we all agreed without any further discussion that our general must be Balafaras.

Ba-la-FA-ras. A first-rate name. Heroic, magnanimous, straight as a ram-rod, broad, pot-bellied. The man himself is equally first-rate: of imposing stature, mustachioed, rakishly handsome, burly. He strides with measured pace, his legs somewhat spread, feet firmly planted. Glap, glop. Even his speech is the same: slow and sure, the syllables emerging leisurely, one by one. In full panoply, they pass in review beneath his handlebar mustache, everything in perfect order, not a vowel or consonant missing.

"Prepare for inspection, MAAAAAARRRCH!"

Everything about him is pompous, because he knows that wherever he goes people will appear at their doorways and windows to point him out and admire him.

"That's the general!"

So he strides about in his boots displaying all his gallant masculinity, head thrown back, abundant mustache upturned, huge triangular lapels of his greatcoat bright red over his chest, visor of his cap solid gold. This is not to mention the spurs that toll away on the foothills of this titan, their peal both dignified and pleasing: ding-a-ling, ding-a-ling. Holy Mother of God, save us! You realize straight off that the Creator intended this man for great-ness. You can smell it from afar. There simply is no doubt about it: his ac-tions are like the eagle's swoosh, his thoughts like the pure gurgling spring-water that wells up in a gush from the heart of mountains. We natives of Lesvos are proud simply to see this colossus tread upon our island. In one of his gloved paws he carries a riding crop with a silver handle. This he strikes incessantly against his right boot every time he speaks.

"We must (swish!) form an army (swish!), an army first and foremost" (swash! swish!).

You'd think he were using it to affix acute and grave accents to his words. Yet would any of these words so much as dare to emerge unclearly or with-out its full military "packaging"? God forbid! In such a case he might well give it a couple of good slashes across the backside and toss it into the clink:

"Three weeks at haaaaarrrd labor!" (swish!)

In the early evening when he goes to the Café Aegean for his post-siesta coffee, that's when we have a real show. All his officers accompany him. He walks in their midst, and his build is so imposing compared to theirs that you imagine you are viewing a hen with her chicks. The others regulate

17

their pace according to his—you won't catch them lagging even an eighth of an inch behind, no sir! Their route takes them along the quay, which is lined with cafés, the chairs all in a row out front. During their progress (the civilians in these chairs rising with respect as the procession passes), Balafaras recites something to the officers, who listen to his words, their jaws and kepis unanimously signaling assent: "Yes, yes." Occasionally, as they walk on either side of him attending this monologue, he halts temporarily in the middle of the road in order to lend additional emphasis to some point. At such times all the officers halt as well—instantaneously and *en masse,* as though activated collectively by a single spring. They gaze into his mouth until he starts out again, whereupon they follow suit. When the procession reaches the "Aegean," Balafaras sits down in the middle while the others place themselves in a circle around him, and smile. Should the slightest suspicion arise that the general intends certain of his words as a joke, their response is so warm, their faces beam with such heat, that if a piece of rock candy happened to touch their lips, it would melt away in a twinkling. If he smiles, they laugh; if by any chance he laughs, they split their sides with guffaws. It is a curious spectacle, to say the least. When they address him they keep their hands next to the vizor of their caps. You'd think his gold braid were emitting sunlight of such brilliance that they had to shield their eyes with their palms. But the most curious pantomime of all takes place when he offers one of them his hand. At such times, the thrice-fortunate being who is about to clasp it lowers his own right hand from his kepi with utmost speed, and for the full duration of his handshake with the general salutes with his left, which is free. When his hand is released by Balafaras, he quickly brings down his left from his forehead, and raises the right again. Only those who have actually witnessed this ridiculous maneuvre in its entirety can appreciate its Punch-and-Judy flavor.

I once had a chance to observe the general at close range, and at a time when he was removed from his circle. The occasion was a tea party given by some friends of mine. There I saw the true Balafaras, saw him at his best— his hooded eyes gluttonously devouring the plump hand of the girl who was serving him (and he a confirmed bachelor in his sixties).

"Would you care for another piece of cake, General?" she asked repeatedly, glancing at him coyly out of her velvet lashes. And as Balafaras kept answering "Merci . . . , merci . . . ," his conversation grew increasingly more languid, garrulous and stupid:

". . . and . . . and . . . well as we were saying . . . we soldiers . . . yes . . . "

A prime example of senile oafdom. Once when he inaugurated a particular line of argument that became so confused that he could not make it come out right, he cut it short in the middle and transferred our attention to the curtains on the French doors.

"Look! Over there, . . . over *there!*" (pointing gravely with his finger). "Do you see that embroidery?" (We saw it, naturally.) "All right, then, which of you can tell me what it resembles? Quick now! On your toes! Who can tell me what that beautiful embroidery resembles?"

The embroidery depicted a pair of flowerpots capped with blossoms. It bore no resemblance to anything else whatsoever. When we told him this, the general was unable to conceal a wry smirk of satisfaction.

"Aha, I knew you wouldn't get it. I'm afraid, you see, that a modicum of imagination is required. . . . All right, then. . . . They resemble two ancient Greek warriors with their helmets. . . . Right?"

This "Right?" was accompanied by a general inspection in which Balafaras surveyed the room with his round eyes while he caressed his mustache with the back of his hand. The entire company was taken aback by the idea, and several of the men exchanged clandestine winks. But then everyone present— the ladies, civilian gentlemen, and officers—immediately agreed.

"Why of course! Just look, look carefully! Precisely! Precisely! With their helmets . . . and the panache . . . , and even their noses and chins!"

The general guffawed with pleasure. "Ho-ho-ho-ho!" And his paunch, one obviously intended for greatness, guffawed animatedly in its own right, so brimming with satisfaction that it continued to chuckle independently for a few moments, even after its owner had ceased.

I have noticed something. As soon as an officer is promoted to major or higher, he begins to let out a bay window.

Now there's a thesis subject for you! In my opinion, if some student in his final year at the Cadet Academy examined it both broadly and minutely in his dissertation for the degree, he would be performing a most beneficial service for the nation.

5

The Ships

*O*ne evening we were given a speech and told that we would all be issued passes for that night. "Tomorrow morning we are leaving for the front."

"Tomorrow!" we repeated, banging our rifle-butts on the ground.

It was still pitch dark outside when the bugles began to sound reveille in fiercely official tones. The sleeping city was cocooned in darkness, as though covered by an army blanket. Vigilant wicks continued to smoke inside the municipality's dim streetlights along the deserted alleyways. The silently tranquil homes possessed the inertness of things in contented repose; behind the windowpanes of several of them, night-lamps gazed out thoughtfully toward the sea, sleepily consuming their peaceful oil. And then, suddenly, certain forms darker than darkness itself, all of them stooping, began to walk at a rapid pace through the empty streets, hastening toward the heights where the bugles were sounding. They wore hobnailed boots whose metal clanked loudly against the cobbles as they passed between the quiet houses arrayed on both sides of the street. A few doors opened and were then shut again with a bang; inside the locked homes a few women sniffled. After that, silence.

The armed forces. Among them, I, too, was climbing toward the barracks with a heavy pack on my back and my rifle slung over my shoulder. At your door I heard muted sobbing. Forsaken, you were weeping in the darkness; you had been weeping quietly the entire night. I entered. We did not speak.

You continued to weep softly, and I pretended to be extremely preoccupied with removing my pack—because if I had so much as opened my mouth to ask you why you were distressed, nothing else, I, too, would have been choked in tears—a state rather ridiculous for a revolutionary carrying his full weaponry on his back and two hundred shells in his cartridge-belt. (Do you realize that even at such a moment I was capable of recalling Hector's farewell to Andromache? I'm a literary animal by nature, wouldn't you say?)

Near you, curled up in a red armchair and sobbing quietly like yourself, was a little girl. She wore a velvet robe, purple in color, and only one sock. I ended by staring at the bare foot with feigned interest, and you, following my eyes, reached for a small basket made of woven cornhusks. Drawing this close, you removed a tiny sock, which you then strove to place upon the child's foot.

"But that sock is a different color," I remarked in a trembling voice, smiling heroically.

At this, you abruptly abandoned the sock (half of which still dangled from the little girl's foot), hugged me tightly, and began to weep without restraint.

I did not shed any tears. But a lump kept rising in my throat, and I kept swallowing it obstinately. Slinging my gun over my shoulder, I left, bowed under my load. I was heavy with grief, but proud of my manly fortitude.

The ships lay waiting out in the harbor, sounding their whistles discordantly. As we began the embarkation, heaven opened its floodgates and torrents of rain poured down upon us. The lighter into which we had been stuffed pitched heavily in the choppy waters, yet quite a few men continued to sing satirical ditties native to our island, while others fired farewell shots into the air, making the cursing N.C.O.s blow their whistles maniacally. Fat drops kept striking the sea in droves, churning it up until it seemed to be boiling.

A thousand and one somber things crossed my mind: things extremely mournful, indistinct, and confused. In my attempt to impose some logical arrangements upon these shapeless thoughts floating inside my skull, the only reflection to emerge was the following perplexity: "Rain on dry land is fine. But on the sea? Why should it rain on the sea?"

* * *

Half a dozen large freighters. Their cargo: young men. The lighters deposited us and went back, leaving us on those filthy vessels that were coated everywhere with thick layers of coal dust and smudges of black grease, and that exuded an inescapable reek of bilge-water. Sledges thundered against steel plating, winches shrieked, heavy chain began to wind onto huge iron capstans—we were weighing anchor. Steam issued from the smokestacks in furious sneezes, the anchors rose out of the sea, whistles tore open our ears and spat their icy spittle into our faces. We were singing, conversing, blaspheming. The recruits dangled their arms from the bridge and pressed against the railings to watch our island recede . . . recede. While the funnels spewed black smoke into the unclean air, we bade farewell to our beloved island. The shores—the verdant shores of Lesvos—followed us up to a point, then drew back one by one, and abandoned us. The mountains were dark. Tiny villages sitting on hillsides kept watching us, and several houses even scrambled up to the summits in order to view us that much longer. Every now and then a tiny pure-white cottage persisted in peeping out of the gray-green olive groves like a handkerchief waved in farewell. Soon this ceased too, and we all sighed.

The heavens continued to empty onto the sea, water onto water, like shotgun pellets being scattered over the waves. (Oh how lovely to be indoors during a rainstorm, watching the torrent from behind a window-pane, close to your beloved, olive-logs crackling in the hearth, a vase of freshly-picked flowers on the table, . . . and a good book in your hands!) But wait, what is this? Something wet on my cheeks? Rain, no doubt.

* * *

Life jackets were issued to every man. These are a kind of vest made from white canvas stuffed with cork. Squeezing ourselves between the vest's two humps, we sensed how greatly distorted our young bodies had become. We looked like victims of rickets, all of us, and when we moved about we resembled a flock of turtles standing on their hind legs. None of this mattered, however, because lying in wait for us beneath the turbid waves, gliding there, stalking us, was the enemy, a huge glittering sea-monster with a steel back. A single torpedo, and all these innocent children impersonating grown men inside their heavy greatcoats would go down to the bottom in a twinkling. Why?

The rain increased. There were no bunks on this ship, just a hold filled with black soot. The entire vessel was one huge, clangorous iron belly, and into this belly we lowered ourselves, clutching some grips that protruded ladder-like from the hold's flanks. Inside, we discovered a cargo of coal.

In an instant, our spick-and-span uniforms became unrecognizable, as did our faces shortly afterwards. This was followed by seasickness, that grave and incurable malady of the oceans that takes a man, takes him with all his grand and courageous resolutions, and turns him into something as disgustingly soft and boneless as an octopus being pounded against some sea rocks by a fisherman trying to tenderize it. You are encased in loathing as in gooey spittle. The soul surrenders, the brain moans. Your joints grow slimy with sweat, your knees buckle, and your abdomen turns into a basketful of putrescent guts shifting first to one side then to the other. Afterwards comes the vomit, the vomit that flows out of all your orifices—mouth, nostrils, eyes—and befouls everything.

Searching for an expression capable of cruelly deflating my enthusiasm, a phrase filled with abuse, cynicism, and heartlessness, I said to myself:

"We are six shiploads of heroes puking 'the nation's destiny.'"

6

Salonika

We disembarked at Salonika. It was in the early evening just after a rainstorm, and the wet streets glistened while a blackish-red sunset set the sky afire. Such tragic sunsets, all flame and blood, are unthinkable in our lyrical islands. The harbor was crowded with the bloated carcasses of animals floating everywhere you looked, and with large vessels puffing smoke into the sky as they unloaded their cargo. As for the city, it is a boundless barracks, grimy and repulsive, swarming with all the tribes of Israel, all dressed in khaki. Men from the Balkans and the rest of Europe are just the beginning. Aside from these there are Chinese crudely sculpted out of filthy, much-kneaded wax, Indians in yellow turbans, and African blacks with round white eyes and scrawny calves—all brought by the Europeans from the four corners of the earth to kill and be killed "for the freedom of all peoples."

The lanes quake, houses and all, every time one of those enormous British limousines passes through them. It is clear at first glance that the British rule the roost, having gained control by means of a copious supply of pound notes, reinforced by their naive magnanimity, at the bottom of which lurks conceit and a generous contempt for the rest of mankind. Everything about them is large: their height, shoes, horses, cars, parties, and teeth (on the rare occasions when they have any). It is a sight to observe the immense pains they take to consume the unlimited funds at their disposal, something they never seem to accomplish. You can be sure that all the tarts in the Balkans quickly caught wind of this state of affairs, with results which must be seen to be believed. They abandoned the weekly wash, abandoned the mopping, and raced to Salonika one and all to play the coquette. One day I observed two English officers keeping company with half a dozen such coquettes. Not knowing how to pass the time with them, they plied them with expensive meals, champagne, and sweets. Every conceivable edible object had been placed before these girls just to keep them from bothering the two officers, who simply wished to be left alone so that they could exchange their inarticulate monosyllables in peace. And the girls gorged and glutted, ate their heads off, driven by their primeval Balkan hunger. They were ugly and badly made up—Jewesses, Slavs, Armenians, Greeks, and Levantines who could hardly make themselves understood, even among themselves.

We Greeks adore the English. Do you know why? Because they smile so affably as they allow us to rob them, anger being beneath an Englishman's dignity. The French are altogether different: a quarrelsome breed, very clever, and so stingy that they'll shout your ear off and turn the world upside down over a matter involving twenty *centimes.* The language they speak is so refined that in and of itself it conveys delicate irony or biting allusiveness. Since the instrument itself is so completely and finely *spirituel,* even the stupidest Frenchmen are able to talk intelligently—which explains why they get along so well with the Jews. Now for the Italians: they're as elegant as lead soldiers, with large black eyes that might almost be described as Hellenic if they didn't have a certain effeminate quality about them. Our recruits feel deadly hatred for the Italians because of their craftiness in retaining the Dodecanese Islands, which are really Greek of course.

We set up camp outside the city on an arid, treeless hill called Tumba, a truly wretched place. Next to us were other camps, each encircled by a barbed-wire fence and all together resembling a row of cages with wild animals locked inside, a description not too far from the mark considering that one night the Italians killed a Greek corporal beneath a bridge there, slaughtering him like a goat, with a razor. The next night our men dragged two Italians to the same spot with two English penknives in their chests, driven up to the hilt.

The English don't act like this; they keep to themselves and never bother anyone else. Among themselves, however, they are so incorrigibly pugilistic that their almost universal lack of front teeth becomes immediately comprehensible. Our soldiers find it difficult to understand how such fisticuffs can occur between two men who afterwards embrace and, for hours on end, indulge in the monosyllabic barking that among them passes for song. At night every man Jack of them gets stinking drunk. Large trucks are then dispatched to collect them bunch by bunch, return them to their barracks, and dump them out like so many stiffs.

* * *

One day when the heat was unbearable we were re-outfitted from head to toe. They gave us a whole collection of greatcoats, spades, tunics, pick-axes, underwear, shirts, blankets, shoes, safety pins, wire-cutters, needles, and thread; they loaded us in addition with an unliftable cargo of "hardware"— a complete line of weapons, none of which we had the slightest idea how to use. Then they lined us up for the departure ceremony. The entire division assembled in a large square. There, against a background of military bands, snare drums, and patriotic oratory, the three regiments took formal posses- sion of their banners.

These regimental flags are of pure silk, blue and white (the national colors), with golden tassels and glittering fringes. A silver apple on each staff indicates the regimental number. They were not unfamiliar to me, because they had been especially prepared for us on our island, woven, sewn and embroidered (at sweatshop wages) by the refugee-girls under the care of the Ladies' Benevolent Society, and donated to us by the island's dowager ma- trons and wealthy debutantes. They smelled of our beautiful Lesvos and of Anatolian shores, these flags; we swore our oaths upon them (Balafaras weep- ing tears as big as plums), took them, and departed.

As long as the band can still be heard and you know that pretty girls are watching you from doorways and balconies, things could be worse. You raise that humpish pack on your shoulders and pretend to be oblivious of that entire hardware store clanking at your belt and bouncing against your legs— in sum, you put on a brave front as best you can. It's a different story, how- ever as soon as you get further out, and the music stops, the companies are commanded "Sling, ARMS!" and that full household on your back starts dragging you down.

The marches, you see, had begun.

7

Marching

Whole weeks of marching beneath rain and broiling sun. The company's log indicates three hundred kilometers to where we've now halted, each covered on foot, one step at a time. In attempting to single out my strongest impressions I find very few: only an incident or two.

I think of one of the hottest days of all. We had been marching since dawn and there was no indication that we were going to stop, although midday was approaching. As usual, we were walking in ranks of four, weighed down by our weaponry, not a man uttering a word. This is always the case after an hour or two on the road. You begin by singing. Everyone joins in at first, but gradually the number of voices diminishes until only five or six are left. These persist in repeating the refrain until they realize once and for all that no one is going to accompany them. (Who can spare any breath for singing?) Then they, too, at last, lapse into silence.

At this point the only sounds from a marching column are the non-rhythmic thumps of innumerable boots upon the ground, and the clatter of metallic equipment. Exhaustion overcomes you sooner or later, begins to unscrew your limbs one at a time, to dislocate your joints. . . . But none of this has any bearing on when the march will end. That is determined by the "Order of the Day." You will proceed to the spot which it—the Order of the Day—has designated. These fearsome Tables of the Law are issued daily by the regiment and transcribed by the clerk of each company. Whatever they say, that's that—no monkey business allowed. On one occasion

I was sent to copy out the Order of the Day. In it I discovered a dangling participle that I had the audacity to set right, an act for which I was reprimanded by the sergeant major who characterized it as sacrilege. When I "begged to inform him" that a syntactical error was involved, he fumed with divine wrath and punished me severely for "tampering with the Order of the Day." (Ever since then I've had an extraordinary amount of respect for the Order of the Day, and even more for dangling participles.)

So you keep marching by some miracle, because that's what the Order of the Day has willed. Exhaustion gradually saturates all the molecules in both your body and your mind, one by one. It spreads to each and every part . . . except the engines that drive your legs. These keep running—hep-two-three-four—as though by magic. All thinking has long since terminated. Both mind and body are carried along now, together with your weapons and gear, by legs that operate on their own: by self-governing and self-sufficient extremities that accept no directives any longer from the brain or nerves, or from anywhere except the Order of the Day. By this time, everything has become automatic. You move according to the dictates of inexorable necessity, as though in some obscure and somber dream. You have no idea where you are heading, and no desire to find out. Others are going in front of you, and others are following behind: your own volition is there, in these others. It is they who exert their will on your behalf; you simply march beneath your pack, which grows heavier every hour. You feel an emptiness in your head, and ought to, for you have handed your brains over to the "leader." The sun stings you, licks you with its flames until the blood entrapped in your swollen vessels (swollen from the straps biting into them) boils and bubbles. You neither talk, think, nor complain; yet you are all too aware of pain and prostration. Your throat is on fire but your saliva is depleted, and not a drop of water remains in the canteen flapping hollowly against your thigh. Perspiration smarts your eyes, tickles your nose, insinuates its saltiness between your lips. You shift your rifle from one shoulder to the other, and each time you do this its loop digs a new foxhole into your flesh. The pack makes you stoop like an old man while its leather straps nip the sinews in your neck, pitilessly. The load of cartridges, wire-cutters, and digging implements at your waist has furrowed your middle with a severe inflammation resembling an annular wound. Your sweaty flesh is everywhere pinched between buckles and straps that seem like pliers methodically flaying you strip by strip.

This is how I felt on that sweltering day.

My soul was oozing drop by drop through my pores together with my dirty sweat. Inside my incandescent helmet my brains felt like they were being fried to a crisp as though in a copper skillet, making me live for hours with the fear that if I gave my head a vigorous shake I might hear them shift inside my desiccated skull like a well-done omelet. My prevailing emotion was misery, a misery as huge and ineluctable as the sea. Yet at the same time that I felt this, I was able to view myself as someone else. Overcome by sadness and tender solicitude for this "other" wretch who was being jostled like a walnut shell on the turbulent waves of misfortune, I felt like sitting down and weeping for him—bewailing his misery. This misery saturated me to the core, infusing its penetrating and obnoxious damp to the depths of my body, the very marrow of my aching bones.

My inflamed eyes, as red as two aggravated wounds, were of necessity trained only on the "outside man" in the foursome ahead of my own. More precisely, they were of necessity trained on his pack with the mess tin secured to the middle, on the small of his back, on his buttocks and on his legs beneath as they moved back and forth mechanically. This rear was indescribably discouraging. (In general, a soldier's posterior makes me feel extremely sad: it is so weak, expressionless and—above all—vulnerable. The anterior is what really matters in a fighting man. Chest, face, eyes, hands loaded with weapons. . . . One day I reflected that perhaps wars will cease only when all combatants have learned to advance backwards.) The only happy thing about the outside man's rear was his pack, which seemed uncommonly pleased to be carried the entire distance. Afterwards I noted that all the other packs displayed this same satisfied air in a manner that I found most exasperating. When I considered how many thousands of kits were comfortably astride how many thousands of goodly backs, I concluded that the whole lot of them were leathery misshapen beasts out for a ride on our shoulders, their claws dug into our flesh. And, like Sinbad the Sailor's demon, there they would sit for the rest of our lives. Sinbad encountered this demon in the form of a weak old man wailing by a riverbank and begging to be carried to the other side. Duped, he lifted the suppliant to

29

his shoulders, whereupon the demon instantly locked his bony legs beneath Sinbad's armpits with no intent of ever letting go. And there he remained, permanently glued to the poor fellow's neck. We were goodhearted Sinbads, every one of us, a large herd of mute, harassed, huffing, puffing, groaning, and panting Sinbads condemned by an unpropitiable Judge to carry those ponderous, hirsute demons forever on our shoulders, demons filled to overflowing with stupid and malicious evil.

Earlier, I mentioned the outside man's mess tin, secured to the middle of his pack. At one point in the march, the strap encircling it worked loose; then the lid began to jingle with a harsh, monotonous, and invariably regular sound. Every time he advanced his left leg the mess tin jingled. Ding! This happened again and again, always with the same rhythm. Ding! Ding! And then again, and again: that unchanging, unfeeling, indefatigable, unsilenceable sound driving its way into my tortured cerebrum like the most slender of pins, then slipping out, then driving back in again, and out, and in, and out, in and out, in and out, forever and ever. I wanted to scream, to sever the chinstrap on my helmet and stop it from tickling my neck, to sever the strap encircling that tinkling mess tin, to sever the left leg responsible for the jingle. . . . Yet I knew I would have to endure this torture for nearly sixty minutes more, until the whistle sounded for our hourly break when we unloaded for five or ten minutes and I could beg that man in front of me to tighten the strap on his mess tin. And indeed, the ordeal did last precisely one hour: sixty interminable minutes of agony.

At the sound of the captain's whistle and the platoon leader's "Halt!" I collapsed face downwards onto some warm clumps of earth and lay there, digging my fingertips into the soil while tears from my eyes trickled down into my mouth, mixed with dust and acrid sweat.

8

Blinded...

*H*ere is another scene that has remained in my memory, affixed there like one of those numbers branded with red-hot irons on the haunches of army horses.

Imagine a rectangular tent, pure white, standing on the verdant banks of an idyllic little river splendidly appropriate for a picture postcard. This tent is an Italian field hospital. Along the bank are thirty-two (I counted them) thirty-two young men seated in a long row on the soft grass, beneath aspens whose birdsong and rustling foliage provide a refreshing chatter. The men have their legs stretched out toward the current, which flows by them quickly, happily. All are dressed in hospital blues, and all have a black bandage bound tightly round their eyes.

They listen in silence as the water sings beneath their sandals, beneath the trees, and as birds converse high above their heads. Their hands caress the grass, or grope with halting, pitiful movements attempting to fill a pipe. One of them strikes a match and continues to hold it absent-mindedly while the flame approaches his fingers and burns them; then with sudden fright he tosses the match into the river and licks his fingers urgently, bathing them in saliva. Occasionally one of these men moves his lips, but we are too far away to distinguish any words. Occasionally one of them smiles pleasantly. All are handsome olive-skinned sons of Italy with raven-black hair and childlike mouths. And all have been blinded by tear gas. All those black eyes beneath the pathetic bandages are dead now, and will perhaps remain so indefinitely. . . .

31

It was then I understood why they sat there in silence, or, if they did move their lips, why they spoke in a whisper as if in the sanctuary of a cathedral. They were listening, listening nostalgically with every part of their bodies, as the secret whisperings of life in all its sweetness told them tales about light and water, about women (who are like fruit, like roses), about the sun and the flowers that they would perhaps never see again. With their sightless eyes they were gazing in horror at a frigid truth hidden from our sight because our eyes are still intact.

Oh God . . . ! I spread my eyes wide in order to take a strong, all-embracing look at thickly woven nature—to drink down its entire meaning in a single gulp, like a man soon destined to be blinded forever.

9

Constantine Palaiologos

*M*y next memory is of a certain captain, commanding officer of the Sixth Company. He is a large-framed man with blond hair, twirled mustachios, pale blue eyes resembling watered-down ouzo, and a little snub nose sharp as a skewer and shining at all times with a greasy luster. He bears a name renowned in our history—Constantine Palaiologos—and is extraordinarily proud of this fact, never failing to write his name out in full, as though the man inscribing this famous signature were the last emperor of Byzantium in person, or at least his very next of kin. Indeed, he subjects his company to frequent historical lectures on the great figure, always commencing: "This namesake of mine, the emperor. . ." When his colleagues address him as Costas he makes an austere little bow and corrects them with the utmost gravity:

"Constantine, if you please!"

He was despised from the very start by his entire company, including the lackeys in his service, because he is a cruel and evil man. During the marches he became notorious throughout the regiment, with the result that he is now heartily despised by everyone. The only trouble is that Balafaras happens to be his uncle and relies on his opinions, which explains why practically all the officers try their best to stay on good terms with him.

One day shortly after we were mobilized, Palaiologos discovered a recruit named Tarnanas in the Sixth Company barracks. This Tarnanas, a sun-baked farmer from Anatolia, had prostrated himself before the authorities and begged to be enlisted as a volunteer so that he could vent his spleen. Everyone knew his story. During the days of persecution in Anatolia the Turks had discovered a Greek flag hidden behind his icons. As revenge they violated his daughter in front of his eyes, binding her face-up to his own body. She was an unripe little girl, only thirteen years old, and they a whole gang of irregulars. Fifteen enormous militiamen passed over her in a row with violent, brutish movements, each one wiping himself on the flag as he finished, while Tarnanas, underneath, kept pleading on behalf of the child, who was gasping and drowned in blood:

"Not so hard, bey, sir, not so hard, bey. . . . She's frail, bey. . . . She'll die."

He was an almost elderly man, with a long gray mustache that dangled on either side of his large mouth.

"Why are you snooping around here in the squad room, idiot?" the captain demanded.

Tarnanas snapped to attention and saluted, stiff as a board, a moronic grin on his lips. After standing there for a moment, he replied in confusion, his long mustache trembling:

"Yes, sir!"

"Blockhead! You're not meant to laugh when I speak to you, do you understand!"

"Yes, sir!"

"What's your company, idiot?"

"Yes, sir!" replied Tarnanas, still harping on the same string, and still grinning moronically and trembling.

This drove Palaiologos wild. Seizing him by the collar and dragging him outside, he tied him with his own hands to a tree in the courtyard, then took a rifle strap and thrashed him like a dog with it. Tarnanas bawled with great ridiculous cries, like an infant. Afterwards we learned that the poor devil was deaf and had been taken into the company solely as custodian of the squad room, since he was an extremely meticulous and honest person. This event embittered us all very much.

Whenever Palaiologos glimpsed a beautiful woman standing at her window when his company returned from maneuvers, there on the spot, in the middle of the street, he commanded with awesome authority:

"Company, HALT!"

Cra—crack—crack!

The curt rhythmical reports of the three movements resounded immediately up and down the lane, joined by the fierce thunder of two hundred rifle-butts striking the paving blocks. Then, delaying the command of "at ease," he kept the men standing this way—absolutely motionless, at attention—while he, astride his horse, one hand thrust into his cummerbund, mustache and nose raised high, gazed triumphantly at the ladies as if to say to them:

"Do you see me, girls? I cut quite a figure, don't I? All these vermin are in my hands to treat as I please. I can thrash them, make them turn somersaults, shave off all their hair, lay them out prone right here in the middle of the gutter, set them running through the streets like raving lunatics; and, when all is said and done, and I—Constantine Palaiologos—give the command at the fated hour, they will fall to the ground, slaughtered, and will twitch in front of my newly shined boots like Easter lambs. Behold! That's the kind of man I am!"

This captain acted like a wild leopard as long as we remained on the island, where the anti-royalist revolution, completely unopposed, had broken out like a folk festival, with public holidays, parades, dancing, band-music, and festive unstitching of the royal crown from our caps. His spurs on the street were clashing armies, his glances pistol-shots. Even the abrupt and stalwart bows he offered at the teas and dances seemed to proclaim: "When the devil am I going to shake the vile dust of this city from my heels and escape this flabby atmosphere of peace that slowly but surely makes heroes go moldy? When shall I take to the hills and roam over jagged peaks, munching four-strand barbed wire as my baclava? Oh when, oh when, shall I light my cigarettes from the shells whizzing beneath my nose?"

Despite all this, whenever Constantine Palaiologos discovered some little female of "inferior station" who caught his fancy, he forgot every scrap of his imperial traditions.

Indeed, he once lowered them all the way to the scullery.

The occasion was a tea party given for the general and some of his officers by one of Mytilene's most distinguished families. Constantine

35

Palaiologos molested some silly little servant girl with big breasts, maneuvering her behind a curtain and pinching her bosom vigorously. She squealed with pain, the lady of the house drew back the curtain with a sudden swish, and the disconcerted captain was left standing *en tableau* in front of everyone, next to the whimpering servant as she continued to rub her welts. The mortified hostess went up to the captain, who had remained there as though frozen solid, touched him with her fan, and then turned to the others and said with an imperceptible smile:

"You see! Now we can all believe the legend that Constantine Palaiologos was turned to marble."

And a pudgy little major added shrilly in his weak voice, indicating the buxom wench with a flourish of his eyebrows:

"But that is not all, Madame. Now we can also believe that he has never ceased to do battle on the . . . er . . . *ramparts* of . . . Byzantium!"

As soon as the marches commenced, the leopard changed his spots considerably. No more of that Napoleonic bravura. Instead, every time an aircraft droned overhead, he lifted his greasy little nose like a rabbit-hound and anxiously sniffed the air.

"Must be one of ours, eh?"

This agonized inquiry was directed at whoever happened to be near him, even if it were a group of privates. And when the reply came back in a happy chorus—"Ours, Captain, ours!"—and he registered the mockery in every eye, he responded with blasphemy and insult, calling down the wrath of Father, Son, and Holy Ghost upon his men from dawn to dusk and hauling them over the coals with the filthiest curses he could muster.

I remember one particularly exhausting day. We had already marched extremely far. Our feet were swollen, our backs breaking, our canteens empty. The sun's rays bore down on all sides, making the cracked earth so hot that we felt we were walking on nails. Our tongues, as dry as shoesoles, were stuck in our throats: thirst had begun its terrible, unbearable torture, causing bright red and blue fireflies to dart in front of our eyes and life to evaporate from our bodies like ether from an unstoppered vial. We all wanted to break down and weep. "If only I could die," each of us kept thinking, "if only I could die—just to bring this to an end." Yet the road stretched interminably between arid fields with no shade to relieve its glaring whiteness and nary a shadow, not even from the wing of a common housefly.

Suddenly, at a bend in the road, something leaped out in front of our singed corneas: a reality surpassing even our maddest and most fantastic dreams.

Two huge plane-trees with dense foliage—robust, green, beatific—and welling up between them a chattering, gurgling spring that sent its pure waters bubbling into a channel along the roadside.

A shout of ecstatic joy rose from the column (you'd think an entire herd of buffaloes were bellowing); in a flash the men broke rank and flopped to the ground along the entire length of the channel. The scene was that of an army suddenly dispersed by terrifying waves of panic. Those fortunate mortals who had reached the water ahead of the rest plunged their snouts into it and began to lap it up with noisy sobs, choking as they swallowed, and grunting happily like animals at the divine moment of sexual climax—completely oblivious of the others who were piling on top of them layer after layer, trampling them painfully underfoot, and muddying the water.

Palaiologos, riding at the head of the column, spun his horse abruptly around and charged like a man possessed. He trampled quite a few beneath his horse's hoofs and lashed out mercilessly with his riding crop at all who did not spring to their feet. Down came the sinews of the large crop, down they came left and right upon the men who lay prone by the channel, their faces submerged voluptuously in the refreshing muddy puddle. Yet none of the soldiers rose until they had taken their fill of the sludge, despite the horrible pain of the lash bearing down on their sweaty bodies, the only sign of which was an occasional squeal of severe distress intermingled with the sobs of happiness that the men released while lapping. The whip caught the cheek of a beardless youth, a young volunteer from Aivaly with not even fuzz on his virginal face, raising a red and bloody welt from jaw to eye. He hurried back to his rank, whimpering plaintively like a child. Meanwhile, the N.C.O.s had begun to sound their whistles with insane frenzy and to abuse the men in the vilest possible language (". . . fuck your grandmother and your mother and your . . .") while everyone hastened to rejoin his rank before the march recommenced.

One old veteran, however—a reservist with full mustache and ribbons from the Balkan Wars on his chest—limped slowly back into line, his leg having been kicked by Palaiologos's horse. Before he reached the column he hooted loudly in the captain's direction:

"Bastard! Don't worry—when the time comes, the first bullet will be reserved for you!"

Everyone turned and glanced at him with admiration. A threatening mutter buzzed through the column.

The sergeants shouted in aggravated tones: "March! Keep moving! Keep moving!"

Palaiologos, pretending not to hear, galloped his mount to the front of the column again and resumed the lead, cursing with bell, book, and candle.

10

Poppies on a Hillside

*T*he horrible time of the marches did include one pleasant day, a "blue and red day"—that is, one filled with the mauve eyes of a vernal sky, with crimson wildflowers, and languidly melancholy songs.

We came upon a hill blessed with abundant springs. Its flank was scarlet with poppies; green vegetation covered the area. A Russian regiment also headed for the front had already chosen this spot to rest, and we were commanded to halt there as well. Stacking our rifles in pyramids, we settled near the Russians and began to eat. Soon we were approached by some burly, rosy-cheeked youths wearing heavy boots and the kind of bottomless blouses seen on children. Their caps had narrow visors.

"Greek?"

"Greek."

"Christian?"

"Christian."

"Orthodox?"

"Orthodox."

They laughed; we laughed in return. Then they welcomed us with almost childish delight, heaping conserves and penknives on us as gifts, slapping us on the back with their huge hands, reaching beneath their blouses and drawing out for our benefit the tiny gold crosses and mother-of-pearl amulets that they wore suspended from their necks on delicate chains, all the while crossing themselves Orthodox fashion and repeating:

"Christian! Christian!"

We ate together; we talked together for hours, neither group comprehending a jot of the other's tongue. Yet we understood each other perfectly, for love as well as hate is an international language.

I discovered an officer who remembered (after a fashion!) some ancient Greek from his schooldays. He was extremely young, and as delicately built as a girl, with large eyeglasses, good-humored lips, hair as yellow as sweet corn, and a golden mustache.

"Ἡμεῖς ρούσιαν λίαν Ἕλληνες ἀγαπώμεθαν. Ὀδνοσόν λίαν Ἕλληνες. Λίαν!"—"We Russian much Hellenes love. Odessa much Hellenes. Very!"

Striking a pose, he then declaimed some double Dutch that he assured me was Homer in the original.

Eventually they sang us folksongs in full chorus, several providing accompaniment on long-necked balalaikas that they slung across their shoulders crosswise to their guns. I did not understand the lyrics, yet surely they must have evoked something like this: A snow-covered wood and next to it a snow-covered village with the flue of every cabin censing blue smoke into the frozen air. Blond women with long braids seated behind closed windows, white foreheads pressed against the panes. Their fingers wipe the befogged glass with slow, deliberate movements, and their eyes gaze out in vain, far, far out over the Russian steppe, whose only termination is the horizon. In the middle of these vast flats: a trail carved in the snow by sleighs, a trail that has taken the village's fine young men and has carried them far far away—beyond the grayish horizon . . . , beyond life perhaps.

The singers' expressions were grave, their childlike, Slavic eyes welling with tears. At the conclusion of their songs they did not move for several moments, nor did we, for we were still traveling on the wings of music, that art which unites all men's hearts because it is the universal language of the heart.

When we lined up in fours again and were about to depart, the Russians placed poppies in our rifle-muzzles, transforming our column into a strange kind of religious procession carrying steel candles alight at the tips with the most exultant of flames.

"Goodbye! Goodbye!"

The young officer tossed his cap into the air with a nimble flourish, his slender form almost diaphanous against the sunlight.

"Hail, very, Greeks! Hail!"

Such great quantities of love exist in this world! Abundant love, covering the earth like a river that floods tidal plains in springtime. Blossoming love, an entire hillside scarlet with poppies begging to be picked. And to pick them is so very, very easy. All you need to do is bend down.

11

M'chaghilous

We marched and marched. At one point we obviously entered the danger zone, judging from the enemy planes that began to spy on us from aloft, keeping tabs on our forces while they circled over our heads like hawks. By a series of harsh all-night marches the regiments and formations of our division were penetrating deeper and deeper into Macedonia, moving closer and closer to the front. We set out each evening at dusk, fully laden as always, and halted each morning at the break of dawn, pitching our tents in recesses of one sort or another: amid thick growths of shrubs, in the secret clasp of a mountain, or deep at the invisible bottom of some defile. As a further precaution against being spotted by the enemy craft, we covered our tents with green branches.

There we remained all day, resting. We sluggishly polished our guns, deloused each other, or slept. But most of the time—whether we were asleep or awake—we dreamed. Our souls continued to inhabit Lesvos, which we had abandoned upon the breakwater calling forsakenly to us with tearful eyes as we boarded the lighters and shoved off, clenching our sorrow between rows of teeth forced into manly smiles. And all for the sake of Greece. Who can explain the magic of that word that sends sudden spasms through a person's vitals?

No sooner were we deprived of the sweet life we had left behind than memories of that life began to regale us with all its precious joys. Pushing their way through the branches of wild pine and terebinth, they slipped into our tents and danced beneath our heavy eyelids, hiding none of their lively charms. All these memories deposited a sediment of sorrow, a haze of sweet melancholy that enveloped us like incense and took the form of muted, affectionate expostulations directed toward all the beloved people and objects we had left behind when, stooped and pensive, we embarked upon the path singled out for us by fate and duty. Oh God, how much more love these people and objects owe us now! I say this to all you men, women, and children, be you friend or foe, who are still able to enjoy tranquil homes and clean clothing and a comfortable bed and the myriad small pleasures of life, while we, like new-fledged monks, advance toward our destiny: toward a fate whose countenance is hidden behind an iron mask.

We proudly relinquished everything in order to protect your happiness by means of enormous sacrifice. If you were honest in recognizing this fact you would be thinking about us constantly. We do not say this to you openly, but we say it with silent forcefulness because we desire your love with all our hearts. We need and want it all the more because we are so far away.

But listen to me—I am talking now to you: a shell, any rosy little shell on the shore of Lesvos. No one knows you, even the Lord God your Creator has forgotten you, yet you continue to gleam in the water or the sunshine, entirely unconcerned. I wonder if you know how fortunate you seem to me, or how fervently I shall kiss you, salty little bud of the seashore, when (God willing) I return home some day.

Dearest, I have said nothing about you, because everything I say in these pages is for you. There are only two things in this entire chaplet whose myriad beads of bittersweet longing I fondle and sadly enjoy one by one in my solitude, and those two things are your thoughtful brown eyes, a tear quivering on their fluttering lashes. It is through these two dear little windows that I view our island with its dancing waves and its natural springs that chortle night and day; through these dear eyes that glimpse caiques with their white sails festively unfurled, and humming copses of pine, and sacred olive-groves, and all the Byzantine castles, and the people of our island whom I love one and all—because they walk and breathe with you along its shores.

* * *

There is a boy named Michael among us (he is known as "M'chaghilous" to our islanders, and this Mytilenian form has stuck, so much so that even the officers use it when they talk about him). The moment this "M'chaghilous" discovered that the business we had undertaken involved honest-to-goodness danger, he attached himself as servant to the division paymaster, like a limpet to a rock. Back in Mytilene-town he had been apprenticed to a watchmaker who also dealt in gold. An orphaned refugee from Pergamum as a result of the first expulsion, he is alone in the world, without a single dear one to bolster his goodly heart.

One day a stray airplane dumped a bomb on us from a tremendous height. The bomb fell far wide of its mark, but the incident nevertheless opened M'chaghilous's eyes to the nature of war. Ever since that moment, he has been deplorably tormented by the fear of death. The division paymaster, a hulking captain with pockmarked features, is a man who subjects his servants to such ill treatment that they all leave him in less than a week. Now he has yanked M'chaghilous out of the company. Although the poor devil is being misused, and is driven insane with work, he swallows everything just so he can remain in the pay-office for the remainder of the war, far from the front lines.

M'chaghilous is merely an extremely frightened and good-natured child, his cheeks still covered with down. And an extremely skilled child as well, judging from the adroitness with which he takes bronze shell-casings and transforms them by means of his engravings into beautifully decorated vases for the officers' tents. In addition, he makes excellent rings out of aluminum, and concocts cigarette lighters from scrap copper—everything fashioned with true craftsmanship.

He is an olive-skinned lad with pleasing features. When he laughs, his large crimson mouth reaches right up to the ears, illuminating his face with two rows of clean bright teeth. His mouth is so large, it divides his face into two equal parts.

I came to know M'chaghilous by accident, since the paymaster, together with his countless boxes, was attached to our regiment for some time, and accompanied us on the marches. Also, the officer in charge of censoring the post fell ill, and they temporarily assigned the job to me since I am educated. Thus, aided by an assistant, I had to read all the letters sent home by our men, and to excise anything that might have aided the enemy's intelligence should a misplaced letter have fallen into their hands. No place-names, no information whatsoever about the march, not even any complaints about hardships.

Now the paymaster was a great one for playing poker and drinking whiskey with his cronies. Every time he wore himself out in these pursuits and turned in, M'chaghilous sat himself down and started to write a love letter, completing an entire page just about every night. The recipient of these missives was a certain Kondylenia, daughter of the goldsmith-jeweler to whom he had been apprenticed back home. He had fallen madly in love with her from the start but, being so very shy by nature, had never found the courage, the entire time she was near him, to declare his love. The moment distance intervened, however (not to mention the war, which gives a man increased rights so far as love is concerned), M'chaghilous gave rein to amorous effusions to which I became privy, and which I often found truly moving. Every dream he had concerning his beloved during those many months when he watched her enter her father's shop yet dared not even raise his eyes to look at her, he now described to her as best he could, given the smattering of education he possessed. He filled up whole tablets, ornamenting the pages with a variety of garlands, poetic couplets, serpents devouring hearts, hearts pierced by arrows, and so on. Each night he sat down and related to her every last jot—every infantile detail—of his dream-fantasies.

"When we're married I'll take you to the movies every single evening without exception. After the show, my sweet, we'll stop at the Public Gardens to listen to the music and drink an ouzo. Then we'll go home. I'll rest my hand on your arm and we'll walk slowly, sweetheart, and I'll be so proud to be with you. Now we're at the door! When we knock we'll hear nanny's voice inside: 'Just a moment, please.' [They would have a nanny in their employ, of course.] She'll turn up the lamp and open the door. 'Come in. Dinner is served.' Our son Alekos (named after your father, dearest) will clap his hands and call 'ga-ga,' which means he wants you to nurse him."

At the very bottom of all these epistles, after the soldier-boy's typical "I give you a sweet, rosy kiss," he never failed to add some couplet or other:

When I donned the colors to do my part,
a drop of black blood oozed from my heart.

45

This he followed with his standard entreaty: "Take pity on me, Kondylenia dearest, take pity on me at long last, sweetheart, and please please please write back to me. I'm alone in the world, miserable and alone. You're the only person I can turn to for some sympathy and comfort. Please! I expect your letter every day."

On some occasions he also set himself the task of describing for her benefit how his love began.

His very first glimpse of her occurred one day at noontime. Her father often became so involved in his work that he forgot to go home to eat, which caused the family dinner to get cold. On this particular day there was a great deal to be done in the workshop, and Kondylenia had been sent to remind her father of the hour. M'chaghilous, as she entered, was polishing a pair of engagement rings, having just engraved "Vaghitsa" inside one and "Orestes" inside the other. When he raised his head from the bench and saw her with her turquoise skirt and her black hair falling in bangs down to her eyebrows, his knees gave way and his heart began to quake . . . deliciously. Kondylenia, her hands on her waist, proceeded to stroll through the shop, obviously enjoying the litheness of her nimble body. She went to her father's bench and stood directly behind the old man's chair. From this vantage point she allowed her gaze to rest for a moment on the agitated apprentice. Then she raised her brows, turned her back on him, and tripped the mechanism of a large musical clock, making it play the National Anthem. She then swung around abruptly and stared once more at M'chaghilous, this time very gravely, puckering her lips as though to whistle a tune (or to make fun of him). Kondylenia then went out, only to halt again on the other side of the glass street-door and press her delectable little nose against the pane making it, the nose, seem yellowish and flat from inside, after which she called loudly to her father while staring the apprentice straight in the eye:

"Didn't you hear, papa? I said: 'Mother is waiting!' The soup will be ruined."

Her father, his face all screwed up as he bent over a disassembled watch with the jeweler's loupe still affixed to his eye, grumbled with irritation, between his teeth:

"All right, all right. I heard you the first time."

Kondylenia tapped a drum-roll on the pane with her fingertips, then turned and was quickly gone.

And that was that. He loved her from that moment, loved her exceedingly, lavished on her the sum total of all the affection he would have bestowed on many other dear ones from childhood onward if he had not been orphaned by the Turks. But he never told her. Month after month went by in this way, with M'chaghilous afraid to voice his love for fear she might respond with mockery (the manner in which she had puckered her rosy lips had left his blood running permanently cold). Yet now, at a distance, he wrote her each and every detail. Item: When he remained alone in the shop each evening in order to put things away and lock up for the night, he kissed everything she had chanced to touch that day with her clothes or fingers. Item: One day a pomegranate flower pinned to her bodice came loose and fell to the floor. He picked it up, kissed it night after night, and even now keeps it secured inside his tunic as a talisman. . . . If only she would send him the letter he craved! Every day he did nothing but wait for that letter. Every day. Whenever the mail arrived, the possibility that Kondylenia's reply had come at last made his heart flip-flop like a fish out of water.

"Oh, write to me, Kondylenia dearest! Tell me that you do not scorn my love."

M'chaghilous composed a letter of this sort every day, and every day he awaited Kondylenia's answer, which showed no signs of ever arriving. In the entire division I was the only one aware of this state of affairs. M'chaghilous knew this and also knew that I took care not to noise his secret about, indeed that I actually sympathized with his plight. All this made him so grateful to me that he was continually ransacking his brains for ways to demonstrate his appreciation and friendship. He put on all sorts of shows to please me. Whenever I walked by his tent he jumped to his feet, snapped to attention and remained that way with a smile on his huge lips, his childish cheeks blushing beautifully (only those with olive complexions can blush in this exquisite way), and his small black eyes—as full of silent devotion as a spaniel's—riveted upon my face. In addition, he frequently brought me some little gift that he had fashioned with his own accomplished hands: a diminutive bronze vase, a letter opener shaped like a miniature scimitar, an aluminum ring. Every time I turned around he would be checking and cleaning my rifle, and he even asked for my underclothes so that he could wash them in the stream along with the paymaster's.

In his present surroundings this youthful Anatolian was rather out of place. He knew none of the sly tricks that pass for cleverness among the rank and file, nor did he possess the facility of convincing others to take him seriously, which is every individual's most important achievement in life. All he possessed was an ardent, tender, and extremely sentimental heart that thirsted passionately for love. And an unspeakable fear of the trenches. And a great expectation, the one and only expectation of his life: that Kondylenia's letter would arrive one day from Lesvos. Yes, it *would* arrive, it would . . . it would!

But there was something else as well. M'chaghilous spoke Greek with a marked Anatolian accent. Like everyone who has grown up speaking Turkish at home, he nasalized his final n's and tended to place the verb at the end of his sentences. On top of this, he could not pronounce either "b" or "d," saying "p" for the first and "t" for the second. The paymaster, who had learned to imitate his servant's speech with great success, liked to amuse himself by conducting extended colloquies with him in front of his cronies, who died laughing. Indeed, the entire regiment, officers and men alike, gradually began to affect a pronunciation fit for Karaghiozis himself whenever they conversed with M'chaghilous, even if the most serious questions were involved. As a result, the poor boy became known far and wide as a ridiculous buffoon.

One day the paymaster began screaming bloody murder because he had scratched his hand ever so slightly on a magnificent sprig of wild roses that had been mounted at the entrance to his tent. M'chagilous, who had placed the roses there in an effort to add some decoration, turned vermilion with anxiety and fright. Jumping up, he opened a field-chest, provided himself with a small box containing cotton, iodine and dressings, and ran with this to attend his master.

"What's that you've got in your hand, muttonhead?" demanded the hulking captain, still extremely irritated.

"I've brought a pox for your cut," replied M'chaghilous.

"You've brought a pox? You intend to treat my laceration with a pox, do you? I suppose you forgot to bring a scurvy, you peanut-brained bastard, or better still a clap, eh? Go to the devil, jackass!"

With this "Go to the devil" he swung his leg and fetched M'chaghilous a vigorous kick in the guts with the toe of his boot, catapulting him head over heels over a distance of five or six paces. The poor boy remained sprawled on the grass clutching his belly in silence while all who happened to be near the tent split their sides with laughter.

After that, "pox" became all the rage.

On still another day, M'chaghilous ran to the paymaster's tent, his mouth agape with wonder, in order to relate a very strange bit of information. It seems that he had seen three blacks—three *arapades*—traveling along the main road, each being drawn by a team of four horses.

"Eh? What's that you said? You mean you actually saw them?"

"I never tell lies. By the Blessed Virgin, I saw them with my own two eyes."

A second lieutenant who felt great antipathy toward the French explained that this was really not so strange since our allies were fully capable of inflicting such torments on their black soldiers—and often did. He described a common punishment that he himself had witnessed: At high noon French officers forced the black soldiers to put on their thick winter greatcoats, to load up completely with all their guns and materiel, and then, outfitted like this, to circle round and round beneath the burning sun for hours on end at "quick march," inside a barbed-wire enclosure, while the N.C.O.s overseeing this harsh chastisement (whips in hand) remained in a well-shaded place. . . . Be this as it may, it soon became apparent that M'chaghilous's three black *arapades* each being drawn by a team of four horses were actually three ordinary *arabades,* a type of heavy four-wheeled wagon employed to carry supplies to the front.

The only somewhat unusual aspect of the affair was the fact that four horses had been pulling these wagons instead of the two normally used on army carts.

M'chaghilous was laughed to scorn all over again. His celebrated blacks went the rounds of the companies for days on end and became a new password triggering merciless ridicule the moment he stuck his nose out anywhere. In short, this servant ended up playing the fool for all and sundry. And when, in addition, the paymaster began to sniff the degree to which M'chaghilous feared the trenches, he allowed his unruly nerves—jaded by ouzo and all-night poker games—to vent themselves freely on his servant's back. In the beginning his practice was merely to give the boy the rough side of his tongue for every insignificant "lapse" (i.e. for no reason at all), using the most shameless language imaginable. Later, when he discovered that M'chaghilous could withstand physical abuse, he started kicking him, fetching him awful slaps every two minutes and, on one occasion, even thrashing him with his riding crop. After such abuse M'chaghilous would slink into his tent and remain there all by himself for considerable time, weeping.

"Leave, you fool," I kept telling him. "Go to your Company Command and lodge a complaint. Report him for maltreating you."

"I can't," he always answered between his sobs, his eyes filled with gratitude for my indignation. "I can't, I can't. He'd get rit of me, and then I't pe sent to the front and pe killt. I ton't want to tie. I want to return home."

At this point he'd cast a significant look in my direction and manage a smile through his tears because of the secret we shared. Then, wiping his eyes with his fist, he'd repeat:

"I want to return home."

But, M'chaghilous remained with his captain, who now subjected him routinely to physical abuse for next to nothing.

"Beast!" howled the paymaster from inside his tent.

"Here, sir!" squealed M'chaghilous in holy terror, from inside his own tent. Throwing aside his mess tin and bread if he happened to be eating, or his chisels if he happened to be carving something, he leaped to his feet and ran with every ounce of his strength, falling all over himself in his effort to respond promptly.

"Is this meant to be a soft-boiled egg you prepared for me? It's as hard as a rock, you filthy pimp!"

"But Captain, sir."

"Good-for-nothing! Louse! Skunk! I hope you fry in hell!"

Whereupon M'chaghilous received, smack in the head, whatever the captain could lay hands on: cartridge cases, ledgers, inkpots, riding boots, marching boots. Then, after he had endured all this and more, he ran with tear-stained cheeks to officers who were friendly with the paymaster, begging them to intervene on his behalf and convince the captain not to post him back to his company, which his tormenter constantly threatened to do.

This state of affairs became a stock topic of conversation among the division's officers when they came to collect their pay:

"Where's the paymaster?"

"Oh, he must be around somewhere . . . , walloping M'chaghilous."

Gradually, the boy grew accustomed to this sort of life. He came to accept it as natural, actually believing that it could not be otherwise, that God apparently had designated him to be the laughingstock of the entire division. So he began to play the clown—as though somehow, if ever so dimly, he half-understood that there is someone who directs the theater of life from the wings, and that this someone assigns predestined roles to people, and to inanimate objects as well, without consulting them or justifying the choice.

When M'chaghilous came to my tent in search of a kind word and I awakened his rumpled pride, he broke into tears (as he often must have done in the solitude of his own tent); however, the moment he stepped outside and exposed himself to our men and officers, he immediately began to play his role steadfastly, hiding behind the mask of M'chaghilous the division buffoon. He laughed in his own right at the ridicule he received from all sides, and even went out of the way to help the others guffaw at his expense.

"Say 'bee,' M'chaghilous."

"Pee."

"'Beak.'"

"Peak."

"Say 'Daddy dresses the darling baby daily.'"

"Tatty tresses the tarling papy taily.

Then: guffaw upon guffaw, and plentiful cuffs on the back of his head. And he laughed, too, along with the rest.

* * *

The marches continued. We walked all night and encamped at dawn. A nocturnal march in wartime is always a silent, melancholy journey, but it becomes positively funereal, pressing down upon the soul and suffocating it, if the night is starless, moonless, relentlessly dark.

The men press up against each other in their ranks of four, like sheep. They proceed without talking and (what is worse) without seeing—

haunted continually by the suspicion that some kind of hidden anxiety is fluttering its wings in that tranquility. The pounding of shoes upon the grass fills the silent darkness; the hoot of an invisible bird slashes night's ebony cloth abruptly in two. The blackness that digests and assimilates all things makes you feel that you are a component of that tenebrous non-existence. Absolute night is one form of complete annihilation, and you become part of the dark chaos that surrounds you. Like it, you lack color, outline, form. (The one thing you do not lack is weight, a somber and invisible burden that keeps shifting in the gloom.) What maintains you on your feet is a tiny hope no larger than the flickering glow in a votive lamp: the knowledge that you are moving toward the ultimate frontiers of darkness. Dawn, in your mind, becomes not the time when the march will end, but rather the place, the march's one and only destination. Everyone walks with weary disgust, in silence, but no one lags behind, not even those with swollen feet, because everyone is afraid of being separated from the security of the herd. Sometimes there is the sound of a mess kit colliding with a helmet, or a bayonet clanking against a shovel. And there is always your rubber gas mask in its ungovernable blue container hanging by a cord from the belt around your waist, knocking exasperatingly against your thigh like a swinging censer. Occasionally the guides botch everything, at which time the column loses its way in an untrodden wilderness like some poor animal separated from its pack, or grinds to a halt on a road that has suddenly come to an end. Despair bites into your soul, accompanied by an exhausted and impotent fury hardly able to stay awake. Now the entire column must about-face and retrace its steps hour after hour. This, too, is executed in silence and with the same weary disgust, because no one has sufficient fortitude even to spew a curse into the darkness. Instead, everyone looks to his despair for consolation, reflecting: "Fate has decreed that we march until daybreak." So we march until daybreak.

When the night march takes place under starlight, the sky sits there and watches us with millions of grave, thoughtful eyes as we pass beneath it in furtive silence at such an advanced hour, like assassins. If the full moon is out, things are much better. No matter how strong the moonlight, all outlines within a short distance appear frayed and obscured by a silvery mist that heavily drenches the atmosphere. At such times, everyone marches as though in a dream. The exhausted brain yawns with sleepiness; the only thought remaining in it is a little spark at the bottom: a tiny coal turning to ashes amid the embers, just alive enough to light a cigarette. For the duration of the march, all the time your body continues to walk with automatic motions, this little kernel of thought stumbles along, or slips and falls, worrying (in a manner suggesting second childhood) about various insignificant and nonsensical concerns, stupid or infantile issues bearing no relation to logic, to the march, or to war in general.

For example, on one such night I suddenly realized that for precisely two and a half hours, while marching with a full load beneath the moon, I had been turning the following ridiculous thought over and over in my mind as though it were a grave problem of universal significance:

"She put one brown sock on Stavrula and one white. . . . She put one brown sock on her and one white." Then backwards: "One white sock and one brown." I was remembering your young niece who was staying with you on the night I came to say goodbye. I sat down opposite you, you remember, with the pack still strapped to my back and my rifle between my knees. I could not bring myself to start a conversation. The tears flowed silently down your cheeks, and you kept nervously stroking Stavrula's diminutive hand. She sat in the armchair, her thin shanks hanging over the side, and she was wearing a single sock, a coffee-brown one on her right foot. Soon, without knowing why, the child added her tears to yours. When this happened, you hastily drew another little sock—a white one this time—out of a basket and started to place it on her other foot with immense seriousness and care, as though she were crying because of its absence. . . . Well, for two and a half hours, this was the detail I saw unremittingly before my mind's eye. I meditated on it with great insistence, fingered its every facet with utmost gravity.

"She put one white sock on Stavrula and one brown."

* * *

Every time we pitched camp, M'chaghilous came to my tent the moment his master fell asleep, and began to talk to me about the letter from Kondylenia that still had not appeared but that would definitely arrive sooner or later, never fear. He was obsessed with this idea; it seemed to have become his entire purpose in living. Each time the mail was distributed, M'chaghilous stood at the very front while the names were called out, his torso inclining forward, his huge mouth hanging open, a palm cupped behind his ear, eyes straining—a perfect model for a sculptor wishing to portray "Expectation."

I made it a point to observe him while he remained in this audient stance as though awaiting some definitive decision about his fate. But the roll-call of fortunate recipients always terminated without M'chaghilous's name being called. Then he would inhale deeply—you'd think he had not taken a single breath the entire time the quartermaster was reading out the names on the envelopes—and would collapse slowly into a ball as though from extreme fatigue, his knees giving way little by little wherever he happened to be standing at the time. There he would remain, crouching and rubbing his cheek . . . until the paymaster bellowed with sudden insistence: "Donkeeeeey!" whereupon M'chaghilous, still in a stupor, twitched as though awakening from a dream, leaped to his feet and raced toward the pay-office, shrieking in fright:

"Here I am! Heeeeeerrrre I am!"

This was accompanied by polyphonic waves of harsh laughter—strong, insane horselaughs as painful as concerted slaps from a thousand open palms—issuing from all the tents in the vicinity, in response to the strange admission that was implicit in the servant's response.

* * *

Having proceeded through Macedonia in this fashion, we were finally approaching Monastir.

The front!

It was just a stone's throw away now, that terrible Golgotha that had been the subject of so many dark stories and horrible secrets transferred from ear to ear in hushed whispers. Even at a distance, we all seemed to be registering its invisible effect: the strange and inexplicable power of its pungent exhalations that came wafting to us in the air, making us nervous and irritable when we inhaled them.

We had to maintain complete silence during the day now while we camped, and absolute darkness at night while we marched—not even the glow of a lighted cigarette was permitted any longer. The atmosphere trembled with the monotonous hum of invisible airplanes passing through the clouds overhead. Using abortive and fragmented strokes, glowworms hastily inscribed fiery green-gold letters in the blackness, letters that were fearsome communiqués—the cabalistic *mene, mene, tekel, upharsin*—inscribed by destiny upon the ebony of night.

Once on the open plain, the platoons halted frequently. If you could have observed them from the distant rises, they would have resembled dusty centipedes of monstrous bulk lined up motionless, one behind the other, in the center of the road because they had grown tired, or had died. The men stood in silence, seeing, hearing, smelling the front. Out of the silence came a distant, woeful rumble. This was the Dragor, Monastir's large river, rolling its waters unseen between its forested banks. The presence of living water in the distance spoke to the men, delivered messages both sweet and sorrowful to their souls. They listened to the river's voice with a deep concentration betrayed by strained, wrinkled brows, yet not one admitted that his soul comprehended or was disturbed by this diffuse, boundless sound, because not one was aware of what was happening.

Suddenly, in the darkness, eyes glowered and arms reached out toward the remoteness before us. Voices full of wonder and secret eagerness said softly.

"Look!"

Pearl-white flashes flared in the distance, begotten in mid-air between land and sky. Large, brilliant stars broke loose from somewhere and began to wander buoyantly through the void like ghostly lanterns. They promenaded at their leisure for a time and eventually expired phlegmatically, or disappeared all of a sudden behind a hilltop as they plunged into some distant ravine. Sometimes when these wartime meteors ignited in the sky they were tinted a beautiful shade of mauve or wine-blue: serpents of green light slowly undulating their multicolored scales high in the air.

The front.

Some kind of terrifying festival was taking place there. From time to time the frightening silence was broken by a sluggish moan that dispersed over the mountains and burrowed into caves and gullies like a huge, dying sigh. A cannon. Cannons lie calmly in wait in their hidden nests, stretching out their monstrous necks that are as long and maculated as a giraffe's. Then they waken suddenly and spit thunder and lightning out of their circular mouths, each slavering and bucking in place like a chained horse. Inside this iron beast is an untamable soul whose absurd wrath can never be appeased.

That morning we had camped next to the river, in a ravine. At midday we were given a tin of meat apiece and some bread. These coarse slabs of preserved meat were still a new experience for us; most of the men threw the tins away untouched and had to content themselves with munching on bread alone, after sprinkling it with coffee and granulated sugar. (On other occasions, if we happened to pass some fields of peppers or fresh juicy corn along our way, we would make short work of them.)

On this particular day we had pitched our tents in temporary fashion, since we were scheduled to break camp that same night and continue our trek. The tents extended lengthwise along the ravine, with my own perched like a large bat at the foot of a small tree weighed down by numerous clusters of blue flowers. Just a short distance away, the waters of the Dragor flowed by with tranquil solemnity, speckled with green reflections. The springtime soil exuded whiffs of provocative perfume on all sides, like the body of a woman. Golden bees, a great swarm of them, buzzed and sucked with intoxicated joy as they gathered the pollen from my blue flowers. Innumerable ground-insects, all frightfully busy, raced in and out among the blades of grass. I sat there listening to their sound while I smoked my pipe and threw stones into the river.

The paymaster had placed his tent at a considerable distance from mine, beneath a wild pear tree whose tufted foliage sheltered him like a green umbrella.

The day was hot and overcast, the air sultry with humidity and the strong odors arising from the soil. But then, at about two in the afternoon, a tepid south wind began to blow with abrupt and irregular gusts. The pungent aromas rose even more strongly now from the soil; a universal whispering arose in the distant woods; ripples appeared on the Dragor's surface, the river's green epidermis shuddered from a sudden chill. All the trees quaked violently, scattering a mass of yellow leaves into the air, while the flaps of our inadequately staked tents burst outward like black wings as the stakes worked loose from the soil and proceeded to frolic in the air at the end of their guy ropes. A merry hubbub arose all at once throughout the camp. Stones hammered against tent pegs, driving them back into the ground; N.C.O.s rushed about ordering each of us to make his tent fast and to dig a trench around it in case of rain. But then a new commotion began, even before the old one had time to subside.

"All men assemble for distribution of mail!"

Every heart began to throb. Each soldier abandoned in midstream whatever he was doing, tossed aside whatever he was holding, left his tent half-secured—and ran. Everyone gathered near the quartermaster, circling him like chicks surrounding a hen. His assistant held a large bundle of letters.

M'chaghilous was one of the first to arrive. (How the devil had he caught on so quickly, way out there beneath his pear tree?) He stationed himself at my side and asked me with his entire face.

"Do you think it has come?"

I smiled at him and placed my finger over my lips: the names were already being called. (When mail is distributed in wartime, it's like the drawing for an important lottery. Who will be the lucky winner?)

The sergeant faltered over several nearly illegible names.

"Private Andon. . . ? Andor. . . ? Who in damnation is this supposed to be anyhow?"

Then, from all directions, numerous anxious and questioning voices rang out urgently—weak voices, heavy gruff voices, shrill voices, voices betraying culture and education, or the blunt boorishness of the peasantry. All were quivering slightly.

"Andonoglou?"

"Andonakas maybe?"

"Please, it is Andoniadhis?"

"Andonellis?"

"Andonreës?"

The sergeant tapped his boot on the ground and gazed out over the assembled heads with a stern expression on his face, one eyebrow cocked, lips mumbling inaudible curses, until he had had enough.

"Shut the hell up!"

Suddenly, something entirely unprecedented happened. Looking at one of the envelopes, the quartermaster read out:

"Private Michael Akindynos Kazoglou."

M'chaghilous's name! I turned and glanced at him.

He had suddenly turned pale as a ghost. At first he just stood there, vigorously nodding his head (no, his whole body) as if to say "Yes! Yes!" Then he looked at me, his eyes dilated as though in terror, and said:

"It's the letter. . . . It has come. . . . It has come. . ."

"Michael Akindynos Kazoglou!" shouted the quartermaster once more in exasperation.

"Here!" shrieked M'chaghilous. He charged through the crowd like a buffalo, opening a passage by jostling everyone with his elbows and knees. Snatching the letter from the sergeant's hands, he took immediately to his heels.

The quartermaster's furious "You!" halted him dead in his tracks.

"Enlisted men receive their letters at attention, idiot! And then they salute, and do an about-face!"

M'chaghilous retraced his steps, snapped to attention, then began to salute—the letter still in his hand. Next, perceiving his blunder, he swiftly raised his left hand in complete confusion and used this to snatch the letter hastily from his right hand, the entire maneuver being executed above the forehead in an extremely ludicrous fashion.

Even the sergeant found it impossible to suppress a smile. As for the men, they hooted the poor boy, jeered at him, splitting their sides with laughter. Soon they began to disperse, all the mail having been distributed.

When M'chaghilous returned to my side he was clutching a small blue envelope between both palms. His eyelids were fluttering, his breath heavy and rapid. You'd think he were gasping for air after a long run.

"It's here, it's here," he panted in perfect turmoil. "I told you it would come, didn't I? Didn't I?"

In truth, the address was inscribed in tiny, delicate letters of exemplary regularity—obviously a feminine hand. The ink was mauve. Written out in full on the reverse side of the envelope was the girl's name.

"From Kondylenia Phanariotou."

M'chaghilous kept examining the envelope, clutching it all the while in his fist. He brought it near to his eyes, his nose, rotated it this way and that.

"Open it for God's sake!" I exclaimed, practically shouting. "You waited so terribly long for it, you never stopped talking about it—and now, are you going to stand there sniffing at it like a cat?"

He gave me a vacant look, then murmured shyly:

"Forgive me, but I'd like to be alone when I read it. You understand, I'm sure."

I laid my hand on his shoulder and gave him a friendly cuff, pushing him away.

He withdrew four or five paces. Removing a penknife from his gaiter, he inserted the blade beneath the flap and set about opening the blue envelope, proceeding with extreme caution, ever so slowly.

At that precise moment the paymaster's ferocious bark resounded beneath the wild pear-tree. He had emerged from his tent and was gyrating his long arms toward all four points of the compass like a raving lunatic.

"Hey, mut-ton-head! You! Where in goddamn hell have you gone? Hey! Swine! Id-i-ot!"

M'chaghilous recoiled in terror. The envelope slipped out of his hand and flew off like a little bird, carried by a strong gust of wind. It sailed for five or six paces, but then became snagged on a trampled-down thistle. M'chaghilous's first impulse was to run toward his captain, but an equally strong impulse directed him toward the letter. After a moment's hesitation he lunged resolutely toward the envelope.

The very moment he reached out to seize it, however, another gust snatched it abruptly away, lifted it high, dandled it playfully for a short while, and then dumped it into the Dragor's green waters, which flowed nearby. The current received it with indifference along with a pile of scrap-paper, twigs, and empty cans, then carried it rapidly downstream, far away . . . far away. . .

12

The Ghost Town

*I*t was night when we entered Monastir and night when we left. The streets of this large Serbian town are unlighted, the houses dark, with no lamps glowing in their windows. The inhabitants—the town is populated by Greeks—walk about furtively, like burglars; they converse in whispers, quiver with fear when they gaze at the sky, and dwell below ground in their basements, or in holes dug beneath their houses. Such holes are called *abris* by our French allies; that is, dugouts. (We first learned this word here, but without comprehending the full horror of its meaning. That was to come later.) We used a large public square as a temporary halting-place and went out from there to get our bearings. This city is directly in the battle zone. The French, who acted as our guides, showed us shell-damaged buildings that looked as though they had been struck by lightning. They also pointed out some houses that had been burned by incendiaries, a type of projectile that spews forth an inflammatory material that ignites piece by piece, each piece then hopping somewhere else and exploding anew, thereby spreading the conflagration over a large area. This burning rainfall (which cannot be extinguished by water) works incurable havoc wherever it lands.

I saw a once-lovely street overflowing with silence and moonlight. On either side, an endless row of burned-out buildings with smoke-blackened walls reaching up toward the somber blue sky. The moonlight marched in and out unhindered, passing through the empty window-frames, slipping behind gaping balcony-doors, and filling the houses with the silent bar-renness of death. They were just skeletons—bare, fleshless bones of mon-strous carcasses—these buildings that once upon a time must have been jubilant dwelling-places. Killed by war.

The people here got wind instantly of the arrival of fellow Greeks. This was remarkable, considering that our uniforms, helmets—all our belong-ings—were French, and that we entered the town on the Q.T. But they darted out of their subterranean holes like mice and swarmed around us—men, women, and children (but mostly women and children), all with gas masks hanging around their necks—they wear these masks night and day as protection against gas. They kissed our hands, caressed our rifles, pat-ted our helmets, buttoned and unbuttoned our greatcoats—and wept calm-ly, silently, beneath the moonlight.

"Can it be true? Are you really Greeks? Greeks from Greece? Our broth-ers?"

"Naturally! What did you expect?"

They explained that during all their years of slavery they had been waiting for us, dreaming about us, invoking us in their songs and worshiping us, without ever knowing who we were. "And now here you are at last, at our sides. May Christ and the Virgin watch over you! And please, brethren, never let us fall into the hands of the Serbs again. They've oppressed us horribly, just because we are Greek."

One old man told me, "They lash us with whips if they hear the Greek language spoken among us. They don't even allow us to celebrate mass in Greek. All our churches have been closed, and our wonderful schools as well. Our women, all our women, have been dishonored, the city turned into one huge brothel. The women have to submit; otherwise their bread-ration is suspended. And no one is allowed to save himself by leaving the city. The Serbs have barricaded every way out, and they shoot to kill."

Good God! Why had we come here, then? Was it to liberate Greeks by fighting Serbs, or to liberate Serbs (our allies, betrayed by the king we had rejected) by fighting Germans and Bulgarians? Something inside us began to crack. Was it our faith in what we had been told in Lesvos? Bewildered, we added our tears to theirs.

They presented us with a thousand and one simple little gifts: in every basement they prepared *loukoumadhes* and other deep-fried sweets for us, despite their tragically inadequate rations. A swarm of boys approached my platoon and all began to sing the National Anthem in hushed voices, caps in hand, touching our sleeves, and weeping. But a French M.P. from the provost marshal's office came over and commanded them to be silent:

"No noise!"

A woman with a black scarf over her head did not neglect to offer us some useful advice about tear gas. "Keep your masks handy at all times, brothers," she said with tender solicitude. "The other day the Bulgarians bombarded us with gas-shells and killed six of our children as they were squatting close together, telling stories to each other in a little huddle (they were in my neighborhood). The French laid their bodies out on the sidewalk, all in a row, and kept them there for an entire day while they took movies of them and also snapshots, some of which they used for picture post cards!"

A girl stationed herself next to me and remained standing there for considerable time, not saying a word. She had dark hair, excessively large eyes, and was as lithe as a cypress sapling. She just stood there and looked at me, stroking my gun-strap absentmindedly with one finger. I stared back at her, a smile on my lips. I could see the moonlight in her eyes. She did not smile. Suddenly she thrust a package of chocolate bars into my pack.

"Take them," she said in a whisper. "Take them. When you're in the trenches let them be a reminder to you that a girl from Monastir, a girl you'll never see again—"

"Why? What makes you so sure?"

She shook her head vigorously. A tress fell between her animated eyebrows and hung there like a black question mark.

"I know what I know. . . . Where do you come from? Tell me, my brother."

"From Lesvos. All of us come from Lesvos."

"Lesvos?" Smiling at last, she assumed the pose of a schoolgirl delivering a recitation, and then mouthed at breakneck speed, most comically, "Lesvos, home of Sappho, Alcaeus, Arion, Pittacus, and Theophrastus, cradle of music and lyric poetry."

How charming! Every one of those names, as they emerged in that pedantic way from her lips, went straight to my heart, as did the girl herself, suddenly. She pushed her way in with the same boldness that members of a person's family display when they barge unannounced into his room. She might have been the ardent soul of Sappho, my sacred Mother; she might have been none other than the soul of Lesvos itself, waiting for me here in Serbia, in order to present me with a package of chocolate bars.

I grasped her hand in the darkness and raised it to my lips, holding it against them for quite some time. It was cool, and it was submissive.

"Thank you. Thank you from the bottom of my heart. . . . You're a beautiful girl, and a kind one, too. . . . Tell me your name. I'll always remember it with gratitude."

At that moment my platoon-commander approached in extreme haste and told me to run as quickly as possible to find our sergeant. "Have him assemble the platoon. But take care—no whistles, no cigarettes, no talking. We leave in five minutes."

The platoon sergeant was my brother. I raced to find him. The girl faded into the darkness and disappeared, nameless.

We left.

Our route followed the course of the Dragor as it ran darkly through the town. At every bend in the lovely river the moonlight jiggled silvery scales. The stream flows tranquilly between two endless avenues of acacias, large robust trees whose roots must never lack for water. "How marvelous they must be at blossom time," I reflected, "when they radiate whiteness on a moonlit night such as this, and suffuse the dark air with their sweet perfume. . . . And that girl, the one who gave me the chocolate: her feet must have trod the paving stones of this embankment many, many times; her eyes must have seen the liquid moonlight flowing in the Dragor's waters. How beautiful she was! . . . And here we are, a column of terrified recruits marching noiselessly without cigarettes, marching for hours behind those enormous frames that have dyed burlap stretched upon them, or wrapping paper covered with painted designs. This camouflage conceals our passage from the eyes, and cannons, of the enemy. . . . That girl, the one who gave me the chocolate . . ."

The front.

We were really and truly there now, at that unknown, mysterious place so full of icy terror—a terror that had come to our souls and sounded the alarm in advance for things that, although still undivulged to us, had already impressed us with their flavor, making the heart of every man flap its wings like a bird suddenly overshadowed by a diving hawk.

Truly, we sat "in darkness and in the shadow of death."

13

The Cyclops' Eye

I am writing to you from inside a hollowed-out recess in the wall of the trench we were assigned to hold. This war, you understand, is just another job, but a most unusual and muddled one that has to be mastered in successive stages. Where we are now is only the third line. If we're good little boys, however—conscientious, industrious, and the like—and if we master our lessons, we'll be promoted to the first line! One thing we had to learn (how hushed the officers' voices were when they told us, how clouded in mystery) was that we are not fighting another Balkan War this time. Zeal is out of place here; there is no call for any hurly-burly or hazzaing. In sum, impetuosity, that lunacy of the Greeks, is a defect here. What we are dealing with this time is a subterranean war. Concealment is all; the best soldier is the one who hides himself best. Consequently, the combatants in this fight cannot be seen or heard. Right now, all of them are beneath the surface, digging sewer-like passageways underground. These engineering operations are soundless and invisible. Nevertheless you can sense them everywhere; you know that they extend as far as the eye can see. The best martial virtues, this time, are guile, foxy slyness, the persistence of an ant, patience of a donkey, tenacity of a goat.

In order to reach this trench where we finally stopped, we had to wind our way for hours through deep ditches carved into the mountainsides. Now I have this recess; this is where I shall sleep, together with my brother. You must realize what a luxury this is for me. He is a sergeant in charge of a platoon, while I am just an ordinary corporal in his platoon. We found only a few other alcoves of this type, hacked out of the wall of the trench; they were allotted to the sergeant-major and the remaining sergeants. The rest of the men, all of them, are bedded on the ground in the middle of the trench, curled up into balls. They all collapsed just as they were the moment we arrived, sprawling out every which way, and fell into a deathlike slumber. They're lying now in heaps on the warm soil, one on top of the other in a confused mass of arms and legs. I hear them snoring, cursing softly in their sleep, shifting their gear about, and farting.

My brother is sleeping, too.

Our recess is carved out of porous rock. The bottom of this human nest is uneven, which explains why my brother's body is in such an unnatural position. In an effort to find some reposeful way of spreading his limbs, he forced himself into such contortions that his arms and legs seem dislocated. Yet his face is peaceful. He is still a child, this younger brother of mine, a child who retains his innocence. His faith is firm; doubts are unknown to him. His dream is to become a commissioned officer in the regular army. In his infancy he used to suck his thumb until he fell asleep. Mother spread quinine over it to break the habit. Right now he is enjoying his sleep just as much as he did then. His respiration fills the empty hours with its rhythm. It is light and regular.

I have attached my tallow candle to the barrel-clamp on my bayonet. When the blade is driven vertically into the ground it makes a very serviceable candlestick. As the unsteady light dances over my sleeping brother's face it produces ever-shifting shadows beneath his eyelids and his golden mustache. It has been doing this for hours, making him appear to grimace continually. A curly clump of blond hair has fallen onto his guileless forehead. Its shadow is animated, alive: it becomes a claw-footed crab that slips out of the darkness, suddenly elongates its pincers, extends them toward the lad's eyes to snatch them out, then retreats and withdraws into itself, only to charge once more. Despite its comical aspects, this shadow-game has made me rather uneasy, as though some hidden danger were truly involved. My brother's adolescent limbs seem excessively motionless to me. Even his fatigue-exhausted muscles seem to be asleep. He looks like a man in a dead faint. All this has aggravated my uneasiness. I want to wake him but do not have the heart—it would be too cruel. Eventually, however, he smiles in his sleep and heaves a deep sigh, which enables me to breathe easily again. I drag myself further inside and huddle against the wall in an effort to occupy as little space as I can so that he may have that much more room and may sleep as comfortably as possible. The trouble is that the dugout isn't deep enough, so his legs extend into the trench from the knees downward. As for me in my sitting position, I feel as though I had a sprained neck. This is because I need to bend my head sharply forward to keep it from being injured by the jagged contours that the mattock left in the roof. As added protection I continue to wear my helmet.

It's a ludicrous and nerve-racking business, this contorting of the neck. It is reptilian, utterly miserable. I remain completely motionless, rolled up tight. My thoughts grow duller and duller. My mind comes to resemble a room being gradually vacated, emptied first of people, then of the shadows and memories they leave behind. Walking on tiptoe, without any haste, they keep withdrawing into the twilight until they vanish. Daylight wanes; lamps grow weaker . . . weaker. . . . I am surrounded by emptiness, by a vacuum drained of the past, drained of recollection. But then, all of a sudden, I discover myself doubled in two like this in a cave underneath a wild mountain in Serbia. What a surprise! Just look at that poor chap, I say to myself. Here it is a warm night without a single sound, and I see Anthony Kostoulas, the university student, huddled in a cave all forsaken and alone, with no trace of human companionship around him. There he sits inside his boulder, doubled in two, a steel hat on his head, his fists supporting his eyes and his knees supporting his fists. This person fills me with commiseration and fright. I want to save him. . . . What for, you fool, what for?

* * *

I must stop now, I have decided to blow out the candle and allow the darkness to enwrap me at last like a blanket. Perhaps I too will be able to get some sleep. But wait—here is a French sergeant. Having trampled everyone lying in the trench (to be sure, how else could he get through?) and having been cursed up hill and down dale in all the village dialects of Lesvos, he has blundered his way to me in order to "advise" me to extinguish my candle—

but fast, *sapristi!* It seems that my dugout entrance faces the enemy line; they might see the glow and level their gun-sights at it. I blow out the tallow at once, then continue to listen to the sound of his voice in the darkness. The only part of him I managed to glimpse before extinguishing my light was his nose, a large appendage extraordinarily enflamed. (I think he speaks with it!) He explains why absolute blackout is essential. Apparently a large mountain looms opposite us. On that mountain the enemy have a concealed observation post, and inside this post sit a pair of ever-vigilant eyes that stare at us night and day. I have a canvas sheet hanging over the dugout entrance, but no matter how well this canvas obscures the candle, the slightest glimmer escaping through a slit or around the edges will be more than enough to divulge our arrival to the enemy. And this, in turn, will be more than enough for their cannons to make mincemeat out of our trench in the twinkling of an eye. I learn from him that this trench has not been occupied for three months; they call it a "dead trench" in army lingo. The Germans and Bulgarians have stopped shelling it, have not molested it all that time, and our job is to give them no cause to believe that anything has changed. In short, we have to play dead here. The only time we can move at all is at night, and then without sound or commotion of any kind, and without allowing any candles or cigarettes to be lighted.

This trench has its history, you see. It is a history full of bloodstained mire, like that of every other trench. "At first it belonged to the enemy. We —*nous les français*—took it from them. Then we turned things around, 'organized' it against them, which explains why these *abris* are dug facing the wrong direction, why in other words they look out toward the Bulgarian cannons across the way instead of being carved into the front wall in order to have their backs to the foe. In short, these nests were hewed out by the enemy. *Eh bien,* we took the trench; then we entrusted it for safekeeping to some Italian conscripts who arrived nattily outfitted in spruce uniforms all freshly laundered and ironed. They raised a rumpus, sang serenades, and behaved like idiots in other ways as well—until one fine day our friends over there sent them a hail storm of lead that cleaned them up good and proper. *Vous savez, mon vieux,* forty men mashed to a pulp. *Oui . . . ,* quite a serving of baked macaroni: rocks, soil, and human meat all mixed together. *Eh bon soir, mon vieux, bon soir!*"

The sound of that enflamed nose continues to reach my ears; a voice at once gentle and mocking continues to issue from the trench's darkness, telling me horrifying tales. Finally it leaves, escorted anew by the curses of soldiers being trodden underfoot. I slide to the dugout's entrance and stick my head out into the trench. The night cools my burning brow. Raising my eyes, I stare over the parapet toward the enemy mountain, straining to cut through the blackness and to see—to divine—the observation post: that invisible antagonist. But nothing meets my gaze except a single star in the sky. It is a small bluish star that twinkles damply, humidly, as though saturated and about to drip upon the land. I keep watching it, and as I do so it gradually increases in size until it becomes a circular blue eye with a biting glance, a large and companionless eye like that of the Cyclops when he ransacked his cave so that he could find Odysseus's hidden companions and devour them. It is the enemy searchlight. Sliding back into my hole, I shrink into a ball next to my brother and try with all my might to get some sleep.

Yet for a long while I cannot escape the sensation of that terrifying gaze riveted directly upon me, upon all of us: the Cyclops' ever-watchful eye ransacking the half-devastated trench with implacable hatred. It has scented us; its icy gaze is laying hands on the sleeping figures in the trench, one by one. We are at the very center of its sights. This evil potency in the distance seems like the huge trunk of an elephant, a trunk composed of light. It reaches out into the darkness from the mountain opposite us, grows longer and longer until it reaches our trench, then proceeds to run its nasal tip carefully, hostilely, over the soldiers whom it has discovered sleeping there, halting over the exhalations of every man, listening to these exhalations intently, and counting them one by one. It slides its beam gently over our weapons like a luminescent finger, worms its way into our cartridge pouches, rummages through our packs. Our young hearts are throbbing, beating their wings as though ready for flight. It comes to rest upon them and remains upon them for many minutes, deep in thought while it waits for them to fail. Finally it draws back into its socket again, ready to turn traitor and divulge to the cannons everything it has seen and heard. These huge cannons are iron brutes whose bodies are nothing but neck. Covered leopard-like in mottled coats, they lurk in the hidden bowels of the mountain opposite us. . . . The eye would divulge all to the cannons and they, in turn, would elongate their necks even more and would spew death into our poor half-devastated trench with the intent of sprinkling its soil and dusty stones all over again with fresh blood. Yet no one here is personally acquainted with anyone over there, nor has anyone over there ever laid eyes on a single one of us.

Killing without hating is strange.

14

Carrion

We have already spent three weeks in this place. Life here slips slowly by, always the same. It's a peculiar kind of life, but unchanging. The only time for work (work here means digging) is night. During the day, the entire day, we have to lie low in the trench, roosting in its holes and recesses. Everyone has dug himself a sleeping den in the walls as best he can—a cranny just large enough to accommodate a man and his belongings. We eat once in every twenty-four hours, the distribution taking place at nightfall. The food is plentiful enough, but always the same, large slabs of meat with noodles or pilaf, so we have already lost all appetite for it. The cookers are tucked into a gully in back of our hill, far enough behind the line so that the smoke will not give us away. The food is delivered to us from a distance of three miles; by the time it arrives it is cold, bespattered with mud and full of pebbles—in short disgusting. I keep the bread and trade the rest with Mitreli, an emaciated, malformed private with a sallow complexion who never tires of eating and never puts on an ounce of weight. It seems that all the victuals he swallows go straight to his hump; this must be his stomach, because it's the only part of him that is nourished (it's been filling out lately). Mitreli gives me cigarettes in exchange for my portion. Thus I not only gain extra smokes, but also escape washing up. To clean a mess tin here is a formidable undertaking since the only source of water for the many trenches in our sector is one small spring on the other side of the hill. All the changes of shirts and underwear carried in our haversacks have already been

71

worn over and over again. Laundering them is out of the question when water is as rare as cologne. It's a royal battle just to fill your canteen at the spring, not to mention the fact that merely to get there exposes you to a heap of dangers along the way, since the trench is so shallow and completely vulnerable in various places. A guard had to be assigned to the spring shortly after our arrival because our men, unlike the French, are not in the habit of queuing up of their own accord. Each one tries his best to break into the line and be the first to fill his canteen. Soon it's a regular mêlée: they take swipes at each other with their canteens and with the walking sticks that all of us carry here to help us keep our balance at night. They throw rocks, too, and knives are drawn not infrequently. A fellow from Plomarion has already been court-martialed because he plunged his jack-knife into the plump ham of a Frenchman from Normandy. . . . But what can you expect from a single canteen-full of water every twenty-four hours? Cleanliness in all its forms, including the washing of face and hands, was dispensed with on the very first day we arrived. Nevertheless, we do refresh our bleary eyes in the morning when we awake. To accomplish this feat we dip our fingertips into the mouthful of water that we have taken but not yet swallowed, and apply the moisture to our eyelids.

At first I thought I would grow accustomed to my unwashed condition. As the days go by, my uncleanliness bothers me more and more. I am constantly aware of gritty dust on my eyelids. When I draw my fingernails through my eyebrow or beard (which has grown long and thorny) the nails come out filled with scurfy powder. If you saw us in our present state, covered from head to foot with dust, you would think that our hair had turned suddenly gray. It's a real torment, one whose intensity I could never have imagined previously. My scalp is full of sand and dirt; my pores are congested. No matter what you grasp, it is dusty. A shudder of revulsion passes through my fingertips at every contact. These last few days we have also begun to encounter lice. (I found one this evening promenading on my bread.) A nauseous antipathy has gradually begun to permeate me; I feel as though the dust and lice had penetrated my skin and were advancing inward toward my vitals. We have become exceedingly irritable and malicious in our contacts with one another. Sometimes all you have to do is blurt out "Good morning" to your neighbor and you find yourself in hot water. All day long we lie beneath a merciless, scalding sun—unshielded, like carrion. Clouds of flies are engendered as this sun bakes us ever so slowly and delays its setting as long as possible, as though deriving positive pleasure from our martyrdom. In cases where it is necessary for us to change location inside the trench, we proceed by crawling on all fours, like animals. You see, despite all the digging we do every night from dusk to dawn, the trench is still too shallow. This place is like a stone quarry, nothing but rock, and cannot be worked with the shovel. So, when dawn comes we stretch our canvas sheets over the trench at surface level, which is only scarcely above the floor, and repose beneath their sweltering shade like a herd of sheep. It's useless for us to try to catch some sleep. An unendurable stench rises from the sweating bodies: the fetor of personal uncleanliness and of males in rut. I had thought that only wild beasts in their cages at the zoo could stink so badly. Many of the men lie on their stomachs for hours on end, without talking. They rest their faces upon folded arms, and occasionally take a deep breath, scratch one-foot with the other, and spit into the dust, their mouths just above the soil. Quite a few have made holes in their breeches-pockets. They lie on their backs with knees raised and one hand thrust shamelessly into the torn pocket and working nervously . . . until their brows contract as though from some mysterious pain, a spasm locks their knees together, the jaws clench abruptly—aching molars straining—, their lids flutter, eyes roll upward and go all white. . . . Then: a deep sigh. The legs slacken flabbily, the fierce wrinkle on the forehead disintegrates, facial features resolve into ugly masses. Sometimes one of the men begins to tell dirty stories. Then everyone crawls close by, gathers in a knot around him, and listens with insatiable relish. Obscenity, just like cigarettes and cards, is indispensable here. It rekindles the imagination, inflames it to a degree that borders on pain. On the other hand, it provides some relief, which is why we all indulge. The obscenity of some of the men is vociferous and aggressive, as if they were looking for a fight. Others among us indulge inwardly. Still others keep diaries, and another group produces love letters of the type concocted with infinite precision by convicts in jail. These letters are illustrated with various symbolic drawings, all very recondite: snakes, the angel of justice, hearts pierced by arrows, hell's cauldron with flames and a black-hilted dagger. The key to all these mysteries is contained in rhymed couplets that can be read only if the recipient is adept at folding the sheet is a special way. Letters of this type are constantly dropped into the company's mailbox and constantly torn up by the censors.

All of us kill time here; many also kill lice. This occupation has turned into a game complete with stakes. The lice are caught by threes or fours and exterminated *en masse* on the cartridge belt with a single stroke of the fingernail. The men destroy these parasites with a grimace of hatred upon their lips, as though murdering the incurable boredom that is the consuming blight of our lives. The more numerous they are, the more frenzied the delousing, until it becomes a veritable mania, The search begins in the tunic. This garment is then removed, followed by the shirt, undervest, breeches, even the underpants many times. The men continue to search for hours, with gory fingernails and inflamed bloodshot eyes.

Those gathered around someone telling dirty stories interrupt the speaker now and then in order to embroider with additional realism certain specific details that have impressed them. Eventually the storyteller falls abruptly silent. Then all the men turn their heads and glance at him in surprise, striving to comprehend something the meaning of which has escaped them. They light cigarettes, their eyelids droop, and they sit there meditating on the devil knows what. If you could observe this mass silence that follows the sudden termination of a pornographic anecdote, you would conclude that it boded some kind of danger secretly infiltrating the areas above and around us, a danger whose purpose was to suffocate us in its coils. Not everyone may suspect this consciously, yet everyone does suspect it somehow, for the absolute silence is never allowed to continue for very long. Someone always begins to chatter away with nervous impetuosity, at which time we all become aware of a certain relief and feel a certain gratitude for this person who has broken the dangerous silence and spliced together the broken conversation—no matter how imbecilic or filthy-minded his chatter may be. (What is it that makes the soul so afraid when it remains all alone? What is this thing that it shuns, that it wishes to avoid hearing in the silence? Its own self, perhaps?) . . . Every two hours with unvarying regularity a soldier wearing helmet and bandoleer slithers along the bottom of the trench on his belly, the scabbard of his bayonet clanging against the stones, This is the duty-corporal. He crawls over to one of the knots of men, draws a crumpled slip of paper out of his shirt pocket and announces a name in full voice—surname first, followed by Christian name and finally the patronymic. One of the men grumbles, dresses with sluggish disgust, draws on his boots, takes up his weapons. He is the sentry who must stand the next watch. He yawns like a howling dog, sighs, and leaves the pack, sliding on his belly.

Then night comes, ever so slowly.

It rises from below, from the bottom of the ravine. This ravine separates us from the mountain opposite, a conical mass whose twin peaks loom before us like the towers of some titanic castle. Sooner or later we'll have to settle its hash, or have our own hash settled instead. We know this all too well, and so do the Bulgarians. The darkness commences from the ravine and then continues to rise ever-upward like a turbid blue-purple mist, gradually obliterating faces, blurring lines, dulling colors, and rendering immaterial the distant trees along the horizon. At this point the mountain across the way is clearly delineated: it stands before us with black solidity, stretching upwards, a terrifying pyramid of gloom and silence. (What weighs most heavily upon our souls is not its bulk, but its silence.) It is without a single light, a single sound, a single sign of life. But everything we do not see we nevertheless feel all the more intensely. The hills in this range are called the Peristeri ridges—"the ridges of the dove." A gentle name for a mountain with such a ferocious soul—a living, billowing, ever-watchful soul that assuredly circulates feverishly inside this black pyramid: a cunningly prescient, ever-active soul of numerous components. This is a ridge with untold thousands of shifting eyes that see without being seen, that direct their penetrating stare in our direction day and night. Upon this ridge are untold thousands of hearts throbbing with blind hatred and measuring out our lives with their beats. Each of its pits, boulders, caves, and trees conceals one heart overflowing with mortal enmity and one pair of eyes searching out human flesh for a target. These eyes do not see; they merely take aim, sighting along the "rear-sight elevation notch" and the "front-sight bar." Every depression in this mountain is the lair of a cannon that slowly sways its muzzle to the right and to the left, looking for warm weak flesh. These innumerable, intolerably attentive glances crisscross in the air like the threads of an invisible net that we perceive somehow and that wraps itself around our poor trench, almost smothering its spirit.

15

Digging

*T*ime passes. Our days are monotonous, sluggish, wearying—heavy with an incurable tedium that coats our bodies with mold and enfeebles our thoughts. Boredom is a spiritual tuberculosis. It consumes the soul little by little until it immobilizes it. . . . Our nights are invariably occupied with digging. This unforeseen aspect of fighting a war is approached without appetite by our men; they dig only because they are compelled to. Immediately after nightfall the squads proceed to an underground storeroom where two constantly ill-tempered Frenchmen hand out the tools. The men file by in pairs; a shovel goes to one, a pick to the other. Each one reaches out without speaking and receives his implement from the custodian of the stores. In this way, the line moves rapidly and everyone can soon acquire his tool. The custodian distributes without respite, forever chanting *"pelle, pioche; pelle, pioche"* in a monotonous singsong, like a priest mechanically grinding out his litany. Illumination is provided by an acetylene lamp with a heavy shade that prevents the light from straying outside; it limits the zone of illumination to the pile of implements, the hands that distribute and the hands that receive. The scene possesses an eerie quality suggestive of an exorcism.

"Pelle, pioche. Pelle, pioche. Pelle, pioche."

Each squad is required to deepen the trench to a predetermined extent. When it has achieved the number of centimeters specified in its orders, it is free to return and laze about until the following night.

We Greeks cannot stomach this incessant digging. "We came to fight," say our men; "we came to help the French and Serbs defeat the Germans and Bulgarians (to help them defeat our own king). We did not come to swing a pick. If we'd known this was in store for us, we would have stayed home and dug in our fathers' olive orchards instead of here in the mountains of Serbia." Our officers and the French advisers in the sector have been striving—to no avail—to make the men understand that digging, more than any other single factor, will mean the difference between life and death. As one captain put it with epigrammatic terseness: "He who fails to deepen the trench deepens his own grave."

We are close enough to the front line to hear the din of battle in the distance, a din that sometimes lasts for many hours. There are shells that rip through the air and burst somewhere beyond. There are machine guns that rattle away calmly like sewing machines, then stop, then resume. And rockets blossoming in the darkness like exotic garlands of light: they travel leisurely through the sky before they wilt little by little and expire on the ground or dive behind the hills and become lost to our sight.

There's something else about us Greeks—we just cannot manage to stop yelling and screaming. We make such a racket, you'd think this place were a Jewish bazaar. The men continually forget themselves; they start vociferous conversations, arguments, and other idiotic pranks of this sort. This drives the French out of their minds.

Our particular adviser is a sergeant named François, a Roman Catholic who sits all day long in his dugout reading a papist rag as big as a bed-sheet. This newspaper is called *La Croix.* He's a royalist besides being a Catholic, and as pedantic as a schoolmaster. If he'd been born a Greek, surely he would have employed our puristic language, have fasted all through Lent, and been a devoted reader of Agathangelos. He keeps telling us: "It's either one thing or the other. You Greeks are either a bunch of maniacs who came here to commit suicide, or a pack of half-wits. How else can we explain why you make such a racket so close to the enemy machine guns—right beneath their noses?" This subdues our voices for a time, and even convinces some of our men to stop talking altogether. But, before long, things are back where they started. Then François starts cursing. He is careful, however, not to take Christ's name in vain, or the Virgin's, with the result that he curses by his "dog," his "pipe" and such like: nothing but innocent Catholic maledictions as impeccably devout and insipid as lenten fare.

Yesterday, however, we all learned a permanent lesson; in a flash, we learned to keep our mouths shut beneath the nose of War.

A squad went to its allotted area and started to dig. But when they discovered nothing but solid rock in the place, they said the hell with it. Throwing down their tools with a bang, they leaned comfortably against one wall of the trench, propped their feet up against the opposite wall, and lighted their cigarettes. The man in charge was Lance-Corporal Zgoumbis, a sniveling juvenile incapable of maintaining discipline.

"We're not digging, and that's that!" the others told him. "What can they do to us, eh? Lock us up in the guardhouse? Fine! The sooner the better!"

The person on duty, a Frenchman, found them lazing about when his tour took him to their area.

"*Allons, travaillez, travaillez!*"

"*Non travaillez,*" responded our men.

Quite a few did not hesitate, even, to resort to fraud, that time-honored Greek practice they had ready-to-hand. Each produced the double stripes of a corporal from his pocket, attached these to his sleeve with pins, and waved the sleeve beneath the Frenchman's nose.

"*Moi caporal. Non travaillez!*"

"*Et moi caporal!*"

"*Et moi also!*"

The only one there not a *caporal* was Zgoumbis, the man in charge! The perplexed Frenchman examined the stripes carefully—"*C'est vrai, mon Dieu*"—and went off to report to the Company Command, where he was enlightened as to the trick. So back he went in a huff and hauled them over the coals in French, but good! He even grabbed one of them by the collar and started pulling him to his feet. He received a stiff boot in the guts for his pains. This touched off a Franco-Hellenic riot whose shouts buzzed up and down the entire trench.

In the midst of this: a whizz (which wasn't heard in time) and simultaneously a bang. Everyone fell flat, became unified with the soil. The night smashed into a thousand fragments, like a piece of fine crystal.

The shell exploded inside the trench at a distance of about fifty meters from the group of "caporals." We all remained where we were, glued to the ground, paralyzed with amazement, resigned to what we assumed would be the inevitable sequel. Trembling, our hearts in our mouths, we waited for them to fire again. Nothing. The first was also the last, the only sequel being a ferocious silence that made us fear that every trace of life had been drained from the created universe. We heard nothing but our own hearts kicking vigorously against our chests. Afterwards, a white light suddenly began to gleam on the flanks of the Peristeri ridge, across the way from us. A bundle of parallel rays moved in the direction of our hill and proceeded to stroll up and down it with great care, as though searching it out, or smelling it. "The Cyclops' eye, the Cyclops' eye," I began to say to myself over and over, rapidly and mechanically. I repeated this phrase many times in similar fashion, as a kind of prayer, a "Kyrie eleison, Kyrie eleison, Kyrie eleison." Coming directly at us from the "Dove's" dark body was this luminous arm that the mountain had extended. I was sure that we would die instantaneously from its touch the moment it laid hands on us, or else that it would snatch us up in its fist and deliver us over to the Dove. But it never reached our particular niche. Instead, it halted at some other point, near a colossal boulder pasted to our hill's nape like a pus-swelled abscess. This the luminous hand fingered first on one side then on the other. Then it sliced its conical blade through the darkness and settled on a spot a little further off, only to return suspiciously to the boulder. It rested against this rock for some time, meditating, until finally it began to weaken and contract little by little. Then it was sucked in by the mountain, like a monstrous tongue retracted into a mouth.

When we got back on even keel again and breathed easily, we concluded at first that the shell had been just a flash in the pan, because we did not hear any cries or moans. Afterwards, however. . .

This random shot had hit a working-party from our third platoon. It landed on solid rock, exploded, and killed all six men in the party. Four were from the village of Mesotopos and two from Ayiassos. The various pieces of only one of them were able to be identified, and those with great difficulty. The others in the party had been mashed into tripe. An entire helmet was found sitting inside a belly, and somebody's intestines had wound themselves round the handle of a pick-axe—rather neatly too, the way a whip, when you give it a smart crack, coils its end around a walking stick. The pulpish remains were placed on some canvas and transported to the rear; this was done in haste, to prevent the men from seeing the gore and becoming aroused. Fresh soil was scattered over the blood, which had drained into a hollow in the rocky floor of the trench and had congealed there (it resembled someone's liver). When I passed the spot again at dawn, I noticed hair plastered onto the stones; also a yellow finger with a long dirty nail. The severed end of this finger had been wedged into the trench wall. It made me imagine that a man had been buried alive in the wall and in his struggle to extricate himself had managed to push out that finger, nothing else. When I touched it with my walking stick it fell down like a dead caterpillar. I buried it as best I could. Its tip was brick-red, stained by cigarette tobacco.

* * *

War had really and truly touched us.

The blood that had been spilled in our trench raised a tempest at first in the somber, innocent hearts of our men, shaking them profoundly. Then this turbulence subsided. What remained was a surface calm even more terrifying than the storm.

Balafaras rose to the occasion. Cheerful and unruffled, he came to Company H.Q. to offer his felicitations.

"Captain, the distinction of baptism has fallen on you. I congratulate your company. All honor to the gallant lads who died. I have left instructions for a lovely letter to be composed on my behalf so that I may dispatch it to their families together with the decorations they so richly deserve. Excellent idea, eh? Heroes must be honored, Captain. As for this little scratch received by my division, I am glad it happened. Things like this kindle the blood and create a genuine zest for war."

These remarks have become common knowledge among the men, who like to repeat them, retaining Balafaras's distinctive pronunciation and adding a tone of chilling mockery (with no intent, however, of humor).

"*As for this little scratch received by my division, I am glad it happened. . . . I shall dispatch a lovely letter. . . . A genuine zest for war . . .*"

Everyone has become extremely circumspect and reticent. The men are quietly thoughtful now. They do not quarrel any longer or shout or kick up a rumpus. All they do is dig, dig, dig. They even dig during daylight hours. This is done on the sly, mostly in silence, and with tiny flashes of terror frequently crossing their eyes. Wielding pick and shovel, each one hews out an improvised nest for himself in the wall of the trench—a hole just big enough to provide a roof over his head. Every whistle, no matter how distant, gives the men's shoulders a nervous jolt, cuts the words short on their lips, and painfully stretches their facial lines into a hysterical grimace. Life for us has grown sadder. It is bitter now, because all of us have had our taste of war, and the flavor of blood refuses to leave our mouths. Yet, in spite of all the justifications (the men nod assent and pretend to find them convincing) an unanswered question dwells within these simple, innocent souls:

"Why must we stay pinned to this spot and let them kill us like that when there doesn't even seem to be a war on?"

16

Animals

*A*nimals in wartime.

All day today I have been thinking of nothing else. It's fine and dandy for the humans involved in war. People have "interests," ideologies, whims, megalomanias, and enthusiasms—just what the doctor ordered for cooking up a truly first-class conflict. And once the war is declared, we have our tricks for saving ourselves as soon as we see that the affair is likely to be a little more than we bargained for. Dugouts and "going sick," for example, not to mention desertions.

But what about the animals? What about the poor innocent beasts mobilized by us to wage war at our sides?

Do you know what I think? I think that even if the human race succeeds one day in driving out the devil that makes it erupt in periodic fits of mass murder, it will still have cause to hang its head in shame for the remainder of its existence. Why? For one reason only: because it dragged innocent beasts into its wars. On reflection, I feel that the day will come when this is considered one of the blackest marks in human history.

Our division carried numerous donkeys along with it when it left the island. An entire ammunition train, in fact. The entry in our official documents speaks of "an ammunition train of mules," but if truth be told, the unit has nothing but donkeys. Getting these animals on shipboard caused them considerable suffering, as did getting them off again at Salonika. The angrily groaning cranes seized them and lifted them aloft in strong slings.

This drove them wild. Their fright was depicted with astonishing vividness in their frantic eyes. They kicked into the void, brayed, rolled their eyeballs. The horror impressed wrinkles on their hides. After this, they traversed all of Macedonia with us, laden with munitions. By this time they had their own accounts to settle with the Germans, Turks, and Bulgarians. When we occupied the trenches, their park was established behind our lines at Koupa, a village devastated by artillery-fire and inhabited only by a few French bakers. There, at Koupa, in a beautiful ravine, our division's "ammunition train of mules" put down its stakes.

The animals were allowed to rest for a few days to recuperate from the prolonged journey that had left them stunned with fatigue. They caught their breath again; indeed, they discovered grass in abundance, ate, and began to feel like their old selves. Invigorated, they suddenly noticed that springtime had covered the earth with its resplendence, and that Love was prodding all things, from grubs to flowers, to join in the age-old festival of reproduction. Obedient, filled like all animals with innocence and unknowing, the donkeys heeded the great summons and answered "Present!" with their amorous trumpet-call. Their ravine droned with jarring epithalamiums; the brayings reverberated through the various defiles until this amorous trumpeting reached all the way to the Peristeri ridges. At this point an airplane took off with a roar from somewhere opposite us. It flew to the ravine and circled it once or twice. As for the donkeys, they did not change their tune. The plane then headed home amid the enthusiastic reception provided for it by our anti-aircraft batteries whose shells, bursting in the sky, surrounded it with an ever-multiplying flock of little white lambs.

Donkeys do not even know that planes exist. In any case, these particular donkeys were so corporeally absorbed in the joy of living that they had no time left to notice anything else.

Shortly afterwards a series of piercing whistles and sonorous bangs set the ravine howling with pain. It was a genuine slaughter of the innocents. The beasts were massacred on the tender grass, disemboweled amid the orgasmic intoxication of their genital pleasure. They expired like humans, sighing. Falling to the ground, they gave up the ghost little by little, bending their necks to gaze mournfully at their entrails swaying like red snakes between their legs. Comprehending nothing, they moved their large heads up and down; shuddered; dilated their quivering nostrils; spread their broad lips and uncovered their teeth; drew themselves along the ground on shattered legs. In the end they died, watering the flowers with their blood, their huge eyes filled with perplexity and suffering. One animal with a broken spine dragged its body for a distance of about fifteen meters supported by its front legs only. Then its knees buckled, it turned its head toward its large wound, and gasped with protracted death-throes until it passed away.

One of the drivers started to run like mad as soon as the bombardment commenced. Though in a daze, he had enough presence of mind to keep a tight hold on his donkey's bridle, and he still had it firmly in his grip when he arrived at the dugout occupied by the French bakers. Here, amidst general jeering from our Gaelic allies, he finally realized that all he had been pulling behind him was the donkey's head, scythed off at the neck.

The animal was still holding a clump of daisies between its clenched teeth, the yellow petals speckled with blood.

17

In the Woods

Where do you suppose I've just been? You'll never guess. In the woods. Imagine! The woods! I still can't get over it. I'm completely amazed and confused, yet when I rest my pack upon my knees to serve as a writing table, look! it is still covered with bits of grass. As for my sleeping sack, it is coated to such a degree with those burrs that cling (like disagreeable in-laws) to any and every part of you the moment you touch them, that I despair of ever getting it perfectly clean again. Everything about me smells deliciously of the forest; my clothes still give off its pungent breath. When I shut my eyes I hear buzzing and soughing inside me; and I hear the many calls that the forest sends out—you'd think it were a powerful beast with innumerable throats, each shouting at full voice. In my mess kit I have a bunch of wild flowers that I collected. They give off a bitter fragrance. I don't know their names, but they are all so beautiful that you could sit and admire them for hours, one by one. If only I knew how to describe all this to you! My hair was showered with dewdrops falling from tall beech trees; right now my dugout is perfumed with resin, wild mint, and fresh oregano.

There is a tragedy connected with all this, however, a tragedy involving human blood. I want to write a thousand and one things—simultaneously—in order to be delivered as soon as possible from their suffocating weight. But I shall have to manage to relate them one by one, in sequence. Otherwise I'll make you just as confused as I still am in this green chaos that continues to stir inside me like an ocean and to dumfound me with its thousand voices. . . .

They roused us in the depths of night. I was placed in charge of a crew of twenty men. The captain summoned me to his dugout. Indicating a corporal in the Engineering Corps, he instructed me to take my crew and follow this man, who was going to show us the way to a forest. "Once there, you will fell trees that we shall use as dugout-timbers and also to make pickets for the barbed-wire entanglements. The quartermaster will give your party sufficient rations for twenty-four hours. You will return tomorrow night. All necessary tools will be found on the spot."

Then he added, glancing at me and smiling: "Not a bad assignment, eh?"

I was almost insane with joy: my ears were aflame, a fiery wave lapped against the back of my neck. If other people had not been present I might have kissed the captain's hand. As it was, I simply mumbled some confused response. But he apprehended the gratitude that was choking me.

In sum, I escaped the trench, spent one long, full day away from the line. Imagine! One entire day filled with the light of outdoors, the shade of trees, and with colors and running brooks and flowers! A day beneath open skies, beneath that vast thrice-lofty vault that raises its broad arches higher even than the stars and allows a man to stretch at will to his full height without fear that his helmet may crash against hewn granite, or that he may become a mark for target-practice the moment he ceases to creep along the ground like a lizard.

We headed toward the rear of our lines, trekking for a half-hour through a network of trenches. When we finally emerged from this labyrinth, I stretched my body beneath God's heaven. Curling up like a pretzel in the dugout had warped and checked my joints; they creaked now like hinges rusted into their sockets from long disuse. We found ourselves in the sharp defile where our cookers had been placed. It is from here that they send us our gritty pilaf that tastes like powdered bricks, and those unchewable slabs of meat from monstrous Australian buffaloes.

After traversing numerous gorges we emerged finally onto a smooth bald expanse like a table laid with silence and warm night. In the sky above this arid plain the stars, millions of them, had all come out just as they do when the world is at peace. They gleamed with festive splendor and sparkled with newness as they twinkled their glances toward us. A fiesta! You would need a thousand eyes to see this celestial revel properly; then, in seeing, you would feel the divine illuminations enter your heart and open it. Surely the stars could never have displayed more liveliness and brilliance than now, not even on that triumphant first night of creation when the Lord of Sabaoth lighted all the brand-new chandeliers of the firmament as an experiment to see if they would work. . . . Attempting every conceivable rearrangement of our metallic equipment in an effort to keep it from rattling, we walked in silence, not daring even to light a cigarette. The trip was wholly uneventful except for one rocket that unsettled us for a moment or two. Our reflexes sent us diving automatically to the ground, where we remained in frozen immobility like the statues at Pompeii until the flare's white glow passed overhead. As soon as the darkness had swallowed this treacherous eye so intent upon betraying our position, we struggled to our feet again (all this without uttering a word) and proceeded once more, guided as always by the corporal from the Engineers. The plain extended with unbroken smoothness, as though leveled by a harrow. Suddenly, unexpectedly, we found ourselves in front of the woods. So this was the black line we had noticed on the horizon when we were still far away. Now, no sooner had a little milky-blue begun to mark the eastern sky than we found ourselves instantaneously in front of the forest. How had it suddenly upheaved itself before us, towering like a colossal fortress with its dense stand of tall, straight trees and its mysterious voice pouring out of its vitals? Strange. Very strange indeed.

A comparable experience would be impossible in our part of the world. To see a large stretch of open country whose broad expanse continues level, silent, and waterless however long you tread upon it, upon this endless roll of carpet that unwinds incessantly in front of your steps; and then, without the slightest alteration in the terrain or the slightest forewarning, to discover looming suddenly before you a frightening wooded area, as though a plot of vegetation had frenetically lunged heavenward in a volcano-burst of foliage with such a roar that it continued to rumble sorrowfully in its bowels, causing you to fall silent and to listen to it with fear in your heart . . . : such an experience could never have happened on our island.

Suddenly, without any preparation whatever, we were tossed from the deadest of silences into the deeps of an ocean filled with unimaginable and uncountable sounds. They raced and intersected high above our heads, quivered there, changed positions, wrestled with each other in the humid air like wild beasts, and grew ever more impetuous: a hovering mesh of calls, whistles, thumps, roars, cracks, rustles, and shrill notes from invisible pan-pipes; an acoustical network constantly woven and unwoven as its waves passed over us. Imagine thousands of insane musicians charging out of a lunatic asylum, each one tooting his instrument madly with all his power. Next, imagine millions of predators, songbirds, grubs, serpents, animalcula and ferocious beasts quarreling among themselves and debating with huge shrieks; also countless metallic clicks leaping rhythmically out of the soil as though in the underbrush thousands of hidden clocks were ticktocking away with irrepressible garrulity, grinding out their seconds.

I said that we were tossed into the deeps of an ocean. This was precisely our sensation as soon as we entered the woods. Truly, we found ourselves on the seabed of a greenish-black chasm rising above us to extraordinary heights and filled to the bursting-point with vociferous uproar. This, then, was the forest—something entirely inconceivable on our island because every manifestation of nature, there, is tailored in amplitude and proportion so that it may attractively and harmoniously fit human measurements, correspond to them quietly, without any fuss. In our forests back home, the only divinities available for worship are charming and graceful sprites who may be propitiated with garlands fashioned from flowers and blue ribbons placed on their grass-covered altars. Contrariwise, this other forest is surely inhabited by a dreadful god fully appropriate to its barbarity: a divinity whose voluptuous, bristling snout and sharply pointed teeth can be appeased only with human sacrifices.

It is a virgin forest of gigantic growth, one of those that established itself on the earth in prehistoric times and has remained intact ever since. The instant we entered it we were painfully crushed—by its bulk more than anything else. Everything was so monstrous and unbridled. The trees stood in clumps, so very tall that they undoubtedly did not even notice us from aloft as we swarmed ant-like at their roots. Creepers unreeled fath-

88

oms of blossoming shoots and tossed these flower-laden swings from one trunk to the next, garlanding the intervening spaces with arches of fruit and large unusual blooms resembling trumpets, or clusters of purple or cherry-red grapes. Reduced to nothingness inside this monster, we halted, our implements and weapons in our hands. At first we even huddled against each other as though sensing some impending danger. We did this instinctively, like sheep that have just scented a wolf. Then, however, one of the men ventured timorously: "Good God, just look at it!" At this, we all began to chatter and gesticulate like madmen. We were striving to make noise, but our meager shouts constituted a sorry and hopeless force compared to the woods' immeasurable clamor, which absorbed them with ease. All at once we seemed ridiculously dwarfed; our axes looked like children's playthings. When Angeletos tilted up his chin in order to promenade his glance to the crown of a beech tree that disappeared in the leafy canopy, his helmet slid off the back of his head—and he is the tallest man in the company. When we saw this mammoth gangleshanks at the base of his beech, despite his height he looked to us like a lead soldier—a little Tom Thumb no taller than a thimble—propped upright beneath a Christmas tree.

What we sensed almost from the start was that we were dealing with some kind of autonomously self-sufficient beast belonging to the vegetable kingdom, a beast whose own very special vitality, primeval and indestructible, gave it life, breath, motion, and voice. The forest was a gigantic, growling animal with a strong smell, its fresh green blood inside the mighty trunks gushing frantically upward toward the sky in an indomitable jet of untamed youthfulness. The ample and multifaceted voice of this forest, something I heard now for the very first time in my life—a voice of myriad ingredients, equal in power to those of the howling sea yet totally different in quality—this forest-voice was a fearsome, unbearable yell devoid of everything familiar to human beings or congenial to them. Instead, the only thing that filled our hearts, surrounded as we were by this monster, was secret and unrevealed terror.

The forest's soul, when we entered, remained completely oblivious of our presence. No bird ceased to warble, no voice in this tempest of sounds diminished its strength, no grub altered its route. Afterwards, when we ridiculous homunculi commenced to lay several young trees out on the ground with our toy hatchets, choppety-chop, and to watch their sap come bubbling out of the fresh sweet-smelling wounds like sacred water from a wonderworking spring, once again the forest remained oblivious, did not change its rhythms by a single beat. Measured against its frightening totality, our activities and presence were apparently just tiny incidents lacking any significance. Life's indomitable spring that gushes miraculously underneath the ground would soon be sending up a multitude of new, supple sprouts to replace every murdered tree.

When our axes bit into a trunk and it began to totter, a dozen hollering men pulled it in one direction with ropes. The entire trunk creaked through and through in pain, inclined with unhurried dignity, and crashed to the ground, shattering in its fall any nearby branches that happened to lie in its path.

The trees were filled with copulating squirrels. Before a given trunk tottered and fell, all the squirrels mating in its branches—a whole multitude of marvelous bushy-tailed creatures with little golden-brown eyes—interrupted their games for a moment to glance curiously with tilted heads at the soldiers who were assassinating their tree. Then, with a leap, they hurtled through the air like hairy balls and established themselves in another tree where they resumed their pranks without devoting any further attention to us. Indeed, some of them hopped down to the lowest branches remarkably close by.

The corporal from the Engineering Corps kept one of these graceful animals centered in the sights of his gun for a considerable time. Although he was sighting from extremely close range, the squirrel did not budge; it just kept shifting its head from side to side and looking him straight in the eye with the shiny beads of its pupils. As soon as the gun went off (the weak pop being absorbed instantaneously by the forest's enormous din) the squirrel fell to our feet and died, extremely perplexed by what had just happened to it. . . .

Our plunge into the forest had brought us into contact with some form of bestiality: that is the strange sensation that filled me at the time and that I continue to feel even now. What I feel, more precisely, is that I spent an entire day wallowing in the green and woolly pelt of a fantastical beast of mammoth proportions that had been lurking there at the edge of the plain for untold millennia, blocking the horizon with its bulk: an immortal brute with a countless number of thick sturdy legs all buried in the ground and anchored there, its flukes reaching to the very core of the earth; a brute that had lifted its muzzle aloft and thrust it into the clouds so that it might lick the sky with its broad green tongue; a brute whose fearsome voice surged like waves of the sea and whose titanic body emitted an astringent forest-smell (the bitter-sweet fragrance still clings to my coat), a smell that saturated our clothes with a heavy reek of arboreal concupiscence that still has not left them.

These blasts of potent bestiality blew upon us from all directions in the forest and suffused the humid atmosphere with their poisonous mists. Gradually it became clear that the men were succumbing with ever-increasing ease. After the initial impression of our insignificance had abruptly come and gone, they began little by little to accept, and then welcome, their situation. Allowing the green monster to gulp them down in one swallow, they commenced to promenade freely back and forth inside its enormous stomach, whereupon the monster in its turn (always completely indifferent) began to digest them with the greatest of ease and to assimilate them into its system. They were like the birds at first, squawking at the top of their lungs so that they could hear each other, even though they were only ten paces apart. Next, the erotic mania hissing and seething on all sides began its stealthy and irresistible work of intoxication. The forest aspersed them with pungent whiffs of the hashish burning in its dark loins. Its wild and fecund soul dripped upon them like semen ejaculated from the treetrunks, which were clasped in the titanic embrace of tortuous elbows, and from the erotically entwined branches all covered with mating animals and with thousands of birds tweeting in response to unendurably gratifying sensuality. The men were infused by this soul as though by a subtle poison, green in color, filtered directly from the heart of the forest while it panted orgasmically in the midst of harsh sexual passion. Although they probably did not realize what was happening to them, they soon became vassaled to the sovereign soul of the green beast, which treated them thenceforth like all the other thousands of beings that inhabited it and that, carried away by the whirlwind of priapic frenzy, joined with it to compose its terrifying vitality.

Eventually the men began to indulge in obscenities and to exchange shameless jokes and gestures, chirping in their own right like the wild birds of the forest. I had never seen them act like this before. In the trench, the morbid cult of sexual gratification had assumed a mysterious, secret and guilty hue, be it from the irremovable shadow of death which weighs relentlessly upon us in that place, or from the obligatory silence and immobility. Here, on the contrary, a pack of inhibited instincts had suddenly been given free rein. The men gamboled about, rolled on the ground, rubbed their hairy maws voluptuously in the untrodden grass as though intending to chew it. Then, like aroused satyrs, they began to wrestle with each other. Soon they had thrown one of their number to the ground, removed his trousers, lowered his underpants, and festooned his testicles with nettles pressed home into the flesh. The victim was as hairy as an ape. He laughed and swore at the same time, bit their hands, kicked into the air like a donkey, and bellowed. When they finally left him lying unconstrained on the ground, he remained gasping for a moment upon the grass, his underpants still down about his ankles, his eyes closed, and his thick lips pulled back into a broad smile. Then he jumped up, kicked off the shorts, spread his legs, clasped his erect penis in his fist, and began to dance in a climax of sexual excitement, flaunting his nakedness and shamelessly gyrating his belly and buttocks.

> Had an old gat, boys,
> > Had an old gat.
> Had all its parts, boys,
> > Had all its parts.
> Had a fat mouth, boys,
> > Had a fat mouth.
> Had a wide bore, boys,
> > Had a wide bore.
> Had a big head, boys,
> > Had a big head.
> Big as my fist, boys,
> > Big as my fist.

Forming a circle around him, the others clapped their hands in time, cheered, and cried "Hey! Hey!" until he collapsed to the ground in orgasm, quivering violently from his spasm.

In the afternoon, following our midday meal, each little cluster of friends remained together as all of us sank wearily onto the grass. Stretched out on our backs, we smoked, talked, and watched the heavens' azure eyes wink at us through the high canopy of foliage as it swayed back and forth in quickstep.

Reclining near me was the party that included Lance-Corporal Beelios, a taciturn young man of retiring personality who had never caused the slightest disturbance in the company. On this occasion, however, he incensed all of us.

The circle consisted of Beelios, Angeletos, and five or six others. This pair—Beelios and Angeletos—had been hand and glove ever since mobilization. They are the two tallest men in the company, you see; accordingly, when each of us was assigned his place for fall-in, these two found themselves side by side in the front row. They came to know and esteem one another, and decided to share their wartime lives. They helped one another when on duty; they ate together, drank together, and roosted in the same dugout.

Stefanis, the corporal from the Engineers, had included himself in this particular group. "Well, what can we talk about now to pass the time?" he asked. Then he spread his lips into a yawn so prolonged that he resembled a howling dog.

"I'll tell you what," replied Mitreli, that malformed sniveler with the jaundiced ears who has been growing continually more shriveled and yellow even though he devours the entire platoon's leftovers and discarded crusts. "I'll tell you what! Listen. Let's each one remember the various women he's had in his life and then tell about the one who satisfied him the most and how he engineered the great event. Without sparing any of the nitty-gritty! . . . How does that strike you?"

"Aha! That's it! Bravo!"

They all applauded.

"Angeletos, you start," said Corporal Stefanis. "Come on!"

"Start!" echoed Beelios, who was half-reclining next to him. He gave him a friendly slap on his broad back. "You're the best looking fellow in the company, and you sure as hell must have plenty of dirty doings to your credit."

Angeletos scratched the top of his head with his pinkie and made a comical grimace. Then, pondering deeply, he began to twirl one end of his mustache while casting wry glances at it out of the corner of his eye.

"What I'm going to tell you happened the year before last," he commenced. "Mobilization, which had brought the Lesvos Regiment as far as Balaftsa and the Lahanas Outposts, still hadn't caught up with me. In other words, I spent that winter in my village and, now that we're on the subject, didn't do half badly either. You see, there weren't many of us olive-beaters left; the army had taken the best of the lot. The time was ripe for us new shoots to act big. So we stepped all over the owners and ended up getting paid like doctors. One of the estates where we beat down the olives belonged to a doctor named Kakourellis. A doctor no less! But he doesn't have to scribble prescriptions for a living, not him, when he produces three thousand jugs of olive oil year after year, and has his own press that serves the entire village. Well, so what if he does! Still, he's as tight as they make 'em, the stingy bum; why he's as closefisted as Judas. At the time I'm speaking of, we were harvesting at Longhi, one of his big holdings. This is an hour's journey from our village, in the direction of Langadara. We cooked there, had our meals there. The plantation has a large cabin on it, you understand. The doctor's regular work force consisted of approximately thirty women: young and old, from our village and elsewhere—all kinds. It rained so much and so hard that winter, we were rotting faster in our boots than we would have in the grave. Harvest began on the first of November. If you had three days in a row without rain it was a miracle. The women who were gathering what we knocked down hardly had a chance to set their baskets on the ground before a fine drizzle started. This would soon increase until it drove down in streams as thick as cord, and lashed us in the face. But, rain or no rain, the boss's orders were that work should stop only at midday for lunch and siesta, and then again at dark when we went home.

"'It's raining, Boss!'

"'And what if it's raining? Do you mean to say you don't eat when it's raining?'

"'Think of the women, Boss.'

"'And what about the women? Do you mean to say they're blobs of cowdung and will be washed away in the rain? Let them light fires in the cabin at noontime—there's no shortage of olive logs, thank God—and dry out their skirts.'

"So the poor things squatted in the rain like a bunch of wet hens, and collected olives. The water flowed down their wimples and onto their backs, filtered through their sleeves. At midday they all ran off to the cabin to eat the herring that was their customary fare. (The number of times an hon-est-to-goodness meal was prepared for Kakourellis's troupe could be counted on the fingers of one hand.) But most of all the poor things ran to dry off as best they could, and to get warm. I have to admit, there was an abundant supply of shavings in the hut, for kindling. They bolted them-selves securely inside and built a huge fire in the ample hearth, so huge that tongues of flame sometimes shot out through the chimney and licked the cabin's roof tiles.

"As for me, I had a slicker and was able to keep dry. At lunchtime I used to sneak into a hollow in direct line of vision with the cabin. We call it the 'cave.' I would open my sack, eat, then roll myself a cigarette (just as I'm doing now), watch the sparks and flames fly out of the chimney, and listen to the women squeal and laugh. But in my imagination I had wormed my way right into the cabin, all the way inside. I had a devilish urge to see what that bevy of females was up to in there. I managed to unearth a crack in a part of the cabin wall that was covered with a luxuriant growth of ivy. This I widened and kept hidden behind the leaves so that no one would see it. One day I went over there on the sly, glued myself to the wall—clutching the ivy—and looked in.

"Well, gents, you wouldn't believe what I saw there unless you saw it with your own eyes, as I did. To put it mildly, it was beyond description! They were all stripped, all the olive-gatherers, and were standing there bare-assed naked in front of the flames, drying their panties and shifts. It was enough to drive a man stark raving mad. Of course I must admit that there were some old hags in that crew whose figures were so horrible that I still feel like puking when I think of them. The world has nothing uglier to offer than an old crone in the raw. On the other hand, gents, some of those creatures in there were so fantastic that I nearly swallowed my tongue when I saw them. You know what I mean: sweet young things never hand-led, with tits as firm as quinces. And the glow of the flames was hitting their bodies and turning them all pink. There was one from Ayiassos, a big red-cheeked heifer with a thick blond braid that reached down to her ass and tickled her in the crotch. She was hefty and tall, almost as tall as I am. Well, this female Hercules strips to her birthday suit and steps up to the wide hearth in the nude. Then she crosses her arms beneath her 'ample bosom,' cups her breasts in her palms and lifts them one at a time, first one then the other, pointing the erect nipples toward the fire. The way the breasts reflected the red firelight, you'd think she'd been holding two large pomegranates.

"There was another lassie, very young with unripe breasts ending in points. Two of her girlfriends amused themselves every noontime by chas-ing her—supposedly in jest—in order to pinch them vigorously against her will, until the poor child wept. . . . But the one who really drove me batty when I saw her in the nude was a harvester from some faraway vil-lage, a refugee-girl who had married young and might just as well have been a widow, since her husband had been taken away into the army. She had unusual eyes full of sparkle, and firm fleshy lips. I can't say exactly what it was about her appearance that excited me, but her body and her airs drove me wild. From the moment I saw her undressed she stayed in my eyes and never left them, no matter whether I was awake or asleep. Hers wasn't a woman's body; it was a flaming inferno. Together with an old witch from the same village, she had come to our part of the island and had contracted to work in Kakourellis's crew. This companion was a first-class harridan, all shriveled up like an empty pouch: you know, the kind the farmers use to carry a few olives with them for a snack when they go into the fields. As awful as this crone was, however, she plastered so much make-up on her face, you'd think she was wearing a mask. She also used henna in her hair, making it sometimes coffee-brown, sometimes red.

"One day I called her aside, stuffed a knitted sweater into her basket, and said to her: 'That girl from your village, Auntie Kanellio, what a beauty she is! What brilliant, darting eyes! She's driving me out of my mind!' Auntie knew exactly what I was after. She hastily concealed the sweater inside her coat and said to me with an ugly smile: 'You're no slouch your-self, my boy; in fact, you're second to none in good looks. And you're a real he-man too, best of the lot. Don't worry, I'll tell . . . the . . . young lady in question . . . that she's caught your eye, and her darling little heart will flutter, never fear.' Well, gents, she said it and she did it—the old panderess! Starting that very same day, the girl lagged behind the others in the harvest supposedly to glean what they had overlooked but really to turn her head on the sly and cast glances at me. As for Auntie, she never left her side and never stopped chewing off her ear: the same and then more of the same. I was working on her from all directions at once, you might say, so with one thing or another I finally won her over. In the be-ginning, for instance, her gaze suddenly shifted elsewhere and her cheeks flushed like carnations whenever I happened to catch her looking at me. Afterwards, the only thing she cared about was that the other harvesters shouldn't notice her stares. If I happened to be singing some especially 'meaningful' song while I sat up in the tree beating down the olives, she would raise her eyes surreptitiously, tilt her head over onto her shoul-der—like this—and smile at me gently, as if to say: 'I know you're singing that for me, my sweet boy, I know, I know.' Her gaze was so coquettish that the song died on my lips, and my stick—imagine!—made random strokes, breaking off twigs and knocking down nothing but leaves onto the women's heads. One evening I sent her a kerchief and bracelet, via the old lady. She kept them. From that day onward I stayed on the lookout for an appropriate rendezvous so that I could lay hands on her. In the villages, as you know, arrangements of this sort are hard to come by. Neither place nor opportunity is to be found very easily because there is always a pair of cunning eyes behind every partly opened window, eyes that wait in am-bush there all night long in order to stare outside and see who enters and leaves the neighboring houses. But good luck came to my aid one day and managed things splendidly. At lunchtime when the harvesters rose to go into the cabin, the girl needed just a few more olives to fill her basket. So she kept collecting. When Auntie Kanellio saw this, she turned, winked at her, and called out loudly enough for the others to hear: 'If you value my good opinion of you, you'll sit there until it's filled right to the brim. In fact, I'm going to stay right here with you to make sure you don't play any tricks on me.' 'I'll fill it, Auntie, don't worry, she replied, and she lowered her head even further than before, wedging it between her knees. When all the harvesters had squeezed into the cabin, Auntie obligingly disappeared, leaving us to ourselves. Then I said to her: 'Don't listen to the old witch. Just go over there and empty your basket into that sack so you can leave and get warm with the others.' Saying this, I pointed to the nearly full sack that I had placed a little way off, near the Toumba. This is a large boulder that sits at the edge of the field like a miniature castle. In the old days it was used as a lookout post. The village sentinels would stand on top of it and keep watch over a whole sweep of sea from our own Cape Korakas to Cape Babas over in Anatolia, in case a pirate ship should happen to appear. Hollowed out of this boulder is the 'cave' I told you about, a kind of massive dungeon-like opening. I dragged her into this cavity, squeezed her good and proper, then spread her out on the ground. She played the bride at first—'Don't Angeletos, they'll see us! . . . O darling, don't, don't, we'll be discovered!'—but then she ignited faster than a dry fern. She went into orgasm like a wild animal in heat; she bit, she flopped around beneath me like a fish. By Jesus, no female that's crossed my path has ever come close to her for passion. Afterwards, we arranged things better. On days when the crew did not report for work—holidays and the like—she and the old lady went out armed with a basket each and a table-knife, supposedly to collect chicory. But they'd proceed straight to the cabin, where the girl and I could then spend the entire day together. While the old one went off to fill both baskets with greens, I lighted a fire and admired the young one as she stood naked near the flames. I tell you, gents, a body like that doesn't come more than once from God's hands. Every woman is a female once over; she was a female multiplied by a thousand—filled with femininity from tip to toe. I remember the brown birthmark she had right here, on the thigh. She told me the story. It seems that when the girl was still in the womb her mother absentmindedly picked up a frying pan on the feast day of Mark the Evangelist. As soon as she remembered what day it was, she wiped the offending hand on her thigh, quaking with fright, but her baby was born 'marked' with that fingerprint. . . . Well, as I was saying, that little birthmark drove me out of my mind. . . ."

At precisely this point in the story, Beelios—who had been lying on his stomach on the ground during the whole of Angeletos's narration with his cheek resting on the grass and his fingers working their way nervously into the soil as though anxious to plant themselves there—asked in a stifled voice without lifting his face:

"And . . . and . . . what was her name, Angeletos? What was the name of this whore with the birthmark on her thigh?"

"Stylianoula," replied Angeletos.

At this, Beelios leaped instantaneously to his feet. His features unrecognizable, blades of grass still sticking to his beard, he grabbed an axe that was lying on the ground and swung it directly at Angeletos's head. But the other dodged in time, and the axe just grazed him superficially on the right arm, near the shoulder. Everyone else jumped up and piled on top of Beelios. They gained control of him before he could strike again—he was quivering all over and bellowing like an ox. Then they bound him hand and foot with the draw-cords used to clean their rifles, while he gnashed his teeth to the cracking-point, overcome by uncontrollable furor. We were all frightened and astonished, but the most frightened and astonished of the lot was Angeletos himself. As yellow as a gold florin, his head reeling from the unexpected turn of events, he gazed at Beelios while the men were dressing his laceration with the bandages we always carry in our kits, and demanded of him in a tone full of grievance:

"But why me, Beelios? . . . Why did you hit *me* of all people? Me? . . . Why me?"

Beelios, however, just kept thrashing about in a frenzy and pleading with tears of rage in his eyes:

"Let me go, let me go. The snake! The viper! I'll drink his blood!"

I sent Angeletos far enough away so that Beelios could not see him.

Evening was approaching. The green shadows had darkened now and taken on an air of sorrow. The trees seemed to be pressing in upon us from all sides and constricting us as everywhere around us the clusters of individual trunks melted together into congealed masses. Night was slithering out of its arboreal womb.

I gave orders for the victim to be conducted to the nearest Mountain Surgery and I appealed to all of his friends not to mention the incident to anyone in the company. Otherwise, Beelios would have to stand court-martial. He was a true stalwart and universally liked, so no one disagreed.

I untied him after the other had gone and took him off to one side where, sitting him down next to me behind a clump of wild brambles, I adjured him to vow that he would never do that terrible thing again. He just sat there rubbing together his spindly hands that were still numb from their fetters, his head lowered between his knees. Finally he replied in a weary voice without looking up:

"I can't, sir. I can't promise you that. It's too late now. Finished! The thing is already settled and there's nothing I can do about it. I'll kill him. It might be today, tomorrow, this year, next year; I don't know when. But as soon as I find him in front of me, 'that' will happen. Unless he gets me first. In a business like this, you understand, there's no way out. . . . I'd rather have you ask me to jump into the Bulgarian trenches this very night. Then you'd see to what lengths I'd go to please you—willingly and happily."

"In that case," I continued, "promise me for the sake of our friendship that the same trouble will not be repeated in our company as long as I'm still with it. What I'm asking you, Beelios, is extremely important to me, and I'll be most grateful if you agree."

He remained silent for several moments during which nothing reached our ears except the forest's deep, serious voice. Finally he lifted his head, removed his helmet, and spoke in a tone that seemed to have sagged in the cool darkness to a lower and more gentle pitch:

"That much . . . I'll do . . . , provided he moves to another dugout."

I laid my hand on his shoulder.

"Do you swear that to me on your honor? As a man of honor?"

I divined the cruel smile that appeared on his lips, and felt his shoulder shrug beneath my palm.

"But that is the whole problem in a nutshell. Honor. I don't have any honor—can't you understand that? You see, I won't consider myself a man until I finish the business I began so poorly this afternoon."

I clasped his big hairy hand in my palm and said to him with genuine feeling: "Despite what happened, I consider you a dignified man of honor and a person with a clean slate. I've always regarded you as my friend; now that I've learned in this sudden way that some secret distress is gnawing at your heart, I feel closer to you than ever. Beelios, look upon me as your brother."

"God bless you," he said in a choked voice. A warm tear rolled down his cheek in the darkness and scalded my hand.

The humidity where we were—on the forest floor—had increased; the air was heavy and stagnant. High above us, however, a strong wind was blowing over the woods' black surface and raising waves in the canopy of leaves. Every now and then a cluster of stars peeked through the swaying crests for a moment and then disappeared again. As night invaded the forest step by step, thousands of marvelous insects with soothing green lights crisscrossed in the darkness, making one imagine that on some unseen loom a golden-green veil was being woven out of fire by invisible shuttles. They sparkled in the air in such great numbers at certain moments, and so thickly, that they seemed like a golden shower of impetuous light-drops. The myriad-voiced drone rising from the depths of the forest suggested the agonized gasping of millions of men, as though the whole of humankind were sighing from the bottom of its heart because of an irremovable burden of chagrin that no god could relieve.

Walking silently beneath our steel helmets, we headed back toward the trench. The forest's voice continued to reach us like the voice of a distant sea, even after we had emerged onto the plain. Our breasts no longer felt crushed beneath that sylvan shadow, and we breathed easily again. Yet how would our souls ever be cured of the infection that had been inoculated into them: the infection of the forest's soul?

The moment we arrived at the trench, I went to the captain and reported everything that had happened. He promised that he would take steps concerning the two former buddies whose mortal enmity had been brought to light in the forest, and have one or the other transferred to a different company, perhaps even to a different regiment if possible. This pleased me very much, for it would now be much more difficult for them to cross each other's paths.

I went to my dugout and lay down, hoping to get some sleep. In vain. Swarms of exceedingly grotesque thoughts were seething confusedly in my mind, flitting across each other like the glow-worms in the forest but never lasting long enough to solidify definitively into any given design.

Indeed, some died away at the same moment they were about to be born. Others were truly monstrous; I watched them with fear and revulsion as they wriggled like eels in my turbulent mind.

The day in the forest still had me, heart and soul, in its clutches. I had begun to understand that the murder that had almost taken place was an incident entirely in keeping with the forest's cruelly inhuman side, that it blended harmoniously with that negative manifestation that had previously been so wholly unimaginable to me. What really held me in its grip, however, was an insuppressible craving to learn the story of that woman whose flame had danced so fatefully upon an axe raised high at midday.

As I sit here now and relate all these sad events to you, I feel secretly ashamed because I know that my concern for Lance-Corporal Beelios had crawling wormlike inside it a curiosity that can only be called obscene. This curiosity spread within me like a cancer and tormented me so much that it finally made me rise in the middle of the night and grope my way on all fours to Beelios's dugout. I went ostensibly to console him, but I realized all too well that this was just an ulterior motive, an entirely hypocritical rationalization. What I really felt was an importunate hunger to learn his secret. A morbid lust had begun to percolate into my fingertips, which craved to paw, one by one, the bloodstained tatters of a shattered soul.

I found Beelios sitting in his dugout still wearing his helmet and cartridge belt, exactly as when he had returned. I brought him outside (I was so marvelously consoling!) and up onto the parapet. The sector was absolutely quiet; everyone, friend and foe alike, was lying low. The sky, with all its stars alight, resembled a closed, faraway palace conducting joyful celebrations for its own inhabitants and exclusive guests, festively illuminated solely for their sakes. Down below, on earth, an occasional flare—those nightflowers of the trenches—bloomed midway between earth and heaven.

I invited Beelios to tell me the full background to this unfortunate episode in his life, and I prompted his memory (with admirable skill, you can be sure!), helping him to bring out all the details, personalities, and crucial conversations involved in this tragedy whose penultimate (presumably) act I had chanced to view that afternoon. Unhappy man that he was, he opened his soul to me like a book (aha! that's what was driving me: my mania for reading). In this book I pored over his terrible secrets, enough to sate my hungry curiosity. I am satisfied now; yet at the same time I feel a certain remorse, as though I had taken a passkey and rifled someone's drawer in order to peruse its confidential documents. On the other hand, my mind is at ease at last and this (wouldn't you say?) is of prime importance for a person's tranquility of soul. After all, we do have to keep our souls in good working order, don't we?

Let me tell you now about Beelios. He is a strapping young man from Mytilene-town. At the time he first met Stylianoula, he owned his own blacksmith shop and was making a good living. The girl, a refugee from Aivaly, lived in his neighborhood. She was a simpering flirt who gave herself airs and had a weakness for finery. She was man-crazy, too, and very pretty—so pretty in fact that her beauty pierced Beelios's heart like a stab. Although she was homeless and destitute, and although her vagaries were fully known to him, he married her. Indeed, this was precisely why he married her so hastily: to rein her in, or as he himself put it, to "break her." He wanted to get her away at last from the doorstep and the window, where she used to stand from dawn to dusk with the express purpose of using her wiles and cajoleries to drive mad every young man who turned to look at those sparkling eyes of hers surrounded by their dark lashes. A strange and lively girl (the devil inside her must have been dancing a never-ending jig), she knew full well the power of her beauty and used it, like a well-honed sword, to play deadly games. There was something entrancingly childish in her manner, a quality available at any and all times to disconcert every young man whom her games had brought to the point of no return. And she employed it—this fake naïveté—with such admirable skill! You would hardly be finished declaring: "That's that! Now I've got her wrapped around my little finger" when you would be thinking instead: "Idiot! What have I done? That creature is untamable!"

Nevertheless, Beelios married her. After all, wasn't he accustomed to softening iron and bending it to his will? He took her into his simple home where he lived with his aged mother, a kindly old soul—one of those old-fashioned Mytilenian housewives who go round from morn to night with brush in hand, keeping everything spic-and-span with fresh coats of white-wash. Stylianoula, of course, was a robust, lithe female with red hellfire smoldering in her sword-straight body, as tart and intoxicating as a jigger of ouzo. Yet the two women got along splendidly. As for Beelios, he wore his bride like a diadem on his head. He loved to lift her high in his strong arms as though she were an infant; she would bite him in the ear then amid roars of laughter, kicking the air and squealing. Soon afterwards, however, came the mobilization of 1915, which took the Lesvos Regiment—Beelios included—far far away to the hills of Macedonia. It was with bursting heart that the blacksmith loaded his haversack onto his shoulders. He feared not only the coquettishness but also the poverty of the woman he was leaving behind him in full bloom, without even a baby at her breast. His fears were not unfounded.

The mobilization lasted through the autumn. Winter was beginning. Their little nest-egg had long since been exhausted; all the blacksmith tools had been sold off one by one. Shops began to refuse them further credit.

"I've decided to hire out as a harvester, mama," Stylianoula told the old lady one day. "I can't stand this any longer. My breath stinks from hunger. Let me go to the olive groves."

The poor mother fought in various ways to keep her back, but to no avail. Among other things, the poverty that pinched them with increasing severity each passing day truncated any argument she might offer. Thus Stylianoula went off, accompanied by an elderly compatriot of hers, and contracted to work in the olive harvests for the entire winter.

When Beelios received his discharge he headed home overflowing with yearning and love. As he approached his house, the gift that he had purchased for her was hidden beneath his tunic, wrapped in tissue paper—a maroon kerchief decorated with a delicate white sprig. The hour was early evening; the whole world glowed with a pinkish hue. A nightingale warbled intermittently in his heart; he was whistling; yet even before he crossed the threshold he sensed that something had changed inside his house. It was perceptible in the atmosphere he inhaled and upon the faces of the two women, as well as in their behavior: something strange. Neither of them could look him directly in the eye for very long. Something shadowy, suspect, and doubtful kept dancing beneath their eyelashes. At first he lacked the courage even to admit to himself that he saw this. Afterwards, he detected certain peculiar shufflings inside the house, and certain glances and clipped exchanges between bride and mother-in-law—like a foreign language that he could not comprehend. To all appearances, his wife and mother had extremely serious conversations behind his back, in secret, because the moment he came into sight the terrified women let the words dry up on their lips, or else they clumsily changed the subject and began to talk about other things. One day Beelios noted that his old mother had been browbeating the girl and making her cry. With each successive day an ever-increasing oppressiveness weighed down upon the household until the atmosphere—saturated as it was with some mystery whose presence he constantly registered—became too close and heavy to breathe. The secret surely must have been a horrible one, since it dared not reveal itself.

"You women are going to make me burst a blood vessel," Beelios used to say to them in the evening when he came home all smoke-blackened and perspiring from the blacksmith's sledge that he wielded now in someone else's shop. "Why don't you let me in on whatever keeps you whispering to each other all day long? You'll wear me to a frazzle, both of you."

With this, he would shift his glance questioningly first to the one then to the other.

"For goodness sake, my boy, what's come over you since you returned?"

This, the mother's customary reply, would be followed by Stylianoula's: "Why, we don't seem any different to you, do we?" accompanied by an anxious fluttering of those butterfly-wing eyelashes. Then both women would do their best to smile, producing instead nothing but two pitiful grimaces.

All this secretiveness was a worm of affliction devouring Beelios's heart.

One evening when he returned home somewhat earlier than usual he caught sight of an old woman leaving the house by the front door. She was tall, with a black wimple tied in a knot beneath her large chin. At the sight of him in the distance she could not suppress a tiny movement that betrayed a certain fright. Going hastily around the first corner, she disappeared.

Something told him that this curious visit portended some indefinable evil for his household. Quickening his pace, he flew up the steps three at a time, the stairway creaking behind him.

105

"Who was that?" he demanded of his mother in a rage. "I saw her ugly puss coming out the front door just now. Tell me who she is. I've never noticed the likes of her around here before."

"Oh, . . . you saw her?" said the old mother, swallowing hard. "Well, she's from Aivaly. An old neighbor of Stylianoula's. Came to pay her a visit. She nursed her in her earliest years, before she was weaned.

Stylianoula, who had turned as yellow as sulfur, confirmed this with a nod.

"She's a long-time friend of her late mother's," continued the old lady. "Her name is Urania. She tells fortunes by reading coffee-grounds, too."

"You keep those witches out of here," yelled Beelios, banging his fist on the table. "I don't like them, understand! If she sets foot in here again, she'll find some mighty bad coffee here, in my house!"

A little later that same evening, when they gathered around the dinner table with their customary bickering and began to eat, Stylianoula suddenly let out a scream with the first mouthful she took.

"Oooch! Oh mama! Mama!"

A terrible pain was knifing through her stomach and abdomen, together with a nausea that made her retch the very lining of her guts. The old mother went berserk. Turning waxen yellow, she ran here, ran there, came back again, grabbed one thing, let go of another—and was of no use whatever.

The blacksmith became frightened in his own right.

"What's the matter, wife? . . . I said: What's the matter?"

Finally, Stylianoula was able to blurt out in the midst of her throes:

"I'm poisoned! The old hag poisoned me. Oh god, oh god . . ."

She inhaled deeply. The shadow of death, passing over her eyes, made them dilate and bulge with dread.

Suddenly Beelios caught on.

Seizing her hair and yanking it until he nearly lifted her off the ground, he brought her contorted and unrecognizable face close to his own at first, then dragged it next to the lamp that was hanging on the wall. In bringing it near to the light in this way, he apparently wished to read the truth in those terror-stricken eyes, for he stared into their depths with his face practically touching hers—drove his gaze into her like a stiletto—until all at once, like a lightning bolt, the truth did flash through those glazed eyes that were goggling in paralyzed dismay. It was a truth that cast light for him, but at the same time burned him to the quick.

"Slut!" he howled. "So you got yourself with child while I was away in the army, is that it? And you had that hag bring you an herb, and you took it to get rid of the bastard in your tummy? Right?"

Still clutching her by the hair, he knocked her head against the wall.

"Right, slut? And with my own mother as your bawd, eh? Viper! Whore! Lousy filthy whore!"

"Forgive me, forgive . . , forgive . . . ," whimpered his wife, who was dangling like a rag from his powerful fist, her body contracted like an injured snake's because of the repeated pangs that were slicing through her entrails.

"Tell me his name! Who was it? Who filled your belly for you? Whore! Bitch! Tell me his name! Tell me!"

Still pressing her against the wall, he began to kick her womb with the tip of his shoe and to slap her face while still banging her head against the plaster. Soon a wound opened in the back of her scalp and blood began to splatter the newly whitewashed inglenook.

In due course she ceased to resist his blows any longer or to implore his forgiveness. Instead, she commenced to groan softly and continuously—unsilenceably. She sounded like an aggrieved child whining quietly in a corner. Eventually this muted wail died out as well, her body suddenly slumped inertly in his grasp, her arms thrashed limply this way and that as he pommeled her, the eyes rolled upward until only the whites were visible, then went glazed beneath drooping lids.

Beelios felt a chill invade the roots of his hair and, after this, something shrink inside of him, shrink gradually into nothingness and vanish—as though his heart were suspended from a number of cotton threads that were slowly but inexorably being cut one by one. He released his grip on her hair. Blood and sweat had pasted some of the tresses to the wall. As her livid corpse subsided onto the patchwork rug that covered the floor, her forehead struck a corner of the hearth with the dry clack of one inanimate object hitting another. Beelios stood rooted in place, gazing at her in dazed incomprehension.

"Criminal! You murdered her," shrieked his mother. "Dog! Filthy dog!" And she fell upon the lifeless body.

Only at that moment did Beelios realize how much he had loved that exceedingly attractive and coquettish little girl and how indispensable she had been to his existence. He understood then that the drooping lids that had closed over those scintillating eyes had also lowered a dark, irremovable sorrow over the remainder of his days. He wept for her, mourned her, lamented—is still lamenting. They brought him to trial and acquitted him. "Execute me," he begged the jurors at the top of his lungs, and they voted for acquittal! His mother died soon afterwards with the same grievance on her lips. From that time onward a sepulcher formed inside Beelios's breast, a tomb surmounted by an ever-vigilant cresset burning with a tiny red flame: the hope that one day he might be able to quench his wounded heart's thirst for revenge. He would dive headfirst into this revenge as into a sea, would devote himself to it body and soul, in order to delight in it all the more.

And now—behold!—the unknown seducer, the hateful object of Beelios's quest, had been identified as someone entirely unexpected: the man with whom he had shared his meals day after day. From now on, however, this former comrade was a marked victim—with a blood-red cross on his forehead, just like an Easter lamb.

18

The Hour Glass

A sudden change.

No digging tonight. We were told to sit tight next to our gear, all of us, and await orders. At dark, the sergeants were summoned to company headquarters. No sooner did they return to their platoons than the trench filled with commotion. Shadows flitted back and forth; hasty whispers were exchanged. We were commanded to pack our complete kit in the regulation manner, to shoulder our haversacks without the slightest noise, and to line up in the trench. No talking. No shuffling about. Next, the N.C.O.s repeated orders in whispers as they squeezed their way along the row. Keep your mess tins from clinking; for god's sake don't light a cigarette; take hold of your shovels so they won't clang against any other metal equipment or the gas-mask case.

We began to move. An honest-to-goodness march it was, through a long communication trench. We groped our way blindly as we proceeded inside that narrow ditch that meandered like a snake, turned, twisted, slid down the hillside, crawled along a flank, clambered upward. No one knew where we were going. We understood this much, however: that we were going closer to Peristeri. Clearly, we were approaching the silent ogre.

Everything in the sky rushed this way and that (although not the slightest puff of a breeze reached far enough down to be felt by us). A miserable chunk of dull-yellow moon sped insanely between innumerable hasty clouds that raced disheveled in the opposite direction full of silence and motion, without halting even for an instant to catch their breath or to glance backwards to observe what was happening hard at their heels—as though some catastrophe were slated to befall their locality, perhaps had already occurred, and they were fleeing in a daze. We were the same. Unquestioning, speechless, activated by an indestructible impetus that kept urging us forward, we walked through the trench.

In places it was so narrow that we skinned our knees on the jagged stones of the walls. If anyone stumbled and fell (the noise sending a chill down our spines) the entire file behind him had to halt. But no one in the rear asked why the column had stopped or when we would resume our march. Each man simply waited in the darkness to discover some motion in the person in front of him. Interpreting this as a resumption of the march, he started again in his turn, and so on down the line. . . . White placards were visible at the various intersections of the trench system. These bore code numbers Al, A2, A3, A4, etc.—in other words, the names of the main thoroughfare and its tributaries. Such-and-such a street, such-and-such a side street. . . . Occasionally we went by a dugout with some Frenchman or other huddled in its recesses smoking a pipeful of vile-smelling tobacco that glowed reddishly beneath his nose like the ashes in a lighted brazier. Hearing our steps, he would turn toward the trench and squinny his eyes laboriously in an effort to see us. But his vision would be limited to a small area inside the dugout, the yellow area illuminated by his candle as it gleamed strangely beneath his large chin.

Finally we stopped. Somewhere. No one found this surprising. We could have continued on just as easily. Then they explained to us that this, our new line, lay immediately behind the front line. . . . The trench we now inhabit is "alive"! Here, in this "second line," one says "There's a war outside" as casually as "It's cold out."

Our company is replacing a French one whose duties are being turned over to us step by step with patient, methodical explanations and guidance. All these examples of sympathy and politeness on the part of the French are the dry crusts of their joy, tossed to us as alms. Their faces shine like those of schoolboys at recess time. I can detect a cry of delight laboriously constrained inside every mouth. They are being sent to a rest camp behind the lines.

We checked out the machine-gun emplacements, sentry posts, bombardment shelters (just what we needed!), the "nests" for hand grenades. We became familiar with the trench's labyrinth: the maze of barbed-wire entanglements whose egress is blocked by the "sea urchin," a door-like conglomeration of iron rods and tangled wire all covered with sharp steel spines. We posted sentries and slept until noon the next day.

This trench is considerably fancier than our last one. It has been kept in better repair and is also much deeper—deeper, indeed, than a man's height, so that in places we can walk fully erect. Most important of all, practically every man in our company has found himself a reasonably secure and ship-shape hole, ready made, as an underground lodging.

I am "rooming" with my brother again in a dugout that is quite unique. Four wooden steps bring you down into the earth and place you in front of a dark burial-vault sufficiently wide for one person but extremely cramped for two. This rocky cave was hacked out of an obstinate block of solid granite, chipped away with a chisel, bit by bit. Sunlight is unknown here. Right now it is noon, broad daylight outside, yet even so I have to keep a candle burning if I want to see. Moving the flame next to the walls and ceiling I find chisel-marks everywhere and my thoughts turn to all those men who must have slaved away in here for so many days and nights before this project could be completed—this project that today is protecting my brother and myself. I feel an affectionate gratitude for them. If they are alive, whether friend or foe, may God protect their fingers! And if they have been killed, may their delicate hands rest in peace!

Something else very impressive: this particular dugout has floorboards—three planks jimmied from someone's front door. They are painted green. I wonder which battered home is lamenting their loss. Traces of the knocker are still visible on one of the planks. It must have been a large village-style ring suspended from a brass escutcheon designed like a rosetta and perforated like lace. We have a similar one, beautifully crafted, on the front door of our home in the village. This hand of peace must have knocked with its cheery sound ever so many times before being wrenched away by war.

Our planks form a sturdy and well-fitted flooring underfoot, but they do not rest on solid ground. Beneath them is a hole whose purpose I discovered with very little delay. It had been excavated in order to collect the water that this subterranean boulder sweats out of hidden veins. The walls are damp, as though covered with mist.

I have found quite a few indispensable items here: a percussion cap taken from a shell and fixed to the wall to hold the candle or the lamp (a tin filled with margarine), which by all means has to be kept burning down here day and night; a horde of quinine pills soaked through because of the humidity; two boxes of matches; a solid wooden case; four nails; a package of pipe tobacco; one half of a thick spermaceti-candle. For each of these things I say "Thank you" to the unknown occupant who preceded me in this dugout and whose elation at leaving it made him forget so many gifts.

Attending to my blankets and fixing the candle firmly in place, I stretched out carefully along the very edge of the dugout. My exhausted brother was still asleep. He had his back toward me. He was without his tunic because of the heat and wore only a sleeveless undershirt that exposed his muscular arm as it lay extended beside him. White and bare, it too was sleeping restfully, completely reposed, its blond fuzz shining goldenly in the light. The only movement came from a small artery pulsating near the elbow, as though it were the arm's little heart. This fraternal arm that I love so dearly was marvelously illuminated by my candle. It was slender, and high up near the shoulder I saw the scar from the vaccination we had received as children— perfectly round, like a coin. I have one, too, just as round, and in precisely the same spot. Here, look!

I clasped my fingers behind my head, closed my eyes, and dipped my memory into our childhood years. I was always quarreling with my brother; I used to wallop him regularly. My reminiscences sailed along over a calm sea of vague, half-forgotten impressions of former times, all of them pleasing. Colors shifted, the outlines of faces began to form—of faces, odors, songs, various shapes. Small pleasures came cruising by: faded flowers pressed between the numerous pages of time's *Golden Legend.* So did tiny sorrows (how readily one would give heart and soul to endure these again!), and dreams, fantasies, incidents, even nostalgic memories from favorite books. They were the sweetly remembered residue from a childhood life that had died and left behind nothing but its buoyant and unapprehendable perfume to hover above the bogged-down soul. You exhume this residue and it smells ever so sweetly, like wilted basil.

Submerged as I was in my voluptuous torpor, suddenly I began to hear the large drops that the boulder secretly lets slide down its sculpted cheeks. They were landing underneath me, water upon water, with a considerable interval between each, like globules of mercury dripping through the hourglass of life. I began to hear myself counting ". . . nine. . . ten. . . eleven. . . " silently to myself. Apparently "someone" had been counting inside me for an appreciable time before I became aware of him. Why was he doing this? What did he fear, or expect? That frigid sound issuing from beneath the floorboards at fixed intervals began to fill me with sadness. I reflected that Death was hiding somewhere here, patiently lying in wait for us. Confidently, his chin resting on his fist, he kept his eyes pinned directly on this hourglass and measured out our lives, mine and my brother's. At some point a final globule would fall, a last drop would drip down, water upon water. Plash! Full stop. Then one of us would die. Perhaps both of us—that was even more likely.

Back home in our village, high on the mountainside, the old folks would suspect nothing, until one day they received Balafaras's "lovely letter." I could see it all. . . . My father would be just seating himself in the little café in the square, beneath the arbor with the laurels. Evening. He has returned from the fields, extremely tired. He takes his regular place near the acacia to "drink down his own sweat" as we say—to spend his hard-earned drachmas on his "one refresher," an ouzo that he swallows as slowly as possible, sip by sip. At this point who arrives in the marketplace but old Uncle Dimitri the rural mail carrier, dragging behind him his donkey with the leather satchel slung over its withers. Calls of "Welcome!" reach him from all sides as he secures the halter to a hitching ring. Knowing his own importance (if nothing else, there is that crown affixed to his cap), he wears an "official scowl" on his face; at heart, however, he is an extremely fine fellow. He fishes in his satchel and draws out a large envelope that he brings to my father. "This is for you, Uncle Thodoros," he says, setting down the thick envelope very close to him. "Must be from the boys, God bless 'em!" The old man's happiness fills him from head to toe. "You don't say," he declares pleasantly to Uncle Dimitri as—smiling, his hands trembling with expectation—he picks up the heavy envelope and moves his leathery palms over its every portion. It is covered with red blobs of wax bearing the division's large, round seal. "You don't say." My father always replies "You don't say" when someone tells him something, no matter what. He stands Uncle Dimitri a drink, stands all of the villagers as well. They congratulate him on his good fortune: "Here's to the boys, God bless 'em."

This is exactly how it happened the last time, in 1912, when I left school to volunteer for the Balkan Wars. I wrote to him from a hospital in Salonika to announce that I had been wounded in the leg by the Bulgarians. Then, too, he stood drinks for all and sundry at Sarandos's café. Tears flowed down his cheeks. Wiping his eyes with that large blue handkerchief of his, he shouted for the proprietor: "Where are you? Drinks on me for everyone in the place. My son has been wounded!"

I began to view all the scenes that would ensue in our household as soon as my father opened the envelope and removed Balafaras's lovely letter. These scenes paraded beneath my closed eyelids, unfolded in my imagination so clearly, and with such an abundance of detail, that they acquired, inside me, the significant vividness of actual events. Above all, I saw my mother writhing with grief. (As for you, strangely, I have never been able to imagine you in a comparable situation, receiving my "news.") I heard her protracted, unsilenceable wail, as harsh as the caw of a wild bird. "My boys, my little boys!" I saw her each and every gesture, each and every manifestation during her outburst of despair. She undid her kerchief, dug her nails into her cheeks, stretched her arms out to us, called to us imploringly, peevishly, caressingly— to my brother and myself. She repeated the old endearments from our child-hood: "My curly-head," "my rosy-lips,"' "my bey," "my gentle-eyes." . . . She went to the green trunk where she has saved all the diminutive clothes from our infancy, removed them, and pressed them to her face, cradled them in her arms, deliriously singing our earliest lullabies:

> *Come take them, Sleep.*
> *come take them promenading*
> *through village, town and city,*
> *then bring them back to me.*

As for us, we would be a pulpish mass of pounded, chewed-up meat packaged in a canvas sack submerged in blood, our hair plastered over this boulder, our fingers— . . . I looked questioningly, affectionately, at my hand. . . . Little by little I was overcome by such great pain, seized by such a razor-sharp yearning and sorrow, both for my mother and for us who had been killed, that hearing her I, too, began to weep, to weep along with her, in loud sobs. This brought me much relief, so very much that it became a strange, sorrowful pleasure. Sitting up and giving myself over with enjoyment to my grief, I continued to weep for the two of us and for our mother. My tears dripped through my beard; I could feel them as they ran slowly down my arm, inside the sleeve, tickling my skin.

I sniffed back my tears when my brother opened his eyes and sat up in fright. Bringing his face close to mine, he asked:

"What happened? You're crying."

Then, all at once, I saw the complete absurdity of my position.

"It's nothing," I said, smiling shamefacedly in an effort to conceal this ridiculous emotionalism from him. "I had a bad dream and woke up crying like this."

"The same thing happens to me occasionally," he replied in a thoughtful tone. "Nightmares. You shouldn't sleep on your left side."

He stared at me for a few moments and then brought out a crumpled cigarette. I picked up one of the matches I had discovered here. I struck it for him, but it would not light. Striking the next one, the next and the next, I had the same result. The humidity had soaked them through; they were good for nothing but the trash. He lighted up from the candle. The glow transformed the masses of silky hair surrounding his face into undulating flames of gold. Some grease from the melting candle had dripped onto his cigarette paper, making him grimace with disgust every time he took a puff.

"I've broken my fast!" he cried, mock fear in his voice. Then he explained himself.

"You know, every time some grease falls like this onto the end of my cigarette, I remember the story that Father used to tell us about the usurer who ruined whole families with his unscrupulous ways. It seems that on the eve of Good Friday a poor wretch who was smothered in debt went and hanged himself from the moneylender's front door. When that skinflint emerged the next morning and saw the corpse, he screamed in a rage: 'Well, now! And who's going to repay my loan?' He was so discomfited that he rolled himself a cigarette and (to avoid wasting a match) went inside to light it at the votive lamp that burned night and day before his icons. In the process some oil spilled onto the cigarette paper, just like now. Failing to notice this, he took a puff and inhaled the awful smell—like burned meat it was. Then he tossed the cigarette away with horror and ran to his confessor. Kneeling before him and beating his breast in desperation, he cried: 'I have sinned, sinned greatly, holy father. Poor wretch that I am, how shall I ever escape the fires of hell? I have sinned greatly and am unworthy. How will God ever forgive me?'

"'What was your sin, my child?'

"'I have broken my fast, miserable sinner that I am! I have broken my fast on Good Friday of all days! O, I'd rather have died.' . . .

"You understand, of course, that he broke his fast by inhaling the meat-smell from the oil that stained his cigarette paper. . . . Just like now."

He laughed heartily at his own anecdote.

Taking his hand, I placed it between my palms and stroked it. He is my younger brother, yet my hands are white and girlish compared to his, with delicate skin and long fingers. They have been that way ever since my childhood, when I couldn't even row a boat for half an hour without my palms breaking out in smarting blisters. My hands have never been accustomed to hard work, and I have always been ashamed of them.

Absolute silence. My brother gradually extricated his hand. I watched him exhale the cigarette smoke, a whole mouthful at a time. Suddenly I became aware of the dripping beneath our feet—water falling upon water; plash! A shudder penetrated my entire body.

"Dear brother," I said, "we shall have to separate. No more sleeping and eating together. You know that, don't you?"

"The dugout is too narrow for you," he replied. "It's true that I sprawl in all directions when I sleep. But you can go anywhere else you like in this trench and you won't find another dugout to match this one for security. Listen to me; I know what I'm talking about. I've inspected them all, one by one."

I wanted to tell him that this had nothing to do with it, that the dugout was a veritable fortress, and that I wished to go to another company—or even to another regiment—so that we would not be together when the last drop passed through the hour glass. I lacked the courage to reveal this macabre thought to him, however. I was on the verge of giving way to tears again for Mother as I contemplated how she would receive the news of her double loss.

What a ridiculous daydreamer I am, really!

19

Anchorites of Lust

*I*nvestigating the walls of the dugout today, I encountered a recess whose opening was covered by a triangular stone. It is practically a cupboard, a diminutive one. Inside, I found two cigars that had been forgotten, some additional quinine (what huge amounts our Gaelic allies seem to require), and a thin book in French.

A book! How many months since I had set eyes on one! Snatching this specimen up avidly, I discovered it to be a pornographic pamphlet meant for young adolescents, the kind that, using the pretense of "science," informs the teenager about the ugliest perversions of the sexual instinct, complete with outlandish details. The booklet made me realize that French soldiers, and indeed all soldiers of the world's nationalities—including the Greeks—dedicate the long and interminable days in the trench to smut. Millions of men everywhere, underground, sitting there in the dirt: filthy, stinking, covered with whiskers and lice . . . , and they babble about women!

Although I am extremely ashamed to admit the pleasure I experienced in finding this booklet, I have read it over and over with a glee that seems insatiable. At first I deceived myself, concluding that the mere possession of a book—of the "printed word," which my spirit had been deprived of for so long—explained my avidity. Now, however, I see my mistake very clearly. No, it was not the hunger for books that caused me to cry out with gluttonous joy when I swooped down, hastily clutched this rotten bone thrown to me by fortune, and began to suck at it as though it were a delicacy; it was another hunger, the craving for female flesh. This lust is inflamed here by our obscene talk. It is a passion that grows from deprivation by consuming its own flesh, an unsatisfied instinct whose embers, as soon as they begin to settle inside the tormented body, are blown again into sky-high flames by the aroused imagination. Not only the officers but the N.C.O.s as well—whoever is privileged to visit the dugouts in the French sector on the next hill—have brought back piles of colored pictures from Parisian magazines and have pinned them on their walls. Before sleeping or eating, and each time they wake up, they cross themselves (half in jest, half seriously) and plant huge, copious kisses on the nude women in the pictures: on their breasts, their legs, their bellies— prolonged, juicy kisses. This is supposed to be a joke, yet they close their eyes voluptuously while they execute this "joke." As for me, I have often caught myself discovering a thousand and one excuses to be assigned some duty connected with the sergeant-major's dugout, the chief reason being that I want to loiter there (without seeming to) and waste my time in front of these shameless pictures—one in particular!

The men here wrestle beneath Death's shadow; they crawl on the ground like snakes, a convulsive grimace of doleful pleasure on their faces. Everyone is aware of this unliftable shadow as it settles over the trench, expands invisibly into the very air we breathe and thence into our lungs. It is cast by a cloud that hovers motionlessly above us, cutting us off from divine sunlight and hurling down its threats upon us. Death is onmipresent; it touches everything, wraps everything in its acrid essence, bequeaths to everything a special appearance and a symbolic meaning. Its taste is uninterruptedly on our lips. We all are its vassals, all of us, living in its kingdom on sufferance. At any moment it may blow its chilling breath into our lairs. Then, the limbs of all these young bodies panting with sexual frenzy will instantaneously stretch out stiff and yellow. The human form will remain frozen in the ultimate posture of "attention" that it assumes when Death's trumpet sounds the ultimate roll call—fingers rigid, jaw hanging loose, eyes glazed. And then, finally, our bodies will be relieved of every lustful desire, for ever and ever.

20

War's Bindweed

*T*he unaltered monotony of our life here creates in us the impression that our present mode of existence is indeed definitive: the ultimate form of life itself. From now on, we tell each other, everything will be the same; tomorrow will duplicate today, a today that exactly duplicated yesterday. Lying inside this repetitiveness, and forming its essence, is motionless eternity, which deprives one of hope. This situation could continue for decades. We exist in a state of patient but despairing expectation, endlessly chewing and ruminating our boredom. We might even grow old and die in this state, still waiting. . . . Waiting for what? For the particular shell that each man expects every time a whistle incises the air (making him twitch his shoulders nervously and cast furtive glances all around him), the particular shell that will deliver his own private destiny. One landed on top of a dugout the other day, caving it in and crushing three men beneath the debris. Two of them suffocated, trapped beneath hundreds of tons of soil and rock. The other's skull was mashed to a cheesecake beneath the timbers. As for the dugout occupied by my brother and myself, it can withstand even the "big boys," the 10.5s—or so I was informed by the inspector of our sector, a Frenchman. Despite this, however, one's whole body waits at every moment, waits and waits, its every limb, nerve, and fiber remaining ever-vigilant, ceaselessly waiting. Even when we are fast asleep, if a mess kit in the dugout happens to drop to the ground, an alarm can be observed to sound throughout the entire body: "Take care!" In other words, our physical self remains watchful even while the spirit is asleep. Its ears pricked up, it stands guard full of suspicion, and waits.

All this, if you ask me, is enough to drive a person mad.

We keep our candles burning constantly, all day long, so that we can see each other. The atmosphere is humid and sweaty, which makes breathing difficult. The darkness smells of damp-saturated mold; it sticks to you like filth. Outside, nevertheless, the earth is flooded all the while by sunlight, by a June sun that drowns the world beneath its brilliance and makes the ground sparkle. (Along the shorelines of Mytilene, on such days, the light dances on the sea with blue and silver sword-strokes, and the fish leap happily out of the water like silver switchblades, the kind that you force downward and then release, whereupon they spring up again.) The ceiling of our dugout is extremely low, making it impossible for anyone to be comfortable, even when sitting. This explains why we always wear our steel helmets; otherwise we would keep bumping our unprotected heads against the boulder's sharp irregularities. The stone is covered by greenish mold as though lined with tarnished copper. . . .

I keep wondering what happened to our initial enthusiasm. Perished from boredom, by all accounts. Or did Constantine Palailologos finish it off with his riding crop? "Enthusiasm," as someone has said, "resembles a serving of oysters; they are edible only when extremely fresh." True enough. It acts as the stimulus, the impelling force, until the Great Wheel begins to turn. Then . . . then . . . it is replaced by Necessity, which brandishes its riding crop and slashes you just precisely where you already hurt the most. The problem is that we Greeks still have not learned to wage war in situations where enthusiasm is lacking. And this war, compared to the last one, is a horse of a different color. The fighter has been transformed into a prisoner sentenced to hard labor. Slaving away continually, he awaits his fatal hour. Your job here is to set up barbed wire while patiently expecting *your* shell. So, we dig; and we reel out the entanglements from giant spools of thorn-covered wire, myriads of such spools (entire hills of them are being constantly delivered and unloaded) that you unwind and unwind and unwind, and still they have no end. We do this at night. Every night thousands—millions—of human beings emerge in order to extend these entanglements, binding together mountains, valleys, and endless plains. The entire terrestrial globe has already become a skein of barbed wire.

This is the wild bramble that has sprouted on account of war and wrapped itself around the universe. It is quack grass made of iron, a leafless bindweed covered with claws and teeth. Watered with warm blood, it sprouts profusely, extending its coils in all directions. Only in darkness does it bud or branch; then its indestructible tendrils cling everywhere. Having wrapped itself around the earth, it has become the crown of thorns of the earth's martyrdom. Wherever these barbed-wire entanglements take root, flowers wither, trees defoliate, apple blossoms shrivel, pomegranates turn yellow. These are the thorns that have rooted themselves in our meadows and our hearts, gained possession over them, left them uncultivated and barren. And it is we millions of prisoners who dig all night, plant the new runners, and drain our heart-blood in order to moisten warfare's bindweed so that it may take root and send out still other shoots all covered with iron claws and teeth.

Strange, wouldn't you say?

Yet that's how things stand. That's how they stand—really.

21

"... this lethargy
anticipating death ..."

S ince yesterday, the men have had a strangely mystical expression
stamped on their faces. No one dares to look anyone else directly in
the eye. Half-naked, miserably dirty, they cluster pensively in their nests
in woeful groups and exchange furtive snatches of conversation, their dust-
covered eyelids sunk downward toward the ground. They converse in
whispers, digging their uncut fingernails into the soil. If, however, some
officer happens to approach the groups, they change the subject or fall abruptly silent, stubbornly withdrawing into themselves, their tormented
souls retreating into this secure defense and spying on you through the
frosted glass of two diminutive windows: their eyes. From this retreat they
observe you furtively, suspiciously, almost with hatred. . . .

The event that produced such a demonstrably emotional reaction here
in our trench-society was something exceptional and unforeseen. A squad
of men detailed to Monastir as a working party—eight of them in all including the corporal in charge—flew the coop and never returned. They
made off for Thessaly, where the royalist faction welcomes renegades and
lets them take up employment freely as civilians. The difficult part is getting past the frontier controlled by our revolutionary government.

It is this first instance of desertion that has given all the men so much
food for thought. They are mulling it over in their conversations, examining it from this angle, probing it from that, discovering its good points and
its dangers. There is no need for me to overhear them in order to know

what is in their hearts. No matter how much they consider me one of their well-liked companions, I know that they cannot help but stiffen in my presence. It's the stripe on my sleeve, you see, not to mention my brother, an N.C.O. so fanatically nationalistic and strict that he would be capable of sacrificing even our fraternal bond if it conflicted with his patriotic duty.

In the midst of all this, Michael Gighandis sent word that I should come to his dugout because he had something to tell me.

Perhaps you remember Gighandis. He is that wan, somewhat puny young man who used to room at Mme. Therapia's house, across the street from your sister's, and who worked in the National Bank. I told you once about the poems he published in various Mytilenian newspapers, a whole series of them all marked by sarcastic melancholy. An extremely dainty and thin-skinned fellow he is, a "weak sister" as the men say. Right now he appears even scrawnier than before. He has grown a huge mop of sleek black hair that seems to have received its nourishment by sucking up all his body-moisture. Yet even in this state he continues to look handsome, with that diaphanous skin of his, always so pale, and those large splendid eyes so darkly filled with languid despair. Most remarkable of all, however, are his hands—a pair that might have belonged to some romantic damsel: slender, always perfectly manicured, and scrupulously clean. Considering our water-shortage, how he manages to maintain them this way is a mystery. I knew him just a little at home; here, however, we have become united in warm friendship. He is an extremely agreeable chap, peculiar, proud, a prey to his imagination, and tossed about helplessly by his lack of resolution. I go to meet with him in his dugout as often as I can. Although our personalities are completely at odds, it is with him that I spend my richest hours. Perhaps I suspect in him the presence of an unconfessed aspect of myself. Could that be it?

Hopeless as he is when it comes to anything requiring a speck of ingenuity or cunning, he found nothing for himself but a jag in the rock behind a slight dip in the terrain. There he dug an oblong ditch that looks exactly like a grave. After stretching his canvas sheet over it at ground level, he burrowed underneath, and that was that. Now he lodges from dawn to dusk in that grave that hardly allows him sufficient room to turn on his side; he lies beneath the ground like a worm in the mire, remains bur-

123

rowed there continuously—except when he is on duty, of course—reclining on his back and incessantly puffing a large French pipe while he stares at the canvas above him. He is awaiting death in this posture, awaiting it with a fatalism that has repeatedly infuriated me. One can always see the smoke from his pipe as it penetrates various slits in the canvas. It is like incense rising from an underground censer.

"Couldn't you be like everyone else and hang up your hat in a regular dugout?" I asked him.

"I tried that when we first arrived," he answered. "I even deposited my things in a sturdy dugout with a good roof. But not for long. Two hulking giants came in and informed me that they had it . . . 'reserved.' Then they gave me a punch that bounced me out into the trench. So, what do you expect me to do? I still had my health, didn't I? . . . and 'Those destined to fall for Greece shall wear a laurel crown that is divine'; 'a man has but one life to give to his country.'"

"Aren't you frightened out of your wits when you lie beneath that canvas?"

"No question but I am," he replied. Then he remained silent for several moments while he leisurely removed the pipe from his mouth and gazed at me with his dark eyes, seriously, calmly. When he spoke again it was ever so slowly, like a person expressing things he had reflected upon frequently and had finally digested once and for all. "Everything boils down to habit. I know that I am going to die. One day a time-fused projectile will burst up there like an overripe pomegranate and will shower its iron seeds onto my canvas. Or an airplane will fly overhead, sight my canvas and manure it with its droppings. Or something even worse could happen. I could be attacked with arrows. Haven't you heard about the arrows? One morning when I was returning here I saw two Frenchmen being carried off with arrows protruding out of the back of them. In one case the point had pierced the nape of the neck—right here. In the other, it had slammed down into the skull. You didn't see them yourself?"

"No. This is the first time I've heard about such a thing."

"Well, I saw them. I tell you, it's a sight worse than death. The arrows are steel and the German aviators release whole bundles of them over groups of soldiers. They fall with terrific force and stick into your back or the top of your head, vertically. I'm sure you know the way a suckling pig is brought out at a rich man's banquet—with the serving fork embedded between its shoulders? Just like that. Understand? This is what bothers me most of all: the thought of dying with a fork stuck into my skull or backbone. . . ."

Raising his narrow shoulders in a nervous shrug, he knocked his pipe against his palm and then continued.

"That is to say nothing of shrapnel. Shells can burst as far as a hundred meters away and often as not their fragments will reach you. 'Frrrnn' they go, like the bass string of a guitar, as they miss you and eat into the ground. You take one in your hands. It has sharp teeth and is still warm. . . . Sooner or later a piece of shrapnel like this will arrive at my canvas to saw me in half. Yes, it will happen without fail, and that will mean the end of everything. I know this, but I have learned by now to be almost calm as I wait for it to happen."

"Calm?"

"That's right. The worry I experienced the first few days was indescribable. The minute I heard a shell whistling or the drone of an airplane, I jumped out of my skin. My teeth rattled; I quivered all over like a freezing dog; the chills passed in waves down to my belly and along my spine; I shuddered right to the bone. I used to squeeze my eyes tight at such times, wedge my head between my arms, and roll up into myself like a snake. Do you remember Cinderella's three garments that fit into three hazelnuts? Well, you see, my whole benumbed existence contracted in the same way into a tiny tiny hazelnut. On the other hand, I felt that I was occupying a whole world of space, and I envied the ant for being able to fit into a teeny little hole no bigger than the eye of a needle, and hide there. This happened one time, two times, three, four, five, ten, a hundred times. Then . . . , well, it gradually became a habit. Death seems to pass above my canvas roof now, to stride right over it as though disdaining a man who is more like an insect and who curls up in the earth like a terrified centipede. Yet I can't be entirely sure. Maybe death mistakes my hideaway for a grave that has already been filled. In any case I've learned by now to wait for it almost calmly."

He hesitated for a moment, smiled, and raised his finger.

"Sooner or later, however, it is going to enter here, even if inadvertently, like an ill-mannered visitor who barges in without taking the trouble to knock."

"And you wait for all this inside a shelter as transparent as Karaghiozis's hut . . . ? On the other hand, why care? Around here, luck seems the only one in charge. Impregnable dugouts have already been demolished and the men inside them killed, while here you are beneath your canvas, alive and philosophizing. You shouldn't let things get you down so much."

This made him look at me in utter surprise. Gazing straight into my pupils, he countered hastily, his astonishment evident in his voice as well as his eyes.

"No! No! No! You don't understand at all. I haven't told you this because I want your sympathy. I *know* that I shall never return to Lesvos. That is one thing I am certain of. . . . How can I put it . . . ? I have grown . . . 'ripe' for death—like an over-soft fig, in fact one that is gluey already and about to fall. My soul is wrapped in its shroud, prepared and waiting. (The only trouble is in the hide, which refuses to accept this.) Every evening I say to myself, 'Another day is gone'; every dawn I open my eyes to the light and cross myself as I murmur, 'Another morning has come.' You see, I regard each passing day as something won at cards, and in a rather dishonest gamble at that. Whether you like it or not, this is something I feel with my entire body: that I am among the condemned. . . . But that's not all. . . ."

"Not all?"

"Listen! As I lie here incessantly on my back, I keep thinking for hours on end how preferable it would be to get it all over with. Heroes and I, you understand, are not cast in the same mold. Since I am going to die anyway, I say to myself, why not here as well as the next place. Here, at least, I have only my own lice eating me, and am forced to smell no one else's stinking feet but my own. But I should also mention the hunger, filth, boredom (that's the worst of all), and isolation. These will do me in, I'm sure, before the shells get me. Look here, I hardly eat any more. The last three days I've taken nothing but a slice of bread sprinkled with coffee and sugar. Even that I've begun to throw up. My stomach refuses everything. Except water. Water is all I want: cool, pure water, a whole huge well of it, filled to the top. What I'd really like is to fall into that well and drown there. When I'm asleep I dream of brooks, geysers, village taps . . . and of a diaphanous sea as clean and smooth as a freshly ironed sheet, just like at home, its water so pellucid that it seems like billowy air; a sea with green seaweed, and with immaculate bluish pebbles on its bottom."

This kind of declaration brought tears to his eyes and ardor to his voice, whose bass tones sounded a plaintive tremolo. He raised his hand above him, palm open. A cluster of sunlight passing through one of the fissures in his canvas struck this fragile hand and its arched, well-manicured fingernails. I observed the rays pass right through his paper-thin palm, which glowed pinkishly, colored exactly like forest leaves at the outset of autumn. Some hidden fever is slowly consuming this young man without his knowledge. He is surely prone to tuberculosis, if he isn't already in the advanced stages. My attention was directed to his ears as well, and I observed that they, too, were so emaciated that they had become transparent, as though fashioned from the cellulose of rose-petals. I felt overcome by the tragedy of it all . . . , the tragedy.

He began again. I had the impression that he was talking to himself.

"There's still more. You cannot imagine how much I suffer from the horrors of this kind of life. My knees buckle when I go out on duty at night; you'd think they were made of cotton. My vision blurs; I stagger this way and that, as though drunk. Sometimes I topple to the ground like a sheaf of grain because in the absolute darkness you walk as if in a void, and each footstep goes out blindly, at random."

"What you need is a doctor."

"Never! If he declared me 'healthy' and I had to return to the others to be their butt and laughingstock, the humiliation would probably kill me. I'd rather die from fear than be crushed beneath the weight of ridicule. . . . I hope you realize that I'm telling you all this—telling you and no one else—because I breathe a little easier when I unburden myself of various thoughts that keep scratching about inside my skull like cockroaches. If only I could describe to you the kind of funk that overcomes me each time I am about to be sent on patrol or to some listening post in front of the barbed wire. But no duty officer or N.C.O. is ever going to discover this. Often I have to strain with all my might to keep my body from quivering spasmodically at the slightest noise. I want to plant some courage in it, to fortify my heart every time it shies and kicks in the blackness: that is, every time a bush sways, a jackal howls, or a dislodged stone rolls away behind me into the night."

"We all experience the same fear, more or less."

"No, for you and the rest it must be different. In my case, when a flare suddenly ignites overhead, I feel its white brilliance pour all over me like ice-water. I can sense its touch upon my skin—or, rather, underneath my skin as if I'd been flayed. I try to block my ears and nostrils, to close my eyes, my mouth and even my pores if possible, anything to keep from feeling that white horror penetrate me. My heart begins to pound with irregular thumps at such times and I keep expecting to die, until the darkness (which is filled with its own kind of terrors) spreads everywhere again. . . . Even our own lookouts send fear down my spine whenever I suddenly make out their murkily immobile shadows. I know that they crouch there muffled in darkness, blacker than the darkness itself, their rifles loaded, fingers on the pins of their hand grenades. I know that these shades belong to our side. 'They're Greeks, you idiot,' I keep telling myself. 'They're our own men, so why do you behave like this? Look, that's Zachariou and the other one is Zourelis.' . . . No use. They're still just as frightening to me, crouching there so motionless and incorporeal, wrapped in silence. . . . But when a person dies he escapes all such torments. As for me, you'll discover how little delay there will be. That's certain now, and has been for some time. It came to me gradually, this lethargy anticipating death, and I have welcomed it."

He filled his pipe slowly, with care, lighted it, and began to smoke without talking further, as though he had been abruptly drained of all his words. I could hear his quiet breathing.

Can you imagine what torments this lad is going through? My own opinion is that of all the men who live submerged here "in the shadow of death" he is surely one of the unhappiest?

You must realize that in this unnatural environment where the only forces that set the life around us in motion are those of instinct and fatality, a person becomes subject very easily to various types of unconscious obsessions or delusions. Even I, deep inside me, have come to believe that Gighandis is some kind of "moribund." Whenever I hear the report of an explosion while sitting inside my dugout, I experience twinges of bad conscience because my shelter is so strong; and whenever I grope my way on all fours to his grave in order to squeeze inside, my heart pounds lest this time I discover him already stiff: a corpse waiting for my arrival. I can even envision those huge eyes of his staring wide open toward the canvas and informing me calmly, in an ironic, almost satisfied tone: "Well, my fine friend, now you know that I was correct. Death did appear at last, and found me."

Each time I discover him alive when I go there, I breathe easily again. On occasion, before burrowing into his hole, I worm my arm through a slit in the canvas and run my fingers over him anxiously. "What's wrong? Haven't you died yet?" I inquire with a forced laugh as soon as my fingers encounter his feverish body. I do this half in jest and half seriously, but he appreciates the suspicion in my fingertips and calls to me from inside with tranquil sarcasm:

"Come in, Corporal, don't be afraid. 'Little children, yet a little while I am with you.'"

I squeeze inside, creeping in next to him. These visits lack any semblance of comfort, which makes them somewhat ridiculous. Squashed inside that tomb, pressed face to face, we carry on our conversations, "The French speak of a *tête-à-tête*," he reminds me with laughter in his eyes. "That is exactly what we have here—literally!" And indeed, we are literally a pair of snakes twined amicably together beneath the ground. I spent all day yesterday digging there in an effort to make the grave a little more commodious so that I, too, could stretch out in reasonable comfort. But this doubles the chances of catastrophe, since it doubles the surface area of the target. He finds these dangerous visits of mine very touching.

"Isn't it rather stupid of you," he asked me once with tender irony, "to abandon your comfort and leisure and expose yourself out here with me?"

"Why, are you afraid that death, when it visits here, will find me as well as you?"

He glanced at me, affection in his eyes, but did not answer.

"Never fear," I continued, "I have my talisman. Don't you know that I am immune to bullets—just like Balafaras?"

"Could it be the True Cross?" he inquired with a smile. "Yes indeed, I'll wager that the cross you're wearing has a sliver from the True Cross.

Your mother sewed it into your tunic the night we embarked. In addition, she gave you some searing kisses soaked in tears, and a thousand and one admonitions: 'Son, be especially careful not to catch cold!'. . . . Guard your cross well, my friend. Simpleminded charms like that don't save the body, of course. But they do save the soul from estrangement, prevent it from slowly perishing in desolation because in its difficult hours there is always a loved one standing by it and talking to it."

Silence. . . . Suddenly he continued:

"Personally, I was never fortunate enough to have a mother."

His dark eyelashes fluttered with nervous obstinacy in an attempt to repress the tear that was striving to fall. This was the first time he had ever opened himself up to me concerning his private life, and I responded in my turn by bringing out your packet, slowly undoing the wrapping, and showing him the circular locket that you gave me on my name day. Opening its golden cap, I removed the tiny plait of your hair. It is still tied with the twisted red-gold "March threads" that you sent me during our first summer together.

"Ah, a girlfriend!" he exclaimed pleasantly. "That's it, eh? You have a girl; she loves you and you love her. . . . That's even better."

"True. And I shall marry her."

"Yes, that's even better. A mother's love is important, but this other kind of love is even more important because it carries the seeds of creation inside it and is directed toward the future, whereas maternal love speaks to you out of the past." Then, turning to me and continuing almost harshly, he added: "But you should not have volunteered for this war. Precisely because of your girl, you should have remained home. You were wrong to volunteer."

"Listen, my friend, I didn't go to war in order to die, if it's any of your business. I know for sure that I shall return to our island, get married, and dandle my children in my arms. But tell me, what about you? Hasn't an enchanting pair of eyes ever crossed your path, a pair of eyes capable of teaching you that life is worth living? As far as I'm concerned, there is only one reason why we should take the trouble to say 'Thanks' to God: because He placed woman at our side. That, too, is the only reason we should throw ourselves voraciously into life."

"Yes, 'voraciously'! Well said, well said. But you enjoy all the best that life has to offer, while in my case I have never yet come close enough to a woman to utter in her presence that splendid declaration that came from you a moment ago: 'I love her; I shall marry her.' The women in my life have always been a matter of . . . 'carnal pleasure.' It's a question of luck, I suppose. Nevertheless, I would be most delightfully surprised if one day I did find a woman whom I could love for more than just her body. It's clear that you have already found such a woman."

"Yes, yes, but don't worry," I said to him with a laugh, "you'll find one also. For every sword there is a scabbard, for every man a predestined woman!"

* * *

Today I discovered Gighandis entirely changed. There was a slow-burning flush beneath his transparent skin. Rifling me anxiously with his eyes, he brought his face close to my own, so close that I felt his hot breath on my cheek. Then he gazed at me doggedly with that febrile stare of his.

"Listen," he said hastily, squeezing both my arms, "I have something very important to confide to you. Yesterday I saw some friends, we discussed certain things, and I made a decision. . . . I want to clear out of here at long last. I've decided to run off with a party that's being dispatched tomorrow to bring back rations. Everything's prepared, including the guide who'll see us through the dangerous terrain between here and Thessaly. We even have a reasonably good map."

I shrugged my shoulders.

"You've decided to desert, then."

Releasing his grip on my arms, he responded to me with an irritation that continued to increase as he spoke.

"I'm talking to you like a brother and you answer me like a corporal: 'You've decided to desert, then!' All right, call it what you like. The trouble is that I want to live, want to live beneath God's heaven just like a blade of grass or—yes—an insect. I have the right to live. Well . . ., don't I? To live is also a man's supreme duty. Like all living things I simply want to be alive. And when the time comes for me to die I want that to happen peacefully, naturally. I want to be washed and shaved when I die—and without lice. Furthermore, when I do pass away I want it to be once and for all. Here I perish a thousand times between one daybreak and the next. Every part of me is in revolt: my entire soul, mind, and body."

At this point he shrugged his shoulders defiantly and continued in a more aggressive tone:

"In any case, all the plans have been concluded and the decision made. I'm leaving. Go and report me to the company if you like."

"Go ahead and leave," I said to him. "But before you do, remember what desertion from here really means. It means a genuine military operation that will last the entire way from this hill in Serbia to Mount Olympus in Greece. It means exhausting battles, and a pitiless manhunt by army detachments, policemen, guerrilla troops, and squadrons of fighter planes dispatched both by us and our allies—all bent on annihilating you. Above all it means true gallantry. Those who desert from here are strong, healthy peasants whose instinct for self-preservation drives them to the insanest feats of daring and whose cowardice transforms them into heroes. If you actually go through with this desertion it will be your salvation. Even if you fail to save your body, at least you will have saved your soul. So go ahead and leave—if you dare. . . ."

He was gazing at the ground. Fiery blotches glowed on his emaciated cheeks.

"I wish you good luck," I concluded. Then I kissed him on both cheeks. He eyed me suspiciously until I was out of sight.

Although I said not a word to anyone, I did not feel uneasy on that account. I knew that Gighandis would never desert, even if he had actually made all the preparations his comrades had told him to make.

And that is precisely what happened. When word of the desertion passed from ear to ear, Gighandis's name was missing from the list of those who had fled.

Poor weak-hearted soul! Yet my own action was just as ignoble; I should never have humiliated him the way I did. Now it will take me many days before I dare seek him out again in his grave, I am so terribly terribly ashamed.

22

Twelve Thousand Souls

*D*o you remember that monster, Constantine Palaiologos? A corporal from his company came to our trench today and told us some juicy anecdotes about his honorable leader. The whole time Palaiologos's company maintained camp in the ravine where the common kitchens had been set up for the entire regiment—that is, behind the range of hills which constituted our line of defense—the captain kept his own tent pitched far away from those of his men. Why? So that he could save his hide if, heaven forbid! some German plane dropped a bomb on his company's bivouac. He used to spend the entire day examining the sky through his binoculars in order to learn the markings of the planes that flew over the lines. But when the time came for his company to enter the trenches like all the others, he found himself a super-impregnable dugout—and he hasn't stuck his nose out since. Word has it that his orderly spends all his time delivering and then removing tinned conserves of various types and sizes. Everyone assumed at first that the trench air had stimulated Constantine Palaiologos's appetite. We found this most perplexing. Eventually, however, word got round—psst psst psst—that the honorable captain uses these cans so that he won't have to poke his nose out of his shelter even for the call of nature. The "conserves" go in to him empty and come out full of shit.

That other bird, our great and noble Balafaras, is the same as always. A French N.C.O. who was detached to the division for a month characterized him succinctly with the following words:

"You marvel as soon as you see him with that super-colossal build of his, and you say, 'Now, there for once is an honest-to-goodness general.' But when you sit down with him and hear his drivel, you say, 'Why of course, the world's most super-colossal saphead!'"

Our latest information is that he is obsessed with the notion of impelling the division's musicians into the front-line trenches. Apparently the idea is for them to play his favorite tune right under the Bulgarians' noses.

> *I enter the vineyard as mistress,*
> *but find there the owner, my wooer.*

Word has it that his granny dandled him to this tune when he was an infant. At any rate, the song has become an obsession with him. The band pounds it out from dawn to dusk on its drums; the general struggles to teach it to every foreign officer who calls at division headquarters.

> *Tread the black grapes, kiss the fair girls . . . .*

Clank-clank go the cymbals, making the whole place roar. An actual obsession, a quirk . . . ; and now it has occurred to him to teach his song to the Bulgarians as well. He suggested this in full seriousness one night at table while he was dining with his staff.

"Let's go with all our brasses and thunder it out right under their noses! Yes, right under their noses!"

Who dared say No? The staff officers ceased chewing, exchanged knowing glances, but kept their silence. As for the bandmaster, he turned white as a sheet and even had the temerity to stammer out while choking on his mouthful:

"But . . . but . . . General, Sir . . . is that . . . allowed?"

Balafaras turned his head ever so slowly in the poor wretch's direction and struck him dumb with a ferocious stare.

"Now what made you say that, Bandmaster? 'Al-low-'d'? Do you know what that word means? When I give an order, whatever I command is allowed. That and nothing else. All the rest is 'not allowed.'"

The bandmaster's digestion was not of the best that night. But the place where veritable wails of lamentation sounded forth as soon as the news leaked out was the area where the musicians had their tents. Now that we're on the subject, these band-musicians are of the unpretentious self-taught variety, the kind who play in the cafés of Upper Skala or at peasant weddings, and who accept donations tossed at them by whoever stands up to dance. The majority are already getting on in years and have no bones to pick either with the Bulgarians or King Constantine, much less Germany. The revolution in Lesvos found them well-nigh penniless. Then, with mobilization, the army hauled in all the merrymakers of the island and with them, naturally, all the potential donations. This caused the most ingenious of the guild, the one who is presently bandmaster, to summon the rest together. He used to play 'cello in the Public Gardens in summertime, and was just another poor devil with a family to support. So he proposed a solution to them: Why not go to work for the division? The rest was simplicity itself. They'd have uniforms, shoes, food, a salary, all the best in life—not to mention English chocolates! They auditioned while the division was still in Salonika. Soon they had gold stripes on their sleeves and gold lyres on their collars. Their leader was made first an adjutant and then a second lieutenant. The oldest of this lot of miserable devils is Uncle Giacomi, or "Uncle Sergeant" as he is known in the division. He plays folk clarinet and from well-established habit tilts even his helmet rakishly over his left ear, just as he used to tilt his Italian *bombetta* in the good old days. . . . Well, this entire guild of hoary elders, when they got wind of the plan to send them to play in the front-line trenches, they let out wails of lamentation inside their tents and nearly lynched the bandmaster, who had gotten them into this pickle in the first place. Fortunately for them, Balafaras's decision was conveyed by surreptitious whispers to the French Army, a bristling memorandum arrived, and thus the band did not perform its deadly concert.

Still another brainstorm hit Balafaras the other day. The military nomenclature here is all French. Suddenly, out of the blue, he conceived the whim of removing all the French names applied to points in our area, and replacing them with designations in Greek. He found it unbearably humiliating, you see, for the stalwarts of the Greek army to be killed at *Quadrilatère, Ravin des Italiens, Arbre Noir, Point O,* and . . . devil take the rest! Didn't we have slews of heroes from the Golden Age, Byzantium, the Revolution of 1821, the Balkan Wars? The French took great pains to make him understand that if such a change were effected there would have to be a simultaneous alteration in the overall terminology of allied cartography, and that new orders would have to be issued all over again from the start (drat and tarnation!) to the multinational forces involved, elucidating and justifying the re-baptism of our positions.

One day Balafaras held a kind of reception at division headquarters, the occasion being one of our national holidays. The French commandant of the general sector, a wily pint-sized old codger with a pot belly, paid him a "state visit" along with his entire staff. Balafaras lined up the band, had them begin *The Vineyard,* and set about explaining the song's important meaning to his foreign guests.

"*C'est un air populaire, vous savez! 'J'entre dans la vigne comme propriétaire!'*"

Afterwards, the "select champagnes, *une chose excellente,*" were opened at his command. These, in accordance with a divisional order, had been purchased by means of obligatory "contributions" levied on all the officers at the front, even though there was never any possibility that the poor fools would taste any. The division paymaster simply withheld a portion of their salary, and that was that.

So, the French officers raised their glasses and the foreign commandant proposed a formal toast. Having taken a sip, he was about to put down his glass when Balafaras, without losing a moment, tapped him patronizingly on the shoulder and shouted:

"*Tiens! Tiens! Tiens! Buvez, mon général, nous en avons beaucoup!*"

When from time to time I reflect that this man holds in his hands the fate of twelve thousand souls, I break out in a cold sweat.

If it weren't for the chief of staff and the adjutant at his side, both of whom have some brains in their heads, and if the Supreme Command weren't French, he'd think nothing of lining us up one fine morning, all twelve thousand of us, unfurling the three regimental banners in the breeze, placing the band and Uncle Giacomi in the vanguard, mounting his colossal steed . . . , and setting out to capture Peristeri!

And he would take it, too, because—after all—he is immune to bullets.

23

Artillery Duel

O ne gets used to anything sooner or later. I have noticed that human beings possess an inexhaustible inner reserve of adaptive capability that rescues them from great misfortunes and especially from madness. Here, for example, our way of life has already become a stable condition. Sometimes it occurs to me that if the stories about eternal torments in hell were accurate, each of the damned would have all the time in the world to grow used to his tortures through and through, and consequently could puff his cigarette to his heart's content inside the cauldron of brimstone, lighting it from the very flames that were harrowing him.

We either sleep during the day, lying on our backs in the darkness, or, our candles burning, play cards and talk. The last we do less and less frequently, however, because no one has the slightest appetite for idle prating. When we open our mouths it is only to pronounce the barest minimum of words necessary for our duties, or to indulge in smut, or to hurl curses at each other. Soon enough, in any case, we are overcome by sleep as though by some disease, a sleep full of exhaustion, nightmares, and wet dreams. The men awake soaked in sweat and semen.

But as soon as darkness falls, this whole world comes to life and emerges from its caverns in order to fight: to wage war. Under the cover of darkness, hordes of implement-laden soldiers peek over the rim of the trench and leap across the top in successive ranks, then proceed sluggishly to slouch toward no-man's land. Deprived of cigarettes, with an absolute minimum of noise, they advance in this robot-like manner in order to dig, or set up entanglements, or keep their ears cocked at a listening post, or lie in ambush. Sometimes the group returns depleted, in which case the Order of the Day strikes certain names off the company rolls and Balafaras obtains certain home addresses so that he may dispatch his "lovely letters," neatly typewritten.

The pyramidal ridge of Peristeri—the "Dove"—looms blacker and fiercer than ever in the darkness. It is swaddled in mystery; its tip touches the sky. The oppressive silence that this fortified mountain exudes is more frightening than a thousand-mouthed cannonade.

Suddenly a slender red line burgeons from one of the flanks and ascends. The men fall flat on their faces then, no matter where they happen to be, because the top of this luminous, fading stem will blossom before long into a brilliant flower of light, a miniature sun. A flare like this ignites high above us in the atmosphere and hovers there, swaying in balance, as it shines down upon us with unbearable brilliance. Then it flounders in mid-air and sails off attentively into the void. It is the Dove's lightly sleeping eye, an eye whose lid lifts suspiciously in the night so that this powerful lantern may search gruffly to see where we are and what we are doing. An area of many square kilometers is illuminated as though in daylight. The lantern advances with such slow-moving deliberation that you would think some invisible giant were holding it in his enormous hand as he strolled from place to place, urgently looking for something on the ground. Eventually it descends ever so slowly and goes out, or else disappears behind some hill. No one budges during this interval; no one breathes. Soon another flare ignites, and then another and another; they follow each other in close succession, coming from both sides now. If a person ignorant of the war observed all this outpouring of light as it bathed the mountains, he would mistake it for a celebration of joy and kindness. The other evening an illuminating rocket like this fell on Magarevo, a deserted hamlet that sits between the Bulgarians and us. It landed on a rooftop and started a conflagration that destroyed three houses, after which the fire subsided of its own accord. (No one went to extinguish it!) The empty village was illuminated funereally all the while, its casements swinging open, the house-interiors filled with darkness. Ignited flares have also fallen into patches of dry grass or amid the wheat that ripened in vain for the absent reapers who will never again come with their scythes and merry songs. The fields burn and burn, until they grow tired of burning. Occasionally an attack, reconnoitering mission, or *coup de main* occurs in a nearby sector. At such times the spectacle is unimaginably grand. Igniting beside the white flares are chromatic ones—green, red, yellow, maroon—that promenade across the sky like multicolored caterpillars or drag their bodies laboriously between the stars as though they were fiery but wounded dragons all coiled in upon themselves. A cherry-dark stalk germinates with a whistle and explodes at its tip, whereupon varicolored stars gush upward in a veritable geyser above our heads, then drip down in clusters, fading as they descend. All this is an agreed-upon signal for artillery barrages and other types of fire.

The cannonade follows close on the rockets' heels. It comes from the Dove, or from us, or sometimes from both at once. The batteries seek mutual annihilation. This is known as an "artillery duel." What happens at such times is terrible but also beautiful. Alas, I cannot escape calling it "beautiful" since it is the most majestic spectacle a man can ever hope to experience. When the action falls outside our sector I creep into the trench, glue my chin to the soil of the parapet, and become nothing but two eyes and a pair of ears diffused into this strange universe, a being who throbs with pride as well as wretchedness.

Diamond necklaces string themselves along the base of the mountains; the gems sparkle each in turn in the darkness, then fade. These are the salvos, discharged in regular succession. Next, the valleys begin to roar. They weep, shriek, howl protractedly, reverberate with imploring moans, and bellow. Absolute silence metamorphoses instantaneously into pandemonium. The atmosphere smacks its lips; it whistles fervidly with its fingers inserted into a thousand mouths. Whole masses of air shift position with violent movements; the sky rips from end to end like muslin. Invisible arrows pass across the void. Angry vipers lunge this way and that. On all sides are lashes incising the air and pitilessly thrashing the weeping hills, which huddle and curl into balls as though wishing to be swallowed into the bowels of the earth, in order to escape. The caves moan and sob in woeful groans. A thousand titans yawp in consternation, chew their fingers with obstinate despair, and holler. The atmosphere vibrates then like a bowstring and men's hearts quake like aspen leaves in a storm.

The passing shells cannot be seen; you sense them, however, with your entire body—their location at every instant, how fast they are traveling, where they will land. Some of them remind you of an object breaking the surface of a lake; they make a refreshing noise, a kind of lapping, as though they were speeding along on peaceful waters. Others create a fearful racket. Imagine colossal iron bridges erected in the darkness between the Dove and us, and rickety wagons passing over them with full loads of clattering metal tools. That is how they sound. Still others whistle almost gleefully at a standard pitch. These have been christened "nightingales" by the men, and in truth they actually do resemble birds that have flown the coop and have soared unrestrainedly into the empyrean, whistling the song of freedom.

Audible amid all these frenzied night-cries, amid this entire chaos of sound, are the amazing wails of exploding shells. A shell, when it bursts, howls with vengeful wrath. It is a blind monster, all snout and nothing else, that charges the earth and rips it to shreds with its iron fangs. Millions of men have packed their hatreds into the ample belly of this mechanized brute, have stamped their enmity tightly in, and sent the beast out to bite. When a shell explodes, all of these hatreds lurking there by the thousands, all of these satanic embryos imprisoned in the steel womb, are released like a pack of rabid dogs that then race to the attack yelping their own disparate cries that are so mournful and strange.

When I find myself near a bursting shell I invariably have this feeling: that human voices are inside it, voices that shriek with unappeasable passion. Inside a shell, I insist, are howling people foaming at the mouth and grinding their jaws together. You can hear the hysterical screech of the murderer as he nails his dagger into warm flesh; you can recognize the victory-cry of the man who drives his weapon into the breast of a hated foe and then, clutching the hilt in his palm, twists the knife in the wound, voluptuously bellowing his satiated passion and drinking down in a daze the agony of the other, who writhes beneath his powerful knee and thrashes about on the ground, spewing his life out through his throat, along with the blood.

Whenever the shells begin to rake our own trench along with the others, we worm into our dugouts and await orders. No one remains in the trench itself except the sentries, and they are relieved more frequently at such times.

A bombardment is the most supremely powerful sensation that a man can experience. You lie flat on your face at the bottom of the trench or in an underground shelter. Your mouth tastes like plaster of Paris; your soul is held in thrall by profound grief and pulsating terror, by a preoccupation that shrinks you, makes you roll up into yourself and take refuge in the kernel of your existence—a kernel that you desire to be tiny as a cherry-pit and hard and impenetrable as a diamond. Your soul is on its knees. Filled with wonder and sacred awe, it prays fervidly of its own accord. You neither understand the words it uses nor recognize them (this is the first time in your life you have heard them), and it directs its supplications to a God whose existence you had never even suspected. Your soul is a tiny lamp-flame, a sickly wavering flicker that totters this way and that in an effort to separate from its wick and be sucked gently upward by the famished void.

A bombardment is extraordinarily cruel and inhuman. It is horrible but also divinely majestic. Man becomes a Titan who makes Earth howl beneath his blows. He becomes Enceladus and Typhon, raises up mountains, juggles lightning bolts playfully in his hands, and causes indomitable natural forces to mewl like whipped cats.

Is it not man "who looketh on the earth, and it trembleth; who toucheth the mountains, and they smoke"?

24

Out of the Depths

I have been spending entire days in the dugout; very often I fail to emerge at night when it is time for duty. The trouble is an old wound I received in my left leg during the Balkan Wars. Whether the humidity is to blame, or our sedentary existence here, I don't know. But the wound has begun to act up again. My upper leg goes into spasm for hours, all the way to the thigh, and a cruel pain knifes into the bone.

The stone above my head has been dripping continually. Yesterday we removed one of the floorboards and with a tin can bailed out all the water that had collected drop by drop in the hollow beneath. It was putrid—as fetid and black as drain-water that finds its way to old neglected cemeteries in wintertime and trickles into sunken graves. It smelled of mold, cigarette butts, and extinguished pipe-tobacco. Yet the dampness remains as bad as before; the air breathed by my brother and me continues stagnant and forever saturated: a secondhand, curdled atmosphere that we ingest with repulsion, as though it were bog-water.

On some days the pain in my leg subsides; on others it is so bad that I feel like screaming. Our captain (an old acquaintance from civilian times) is extremely sympathetic; indeed, he often displays his concern in a manner that I find annoying, because he transgresses the limits ordained by subordination and rank. When I told him everything about my wound he showed a lively interest and proposed to send me to the doctor. I refused. (I remembered how Gighandis had also refused when I suggested that he

report sick.) The captain also proposed time and time again to place me in
company headquarters as a quartermaster's aide so that I could move to a
dry dugout and assuage my wretchedness in more humane surroundings.
But it never even occurred to me to accept this proposal, no matter how
much I considered it. Keeping incessant company with officers and adding up loaves of bread from morn to night in those stupid ledgers would
have been an even worse torture than my leg. Imagine: to volunteer for the
army and end up a grocer's accountant! Beyond this, I am of no mind to
abandon my brother. I want to remain here, together with him, so that I
can observe him healthy and alive every time he returns from an ambush
or patrol. Besides, to cut myself off from the camaraderie of my platoon
would be very bad for me. Shared boredom, nostalgia, and incessant danger have welded our souls together into a kind of primitive kinship and
love. To leave the others and go away would be equivalent to desertion. I
asked the captain, therefore, to let me remain here despite my condition
and simply to have me excused from duty, if possible, so long as the leg
continued to hurt. In this way we could see whether or not the trouble
would go away by itself. He agreed. I was brought a box of sugar at his
command and also a large lump of solidified alcohol so that I could brew
myself some tea. He also sent me some kerosene to rub on my leg.

As I remain here for interminable hours sitting on the planks with my
shoulders hunched over, scores of lugubrious thoughts arrive and seize
control of my mind. This happens gradually. I clutch at a reflection as
though holding the end of a thread, and then my brain unwinds and unwinds until I become completely tangled in entire spools of cogitation. Inside this net I thrash about in confusion like a caught fish, with no way
out. Especially when I am completely alone, such thoughts gain absolute
control over me. If I close my eyes or extinguish the light in the hope of
bringing my galloping mind to a halt, things become only worse. Then I
can feel my anxieties spinning round inside my skull with a hum, like a
swarm of black flies inside a cranium that seems to me as huge and hollow
as a large earthenware jug. Up they rise, whole colonies of these black flies,
and fill my head with droning grief. At various times they subside momentarily, not in order to leave me at peace, but rather to thrust their
needlelike stingers into my brain. I try my best to obtain help from the

theories of various philosophers whom once upon a time I used to read with trust. Thus I toil to place bodily pain outside my soul so that I may observe such pain at a distance; I toil to separate thought from flesh, brain from nerves, soul from corporeal woe. Then I realize that all these theories are just crude, unbeneficial idiocies indited by great fools who happened to be in sound bodily health. One feels like taking these hypocritical jackasses who go about loaded with their quack nostrums, taking every last one of them and smashing in their teeth! There is nothing more potent than physical pain for making both the soul and the spirit completely wretched. These too are corporeal, and they go to the devil along with everything else if the body suffers. Only when the body enjoys good health is the world beautiful; only then are human beings openhearted, magnanimous, happy or in love, so that all of life's benefits seem worthwhile. The whole of creation exists only through the flesh; bodily equilibrium determines universal equilibrium.

* * *

I am horrified to see my rifle resting at my side and looking so deceptively peaceful. The truth is that the bayonet, as it rusts away in its scabbard, is anxious to lap up human blood. It is extremely thirsty, this oblong tongue of steel, but it knows that its time will come. I feel like inserting the blade in a crack in the rock in order to break off its sharp tooth-like point. Outside of our dugout, I reflect, the days and nights are passing over the earth in succession like a row of alternate white and violet birds—an endless row of cranes that fly off toward the horizon and vanish. They are the days and nights of my life. They exist beyond my stony carapace, passing away and carrying their allurement with them while I remain sprawled in the darkness within—I and my twenty-two years—a dirty cripple with an aching body all laced in cobwebs. These beautifully ardent birds of mine fly off into the airy void, head for the dead past with nary a hope of returning, while I, unworthy soul that I am, fail to reach out my hand to catch them. Nor do I even extend my arms in prayerful supplication that their pitiless course may halt until I emerge from my tomb into the open. Alas, not one of these fleeting days and nights will ever return to me. And yet they belong to me, each one of them. Only now do I realize how precious they are. I attempt to get up, to creep on my hands and belly, and I am like some foul and ponderous reptile in its lair. I attempt to drag myself toward the entrance-hole, to project my head entirely outside the trench, outside into the sunlight, so that I may feel its warmth pour over my neck and in back of my ears like golden water, feel it penetrate my hair, rest a friendly hand on my sunken cheeks, . . . But I cannot, because of that pain that shoots through the bones of my leg as though an auger were spinning inside the knee-joint. And if the pain happens to subside, there are always enough lice running over a soldier's odious body to make him scratch himself with his filthy fingernails that are so long and sharp, to scratch with voluptuous obstinacy, tears in his eyes, until his hand grows tired and, drawing it back, he sees his nails covered with blood. Many men have ended in hospital because wounds made in this way have become infected and have started to fester. One sees long gashes all the way up the leg from ankle to thigh, or on the chest around the nipples, or between the shoulder-blades, the last being accomplished with the rifle-barrel or bayonet tip since the fingernails cannot reach down far enough in back. I know one of our comrades here, a somewhat elderly volunteer from Constantinople, who has already given in completely to the lice. Vilely defeated, he surrendered his body to them. While they devour his living corpse he simply stares around him in a senile daze. His eyes are lusterless and the lids droop continually, as though he were always sleepy. If you look at the belt that supports his trousers, you will observe that all the holes not kept open by the buckle-tongue are sealed by gluey white nits.

* * *

Our captain is a fine officer and I am very fond of him. Of all the career-officers I have known at close hand, he is the only one who inspires affection in me and for whom I can feel unqualified esteem. On the other hand, he is not the sort of person who occupies himself very much with thinking. He is just an extremely simple character, girlishly chaste, one of those men upright in both body and soul that are still produced from time to time by Crete. He believes in his profession with all his heart and spirit.

Not a single doubt torments him. I love him for his sincerity, and envy him his monolithic soul. His faith in the war and in the colors he serves is absolute, just like my brother's. (Once-upon-a-time mine was too.)

He returns my affection and thus strives as much as possible to make my days of suffering less harsh. On occasion he even invites me to his dugout. If my leg is feeling better I get up and manage to arrive there by dragging myself along. It is a truly sumptuous dugout. A man can even promenade in it fully erect! We drink tea together, smoke lots of luxury-brand cigarettes, and talk. When no other officers ate present we converse with complete freedom about anything and everything. For me, these are occasions of great pleasure. Once I asked him if the following thought had ever chanced to cross his mind: that all the so-called ideals offered us in this "lower world" might very well be hollow and inflated entrails whose value is anything but absolute. I told him that men had once killed each other, just as we were doing, but for religious reasons, that in Byzantine times the various factions had stabbed each other at night on account of a single diphthong, one half wanting the Son *homoousian* with the Father and the other half wanting him *homoiousian*. Could he make sense of people knifing each other in the dark for such a reason?

He laughed heartily, showing all his large teeth, which are as white and firm as fresh almond-cloves.

A few years from now, I told him, perhaps others would be killing each other for anti-nationalistic ideals. Then they would laugh at our own killings just as we had laughed at those of the Byzantines. These others would indulge in mutual slaughter with the same enthusiasm, though their ideals were new. Warfare under the entirely fresh banners would be just as disgraceful as always. They might even rip out each other's guts then with religious zeal, claiming that they were "fighting to end all fighting." But they, too, would be followed by still others who would laugh at them with the same gusto.

He bit off a corner of hardtack and, taking a red pencil, drew a line on the chart that depicted the Bulgarian trench opposite us in its every detail.

"First let's throw the king out of Athens along with all his German-loving; friends—the dogs! Then let's throw the Bulgarians out of *our* Macedonia. After that we'll have plenty of leisure to ponder your ideas and

talk about them. Everything in its own good time; vintage in August . . . .
Have a cigarette!"

In my opinion this man, even if he tramples over whole mountains of
human corpses, will be as entirely innocent in God's eyes as a newborn
babe. The same holds for all innocent criminals of every ideology, because
faith can work such miracles. I, too, had faith once-upon-a-time. I had it
until just a few months ago. Now, however, I am horrified when I think
that once, when I was still a fuzzy-cheeked adolescent, I sent home a black
cavalry-belt with bronze buckles and half-moons, sent this with arrogant
satisfaction to my peaceful home as a wartime memento. A Turkish hussar
had been wearing it across his chest. He was the first man I ever killed in
my life, and I dispatched him with cheerful innocence. He simply appeared
in front of my muzzle, in a way neither of us had expected. I was lying on
my belly in a wheat field; he rose in his stirrups and began to survey the
area around him, a gold button on his chest flashing in the sunlight. I aimed
in a line with the horse's head and pulled the trigger. He lifted his hands
high, still holding the reins, leaned to one side, then tumbled off his mount;
but his boot remained tangled in the stirrup and he was dragged along the
ground when the startled animal began to run. The horse stopped eventually, and snorted; it kept turning its head toward the suspended cadaver,
snorting. I went near, my heart pounding. He was blond, a young man as
blond as my brother. The dragging had lacerated his scalp; warm blood
flowed from his nose and mouth. Though my temples were throbbing,
basically I was happy. I had vented a tiny particle of the rancor felt by my
nation against the Turkish nation. When I sent the belt home to my village, the respected headmaster of our local school wrote me a letter that
filled me with pride. This was Anagnostou, the same man who used to
lock the school's front door, during the years of Turkish rule, whenever
he intended to give us that scathing speech of his about the "Great Idea" of
recapturing Constantinople. His eloquence made us clench our tiny fists
as they rested on our desks. But all that is over and done with now, along
with my faith. I engaged in insurrection against our lawful government in
order to honor the Greek promise to stand by the Serbs as allies. Now I am
helping the Serbs to enslave the Greeks of Monastir. I came here in order
to stand side by side with the French and to be killed with them for the

sake of democratic ideals. When I arrived I found them thrashing their black troops and heard them greet us in the trenches with the cry *"chiens grecs."* . . .

In trench warfare, as you can see, a soldier is granted ample time to think. This is not good, because the more a soldier thinks the more his faith deserts him. The truly horrible thing is to wage war without believing in it, and in addition to lack an "unbelief" sufficiently strong to push you to the other extreme of denying war completely, come what may.

In any case, my own faith is flapping about at present like a rag tied to the top of a telegraph pole, where it is lashed and slapped deplorably by all the winds of doubt. What constitutes the good? At what point does evil begin? Our headmaster Anagnostou is no longer here to explain such things to me. If only I could visit the Lord to implore him to restore some faith to me—any faith whatsoever: in Him, in good, in evil. I cry in anguish out of the depths of my stony dugout; I weep, I beg:

"Lord, Lord, help Thou mine unbelief!"

If He cannot give me anything new to believe in, let Him at least grant me a massively fortified unbelief, because the human soul knows no disease more horrible than doubt.

25

Uncle Stylianos the Hunter

I 've been thinking of Uncle Stylianos since early morning. You never met this character, a hunter from one of the most precipitous villages on Mount Lepetymnos. He used to wear old-fashioned breeches and was a tall, big-boned fellow as lean and trim as a sturgeon. Around his waist he had a leather weapon-belt complete with bronze cartridge loops, a knife with decorated hilt, and numerous cigarette holders whittled skillfully with a delicate blade out of cherry, rosewood, pine, and jasmine, all arrayed neatly along the belt together with his tobacco pouch and a leather purse containing flints. The mountain sun had roasted his hide and plated it coppery red, leaving him not a single grain of lard on his body. His entire frame—which, with his tattered breeches and unbuttoned shirt, he left half-naked both winter and summer—was a complex of nerves, muscles, and large veins all swaying and coiling animatedly beneath his singed hide like so many robust snakes. No wife or children. A bachelor. Hunting was his sole passion and his unique skill. Now this mountaineer, whose bark was as gnarled and indurate as an olive trunk's, maintained in his heart a tender compassion for the lives of birds and beasts if he happened to find them drinking. He had four dogs that he adored as though they were his own children. How he cared for them, loved them! Compared to the dogs, he himself was nothing, yet one day he shot the one called Phlox in the right front paw because she had attacked a brace of partridge refreshing themselves in a puddle! All the while the birds drank, he pointed the muzzle of his double-barreled shotgun into the grass. They were unsuspecting souls imbibing God's water beneath God's heaven, a fact that filled his mountainous soul with piety and reverence. He even had the notion that birds are the most blessed of all living things because after every sip they swallow they lift their little heads toward heaven to say "Thanks."

You'll ask why I happened to recall Uncle Stylianos so suddenly. It was not by chance, as you will soon see.

If a person emerges from my dugout and follows Trench B1 bearing always to the right and traversing each of its branches with their numbered placards until the end of B14, he finds himself in a cleft in the mountain, entirely out in the open. There are no trenches in this place, for one thing because the terrain is nothing but impenetrable marble, and for another because the hill you pass in order to reach this cleft shields you from the enemy's observation post. In addition, this defile is so steep that the officers term the place a "safety zone," "dead spot," and heaven knows what else. What this means, supposedly, is that even if the enemy directed shells at this target, the missiles could not possibly drop into the cleft because that would require an abrupt right-angle turn in their trajectory, breaking their elliptical course. This is a godsend for us since precisely there in the cleft, bubbling out of the marble, is a column of diamond-clear water, a vein that supplies four companies in all, three Greek and one French.

To assure oneself of a full canteen every day has become a matter of exceptionally good luck. Several men have turned "professional" (entrepreneurs are never lacking anywhere). For a price, they risk their lives in broad daylight in order to fill other men's canteens. It really is a feat of daring to traverse all fourteen branches of our trench at high noon. In quite a few places the ditch is so extremely shallow that you are visible to the enemy across the way even if you slide along on your belly like a lizard. The German and Bulgarian forces, moreover, have ranged the spring's position and are in the habit, when the spirit moves them, of searching it out at random with what we call "curved fire"—projectiles shot with low muzzle velocity so as barely to clear an interposing cover and then to descend upon the object. Among the water-dealers is Dimitros Zvingos, who is in my platoon. His wife Paraskevi, you may remember, used to come to our house every Saturday and wash the floors, until her rheumatism got the best of her. Zvingos can hardly be described as a valiant young stalwart, yet with all the canteens he fills (at two drachmas apiece) he manages to dispatch a modest hoard to his wife with every post. It's one way to make a living, after all.

Early this morning I, too, went to the spring, hobbling along as best I could. Mainly, I wanted to dry out my musty lungs. The moon was still up when dawn began to whiten the sky. The men were returning in continuous streams from their nocturnal duties; therefore the spring did not have many customers. From our platoon Gighandis was the only one. When he saw me he gave me a friendly wave, without relinquishing his place in line. Some French orderlies were filling their officers' canteens just then, and newcomers went to the end of the queue. How wonderfully quiet it was! The cannons were napping (warily) beneath the ivy that camouflaged them. Not a sound from any of the sectors—just a single machine-gun loquaciously rattling as it stitched the motionless air far in the distance. In the midst of all this tranquility, however, a shell took flight from behind Peristeri. It was of medium caliber, one of the type that our men have nicknamed "puppies" owing to the barking sound they make as they pass overhead. No one noticed this shell until the instant it landed and burst—at a distance of two meters from the spring. That was all; no other shell was fired. When I rose from the ground in a daze I had no hearing in my right ear and felt a strong pain in my stomach. Gighandis was seated on the ground with his head reposed on his knees and his hands hanging down at his sides like broken wings. The empty canteen hung by its leather loop from one of his nacreous fingers. I ran up to him. He had been killed, though without receiving a single wound. It was as though he had suddenly fallen asleep and had remained that way. Poor Zvingos, loaded down with his twenty-odd canteens, had been hit in the face by a wide fragment that, without finishing him off, had destroyed his nose and eyes. He appeared to be wearing an extremely crumpled mask colored black and red. He might live; yet he will never regain his sight.

Ten or eleven others were groaning or dying, their guts hanging out. A husky Frenchman with a beard as yellow as ripe wheat sat cross-legged on the ground. Without moaning at all, he kept rocking his torso rhythmically forward and back like a muezzin reading the Koran while he lifted his hand slowly to his head and then used his finger to probe a tiny hole in his skull from which a small amount of bloodstained brain-matter was oozing. After lowering the finger in front of his face and attempting to see its tip, he lifted it again and again to the diminutive wound.

All day today I have been thinking of Uncle Stylianos the hunter, who never in his life killed birds while they were drinking water.

26

Moonlight in the Trench

*I*t is a gorgeous moonlit night outside. I am here in my shelter, all alone except for my repulsive shadow that the lamp-flame forces to dance without respite upon the walls. Everyone else has gone on duty. I cannot detect any noise coming from the trench. Although my leg was exceedingly painful this morning, it began to feel somewhat better in the afternoon, and I actually managed to get a little housecleaning done. Taking hold of my pack (I have been using it as a pillow) I noticed that the dampness had covered the leather straps with a kind of green fungus resembling a mossy growth of delicate, rotted hair that could be parted with the finger, leaving a wet line. I spent the entire afternoon oiling these straps with vegetable fats, which I rubbed in well. I also noticed that the bore of my rifle-barrel had begun to rust and that considerable force was needed to withdraw my bayonet from its scabbard.

Now it is nighttime. As I drag myself to the entrance of my shelter and peep out, I see the August moon coursing through the trench, which resembles a canal brimming with light. I am reminded of that sweet legend about the island girl who used to embroider her dowry beneath the August moon while she sat on the flat roof of her house and waited for her lover to return—waited to glimpse his sail upon the waters. Extinguishing the flame in the tin can that serves us as a lamp, I crawl into the trench on all fours and install myself at a vacant sentry-post, to enjoy the moonlit evening.

What tranquility!

Everything has been dipped in moonlight. Lines and shapes fade into softness as they soak up the deluge of light that pours out of heaven's silver spout and, dropping without the slightest clamor, bathes the earth in a half-transparent dust of bluish radiance. No sound whatsoever, not even a machine gun. No rifle shots; no flares.

All things are at rest tonight beneath the sky. They lie beneficently there in comfort while inhaling with controlled ecstasy the merry light that dissolves into the motionless air. The low ridges of the nearest hills can be discerned in full detail from the parapet. The thorn-bushes and jagged lumps of gravel that cover the yellow slopes of these hills and are chastised all day by the flaming sun remind one of the shriveled framework and well-licked bones of certain flowers and other creatures whose flesh has been vaporized by sun-fire, leaving nothing of their corpses but a few desiccated remnants. These mountain slopes are also pocked with cavernous dens excavated by the snouts and claws of unknown beasts who desired to nest within and reproduce. Each lair is normally a stride or so away from the next, but in some areas they are so densely packed that the ground resembles a harvested potato-field. Dug by the shells that have been landing in this region for many months, they gape upward toward heaven's mystery and are filled, in their turn, from the moon's spout. Most resemble large earthenware cups brimming with incorporeal honey, but those that receive the moon's rays obliquely are stuffed with neatly cut slices of black shadow. With equal beneficence the moon rains down its peacefulness upon those endless fabrics of woven steel that stretch into the remote distance and vanish in pearly darkness. Even these—the barbed-wire barriers—it bathes as though they were wild or trellised grapevines, indulgently suspending its globules of light from their iron barbs that wait in ambush like claws and fangs.

Far in the distance is the Dragor, invisible in its tenebrous gully. Although the river cannot be seen, if you listen very intently while resting your cheek upon the parapet you can hear its triumphant huzzas as it cascades downstream and exults with aqueous snouts over the unrestrained freedom it enjoys. Squealing provocatively and whooping, it hawks the pleasures of movement, proclaims these delights in a serious, languidly

protracted song. I always feel melancholy when I observe water imprisoned in tanks. God created it a free element; it should never stop running.
Looming in the background, enigmatic and mute, is the Dove's murky
pyramid. All things in the vicinity are pricking up their ears and maintaining their silence so that they may hear the Dragor rumble in the distance
as the happy river charges freely across the plains, dangles serpentine
tongues of elongating whiteness down the cliff-faces while guffawing at
the tops, strides over stones that have been soaked for centuries and bloats
their velvety green moss as though saturating a sponge, froths its way round
fallen tree-trunks or overleaps them like a powerful unbridled foal that
rejoices in its wildness and with dilated nostrils whinnies its absolute freedom to the heavens. On the other hand this beast also remains still on
occasion, adorning all the maidenhair ferns with tiny diamond-studded
earrings. My thoughts tell me that after a certain amount of time—that is,
when people grow tired of killing each other—the war will end, the
trenches will be vacated, bears will enter the dugouts to beget their young,
and wild brambles will nonchalantly festoon the abandoned barbed wire
with blossoming garlands. Here precisely, here where I am crouching at
present, a wild animal will stand in similar August moonlight one evening
before too long, will stand innocently here in the divine night, teeth glistening, ears cocked toward the river's distant song, tongue hanging out,
lungs contentedly inhaling moon-dust. And these mountains—once they
are rid of us humans and of the war we carried into their deepest bowels—
these mountains will remain firmly planted once again on the earth's great
back, comfortable in the repose and indifference of eternity. My thoughts
tell me that for Nature-of-the-myriad-eyes-and-mouths, for Nature that
stands by disdainfully in its glory and surveys the whole human drama
with callous disinterest, there is not the slightest difference whether the
creature placed here in this sentry-post is a wild beast with its tongue hanging out as it inhales the summer night, or a human being whose intelligence is capable of apprehending both Nature herself and all his fellow
humans, and whose heart overflows with love and sorrow.

Covering all these mountains a few years hence will be a snow of granulated bones, remains of the soldiers who arrived from the four corners of
the earth to die for "the freedom of all peoples." (This slogan, even if mean-

ingless when mouthed by diplomats and journalists of every faction, does produce an agitating effect upon us Greeks because of the millions of our fellow Hellenes who are still slaves in the hands of oppressive conquerors.) Heroic skulls, gaping even then with continued incomprehension, will be the nesting places of all kinds of insects, vermin, and centipedes, the whole filthy lot of them making themselves splendidly at home in the very cavities in which ideals and perceptions formerly swarmed. It goes without saying that the moonlight will wander in and out of the vacant eye-sockets with celestial innocence and that the snail will enjoy its bit of fresh air by relaxing on the cranial balcony of someone's illustrious skull. All the mountains will be arrayed imperturbably then on every side, just like tonight; they will be awaiting the new centuries with patient indifference and bathing their humps in the August moon.

Hosanna!

27

The Concealed Poppy

 y leg felt so very much better tonight that I decided to get up
(slowly) and go for a walk in the silent trench. How peculiar
trenches are under such a bright moon. You'd think it were daylight outside; on the other hand, I had nothing to fear, because moonlight does not
reveal anything to a distant observer unless it reflects off polished metal.
Consequently I was able to enjoy a casual stroll beneath this protective veil
of pale-silver darkness.

For a moment the thought occurred to me that I was truly alone, as if
all the others had risen and fled, leaving no one but myself here on this
Serbian hillside. This thought caused a chill to pass like a knifeblade
through my heart. To have known that other human beings lived around
me, even if they were hidden and every one of them an enemy, would
have been preferable to remaining here in complete isolation.

I advanced to the end of our company's trench, to the place where we
exit from the entanglements. There is a secret door here that closes by
means of a shaft plated with barbed wire. Since this area is solid rock and
cannot be excavated, a protective screen was constructed long ago out of
sandbags that have been exposed in the meantime to dampness, rain, snow,
and sun. The burlap—rotted by water, singed and baked by sunlight—
disintegrated at my touch, just as grave-wrappings of exhumed bodies
unravel and crumble to powder the instant one's fingers encounter them.
Some of the sacks remain as fully stuffed as when they were originally

filled; others droop flabbily, half empty. All together, in the strong moonlight, they resemble an orderly heap of dogs' carcasses, some bloated and others disemboweled.

I sensed that here at the end of the trench the view would be more beautiful—the distant call of the invisible river can be heard more clearly here, issuing from its deep bed—and I felt like lifting my head high above the parapet (or even sitting astride it, if that were possible) in order to look out. As it was, I leaned my walking stick against the wall, rose up on tiptoe, putting pressure only on my good leg, and hooked my fingers into the screen of sandbags that extended above my head, whereupon one of the sacks fell to pieces all at once and dumped its sand onto my scalp. But this was followed by a revelation. The moment this sack deflated, the moment its hump sank, it uncovered to my sight a tiny bit of happiness that benefited my soul to such a degree that I was a hair's-breadth from shrieking with joy.

What I saw there was a flower! Imagine! There, among the rotted sandbags, a flower had grown and had suddenly been revealed to me on this night so filled with miracles. As I stood there gazing at it I felt almost terrified. My heart pounded as I touched it. (I might have been touching an infant's cheek!) It was a poppy: such a large well-nourished poppy, open there like a small velvety palm. If one could have relished it in sunlight, he would have observed its scarlet hue, the black cross over its heart, and the tuft of deep blue eyelashes in the middle. A robust plant full of joy, color, and health, with a firmly erect stalk covered by fuzz, it also possessed another bud that remained unopened, still tightly wrapped in its green swaddling-bands, awaiting its proper time. It would not be long in opening, however, and then there would be two flowers—two flowers in the garden of death! I felt a sudden emotion that reached to the depths of my soul, and at the same time a sudden fatigue that made me lean against the parapet while tears of release welled up from inside me. In this posture—my sand-covered head resting against the rotted sacks and two of my fingers gently, carefully, touching the poppy—I remained for some time, until I was suddenly overcome by an anxiety: a lively worry that some harm might befall this flower that God had used on this night to reveal Himself to me. Then I lifted one of the still-intact sandbags onto my shoulders (biting my lips from a sudden stab of pain in my leg) and placed it as a precaution in front of the flower, telling myself that this would serve to conceal the plant once again from everyone else. Sniggering at my craftiness, I rose on tiptoe once more and extended my arm. Yes, I was touching it again! Shudders of happiness passed through me as I felt its tender petals contact the balls of my fingers. What an unexpected joy was granted me solely by the sense of touch! A sweet shiver tingled inside my arm and mounted all the way to the shoulder, as though the eyelashes of some beloved woman had been fluttering against my skin. Withdrawing my fingers and kissing their tips, I addressed the poppy ever so softly: "Good night . . . . God bless you." Then I returned quickly to my dugout. If only I could have flooded the whole place with light, could have suspended banners and garlands on every side! Instead, I lighted four wicks in my lamp and began to wonder how such a great joy could possibly be squeezed into this cavity that is so very very constricting. My soul gamboled like a large butterfly as I reclined on my back, smiling. Something was being sung inside me; I pricked up my ears and listened. It was a lullaby:

O my bright moon . . .

Suddenly I thought of Gighandis, and the skies of my heart blackened. I would have been able to confide the happy secret to him if he were alive—to him and no one else. Dearest comrade! For you I might even have picked this flower and delivered it in a cupful of water, delivered it to you beneath your canvas. My friend! If only you were alive! You had an affectionate, childlike heart, the eyes of a grieving archangel, and clean, tender hands. I was filled with both joy and sadness; I wept from both joy and sadness. My heart overflowed with the lovely secret that a poppy was in bloom—in bloom for me, 0 Lord—and that it had issued from one of the fetid sand-bags protecting the trench, like a "Hurrah!" from the mouth of a skeleton. There it was at placard B1 near the exit from the barbed wire. My reflections told me that it constituted a promise, a tiny red pennant of flaming life signaling to me. It was a good sign, Lord, was it not? Was it not the hem of Thy regally purple garment? I had touched the Almighty even if I could not comprehend Him.

I curled up under my blanket and closed my eyes in order to savor my joy in greater solitude. My heart danced in exultation but at the same time was filled with tender sorrow because of my more intense awareness of Gighandis's death. I bewailed him with searing tears while on the other hand a hidden but momentous smile spread over the face of my soul, which possessed its lovely secret: The soul lives! It lives!

Once again I rose. With sly, guarded movements I projected my head out of my nest and into the trench. Then I gazed in the direction of the exit to the barbed wire, the site of a joyous rendezvous that awaits me but that I am not going to keep twice in the same night. On all subsequent nights, however, I shall spend a few moments with my poppy; and whenever I pass the spot with others on our way to patrol-duty or "works," I shall keel over laughing (internally, of course) because my companions will know nothing. As for me, I shall secretly turn (in my mind, of course) in order to observe the red flower and salute it: the concealed blossom sent to me by life as a summons.

What I desire at this point is to fall asleep while still in such a happy frame of mind. I cross myself before closing my eyes, just as I used to as a child. A certain something—I cannot distinguish whether it is sorrow or jubilation—has begun to vibrate inside me, musically. The Lord suddenly touched me tonight with His finger, and I am trembling in the depths of my soul. If only I could believe in the lovely fairytale of Divine Providence, believe in it just long enough to kneel and give thanks to Someone for this joy, then to raise up my young body in the glorious moonlight as straight and spare as a taper and to feel his beatific gaze spreading everywhere over my limbs. If only I could pray with one of those old-fashioned supplications appropriate for children, the kind we were taught to recite in ancient Greek. We possessed not the slightest idea of what we were saying to God by these means, yet we agreed unquestioningly to recite the prayers, and the thought that we might forget one or two of the mysterious words made us quake with fear. We never asked our teacher to explain what the prayers actually meant, because we suspected that they made use of God's secret code-language, the official idiom of heaven employed in all audiences granted by the Almighty to his servants.

I wish tonight that I could recite such a prayer, one whose meaning is unknown to me, because only then could I make it contain the infinite concepts and sensations that, formless and incapable of expression, are welling out of my arid soul like the water that gushed from the red-hot stones of the wilderness when they were touched by Moses' rod. You see, my soul is frisking tonight; it is an abundant and joyous spring even though it lacks anywhere to send its water or its songs.

Once more, however, I find it impossible to speak to God, despite my feeling that He is so close to me, so very very close. . . .

28

Jacob

*L*ast week we were brought a bunch of newcomers to fill the "gaps" left in our ranks by sickness and explosives. Among them were a Jew and also one of our own, a Thessalonian named Dimitratos, sent over from the Hospital Corps of the Serres Division. He seems a jolly, entertaining wag: a sly case-hardened tease. And a real blabbermouth, too. As for the other, the Jew, how the devil did he get here, and in a Mytilenian regiment no less? God only knows! He is an exceedingly lean, gangly character with cinnamon-colored eyes as tiny as two coffee beans. His brows sport the same cinnamon tint; his hair is reddish-blond and curly. I was reminded instantaneously of that straw effigy of a "Hebrew" that Kostas Patlaktsis sets up annually on our island on Good Friday, and that is then burned by our gleefully shouting urchins. It is stuffed to bursting with caps and various other kinds of fireworks that explode one by one as the flames progress through the straw man. The children's greatest pleasure comes when the "whistler" ignites. Patlaktsis always hides this in the Hebrew's backside, and the minute I saw Jacob from the rear I involuntarily directed my glance downward to his behind to see if the whistler's white fuse were hanging out between his legs. His mug is as white as snow, with reddish freckles everywhere, as though splattered with wheat-and-raisin soup. The same with his hands, giving the general impression that his skin—which is as gossamery as the finest cigarette paper—suffers from an inflammation. Indeed, you think twice before touching him lest you excoriate him and cause him pain. Yet he is a humble, obedient sort despite all this, willing and eager to undertake the most difficult assignments. Still, I cannot bring myself to like him, I just cannot. Certain people are actively repulsive. No matter what you do, no matter how logically you try to approach the situation, you cannot accept them or go near enough to let your breath mix with theirs. Your soul spews them out like castor oil. This accounts for the inexplicable satisfaction I had, a feeling approaching active pleasure, as soon as I heard that he was given a trouncing yesterday while on mess detail with some others. The man who did it was Giorghalas. (More about him later!) You must realize that I have no prejudices whatsoever against the sons of Israel; I had never even laid eyes on one until we arrived in Salonika. On the contrary, I marveled at the beauty of their daughters, which makes the insufferable ugliness I observed in all the elderly Jewesses an entirely incomprehensible phenomenon. At any rate, I treated the thrashing of gangling Jacob as a laughing matter, and even enjoyed learning all the details of this episode. Now that I'm thinking about it again, I wonder if it isn't the foxy way he darts his brown, beady eyes about that makes it so difficult for me to stomach him. I've also been pondering the sad plight that his repulsive appearance and ridiculous way of pronouncing Greek must create for him now that he is among us, and I realize how much indignation and justified malice must be concentrated inside this poor soul that is sacked in such a vilely speckled hide. But it's no use. I cannot, I simply cannot view him sympathetically. All of my senses find him antipathetic, and it is clear that the same is true of the other soldiers, every one of them. When they look at him it is with aversion.

Giorghalas was obviously nothing but this shared, inexplicable antipathy in concentrated form. When he and the Jew found themselves in the ravine where the camp kitchens are located, he suddenly grabbed Jacob by the shoulder strap, using the four fingers of his left hand (the pinky was nipped off at the base by an electric catfish once while he was fishing). He shouted in the other's face, thrusting his own hairy kisser beneath the Jew's rapier-sharp nose:

"Hey, Jacob, why the goddamned hell did you Jews nail up our Christ and lace it into him like he was any old cutthroat? Eh?"

Jacob could smell the wine on Giorghalas's breath. Realizing that he was dealing with a drunkard, he struggled to wriggle out of it by pretending to die of laughter at his assailant's joke:

"Hahaha, hahaha, hahaha . . ."

But Giorghalas was not joking, not even slightly. He gave Jacob another good jolt, making him look like a quivering springboard, and thrust his dilated eyes right into the Jew's little brown beads.

"There's nothing to laugh about, Yahoudi! Tell me: Why did you Jews crucify our Christ? Eh? Why? Lousy skinflint, what did he ever do to you?"

"I . . . I didn't crucify him," replied Jacob with quaking limbs. "You shouldn't believe such fairytales."

This drove Giorghalas out of his mind. His eyeballs nearly sprang from their sockets, such was his divine wrath. His mustache waved about like a sea urchin's spines.

"*Fairytales!* Do you call a fairytale what's written in the Gospels? Eh? Are the Gospels fairytales? Judas! Unbaptized heathen!"

And he laid him out flat on the ground and beat the living daylights out of him.

Jacob was an awful mess when they brought him back. He approached the captain and asked to be transferred to another company. But when the captain attempted to comfort him by promising to punish Giorghalas severely, Jacob's despair only increased. "What?!" he cried as he heard this new horror that was about to descend on him. He implored the captain not to grant him this satisfaction, because then Giorghalas would truly wipe up the floor with him. In short, he begged with tear-filled eyes that Giorghalas not be punished. The captain finally gave his word, but when he summoned Giorghalas to his dugout he was ready to explode. Pacing up and down in silence, hands clasped behind his back, chin held high, he suddenly halted in front of the ruffian and demanded curtly:

"You dog, why did you hit Jacob?"

Giorghalas was still under the influence. Strive as he might to stand properly at attention with his hand at his helmet, all he could manage was to rock his large, sagging body back and forth as he fought to remain balanced atop closed legs and joined heels. In the end, unable to restrain himself any longer, he broke into a flood of those tears that drunkards seem to possess in such abundance.

"Captain, Sir . . . I have the honor of . . . Captain, Sir . . . Well, what did Christ ever do to them, Captain, to make them crucify him? Eh? I'm asking you, Sir, what did he ever do to them? He healed them . . . he cast out their demons . . . he raised up their dead . . . . So why did they torture him like that, Captain, Sir? Eh? Why did they torture him? Tell me why!"

29

Balafaras at the Front

*A*t ten o'clock this morning, in the full heat, we received an unwanted visit.

Balafaras, you see, had conceived the bright idea of gathering together his staff and coming to inspect our sector. Major Kondoulis of the Engineers appeared on the general's heels, as did Politis (his interpreter), the French officer in charge of this sector, the adjutant, and naturally our own captain. Balafaras executes these demonstrations of valor adorned with full display of gold on his shoulders and forage cap. These escapades—these sweeps through the trenches in the heat of midday whenever his whim moves him to "see how my boys are getting along"—are accomplished without benefit of a helmet, even. The man's ostentatious scorn of death is something to behold. He strides nonchalantly through the trench, as tall and upright as a tower, with his entire head above the parapet. He struts with ramrod back as though on parade. You're at a loss whether to marvel at his idiotic recklessness or at his bravery. What goes without saying is that the poor officers he drags along with him dare not utter a single word against this numskullery. So they follow him, their hearts in their mouths, and are obliged in their own right to stride along all stiff and erect, directly in the sights of the Dove.

These erratic caprices drive the French commander of the sector out of his wits, because they backfire against us, indeed give us a good kick in the rump. What happens as often as not is that the enemy sentries across the way make out Balafaras's gold-laden cap as it flashes in the sunlight. They telephone to their artillery and then the fun begins, "big boys" and all. Sometimes the shells wreak havoc on a trench, but Balafaras continues on. Yes, with a decorous motion of the back of his hand he sweeps the ends of his mustache upward, and says in his drawling voice that accents each and every syllable as though the whole row of them were lined up for inspection, "It's noth-ing, noth-ing at all. These are in-ter-na-tion-al cour-te-sies. The enemy is firing a salute in the gen-er-al's honor . . . ."

His attendants pretend to find these jokes amusing. They have no choice. God only knows where they find the spunk, but they are obliged to prove themselves equal to him in courage, even if they are green in the gills with fright. The miracle is that not a hair of his head has been touched so far by either hot lead or shellfire. Maybe it's just plain luck. Or maybe it's the incessant walking that makes him a "moving target." I don't know. His own belief, and an unshakeable one, too, is that he is immune to bullets. He escaped without a wound even in the Balkan Wars, where he commanded a battalion of evzones and undid practically every one of them in a single bayonet charge at Bizani.

One of his sayings is: "Death, like a well-schooled whore, chases whoever tries to escape."

Well, this is precisely what regaled us again today at Balafaras's arrival: the fun-and-games of an "honorary salute"! They caught wind of him across the way and began to pound our miserable trench. Whizz-bang! Whizz-bang! Fortunately, our captain anticipated this the moment he laid eyes on Balafaras, and was able to order all of us into our dugouts in time. Suddenly a shell exploded just outside the trench's ramparts in the region where the general happened to be, one of its fragments burrowing into a sandbag and sprinkling his cap with dirt. While everyone in his entourage turned white as a sheet, Balafaras halted in order to scold the Bulgarians across the way:

"Now, now, dear me, what have we here? This is disrespect toward superior officers!"

Removing his cap, he blew on it. Then, using his fingernail, he flicked off some grains of sand that had worked their way beneath his gold braid. Finally he turned with complete nonchalance to his adjutant and said, "Do me the favor, Adjutant (since you are younger than I and more nimble) of popping over the top of the trench for just a second. I'd like you to get me that large fragment from the projectile so that we may . . . determine . . . precisely what caliber we are dealing with."

That was the last straw.

The officers turned pale as wax and glanced at each other in despair. The poor adjutant, saluting like a Roman gladiator, prepared to vault over the top. But luck was with him, for the French officer intervened. Speaking respectfully, yet in a forceful tone, he pointed out to the general that such purposeless exposure of soldiers' lives was strictly forbidden by army regulations and that he would be obliged to report to the proper authorities any infringement witnessed by him in our division.

Balafaras patted him on the back with his huge palm. "Fine, fine, *mon camarade* . . . . We never intended . . . No hard feelings, eh?" . . .

And he commanded Politis, whose face was transmogrified with fright, to provide a translation of his words to the Frenchman. Then he continued, accompanying his remarks with explanatory gestures.

"Tell him, my boy, that we Greeks and those fine fellows across the way are old friends. We understand each other perfectly. There is no contention between us, right! They are former acquaintances of ours, *des anciens connaissants, comment!*"

Luckily, we suffered no casualties as a result of Balafaras's visit—except one man who was hit in the eye when the explosion slung a pebble at him. The shelling continued all afternoon, however, and that night the company, cursing Balafaras's ancestry back for fourteen generations, was forced to labor until dawn to repair the damage and clean away all the dirt.

* * *

What hidden palpitations I experienced while the shelling lasted! As soon as night came I accompanied the others as they proceeded to their work details. Dragging my leg, I continued to the end of the trench, all the way to the thorny sea urchin that bars the exit from the entanglements. Gropingly, I advanced to the place where the trench wall consists entirely of sandbags: to *the* place, the exact spot where I had crept like a thief (and a lover) every time the opportunity arose, and where I had stretched my arm behind one of the sacks, closed my eyes, and with secret exultation caressed the hidden poppy-blossom with the tips of my fingers.

The trench was devastated in this area; disemboweled sandbags lay scattered hither and yon. A tornado seemed to have struck here and laid waste everything. Not the slightest trace of my poppy. War in all its brutality had found it out and trampled it underfoot. Returning to my dugout, I began to read one of Gighandis's poems, and to weep.

Was I weeping for Gighandis? Or for the wretched flower that had decided to sprout on a trench-parapet (of all places) directly opposite the Dove's batteries? I could not tell.

As for Balafaras, he continues to make his rounds, invariably laden with gold. Nothing seems to hit him. He is self-satisfied, obese, and . . . invulnerable.

30

Three Nights

*H*ow very many pleasures lie in wait for us behind life's misfortunes! Unexpectedly great ones, too. Yesterday the captain confided to me an extraordinary piece of news that has kept me topsy-turvy ever since. We shall be leaving the trench! Tomorrow night! We are being sent to a village behind the lines—to a "rest camp." The division's morale has been reduced to a shambles by desertions, incessant casualties, and the dysentery that an unaccustomed diet of margarine and canned meat has inflicted upon the constitutions of our men. Thus we shall be conducted behind the lines in order to rest, to put on a little weight, and be reconstituted as a fighting unit. That is the extraordinary news. Because I promised the captain not to breathe a word of it to anyone, this good fortune has become an almost unbearable burden for me—which explains why I am sitting here and writing about it to you. Sleep evades me. I even find it impossible to eat; I can't swallow a single morsel.

As I watch the men crawl through the trench with bleary eyes, their faces brutalized by hardship and filth, my impulse is to embrace each in turn and whisper the great news into his ear. But I promised not to. . . .

From now until tomorrow night I shall be counting off the seconds that separate us from the rest camp, the Promised Land. All of them, one by one. What an agony this is! On the other hand, fortunately my leg seems to be improving. I massage it vigorously with kerosene, up to the thigh. I unlock the knee, swing the calf back and forth, stretch the muscles. Then

I give it a try. You'd think it were a machine subjected to a thorough oiling to insure that all of its articulations will perform with top efficiency. In any case, this leg will be the test of my fortitude on the coming march. I am counting on it to prove me a true stalwart.

* * *

Three nights of marching. Three whole nights. Never in my life have I suffered such pain. At first I thought I would be able to manage with my leg. The captain asked me if I wished to relinquish my pack to the transport wagons. Naturally I would have been only too happy to say yes, but he made his offer in the presence of the sergeant-major, who turned toward me and stared with half-closed, mocking eyes all the while the captain awaited my response. This sergeant-major is a warped specimen of the professional N.C.O. His sole ambition in life is to wear epaulettes, and he possesses an apparently instinctive hatred for any recruit who happens to be educated. In Salonika he invariably assigned Gighandis to sentry duty at the latrines. I could read the thoughts behind his vulgar stare:

"Well now, just look at him: Kostoulas the volunteer, Kostoulas the university student—he can't even carry his own pack. I've got your number, all you patsies. Infantrymen de luxe, that's what you are. I know you!"

I thanked the captain and told him that I would carry my own pack by hook or by crook. Thus I started out with all the others, my full gear on my back. Stubbornness and pride. It did not take me long to realize, however, that I had bitten off more than I could chew. Early on the first evening I was forced to leave my rank and fall behind with the stragglers. But I lost these as well, one at a time, and eventually found myself entirely alone in a wild gully. Night had fallen; I feared I might lose my way. This would have been at terrible cost, because every step I took sent such a strong stab into my bone that I had to bite my lips from the pain. Just as I was planning to look for some protected corner in which to put up until dawn I spotted the debris of a circular edifice partially hidden behind dense foliage. Having resolved to accommodate myself there as best I could, I began to drag myself toward it—until suddenly I was nailed to the spot by a high-pitched shriek.

171

"Halt!"

This was more than a simple "Halt"; it was a monosyllable well-honed to a point and ejected by the night like a bullet. The gully took up its harshly menacing sound and reiterated it with sarcastic, booming distortions. I stopped and waited in desperation while the syllable recurred just as sarcastically as before, mingled in confusion with echoes and cutting reports, as though the gully itself were sneezing it out because of the nighttime dampness.

Full of pain, my heart thumping, I waited. Not a sound. I waited some more, fixed to the same spot. Nothing. Then I heard the voice again. It was saying something to me from a distance, from inside the ruin. It did not resemble a human voice; rather, it resembled a chirping bird attempting to reproduce human speech. I concluded that it was asking "Who's there?" in some language or other and I called out loudly:

"*Ami!*"

Then I heard an extremely familiar sound: the dry clack of a breech-block forcing a cartridge into place. After that I discerned a formless shadow detach itself from the murk and advance slowly, suspiciously, toward me, halting at a distance of about ten paces. It turned out to be a dwarfish infantryman wearing over his greatcoat a sheepskin tied at the waist with the loop from his cartridge belt. He kept his rifle trained on me, bayonet fixed, until I laid my own on the ground, raised my hands high, and recited my identity to him in French. Then he advanced to my side and lowered his gun, though not until he had actually touched me with the bayonet. After this he removed a flashlight from his pocket, turned it on, and helped me drag myself to the ruin, cackling his double-Dutch all the while. Once we were there he lighted a candle, enabling us to regard each other at our leisure.

He was Chinese, an extremely skinny man who happened to be traveling with a cart and two horses. These were grazing unbridled somewhere in the vicinity. Although I could not see them, I could hear the refreshing rustle of the grass as they tore it off with their teeth. This Chinese soldier had two diminutive slanted eyes and two tiny, infantile hands whose tips scarcely protruded from his coat-sleeves. From bottom to top his stature was exactly like a child's; he barely reached my shoulder. We were inside the debris of a water mill devastated by shelling or aircraft. Still intact, however, was a wooden bench with a section of wall surrounding it. You might say we were in a half-demolished room with a semicircular wall. I unfastened my equipment and collapsed to the ground under the weight of pain and indescribable fatigue.

The Chinese strove to attend to my needs. He kept pointing to his canteen and mess-tin while saying something to me in a voice once more like birdcall attempting to be speech. I was not hungry, but I accepted a cup of wine, which did me good. This homunculus was ignorant of French except for a few service-terms, and I was obliged therefore to begin a pantomime with him in order to convey my needs. My regiment's stopping-place was a village called Velušino. Taking out my tent pegs and pretending to drive them into the ground, I repeated this name over and over. The Chinese fixed his gaze attentively upon my lips but was unable to conclude anything from my dumbshow. He just smiled. Suddenly, however, an illuminating flash of apprehension passed across his clever little eyes. He had understood something at long last, and he celebrated this progress in our deliberations with a cascade of monosyllabic ejaculations and apish gestures. We were both filled with enthusiasm at having advanced somewhat in mutual comprehension, but after this we were at a loss regarding what more to say (with our hands). He uttered a few additional soliloquies in Chinese, to which I responded mostly with my shoulders and head, but also with a few protestations in French: *pas compris.* I had understood nothing. Then I addressed him in my turn, telling him I had lost my way and asking him to serve as my guide. He answered *"pas compris."* At this point we both broke into hearty guffaws (he laughed in a most peculiar fashion, as though overcome by hiccups) and we ended our attempt to converse.

Next came smoking. He offered me a miserable Caporal, ineptly rolled and adulterated with sawdust. I gave him one of the captain's luxury-brand Greek cigarettes, which he enjoyed immensely. He inhaled the smoke, retained it for the longest time, then puffed it out through his nostrils, bursting with laughter. Afterwards we just looked at each other silently, exchanging friendly smiles, until my companion reached abruptly into his breast pocket and removed a wallet from which he withdrew a photograph showing a Chinese lady and two little Chinese children like those painted on cups, all three seated on low stools. They looked like him (all Chinese look alike). In order to elucidate the fact that they were his wife and children, he was forced to allude, by means of a gesture, to the sexual act that united them. Otherwise, you see, it was impossible. This man was just another wretched human heart snatched from Indochina by the war, without being asked, and tossed all the way to this echoing gully in Macedonia.

What joy flooded this poor, tender heart at the opportunity to express the pain of separation from loved ones, albeit in huggermugger fashion and to a perfect stranger! Moved by this sentimental outpouring I responded in kind by showing him your photograph. He asked me in his unique manner if you were my wife. Now that I am writing this, I note that neither did I feel the slightest anger at the gesture he used as a means of expressing himself, nor did I find it unseemly. After we had remained there for some two hours in this way, reclining and at ease, the Chinese stood up, began to make himself ready, and indicated my things to me, obviously meaning for me to make myself ready as well. He hitched up the horses, then nodded to me to climb into the cart and lie down.

"*Allons?*"

"*Allons!*"

"Velušino?"

"Velušino!"

I scrambled into the cart. As soon as he assured himself that I had stretched out comfortably on the bundles of blankets that he was transporting, he flapped the reins and the horses moved forward. Clacking his tongue against his palate, he chirruped the animals into a trot. Despite all the discomfort caused me by the incessant jolting of the cart, my leg hurt less than before.

Only a few dim stars shone in the sky, providing no illumination. I heard nothing except the racket of the wheels on the interminable military road. Turning, I gazed in the direction of the range of hills that provided our cover. Several rockets succeeded in overtopping the crests of these hills. They oscillated slowly, like dying stars, then plunged behind the squat mountains and disappeared. The existence of several others could be surmised only from the pearly glow dawning weakly for a moment atop the ridges. At one point, four green rockets rose from a single spot in quick succession—one, two, three, four—followed immediately by a hasty but dense barrage that lasted some two minutes and then subsided as abruptly as it had commenced. Strange, how all this already seemed so very far away. At another point the Chinese turned and called out:

"*Camarade!*"

I raised myself onto my elbows to see what he wanted. He indicated the cigarette I was smoking, then gestured with his hand.

"*No tabac!*"

Thinking he desired a cigarette, I took one out and offered it to him, but he pushed back my hand and shouted again:

"*No. No tabac! Kaput!*"

Understanding at last, I snuffed mine out. The road at this place formed an almost perfect crescent that gleamed whitely in the night like a ribbon. The Chinese gave the horses a hard smack with his switch and we traversed this stretch at full speed, galloping madly, while I clutched the sides of the wagon lest I be thrown out by the abrupt jolts. The road here was full of potholes made by shells, some of which lay intact and unexploded at the verges where they had been pushed out of the way. Their hulking forms made one think of dark animals lurking in clusters upon the road's white dust. This stretch had apparently been ranged by the enemy, who pounded it the moment any motion, illumination, or noise caused them to suspect it was being traversed. "Ranged" means that they keep a couple of cannons permanently pointed at this spot, having aimed them at the target with precision during daylight

A lusterless moon past its prime emerged from someplace in the sky about two hours later, its presence above making no impression whatsoever. At the first light of dawn, the Chinese halted his vehicle before a fork in the road. Using a sweeping gesture he indicated the right-hand division to me and drew my attention to a marker by the roadside. It was black, with white letters.

"*Allons . . . Velušino . . .*"

Afterwards, he placed his palm over his breast and then used the same hand to indicate the road's other fork. He was heading that way; I would have to get out. Taking his hand between my palms, I pressed it firmly while saying to him repeatedly in Greek: "Thank you, thank you, thank you!" He began to laugh, but the laughter sounded more like a series of tiny, incessant sobs. He cackled some words to me, who knows what. I stood there, overcome with sadness and pain, as I stared at his shadow in the diaphanous night. He inclined his torso forward and flapped the reins gently. The animals started up. But then he abruptly reined them in again, signaling them with a hissing sound. When he had stopped the team he turned to me one last time and cried:

"*Camarade!*"

I drew close to the cart again. He rose from his seat, which was like a little chest, opened its lid, and brought out a quince, which he placed in my palm. Then he rested his hand on my haversack and gently pushed me away from the cart, which I had been leaning against. He clacked his tongue for the horses to move, and was off.

I remained standing in the middle of the road even after he had disappeared from sight. Holding the quince, I listened to the clatter of the receding cart. . . .

The following night I was caught in a persistent drizzle that made my journey all the more excruciating. The pains in my leg multiplied at every stride. In order to advance I had to support myself on my rifle as though on a crutch. Yet every particle of my spirit was dedicated to a despairingly obstinate resolution: I must arrive.

The Chinese's quince—the first piece of fruit I had laid eyes upon since leaving our island—was the only food I had put in my mouth for three days. I experienced spells of dizziness, also a continuous sensation of feverish heat in every part of my body. Realizing that if I allowed myself to sink onto the muddy ground it would be never to rise again, I concentrated all my strength on the effort to keep walking. Though each step was one more spike driven into my bone, I gritted my teeth and continued on. The fact that the night had grown completely black added to my harassments. From time to time I was aware of soldiers passing next to me in clusters. They seemed wrapped in their tents, their shapeless bulks blending confusedly with the darkness. I proceeded along the right-hand side of the road so that none of the markers would escape me. I knew that Velušino would be written on one of them, and that I should have to turn there. The darkness prevented me, however, from discovering what was written. At first I struck a match each time in order to see. After I had exhausted all my matches, I propped myself against a nearby rock whenever I found a marker and awaited some passer-by who could give me a light and tell me where I was. I had to remain stone still like this in the rain for tiresome intervals of great length until someone happened to come along. I was loaded down with my entire kit and the rain-bloated blankets were heavy as lead. Clenching my teeth obstinately, I listened to my own voice (it seemed to belong to someone else) as it stopped each passing shadow:

"Halt! *Écoutez . . . Écoutez, mon camarade!*"

Some of these dark shadows fingered their rifles the moment they heard me in the blackness; others refused to answer; still others cursed in unknown tongues and continued on in a rage. But I did not abandon a single marker before determining its inscription to my satisfaction, because if I had passed the sign for Velušino I would never have encountered it again even if I had covered the whole of this vast military route, which runs from Monastir all the way to Florina.

Day was breaking when I finally did reach my regiment's bivouac and collapsed in a swoon in front of my brother's tent.

31

The Song of Life

I remained prostrate there for two whole days and nights—without moving, without putting a single thing in my mouth, even without thinking. Exhaustion and pain, my intoxicating pain, had brought me to a state of absolute (and beneficial) stupefaction. The soldiers who went back and forth outside the tent were like incomprehensible creatures from another planet, their indifference toward me matched by mine toward them. My brother had kept Lance-corporal Dimitratos as an orderly, and this character performed the "household chores" with amazing diligence; indeed it was extraordinary how he managed to accomplish all the tasks of a servant without losing any of his self-respect. He added me to his concerns during the time I lay bedridden there, caring for me with a readiness (not to mention a skill) that even a professional nurse could not have equaled. With blurred sight I observed his ridiculously large nose above me, also his clever eyes beneath enormous brows as bushy and tangled as an ungroomed mustache. Sometimes I felt him tucking the covers in beneath my back. At other times I was aware of him dipping his hand into a supply of kerosene contained in a mess-tin lid held by my brother, who knelt next to him. He would then massage my leg from knee to ankle with his large fingers. This vigorous rubbing brought such a soothing pain to my leg that I would close my eyes and clench my teeth so that the golden feeling might continue. Afterwards I abandoned myself to the torpor that dulled my senses and held them sweetly benumbed, so that every sound seemed muffled and distant. There was as much life in me as in a tuft of grass fated to remain fixed where it sprouted while someone mashed it beneath his boot. On the other hand, if my ear registered the least talk about transfer to the hospital, I demonstrated the vigorous power of denial that was still in me.

Two or three days later, when the massive fatigue had passed along with most of my pain, life began to greet me with renewed freshness; it tickled me and smiled in an effort to make me open my eyes and move about once again. I first became aware of this when I was roused from a nightmarish torpor one noontime and I could feel life teeming inside my body like a tangy, sparkling wine mixed into my bloodstream and circulating there. I was alone in the tent, both Dimitratos and my brother being away in the chow line. Opening my eyes, I rolled onto my back and kicked off the covers. Suddenly, all my awakened senses had become hungry and demanding.

To conceal our tents from enemy aircraft we cover them with freshly cut branches. The sun was at the zenith and its plummeting rays drew a lively sketch of these charming branches upon the translucent canvas: leaves, filaments, stems, nodes, tiny flowers. I undertook to admire this ornamental masterpiece that was outlined on the stretched canvas. With voluptuous delight I examined all its charms, scrutinized its every detail. Interlaced branches and leaves formed individual patterns of completely unforeseeable originality that were placed there ever so stylishly (or thus one would have suspected) in a composition displaying that artless simplicity of technique that results only from careful premeditation. This superb shadow-embroidery, worked from a few unprepossessing branches randomly posed, suddenly brought back to me the aesthetic pleasure that had been denied me for so long. I felt inundated by the powerful wave of beauty that rolls continuously over the created universe and causes our soul to sing forth like a maiden recently betrothed. My heart responded with a deeply felt exclamation of joy.

Oh, how very fine to be twenty-two years old, still alive after returning from the trenches, in love, and a son of Greece! Life is inexhaustibly beautiful. I am in a position now to weigh it responsibly and to proclaim its immeasurable worth. I am in a position to savor its wine, drop by drop, like a habitual drunkard grown old and wise. In the depths of my heart I can feel how uniquely precious is every moment that passes over me. I would like to stop each one individually and whisper in its ear, "Godspeed to you as well, but remember that I have been aware of your passage. I perceived you, enjoyed you, and now I thank you!"

I am full of a bliss that is deeply moving. This strange sensation, which overcame me all at once, makes me apprehend my entire being as a noble instrument of great resonance and amazing sensitivity, with thousands upon thousands of golden strings stretched across it—strings as golden and exquisitely delicate as blond hair. This instrument vibrates with musical sound, throbs and hums sweetly as though inhabited by a colony of warbling insects as tiny as specks of dust, all sonorously fluttering their multicolored wings and producing countless minuscule cries. Its myriad strings shudder harmoniously; they vibrate with both joy and complaint, bringing forth a marvelous drone. A verse, a sound, a few words, a glance, a smile, a yellow butterfly, a bit of color, a fistful of sunlight, two or three branches thrown down at random on top of a tent—any of these is sufficient to make this instrument sing and weep. I clench my fists tighter and tighter until I can feel the nails bite into my flesh. I myself am this instrument of such extreme delicacy and sensitivity that, in humming softly, sweetly, and plaintively with its countless thousands of blond strings, is responding to life's summons. I am an enthusiastic connoisseur of life, and I affirm that my life is worth living! Yes, by God, it *is* worth living! If I weep inwardly I do so because the miserable days of my human existence are nothing but a handful of yellowed aspen-leaves: feather-light leaves jettisoned into infinity. The days of my existence light up and then darken again in the twinkling of an eye. They resemble those iridescent bubbles of foam on the seashore that are annihilated as soon as they blossom, but whose short life is sufficient to mirror the sun in a hurry-scurry way for one infinite instant. Afterwards, who cares if they die? What they accomplished is extraordinary. Despite the brevity of their existence, each one succeeded momentarily in incorporating into itself every particle of the immense, immortal orb.

Before I entered the trenches I had not the slightest inkling of life's true worth. From now on, however, I shall savor its moments one by one so that, like the miser I have become, I may expend it a farthing at a time. A man's days on earth are strictly numbered, after all, just like a soldier's on home-leave. I am an arrow shot into the air by life's bow and speeding now along the earthbound arc of its trajectory, a waterdrop tossed into the light from the surge's frothing nostrils, falling back now into the vast deep. At last I am worthy of planting myself firmly here and enjoying life's passage from the very first moment it began to stir and to creep out in reptilian form from the darkness of non-existence, to the very last moment when it shall expire. No matter, Life, if I am thy final eyelid that will droop and close forever! No matter if I am the terminal grain in thine exhausted hour glass, or the last infinitesimal full stop closing thy concluding sentence, or even just a humble shellfish mixed into the sands of a Greek littoral, a shellfish that will drink nothing but sunshine and be shifted this way and that by the refreshing surf.

* * *

The fields around us are cultivated; some trampled, half-dead pepper plants can still be found here and there with ripe fruit the color of flayed flesh and the shape of a bitch's pudenda. I captured a ladybug on my hand. Afterwards I noticed scads of these charming insects promenading inside our tent. They have a small roundish back colored cherry-red or brown and sprinkled with little ebony spots. When I turned this lovely beetle upside down on my palm, the frightened creature held its diminutive legs motionless and tried to deceive me by playing dead. When I turned it rightside-up again it remained motionless a little while longer, looking like a precious gem set in enamel, but gradually it grew bold, straightened its tiny legs with care, and made a dash for freedom. I brought it back to its starting point. It began to race about my hand again, disconcertedly, not knowing how to escape. It sped to the tip of my up-stretched finger, looked to the right, looked to the left. Chasms on all sides. So then it discreetly produced two transparent wings from its mottled waistcoat and took off! I applauded it.

Gazing out through the tent's triangular entranceway, I encounter, as far as the eye can see, nothing but warm, pliant soil covered with stalks of harvested wheat. The stubble is short, the ground like the scalp of an extremely towheaded boy after a close but uneven haircut. Ants are slaving away indefatigably, carrying off wheat-grains and tender bits of chaff. They work in silent haste, without respite, like troops transporting their provisions with all possible speed lest they be attacked before finishing. The ants appear to sense a coming storm.

A tiny green lizard (an okra-pod come to life and running) has scampered up the tent post and halted on the blue box (the gas mask container) that is hanging there. It is striking poses now, apparently delighted to be gazing out at the world from such an eminence. It gives me funny looks with its beady eyes as it executes graceful movements without shifting ground. Short of breath, just like a *grande dame* whose frantic haste to be part of the latest gossip leaves her panting, it also has the double chins of the matrons in our Ladies' Benevolent Society. To be sure, I am filled with admiration at the way it is dressed in matching colors from tip to toe. As I return its glances—I, too, without shifting ground—I am suddenly overcome by laughter so generous that it shakes my entire body. This frightens the lizard out of its wits and causes it to scurry off without so much as turning to look behind it.

Clasping my hands in back of my neck, I lazily stretch all my stiffened joints, which respond with creaks of relief. My muscles move with elasticity; they are full of unused power. The pain in my leg has decreased somewhat. My youthfulness is flooding me, gaining control. How can I dispose of it and be relieved of its weight?

I emerge from the tent, half-crawling. I want to feel the sun rest its warm hands upon my shoulders and bare arms, to feel it run its fingers through my huge mop of hair, which is clean at last and crackles with static electricity when combed.

I see my brother and Dimitratos approaching in the distance with three mess-tins filled to the brim. They are holding them ever so carefully by means of the spoons that have been slipped through the handles, and are walking with weighty solemnity for fear of spilling even a single drop.

The moment they catch sight of me outside they halt and explode into whoops of joy; my brother, with a laugh, raises his free hand aloft into the sunlight like a victory banner.

I respond loudly in a voice that I am pleased to note is clear and full: "Heeyyyy!"

They have brought me a splendid bean-soup garnished with tomatoes and red peppers. Famished, I tear off a large chunk of expertly baked army-bread and ladle up the beans with it until I scrape bottom. Dimitratos, swallowing words and beans together, blurts out through a mouthful:

"Just wait and see what treats I have in my sack—for our invalid!"

Thrusting in his hand he extracts a fistful of refreshing green peppers. Thrusting it in a second time he offers me triumphantly a marvelously appetizing ear of milk-juicy corn still adorned with its soft silken beard. I bite into it with all my teeth; I laugh with all my teeth. The wave of life makes me want to shout, to howl like a wild beast.

* * *

Why must we kill and be killed? Why is this so unavoidable? Who can I ask about such things? When I wonder in what womb this evil was engendered and why it should have emerged so much stronger—so very much stronger—than the good, I hear as replies: "Make war against war!" or else "Class war!" Ah yes, I know. But what is this if not just a new deception—war all over again with a more modern, more odious mask? Then I wonder if perhaps the trouble lies elsewhere—specifically in this: Hatred is organized, armed to the teeth and disciplined, while love, unorganized, vents itself in sentimentality and religious exorcism. But who will come along now and organize love, arm it, make it worthy of respect? Christ sought to accomplish this by gentle means and failed to produce anything worth mentioning. Yet if it is accomplished by force then love ceases to be love.

I am all confused.

32

In the House of Kindness

A great event, something I'm growing more and more aware of: I've had a roof over my head since yesterday afternoon. The doctor told me that if my leg were going to heal, the first thing I'd have to do would be to get off the bare ground and away from the dampness of the tent. I refused on any account to be sent to the hospital, so he billeted me here in one of the village houses, where I'll stay until the regiment is transferred. Exactly when that is due to happen I have no idea; at this point I refuse to think about the fact that it is bound to happen sooner or later.

For the present I am simply enjoying my new good fortune, enjoying it to the hilt. I constantly raise my eyes to admire the wide-planked ceiling. I am actually beneath an honest-to-goodness roof! Beneath roof-tiles! ("Tiles!" That was the term the men used as their own special code-word, sometimes pronouncing it right behind Balafaras's back, and not too softly either. "Tiles!" "What's going on there?" snaps Balafaras, twirling around. "They're cheering you, General," replies the natty adjutant.) . . . Inside me I feel a wonderfully vivid exultation singing away like a loquacious swallow. Yes, my heart is a warbling swallow flapping its wings. I am still in a state of incessant spiritual restlessness (how extraordinarily pleasant that state is). There is a sparkling sea inside me, a sea whose surface quivers with flashes of light and also with sudden tremors. If only I could pray, could sing out the triumphant hymn: "Glory be to Thee who hast shown us the light!"

The peasants who are my hosts welcomed me cordially, without any fuss. The moment I remained alone in their midst they began to talk to me all at once in a language that I do not understand but that I never tire of hearing. There are two old men, one youth, five or six women, and a whole army of babies. They all live in two contiguous houses sharing a roofed verandah that is extremely long and wide. They kept speaking to me energetically, all at once, and smiling, until they realized that their language was completely incomprehensible to me.

"Ne znaish . . . ne znaish?" (Don't you understand?)

"Ne znai?!" (Doesn't he understand?!)

Then, all together, they stopped talking to me and instead began to discuss me among themselves, struggling to divine what answers I would have given to the questions they had been asking for such a long time. While talking they kept turning and looking at me. I looked back at them, and smiled rather stupidly. Then they burst out laughing.

"Ne znaish." (You don't understand.)

But I did understand one thing extremely well: that these were simple, industrious, tormented people. I understood moreover that their words were benevolent, as pure and unadulterated as their bread, all fragrant with compassion and sympathy. That was why tears had welled into my eyes when they surrounded me and wrapped me in their kindhearted loquaciousness; why my hands had strained to enlarge themselves sufficiently to clasp the immense, rough palms as cragged as the bark of an oak.

I tremble in the very depths of my being when Anjo's two little daughters scramble onto my knees. I am bewildered and awkward in their presence; I have been away from children for so long that I don't know how to behave. They rummage endlessly in the bottomless pockets of my greatcoat. Just as they think they've come to the last one they suddenly discover still another (there is no end of pockets in these French coats). I understand their exclamation: "So many pockets!" and I see that the adults share their wonderment. These two little girls are twins, so identical that they seem like two brightly colored gumdrops pressed out of the same mold. They have red cheeks, blue eyes, and blond hair. In their corn-colored pigtails Anjo has braided strips of red and blue cloth with turquoise beads at the ends. The children are always full of mischief, their tiny noses and entire faces always filthy from the roasted corn that they never cease munching. As for their mother, she works away at her loom, her bare feet large and white as they move up and down on the treadles. She, too, is blond, tall. She speaks slowly, with measured words. Quite frequently she stops, shuttle in hand, and cheerfully scolds my tiny girlfriends who, serious and vociferous, hold veritable conferences about the insignia on my cap. Am I "Grrts" or "Srrp," Greek or Serb? Declare yourself! Their mother tells them that I am "Grrts," a "dobar kristianin," and . . . to be careful of my aching leg.

But truly, at this point I am neither a Christian nor a Greek nor a Serb, but simply a human being filled with expectations, nostalgia, and fatigue: an exhausted, contented human being who admires these people—envies them—for being the lovely, openhearted creatures of a beneficent God. I marvel because every one of them (with the exception of the emaciated son) is strongly built and tall, with the simplicity possessed by mankind as a whole before it departed from the strait and narrow path. They are near God and near the earth, all of them. This you perceive from the very moment you set eyes on them. Their home, lamps, clothing, bread, plough, furniture: each is a piece of work that has passed through their industrious hands. Everything inside this house represents a victory in the never-ending battle that these hands have waged against raw material. That is why the hands are so gnarled, all calluses and knots, as though made of oak.

Their diet consists of cheese pies, peppers, lentils, flour-thickened soup strewn with red pepper, whole-wheat bread, and large baked squashes that they cut into immense slices and eat the way we eat melon. They drink cold, refreshing water. They work the soil, which accords them a simple, monotonous happiness. Afterwards, when they grow old and infirm, their large tormented bodies spread over the ground like overripe fruit fallen from a tree, and they return to the earth. There they peacefully dissolve together with all their ancestors. Above them the golden wheat sprouts to its full height once more, the corn soughs throughout the night, and the reapers sing their ancient meandering songs. As for their souls (if we must assume that such things exist), these ascend toward heaven from the earthen thurible, like incense.

I watch these people in the evening as they stretch out on the floor to relax. Propped on one elbow, and using coarsely whittled holders, they silently smoke a kind of colossal cigarette that they roll ever so slowly and lick with infinite care. The smoke rises to the ceiling and disappears. They watch absentmindedly as its slender bluish-white ribbon leaves the end of the cigarette and, with gentle quavers, ascends either directly or with undulations into the peaceful air, which smells of haystacks, threshed corn, and newly scythed grass. This is how their souls will ascend toward the Lord's feet when the proper moment arrives.

Reclining like this for hours, they smoke away in silence. Perhaps they are thinking. Now and then they utter a word or two in a conversation as brief as the exchange of passwords; then they relapse into silence. On the other hand, they may not be thinking at all. This should be hardly surprising, for simple people have the habit of relaxing not only to the depths of their bodies but to the depths of their minds. Thought for them is not a sickness; it is work. Until recently, they never even realized how happy they were. Only now have they recognized this happiness, now that they have seen the foreign hordes pouring in from the four corners of the earth, rushing to the attack across their fields and cemeteries, trampling their unapprehended well-being underfoot. "They are trampling it," their philosophy must stammer; "*ergo* it exists." Crossing themselves energetically, they pray God to restore their peace. Months ago a shell came through the ceiling of the verandah and scythed away the thick hatch-beam holding up the roof. The war left this House of Peace gravely wounded. This happened one summer; a bit of swallow's nest is still attached to the splintered beam. If only all those responsible for war could come to this place where I am sitting and writing, could fall on their knees in the center of our large verandah and gaze upwards through the gash that the cannons have left in the ceiling of this beneficent home, murdering its swallows! Through this gash they would perceive the blue eyes of an austere, wrathful God—and then (perhaps) they would stop making war;

I am filled with reverence for this wounded roof that covers so much kindness. Blessings upon this holy sanctuary that has received me so hospitably beneath its red tiles and has stretched its protection over my suffering body. May heaven repay it for everything, and restore its persecuted swallows. Amen.

A feeling of comfort and cheer emanates like incense from every object in the house. It is with confidence that my lips touch the thick earthenware mug that Anjo holds out to me filled with foaming milk, and it is with the brush of a kiss that they leave it. The women have a large oil-lamp with three wicks that they light at night so that they can do the evening chores. The three flames diminish mischievously hour by hour, then suddenly open into full blaze like living flowers. They are three little eyes of gold that droop with apparent fatigue and then prop themselves wide again, focusing brightly. The women usually remain silent as they attend to the work that is spread all around them. Sometimes, however, they converse quietly, peacefully, and every so often a refreshing laugh spills out into the air and vibrates there, reminding me of the rattle on a tambourine, and also of other refreshing sounds, as, for example, when wet pebbles on a beach are drawn along by the wave that has broken over them and is receding.

I am lying back on a comfortable mattress that Anjo made for me by first sewing a hem around my two canvas sheets and then filling them with dry cornhusks. This bedding creaks a great deal, but it is an undeniable pleasure to plunge into it. To make a bedstead for me they took a wide door off its hinges and rested it on two solid logs. *Dobro!* Everything here is dear to me, and good, and friendly. The children have washed and said their prayers; they are sleeping. One of them received two strong smacks on the behind. She went to bed sobbing, but in a little while slumber erased all her troubles. The old men smoke incessantly. Each time a cigarette is almost finished they stick it to their shoe until, working ever so slowly, they have rolled the next one, which they then light from the butt. The women spin wool, chattering around the oil-lamp like a flock of birds. Apparently they talk about me from time to time, and when this happens they turn, all of them together, toward the dim corner where my bed is placed. Squinnying their eyes strangely because of the absence of light, they try to make out my shadowy form. The older ones laugh openheartedly; the girls manage just a hesitant smile, and nudge each other knowingly with their elbows. All of them have fair complexions and blue eyes, except for a young one of about fifteen or sixteen who is swarthy, with fuzz-covered skin. Her figure is so supple that she quivers like a branch of cherry-wood. Every time I bid her good morning her honey-colored face, together with her ears and neck, flames poppy-red, and a pair of thick velvety eyelashes flutters above her chestnut-brown eyes. When she laughs, her large well-shaped mouth blossoms, overflowing with animal health. Her lips are as scarlet as arbute berries, and fully fleshed. If she happens to laugh in direct sunlight her teeth flash, illuminating her entire face, which then resembles the contorted snout of some nimble forest-beast craving to bite away in erotic frenzy. When I stare at her she frowns and disappears, as though she were being hunted. She is a strange child, extremely high strung and charming.

Yesterday I sat and watched her as (suspecting nothing) she gazed pensively at her reflection in the windowpane. The sun, entering through the gashed roof, deposited a halo of light on her hair. She was superb.

I shifted position. Hearing, she shuddered with surprise and fear. Then she gave me a solemn look. I glanced back in a friendly way, and smiled. She knit her brows. "Why are you laughing?" she demanded in a rage, and sped off like a doe.

Her name is Givezo.

The sonority of that name is strangely harmonious with her being. Around her, as around a rosebush in full bloom, one inhales an atmosphere ardent and warm. On reflection, I am certain that this is the one and only name they could have given her: Givezo. . . .

33

The Judgment of the Lord

What a joy to be in underwear and a clean white shirt still bearing the sweet aroma of laundry soap, to have a fresh shave, and not a single flea! I feel as though I've emerged from a spell. Some evil demon from *The Thousand and One Nights* must have bewitched me and crammed my human selfhood into a swinish, filthy body; my soul remained imprisoned inside that body, that filthy attire that it detested but could not remove in order to escape the disgust that was tormenting it. But now the compassionate enchantresses of those same tales had encountered me on their journeys, had exorcised the demon and enabled me to resume my previous form. Bathed, laundered, darned, mended, dressed in fresh clothes—I had become a human being again. After I'd had a shave in addition, I felt as though I had been born afresh with a new skin as tender and velvety as a babe's. When the barber was gone, Givezo brought me her mirror—secretly and confidentially, because mirrors are considered sinful here. How pleasing it was to see my face again after so many months. I smiled and said "Hello" to myself as though to some cherished acquaintance of old whom I had not encountered for years. I'm not at all bad looking now. My hair, left to itself, has grown in all directions like an unpruned bush, while my face, there in its midst, shines out glamorously pale and ever so white. Givezo is secretly watching me as I smile into her cheap little glass. I can see her reflected in it; she seems extraordinarily happy. Painted on the reverse side of this mirror is the hairy, contorted snout of a monkey with protruding teeth. If you move the mirror adroitly, five white beads line up in place of the teeth, in little indentations.

"See, that's just the way I looked," I said to her.

Covered with blushes, she protested vigorously: "No, no."

"Why are you angry with me?" I asked.

She opened her mouth to say something, then changed her mind, turned red, and flew off like a bird, her supple figure quivering as always like a branch of flowering cherry.

I have discovered two gray hairs on my left temple. They are my first, and I cannot deny my chagrin. I've been out of spirits all day. Now that nighttime has come and I am writing this down, the evil tidings are still haunting me. So soon? Ah, those poor beautiful years: our youth miserably destroyed in sunless tunnels and caves filled with cobwebs. Those poor years as refreshing as the heart of a red watermelon.

I believe that when the lies are terminated and we appear before the Lord—before the Maker of heaven and earth, of all things visible and invisible—, our Creator will turn in furor and declare:

"Eh, you hunchbacks and cripples down there; you with the hare-lips and sightless eyes; you consumptives, paralytics, rheumatics; you wretched buffoons with contorted jaws and crutches and squinnying glass eyes; you who are bent in two, you degenerates who have gone soft in the brain; you ugly, misshapen physical wrecks; you with the miserable bits of tin on your chests—tell me who you are and where you come from! What have you done with the 'talents' I entrusted to you? Where are the eyes that sparkled with love, the hair that was blacker than the darkest of grapes? What happened to the torsos that I erected as lithe as the beechwood lance that the harpooner drives into the sea floor, where it remains quivering with suppleness? Your arms of steel: have they enjoyed the creative act, opened new paths to happiness? Have they taken blond redcheeked boys and lifted them high? Have your virile palms grasped either the plough or the firm breast of a woman? Have your lips had their fill of exultant songs and crimson kisses? Your solid legs: have they raced through life's pastures, have they fluttered on the dance-floor? Have your knees of steel squeezed the female between them as in an iron vice? Have you produced new life inside a woman's mysterious loins, where Pleasure dwells with Creation? . . . Tell me, how have you spent your 'talents'?"

191

And we, when we have heard this harangue by the Lord (standing as best we can at the most impeccably correct posture of attention—we shall salute smartly one by one, as in the regimental review, and shall each "have the honor to inform" our Maker with the studied modesty of all the best heroes in books:

"Lord, we have done things above and beyond Thy requirements. Look at these ribbons of every description. Look at these medals, wounds, silver-colored chevrons each signifying a six-month tour in the sunless trenches. Look here: favorable mention in the Order of the Day, citations in official dispatches, and all kinds of other marvels. These are our credentials, Lord, proof that we struggled for 'The Freedom of All Peoples.' As for our youth, we tossed it away in such-and-such a dugout or upon such-and-such a hill. Our best years? We spent them bending double in a subterranean chamber, crawling in ditches, stooping beneath a full donkey's-load of hardware and all kinds of implements designed for slaughter. Look at our spines: we offer them to you arched like warriors' bows. Our backs are full of bedsores from confinement in hospital. Our feet have been hacked away by shells, crippled by arthritis and frostbite. With our eyes we have viewed every conceivable horror and ugliness, with our hands have dug pits and tunnels to conceal ourselves because we were trembling like hound-dogs. We dug graves as well, many graves, and trench latrines. All of us took up our knives, our fire—and one half of us did away with the other half. In our palms we clasped hand-grenades, which are harder than a young girl's breasts. Look at these hands: black from the gore that remains stuck between the fingers. We embraced no women, begot no children. Our Country was our bride, machine-guns our spawn. The seed of Thy creation we spilled on the ground along with our blood. Though we planted no wheat, we ploughed up the rocky mountainsides and wrapped barbed wire round the earth as though the world were a gigantic spool. We died 'gloriously' in the flower of our youth. We are genuine heroes—of that there is not the slightest doubt. Has it not been confirmed by Balafaras himself? Does not each of us carry in his pocket the 'nice letter' sent out by the division? We are 'demigods,' a status assured for us by all the Athenian and provincial newspapers in long leaders—just take a look at them Thyself and see how long! And now, Lord, because we fell for Faith and

Fatherland, we expect our recompense, just as it was promised us by the division chaplain acting on Thy behalf."

Whereupon the Lord Almighty will expectorate smartly in our eye with his holy spit.

"Away with you all, you miserable swine," he will declare. "Wretches, ingrates, you have trampled upon my most precious gifts; may they rot before your eyes. Off with you; out of here! Get you down to the darkest bottom of the coldest sea, and out of my sight! I shall turn you into sponges and keep you there for all eternity until I discover what breed of things can be developed even more imbecilic than yourselves. . . . Scat!"

And straightway all of us, in the midst of our attempt to salute as best we can in the most regulation manner "with the right palm (fingers joined) at the peak of the cap (elbow at shoulder height), left hand extended along the length of the thigh, pinky at trouser seam"—exactly then, suddenly, all we thousands and millions of heroes of the trenches will find ourselves, good Christ!, transformed into sponges at the bottom of the blackest and coldest of all seas, where light and thought do not exist. Millions and millions of heroic zoöphytes, then, will abruptly cover a tenebrous plain of unlimited extent beneath the waters; whereupon at one fell swoop we shall begin to sway our slimy, glutinous limbs in the most regulation and disciplined manner, first this way then that, first to the right then to the left, according to the movement of the turbid waters.

"Hup-two-three-four. Hup-two-three-four. Hup-two-threeeee-fooouuur.

And this will endure forever, to the very end of eternity, world without end. Amen.

34

Zavali Maiko

*F*or one week now my life has been like a ribbon of water flowing through grass. I've felt an inward compulsion to communicate with the primitive souls of my hosts, a compulsion that has grown stronger every day. This has made me set myself the obstinate task of cracking the meaning of their linguistic idiom. Immediately after my arrival I began to compile a glossary; I've been supplementing and enriching it day by day. They speak a language that is a branch of Slavic, with many Turkish and Greek elements. Its virile sounds give me a bracing sensation. The vowels are rare, their soft femininity drowned in a cascade of obdurately burly consonants. When these people speak, you hear gravel and rounded pebbles passing downstream in the impetuous current of the Dragor. Various words display the virgin descriptiveness of newborn languages, which were nothing but phonic mimicry of the thuds and clangs of vigorous life. To express the idea that a bird should fly away, they say "p'rrlits." In no other language have I heard the flight of a bird conveyed so sonorously.

I have already progressed far enough in this study to make them split their sides with laughter at each group of words that I manage, by dint of much sweat, to fit together. Most of the time I apparently dish out extremely hilarious linguistic blunders that the older women comment upon with loud guffaws until their eyes water, while the girls blush and bite their lips. The important thing, however, is that in the long run I almost always succeed in making them divine the simple ideas that I am struggling to convey to them. This of course is all the more proof of their intelligence and the flair they have for intuiting things. But just imagine the carnival of confusion that takes place simply because their word for "no" is the same as our word for "yes"!

Nevertheless, with this extremely poor linguistic tool that I have constructed all by myself in my isolation, like Robinson Crusoe, today I discovered a hidden treasure—a true horde of human innocence, the kind of treasure that makes one proud to be a human being.

It concerns the "lady of the house," Anjo.

Every day she fluffs out the mattress of cornhusks that she made for me, and airs it. Every morning she brings me a hefty cup of milk, then sits with her head bent to one side, looking at me seriously and placidly, her hands clasped in her lap, while I sip the contents. She dotes on me as though I were a sick infant. It is a thoughtful, anticipatory concern, as knowledgeable as it is simple in its manifestations. She offers it to me with a tranquil and unassuming naïveté that nevertheless sometimes assumes an official, almost ceremonious character. This dignified mother, with her austere white face, her clean, bare feet, and the horsehair sash tied tightly round her waist, is a woman of another people. I have known her less than twenty days. Nevertheless, in a marvelous way, she foresees a mass of tiny details connected with my needs and habits, none of which were ever hers. She smells them out with an instinct that is drilled into women by maternal love, and only by maternal love. And she ministers to them with a kindness so solemn that not even once have I dared to say "Thank you." I feel that this trite, citified expression would insult her, that if I employed this phrase from our conventionalized civilization I would disturb this pure and effortless welling up of kindness from a deep source, this spring that flows next to me in such a natural way that it seems to issue directly from the hands of God. Besides, the whole situation would be ridiculous. From morning until night I would be doing nothing else but saying "spollat gospodina" over and over again for all the tiny benefactions accorded me each and every moment in her home. What I know is simply this: that overflowing inside me is an ocean of silent, restrained gratitude, a potent myrrh that is being stored with undiminished pungency in my heart, as though in some sealed chrismatory.

What I learned today is that Anjo has two sons in the army, two boys serving in the trenches at Peristeri along with the rest of the enemy who are confronting us. That is the treasure I gleaned today from this peasant soul that is as pure as untrodden snow.

The people here speak a language that is understood by both Serbs and Bulgarians. They hate the Serbs, who treat them like Bulgarians, tyrannizing over them. They hate the Bulgarians because they have conscripted their children into the army. As for us Greeks, they accept us with a certain sympathetic curiosity on account of one, and only one, fact: our status as genuine spiritual vassals of "Patrik"—that is, the Ecumenical Patriarch. The idea of the Patriarchate still hovers over this simple Christian people. It is an idea encased in an extremely peculiar mysticism, peculiar because, considering the kind of bishops the Patriarchate has sent to the Christian populations of the Balkans, the only natural consequence should have been to insure their hatred. Anjo's elderly father-in-law Kyrillos, who characterizes the new generation to me as faithless and apostate, still remembers how the bishop made his circuit in the years of Turkish rule when the time came for him to collect "contributions" from the provincial villages under his care. He came in a velvet-lined brougham, reclining inside on thick cushions, while the deacon sat in front next to the coachman. All this was fine and proper, except that the heavy brougham had peasants in the traces instead of horses. The coachman held a strong whip, and the deacon sometimes grasped it as well. But despite everything, the fascination of Greek Byzantium endures. In addition, they have the tombstones of their notables and priests, carved as they are with those mysterious and sacrosanct Greek letters. The same letters are inscribed around the ascetic heads of the Byzantine saints on their old warped icons, and inside their yellowed Bibles. All this makes us privileged in their sight. Nevertheless, they want to be neither "Boulgar," "S'rrp," nor "Grrts."

For Anjo, therefore, the conscripting of her two stalwart sons was a great evil that fell upon the house like the wrath of God. She submits to this incontestable misfortune humbly and with patient endurance, her hands clasped in her lap. All she does is pray. And I—who stood across from her children for so many months with weapons in hand; who for all she can imagine might well have killed them—I am viewed by her in the same way, as one more victim of the identical divinely instituted scourge. Her compassion falls upon me cleansingly like rain from heaven, without reservation, rancor, or complaint. In her sight, I, too, am just another "ashker," a "zavali ashker"—poor, unfortunate soldier. On the other hand, her two boys could all too easily have chanced to be in front of my weapon in one of those clashes between patrols colliding blindly with one another in the dark of night. My bayonet then would have penetrated deeply and coldly into her children's hearts. It would have penetrated into your own heart as well, my poor Anjo. . . . But she would never even dream of allowing such a thought to defile her broad gesture when she offers me, in the heavy earthenware mug with the red and blue flowers, the fresh milk just taken from the cow—the milk that her daughter Givezo, the sweet sister of my two unknown enemies, collects for me down below in the stable, singing while she milks. And as Anjo airs my mattress to make it as comfortable as possible for my aching body, it never enters her mind that in a few days I—yes, I—might disembowel her sons. She frequently questions me about my mother, however.

"I'm sure she's weeping now, isn't she?"

"Yes, she must be weeping."

"And I'm sure she's waiting for you and your brother."

"Yes, she's waiting for us."

"Zavali maiko!"

Falling silent, she looks at me with her kindly blue eyes, holding the shuttle. Then she says in an expressionless tone:

"First the Serbs took them. They dragged them out of our cart, beat them, and stole them from me. 'You are Serbs,' they shouted. 'Why don't you want to fight the Bulgarians?' Next came the Bulgarians together with the Germans. These shouted: 'You are Bulgarians, forward march to fight the Serbs.' And all over again from the beginning: beatings, prison . . . "

"Zavali maiko!"

35

A Letter from Home

*T*oday I received a letter from you—not a letter, a whole packet! It was brought to me by my brother, who got it from a soldier just arrived from our island laden with all sorts of goodies sent to the boys from home. I received quince jelly, chocolates, and a crate of dried figs stuffed with almonds. But what delighted me most of all was your letter. I've read it over and over again, insatiably. Blessings upon your sweet little hand! Such happiness never comes via the regular military post. The previous letters I received from you contained a mass of erasures and excisions, plus repeated admonitions from the censors. Those skunks noted for me each time: "Inform sender (you are the *sender,* dearest) that persistent expansiveness and verbosity will entail discarding of letters by Censors' Office." Those shirkers! Those lousy skrimshankers! Those ink bottles! Those blotting papers with their rheumy eyes! But this letter has been ample recompense—more than ample. Do you know what it has placed in front of my eyes? The diagnosis of my mental illness. Dearest, I have a serious case of homesickness!

A fever is quietly melting away my body as though it were wax. A liquid flame is smoldering in my veins and my heart is continuously brimming over. I want to go back, to be near you, near Lesvos, near all the things we love. I pine so strongly for them all; I cry out for them; only now do I realize how badly I need them. My soul has been deprived of Lesvos's air; it can no longer expand its lungs to the full. Well then, those many joys

you wrote about have continued to exist all the while, scattered with such
liberality over the island. Alas, I sense their existence; I had a taste of them
in your long letter. A sea breeze blew out upon me from its azure pages, as
did the breath of pine, laurel, and oregano. Ships sailed between your lines,
coasters whistled as they hauled up their anchors, merry houses clapped
their green shutters together like applauding palms. Your letter made everything alive and exultant in the joyous sunlight. The atmosphere smelled
of flowers, all things were anointed with myrrh by the touch of your shadow;
yet I was not there. . . .

Now I can see you once again as you traverse the full length of the quay
at night with your hurried stride. Your chestnut eyes, weary from study,
are circled with sleeplessness. All the fishing boats are moored—ah, the
boats of Mytilene: there they are, all in a long, constantly undulating row.
Every one of them is white; they differ only in the colored bands around
their gunwales. They sit tied to the pier one next to the other, colossal
white birds of the littoral that have folded their wings and have arranged
themselves along the length of the pier in order to peck at crumbs. They
bob up and down upon the illuminated water, clasping hands all in a row
like dancers in a *syrtos*. Plunging all around the harbor are scimitars of
reflected light, sword-strokes of gold, silver, green, and red. Any turbulence on the water transforms them into multicolored serpentines of light
that unroll and sway like snakes. The large aspens of the Public Gardens,
so dusty and well-loved, always shake their leaves, even when no wind is
blowing. The gentle swell of the sea makes the coasters' masts creak with
stately regularity. A ship-dog barks heroically at the moon, then stops for a
moment and listens to its yelps as they are echoed by the fortress. A bugle
sounds taps. The notes are copper balls tumbling down the slope one behind the other, then receding and expiring in the half-lighted alleys. When
you finish work you skirt the patch of woods at the waterfront and call at
Apellis's little café in an act of homage to our happy days. Do the little
Apellises still greet you in the same festive style now that you are alone?
What has happened to those evenings when we used to take the café's
shabby chairs down to the shore, place them in the water, and listen (ah,
so many many times!) to the exhausted waves dragging themselves between our feet? Floating buoyantly nearby, just a rifle-shot away, were the

Anatolian Mountains. No, they were not mountains; they were pyramids of violets and hyacinths; floating hampers of roses; islands of flaming copper, like Calypso's isle. Has anyone seen more beautiful sunsets than I have? They were the sunsets of Lesvos. I used to watch them pass ever so slowly across your eyes where, deep down, your love-sick soul was trembling with the anguish of a pinned butterfly. Sometimes a caique with slack sails passed by, the rowers dipping their oars sluggishly into the golden-pink waters. They would come close to us, lazily, without talking, carrying with them their silence and their slow rhythm, and would then pull away in this speechless manner, as though dreaming. There was a young boy who had a red kerchief on his head and kept gnawing one end of it between his teeth. After the caique went by, he turned two or three times to look back at us. His little face was copper-colored. Soon the boat disappeared behind the Fykiotrypa, with only the tilted mast remaining visible above the rock for a moment longer, sketching clumsy capital letters against the sky.

The Fykiotrypa Rock used to turn gradually into a monstrous frog that had been instantaneously transformed to stone when it emerged from the sea to inhale the pine-filtered air. Somewhere in the vicinity is an oblong, quadrilateral sea-stone that rises out of the water like an altar for maritime divinities. "The Altar": that's what you called it again in your letter, and that's how I saw it, too. A curly garland of green seaweed and chocolate-tinted moss is revealed all around it at low tide, and beneath that a red-white girdle of fossilized shells left glued there by the dead mollusks. All this is covered at high tide. However, when the north wind blows afresh, mauve waves with white shawls clasp hands, form a circle, and dance around the Altar. They come one behind the other, a whole line of them, and try to mount it. Do you remember their extraordinary struggle, their resolve? They bend in two, roll up, pitch forward, slide, clutch at the tiny cavities with their watery fingers. All in vain. In the end they fall back again in order to gather momentum by charging from afar. Once more they try, with fresh impetus now, with fresh efforts hedged by grace. And if one of them finally manages to mount the Altar, it races along the near side and through the cool moss like a small cascade, gurgling happily with aqueous laughter.

Nearby is another rock, this one red-green. At high tide there is nothing very special about it, but at the ebb it is stripped of its water right down to the base. There, the waves have licked at it for ages and ages until they have eaten away a ring and made it as slender as a stalk. At such times it resembles a huge red and green bouquet.

That's what you called it: "The Bouquet."

I remember one night when the sea was like glass and there was not a sound. Suddenly a ship passed by in the distance and the ripples of its wake reached us. Then, all around the harbor, the hollows in the rocks began to go "cluck-cluck" as though billowy kisses were being exchanged inside huge lascivious mouths.

One day you suddenly asked me if it were possible that not even a single grain of soul or a single drop of love existed in all this struggle.

And I said to you: "How many things worthy of adoration, how many marvelous, divinely beautiful things like this happen everywhere, all around humankind! They prod us to look and listen; they invite us graciously to partake of their joy and beauty. But what is the response? Nothing. People pass their entire lives with hermetically sealed souls, not even suspecting that miracles are bursting forth every moment in front of their faces and next to their hands. In the end these people die completely unaware; yet they seriously believe that they, too, have lived."

You remained silent. You were casting tiny pebbles from your hand into the water and listening as they were swallowed. After a long time, so long that I thought you were not pondering this at all, you said thoughtfully:

"Perhaps when everyone is able to see life's beauty, perhaps only then will the whole world become first good and then happy."

And I recall the triumphant definition you made:

"To be unhappy is to refuse to be happy."

What faith in life! But I, too, possess this faith, even now in these terrible times that we are enduring.

36

Longing for the Aegean

*T*he word "sea" occurs so many times in your letter—enough for me to perceive that your love for me and your concern for the sea must fit together to form some secret meaning. For hours on end I've been sitting here and asking myself how I have been able to live without the Greek sea for such an extended period. Longing for the Aegean: that is the sweet illness that is consuming me. Sea . . . *thalassa.* No other word in our language locks its emotion into itself so magically. *Thalassa . . . thalassa . . .* : that marvelous word that possesses a voice, a perfume, a breath. I close my eyes and repeat it over and over again, sounding both the s's. I pronounce it slowly, listening intently to my voice. And as I do this I hear the rustle of summer waves as they recede along our smooth beach and slide over the clean-licked shingle. This word rings out and sings. It is like the conch that lets you hear the voices of the sea coming from afar (even the muted cries of the drowned) when you press its opening against your ear.

Despairingly, I turn and measure out the unliftable hemisphere of the Macedonian sky as it weighs down everywhere around us and rests firmly against the level plain. From my schooldays I remember a finch suffocating beneath a similar bell jar when our teacher slowly sucked out the air with an exhaust pump. I feel my own breath restricted in the same way. But in Lesvos nothing stands still. The mountain-crests dance, the horizon rotates like a multicolored undulating garland of islands and waters; the sea has a thousand ways of bounding, cowering back, darting forward again; and the sun plays with every color. In Lesvos the very air—even the air—has its own very special taste and smell. It is salted with sea-spray. You savor it as it spices the tip of your tongue; your nostrils welcome it as though it were a freshly opened oyster. Then there are the sunsets over the sea. So many of them are locked inside me; their memory hurls bolts of pinkish gold light into my soul. The sun is a young flashing-eyed prince who hauls his purple satin and its rose-colored train over the waters, then departs, tip-toeing lightly upon the surge with his gold and orange slippers. Waving a kerchief of greenish fire from the distance, he nods: To-morrow . . . tomorrow . . .

The sky rains down cyclamen. The mountains grow dullish blue and half-transparent, just like the vases of antique glass we see in museums. The seaweed sways on the tips of the rocks. As for the rocks themselves, they laze about at their ease, seated grandly on the shallow bottom. Then the crabs emerge onto the sea-stones. They come out one by one, full of suspicion, looking like small metal cigarette-cases to which tiny legs have been appended. Their wee eyes are the hinges; the lid opens at that end. The sunset transforms their shells to gold, their sea-washed eyes to ruby beads. Each one wears a shirt with an embroidered monogram, a "B." A whole nation of them lines up along the rocks of the shoreline. Then, ranging over the cracks where the marine grasses and the moss are most tender, they begin to eat with their two little forks, first with the one, then with the other, hurriedly. A single clap of your hands and frrr! they take to their heels in a general rout—devil take the hindmost!—and then it's as though they had never emerged, had never even existed.

The island's mountains, dressed in their beauty like priests in their embroidered vestments, stand admiring their shadows, which are cast far far down, right into the sea, and seem to constitute their foundations. Even at this late hour a carpenter is banging a thick wooden peg into a warped plank with his maul. The noise swishes into the water. The fragrance of sawn cypresswood and boiled tar issues from the shipyards. A net is spread out in the shallows, its corks bobbing on the surface all in a line, like periods forming an ellipsis. Standing at anchor outside the harbor are two large ships, the one lead-gray with a red keel, the other walnut-brown. Their masts loom even higher than the blue peaks that line the Anatolian hori-

zon. On a trawler's prow a sailor chants with wistful ardor as he hauls
water up from the sea in a green bucket. A man on the end of the mole is
dressed in flowing white jodhpurs with the *sela* raised in front and inserted beneath the black waistband. He cups his hands over his mouth
and shouts to the two ships that are moored in the open sea, standing there
so solidly that they seem to be resting on foundations:

"It's near the aft cable, near the a a a a a f t c a b l e."

The sun continues to sink.

In the villas, several windowpanes burst into red flame. Some clouds
above Amali are rimmed by a selvage of burning gold.

Locked inside me, frolicking their many-colored lights, are so many
Lesvian sunsets!

Turning, I see these humble people of the plains. They are like so many
dung beetles as they roll their sheaves along the expansive yellow fields. I
see these women gathered one next to the other around oblong piles of
corn-ears, each with a large flail, threshing the corn, threshing it, threshing it, with these cudgels. And I feel that they are thrashing their own fate.
I see their ponderous carts laden with mountains of straw and slowly swaying on solid wheels behind colossal mud-bespattered buffaloes, the joints
screeching out a horrible song of boredom, torpor, and sluggish delay. I
declare to myself: if only I could inject into their imaginations, just for a
single instant, the vision of a Lesvian shoreline with its unrestrainable play
of colors, with its festooned trawlers and its sun that promenades over the
waters on tipy-tipy toe, shod in golden slippers! It is truly incomprehensible to me how all these people can fail even to suspect the existence of such
a miraculous reality, something much more miraculous than the heavens.
The sea! *Thalassa!* How can they shut their eyes forever before they observe—if only in a dream—the waters and islands of the Aegean? But it
would be criminal to fill their plainsmen's landlocked skulls with nostalgia for the sea—to make them understand why the ancient Greeks located
their paradise in the "Islands of the Blest"—and afterwards to place a flail
in their hands so that they might go on threshing wheat here in this inert
plain that steams from heat, until they die. . . .

One day I attempted to convey a small impression of the sea to them.
Fortunately, I did not succeed.

Anjo sat there motionless as was her habit, holding the shuttle in mid-air. "Is there really so much water?" she asked me, full of perplexity. "Is there more than in the Dragor?"

Then Givezo glanced at me with friendly condescension and, lowering her thick eyelashes, declared:

"Ne videl maiko na Dragora vodata da gi plavi nivite!" But mama, he never saw the Dragor flooding the plain!

37

Face to Face

*H*ow hot it is tonight! Hot, moonless, and starry. The moon is a golden sponge that wipes the heavens clean of stars the moment it appears. Tonight, however, the entire celestial embroidery is unfolded, threaded with starlight. I took my crutch and went out to the field surrounding Anjo's house. That's where I am now, reclining on a mound of freshly harvested corn-ears. They smell of greenness; they creak.

I am lying on my back, gazing straight up at the stars. My fingers are running through the beards of the corn. How cool to the touch they are, how soft—like silken tassels. Extended above me is the firmament: a mauve steppe flowered with magical springtime. Thousands upon thousands of silvery camomiles are trembling there. Millions of tiny argent faucets have opened and are spilling delicate fountains of mystic light onto the darkened soil, are drizzling sparks into black forests, are dripping fire upon fearsome seas. The earth travels through frozen chaos, between calms and storms. It is lashed and pushed by sun, by winds, by rain; yet it speeds over Fortune's waves, firmly guided by the Great Hand. It teems with creatures and it hums with life's myriad forms, all of which struggle in vain to penetrate the meaning of its history.

How extremely strange it is to lie on your back and watch the sky when all its little eyes are opened! You find yourself "face to face" with God. The newly picked corn exhales a fresh sweet-and-sour odor that can be tasted as well as smelled. On all sides the crickets fill the holy silence with their tremulous song. Where do so many thousands of insects hide? They sing only at night, after everything is hushed, and they make the darkness vibrate plain-wide with refreshing trills: crisscrossing tremulos of silver sound coming from above, from below, from everywhere. And no one knows whether these tiny voices belong to the plain, the crops, or the stars. They might even issue from the lovesick seeds that are cracking open and grating beneath the soil.

Our dead comrades will never enjoy this divine night that gazes at me with all its stars and summons me with its cricket-voices. (Gighandis! . . .) These calls that emerge so plaintively from the bowels of the earth, rising with the roots and sprouts—could they be the voices of our dead stalwarts?

I reflect: For so many millions of years these insects have been born, have sung out in unison every night, and before dying have yielded up their tiny mandolins to the next generation so that it might do the same. All this for eons and eons. But there will come a night when the earth will finally be too old and doddering. All these people whose ingenuity is so dazzling, all those who spend their time concocting mines and aircraft and melinite, will be nothing but finely sifted dirt. At that point, mankind will be just a legend, a bad dream that came and went. Only the ancient trees will remember it. They will pass it down from generation to generation, relating it to their descendants whenever the breeze blows and their foliage begins to whisper memories. On that night, however, the tiny crickets will emerge as usual to sing their accustomed song in unison beneath the countless stars. And all the silver daisies of the sky will blossom once again, and the heavens will bow down in order to harken to the infinitesimal crystalline mandolins. And the same frozen mystery will extend everywhere. The young forests will rumble, unaware that no more poets exist to capture their murmurs in rhyme, nor any more soldiers to saw them into stakes for barbed wire. The seas will lash the indomitable shores and will bound without respite onto the defiant reefs, without caring a single jot about those vainglorious blockheads who, once upon a time, honestly and truly believed that all of God's superb works and actions took place solely for their own dear sakes.

In the meantime, however, we go on killing and disemboweling for "The Freedom of All Peoples." Just ask one of those blacks brought by the

French (the ones who Anjo swears by the cross bake and eat little children if they catch them when no one is looking). Just ask an Indian or a Chinese. All these slaves will assure you in a single voice that they are fighting for "The Freedom of All Peoples." None of them intends to fight for his own blasted freedom—no, not even one little bit!

* * *

Oops! What's this?

Such a darling little star—one of the tiniest, the sweetest. It broke away from the sky and plunged right down onto my coatsleeve. Is it a star? It might be a sidereal crumb, a little fluff of pale green light. All right, you, come here, here into my palm. It's a glow-worm! A romantic Madame Glow-Worm, a gadabout who forsook her household chores at nightfall to go promenading in the fields. She lighted her little lantern just for me— the tramp!—and went out for a stroll. All right, come here, you, and sit down a minute for god's sake so we can talk things over—quicklike! I gaze at her carefully, in a friendly manner. She has her little lantern hanging on her backside—yes, by Jesus, right on her backside. It's a twin lantern with a delicate green glow that shines intensely in my cupped palm, shines as brightly as a lighted cigarette. Miraculous! She can increase or decrease the brilliance as she pleases. Assuredly a perfect mechanism. But there is a vexed question that keeps bothering me; a puzzle that, without fail, I must ask a learned entomologist to solve for me. Why, my fine lady, do you hang your lantern from your backside? Why the devil do you bother to light it at all, since you don't employ it to help you go in a straight line by illuminating your way in front? Supreme God, there can be no further discussion about Thy works: in wisdom Thou hast wrought them all. But the backside of the glow-worm? Explain that one if you can! The backside of the glow-worm?

38

Court-Martial

*T*he domestic routine and loving concern of these people of the soil has swaddled me in a cocoon of soft silk, isolating me from the war. A little more and I would have forgotten the terrible laws governing life just a stone's throw from Anjo's front door. Today, suddenly, my brother came to remind me; indeed, it was a sudden shock. He says that our regiment is all topsy-turvy. Desertions have begun to increase at a frightening pace. The day has come when in a single company five or six men will be missing all at once when the morning roll is called. They make off in groups after first equipping themselves lavishly with hard-tack, cartridges, hand-grenades, and as much rope as possible. (No one has been able to understand yet why all deserters equip themselves with rope.) A few notes with passwords and directions have been found among the odds and ends they leave behind as useless. Apparently it is a question of organized propaganda by the pro-Germans—or so people say. A captain has already been sent down in fetters for complicity. After this came a council of the Corps Commanders, and there is talk now of "drastic measures." I know what that means. In army language this short, hackneyed phrase always contains a great deal of human blood. That's how it turned out this time, too.

They have instituted a special court-martial that will try three men for abandoning their posts in the face of the enemy. The trial (i.e., the conviction) will take place in the village church. That's where everyone is headed today, confident that something significant will happen. This trial is being conducted for the sake of appearance because an exemplary model is needed. It is symbolic, but the symbol hiding behind it is a terrible one with twisted, grimacing features. At this "mass" that will be celebrated today in the village church, every single man in our division will receive communion—but the blood and the body will be real.

Since my leg is progressing nicely, my brother managed to convince me to venture out-of-doors with himself as escort. Together, we made off slowly toward the church. By the time we arrived, the trial had already begun and the place was filled inside and out with officers and men. The porch was full, so was the churchyard, and group after group continued to approach. The men chattered idly and shouted on their way but fell silent the moment they drew near. Squeezing themselves in among the others like sardines, they stood there in the heat and waited in silence. My brother and I separated at the narthex. Climbing onto a stone bench, I waited, too.

Eventually there was absolute silence. It commenced inside the church and spread to those who were outside. The president of the court had begun to speak; the decision would come momentarily. Everyone stood on tiptoe, held his breath in order to hear, and craned his neck in an attempt to bring his earlobe as close as possible to the door. All eyes were focused on the low whitewashed dome of the narthex or wherever else they chanced to fall, but they looked without seeing, as though they, too, were struggling to hear. Everyone was breathing more rapidly now, and waiting. The expectation and silence magnified every noise. A buzzing horsefly was revolving around my head; its wingbeats sounded to me like the whirling propeller of an airplane. The president's voice issued from the depths of the church but we could not distinguish his words. It was just a continuous flow of talk in a hoarse, monotonous tone, without intervals. But then it ceased abruptly and straightway from the church came a myriad-mouthed commotion that spread to the outside exactly like a breeze that suddenly vents from a narrow lane and sweeps up the dry leaves nestling on the ground. Issuing from there, from inside, passing from mouth to mouth and from ear to ear, came the word that put the final seal to the president's peroration: death. Its import spread over the mass of soldiers like a cold sheet over naked bodies—a serious import, making all eyes stare with surprise and terror. The men's faces, which had retained the pallor of life underground, appeared more pallid than ever beneath the low-roofed narthex. Yet all of us who had gathered nearby had been sure of "this" from the start. We had all known that this horrible word would be uttered in the half-lighted church. The word passed among us nevertheless as though its import had just now been freshly revealed and could not be grasped by the human intellect. The soul kept pushing it away; the heart refused to accept it. "Death"? Each man stared austerely at his neighbor with thoughtful, inquisitive eyes, and with knitted brows.

This momentary shock was followed by the great hubbub of people leaving the church and striking up conversations on all sides. Everyone began to chatter now about the three men who stood condemned; everyone had some bit of information to contribute; in an instant a thousand and one relevant particulars became general knowledge.

All three men had been apprehended up front, in the line. One of them had been on sentry duty on a day when the enemy suddenly began to bombard the trench. Panic overcame him like a sickness at the first explosion. Deserting his post and abandoning his gun, he burrowed into a dugout, squealing. There he flopped up and down like a fish and howled: "I can't face it! I can't! I can't!" He was very young, this boy—just a fuzzy-cheeked infant, a refugee from Anatolia, his father butchered by the Turks. He had enlisted in Mytilene for one and only one reason: so that he could convey his bread ration and full mess tin to his aged mother and two sisters. Everyone who "donned the colors" was carrying home all sorts of goodies. So one day his people said to him: "Come on, you good-for-nothing loafer, everyone else is bringing things home while you roam the streets unemployed and hang around in alleyways, you overgrown beanstalk!" He was tall. He went and falsified his age so that he would be accepted.

The second decamped one pitch-dark night from a working-party as it was digging beyond the barbed wire in order to set up, in great haste, a new advanced machine-gun emplacement. There were eight in the party, with a sergeant-major in charge. The parapets had to be ready before dawn, without fail. The work progressed with great difficulty because the Bulgarians across the way had heard the grating of the picks and shovels. Suspecting that our men were "organizing" the point, they started to plant shells all around in the darkness. They would probe the night blindly with rockets, then fire away. The crew, from the moment the lookout signaled the cannon-flash at the artillery position across the way until they heard the report of the bursting shell, had to abandon their digging and lie motionless on their bellies. Similarly, they had to lie stiff and motionless from the moment a rocket shot skyward until it expired. In the intervals they sprang up on the double and dug like madmen for as long as they could—until the artillery flashed again or until the red stalk of a rocket loomed anew. It was a galling night, full of congealed darkness, thumping hearts, and sudden terror. Four of the party had been hit. One had died on the spot; they left him there until dawn. The wounded they carried off lickety-split lest the groans be heard across the way. As for the man who stood trial today, he had absconded, overcome by fright. They found him in his dugout, trembling and raving away with his features so contorted that be was unrecognizable. This condition lasted for two days. In his delirium he said that he had seen the sergeant-major finish off one of the wounded on that night because he took a long time in dying and his screams, audible across the way, were betraying our position. The third man had the strangest tale of all. I heard its every detail from a friend of his, an old reservist. The man in question was a little orphan who held a job in Salonika in a chemist's shop. For months he struggled to set something aside in order to buy a pair of new shoes. His old ones were a mess, and once when he went to make eyes at the girl of his fancy, she halted, raised her brows and, without uttering a word, fixed her gaze on his dilapidated footwear. Then she looked up, stared him straight in the eye in a nonchalant manner that froze him to the spot, and continued on her way as though he had never existed. This was a terrible blow. He remained paralyzed there in the middle of the street, left now to gaze shamefully in his own turn at this worn-out shoes, as though seeing their deterioration for the first time, through the girl's eyes. After a long struggle he managed to put aside enough cash to buy a pair of new, ready-made shoes. When he tried them on they seemed a perfect fit. He paid for them and jaunted proudly off. But by the time he reached the chemist's—this required him to walk the full length of the quay—he realized that the shoes were too narrow. Every step had become an unbearable torture: he was biting his lips and trodding as though on nails. At the midday break, bowed over and miserable, he returned to the store where he had made his purchase. There he related what he had endured and asked to have the shoes exchanged for a wider pair. He begged, whined, supplicated. No use. The owner packed him off, drawing his attention to a square block of crystal inscribed in golden letters: "No merchandise removed from the premises . . . ," etc., etc. The boy steeled his heart and began to retrace his road of torment, limping so badly that you would have thought a pair of horseshoes had been nailed to his bare soles. Then, completely by accident, he encountered his friend the reservist outside some barracks of the National Guard. This reservist, the same one who told me all these details, had that very instant emerged from the quartermaster's. He cut a fine figure, nattily dressed as he was in his English-made uniform and planted comfortably in a superb pair of double-soled shoes which he had just put on. To the boy's eyes he seemed the most fortunate of men—so much so that the lad, without a second thought, went inside and enlisted as a volunteer, whereupon he was issued a pair of shoes. And now: now he was about to be shot because one night as his patrol was advancing to affix proclamations to the Bulgarian barbed wire, he had left it, returned to his dugout, and gone to sleep. In other words, he was going to be executed solely because he had once had the ill fortune to buy a pair of shoes a single centimeter narrower than what was needed. This strange story was disseminated from mouth to mouth even more widely than the others, and became the subject of endless discussion. But no one found it funny. On the contrary, everyone pitied this chap more than the other two, because it was ascertained at this same time that he lay bedridden in prison, gravely ill with typhoid, and that even if they failed to execute him, it was his lot to be condemned by disease.

A quartermaster's aide, an extremely short soldier with nearsighted eyes, tilted back his cap to rub his forehead. He told us that military law provided for such cases where someone infirm had been sentenced to be executed. It ruled that the condemned man must be made well before he is killed. None of us had been aware of this and no one noticed the implicit contradiction. Instead, the minute we heard it, we all declared: Yes, of course, entirely right, this really is what the law says; they can't shoot the chap until he's been cured. . . .

After some more time had elapsed, an aisle was formed amid the mass of chattering soldiers. The members of the court-martial were leaving the church. They passed silently through our midst one behind the other, sullen and covered with sweat. Of all of them, only the recorder of the court-martial looked happy. He was a handsome, idiotic adjutant with pencil-line eyebrows and the pictorial little phiz of an operatic tenor. He held an expensive briefcase under his arm. On his face he wore a satisfied smile. Finally, bringing up the rear, out came at last the president of the courtmartial, the colonel of the Third Infantry Regiment.

I don't know if you can imagine this squat, blubbery, pot-bellied man. He was billeted in Kioski and had a skinny wife (without eyelashes) who invariably stood at his side with a whining expression whenever he reviewed the regiment. He also had a jaundiced little daughter who wore artificial cherries in all her hats. Nor is he himself without quirks. They say that he once punished his mare with a ten-day cut in rations because she had tossed him off like a sack. They also say (among other things) that he used to apply the regulations in his own private manner even inside his household—to his wife, his little child, and his servant-girl. This man is very cruel. Maybe he's perverted as well. I learned that in Samos, where he was formerly military governor, he seduced and shamed a young teacher who afterwards hanged herself from a rope attached to the ceiling. This, then, was the president of the court-martial. Everyone says that it was he who pressured the judges to declare the extreme penalty, insisting that all three defendants must be executed "as an example." We have even heard that he threatened to submit his resignation and to report the others to the ministry for "slackness" if they allowed themselves to be influenced by sentiment. We gazed at him with fearful hatred now that he was passing through our midst. He was as round as a top. His paunch went first, carving out a path for him. Then came the bloodshot face, so red that it seemed his whole mug was in eruption. His eyebrows were very fair, his mustache like clipped stubble. Letting the other officers continue on, he halted in front of us. I was standing on the stoop, from which height his stunted bearing appeared even more humble, even more inconsequential and ugly. He kept banging his crop nervously against his boots, and repeatedly opening and closing his diminutive sweaty eyes, which are faded and have a feline air. To all appearances he was extremely perturbed. We realized that he wanted to say something to us but was hesitant. We expected angry and abusive words. But this is not what we got. By dint of great effort he managed to form a repulsive smile on his apoplectic face. It was constructed chiefly of two little fans of delicate wrinkles that spread radially from the corners of his eyes. Armed with this smile, he swept his gaze over the whole company with optics that seemed to have lost their lashes. We were all surprised, and kept our silence as we waited. It was evident that the colonel of the Third Infantry Regiment did not know how to begin. Finally he commenced his speech as follows:

"Well . . . how're ya getting along, lads? Feeling more fit, eh? I see you're beginning to recover from the trenches. . . . That's the way, boys! Gallantry and fitness, that's what we want, isn't it? . . . A Hellenic soldier suffers all for his Fatherland! . . . Yes, that's the way; you're doing fine.

". . .We superior officers, you understand, we have great and. . . mmm . . .difficult obligations. Look here, 'this' had to happen. It was required— for the sake of discipline. . . . Our country . . . Indeed, I insisted as strongly as I could. . . . It was right for 'it' to turn out like this, don't you agree?" (He gazed at us questioningly, maybe even imploringly. No one responded, not even with a nod of the head. We were all looking and listening without comprehending anything.) "Eh?" (He then proceeded to answer his own question.) "By all means, yes, it *was* right for it to turn out 'like this'! I did well to persist in seeking the death penalty for the deserters, don't you agree? . . . Eh? . . . Of course I did. . . . Because . . . because the exceptional circumstances in which the nation finds itself . . . Because . . ." (furiously:) "You, there! Why aren't you standing at attention, eh? Swine!"

These final words were uttered in an abruptly changed tone of complete ferocity, and with a face that had broken instantaneously into a raging storm. They were hurled at a poor devil of a soldier who was stooped over with fever and who happened to be standing next to the colonel and listening to him with drooping mouth and dangling arms. The man shuddered with fright, then stretched himself out as straight as a clarinet, as did all the rest of us, because no one had been standing properly at attention. The colonel! He glared at us severely with his sweaty little eyes whose upper lids kept fluttering. The little fans of kindness at their corners had folded immediately; the worried smile was gone. He banged his crop against his boot and departed quickly, with vigorous strides.

We all remained at attention for a few moments longer, petrified by the clink of his spurs as they receded. But when we fell out we all knew secretly that this unfortunate man was not at peace with his soul. What had he been doing for such a long time? Nothing but inviting us to aid him in his battle with it over "that thing" he had done. Who knows—perhaps lurking in the blackest of men is a saint in chains, praying.

In the end, I felt only a profound sadness for the colonel of the Third Infantry Regiment.

39

The Condemned

*C*lear skies today. I rose very early and watched the dawn as it opened its petals one by one above the plain like a golden lily spreading glory across the entire earth. This is the day on which the execution will take place; the three condemned men will be shot in a field of reaped grain outside the village. All units have been notified to be present—infantry, artillery, pioneers and drivers: every branch, corps and service, all mixed together. They have been assembling on the site since daybreak. Officers of every variety are pacing back and forth with hands clasped behind their backs. They are smoking, chattering about pleasant subjects, and laughing genially. The crowd grows denser as time goes by; it is rumbling now like a sea. The sun has begun to beat down; people have shifted their caps into the most serviceable positions and are impatiently raising fist-clenched hands in front of their noses to glance at their wristwatches. What is this irresistible magnetism that draws men to the spot where they are about to enjoy (from a safe distance) the slaughter of their fellow creatures? Much has already been said about this diseased curiosity. I would add, simply, that this unconfessable pleasure is perhaps nothing more than a need concealed within the instinct for self-preservation. To see others die is a frightful confirmation of our own vitality and good health. A secret and unconscious joy invades us, giving us a palpitating awareness that our own lives have not been lost. A small confidential voice emerges from the hidden sources of existence and whispers: "*He* is done with; but *we*—we have wriggled out once again." It whispers this with relief because all of us know for certain, deep down, that somewhere, be it near or far, "our hour" is maintaining its place in the queue and waiting to come. If you observe well, you will acknowledge that you hear this voice even when you are returning from the funeral of a dear departed friend. You are basically in a fine mood; indeed, you lavish wishes for "long life" upon those who have been grazed by death. Why? Because you are sure about your own life. Your body is the part of you that feels this joy, that "reflects" with its warm blood, its muscles and its strong joints: "That other fellow has turned to dust. But I am able to pace up and down if I please; to raise my arm straight into the light; to see the sun as it strides over the trees and drips from the vibrant foliage; to gaze at a hawk hovering in the blue sky and to shout at it: 'How do you do! Looking for me, are you? Well, here I am—still!'"

The fine weather has also been playing its part, transmitting its joy to the impatient swarm buzzing in the wheatfield. There is a rushing brook at the field's edge, just beyond the fence. It chatters away refreshingly, shaded by two rows of wild shrubs that incline along its full length on either side, bowing romantically above the clear water as it slides like running light across the rounded stones and gurgles in the hollows. Flying above the stream are some winged insects that resemble blue mosquitoes. They are a kind of lepidoptera; the sun is iridescent in their transparent wings. From time to time they rest their long delicate legs on the water, taking utmost care lest a drop or two splash their impeccable Sunday *toilette*. A gang of barefooted village boys with rolled-up trousers is dislodging stones in the stream, looking for crabs. Standing next to me is a group of division clerks, very cleanly and elegantly dressed. They are exchanging obscenities as they eye a party of village women gathered off to one side beneath the shade of a terebinth-tree conversing seriously among themselves, their large hands clasped beneath the curve of their strong massive breasts, which protrude like huge fists inside the black homespun of their dresses.

Four infantrymen are vociferously discussing the execution. Apparently they come from the same village as one of the condemned. They say that the sentence was read out in prison last night to those about to die, and that the division chaplain remained with them a considerable time to give comfort and administer communion. Two of the three wrote long letters home to their families, the underaged chap apparently supplementing his with separate two-page poems for his mother and sisters. The third man, the one with typhoid, was in such poor condition that he remained completely oblivious of everything. He kept bellowing all night long, raving about the sea and fishing boats.

All the men in the vicinity have begun now to contribute to the discussion. They are asserting once again that the sick prisoner cannot possibly be shot today. He'll be escorted under guard to the hospital, where he will remain until he is cured. In everyone's mind, moreover, is the thought that since the poor devil will squirm out of it at this time when the expediency of "setting an example" is a contributing factor, he will eventually escape for good. "When you're in luck why run, and when you're out of luck why run either?" asks a corporal with new stripes, tapping a cigarette against his fingernail. They discuss the regulation that prohibits a condemned man from being executed so long as he is ill. Everyone finds it touchingly humane. No one stops to consider what kind of "philanthropy" this is that in order to kill a man sits patiently waiting until he first becomes entirely well, spoonfeeding and coddling him in the meantime with meatbroths and physicians, precisely so that it may deliver him in perfect health to the hands of death. Is it attempting to make the deprivation of life all the more cruel for him? Or has it perhaps entered into a pact with death to surrender nothing but complete lives to it, and none that is half-alive or deficient in any manner? . . .

But the hour seems to be drawing near.

They have already begun to clear away the throng of soldiers from the "field of execution." This is a stretch of ground with an uphill grade and rich soil, bounded at the far end by a long, low mound of earth that will prevent the detachment's bullets from ricocheting blindly over the plain. It is precisely because of this mound that the field was chosen. In order to anticipate every eventuality, however, three buglers have climbed to the top of the mound. They are sounding the "Theodora" at frequent intervals so that any passers-by who still have not caught wind of the execution will hear and withdraw from the vicinity. The notes of the retreat dash smartly forth in march-time and gambol in the light, full of nimble animation. The trained bodies of the buglers rise up proudly in the festive atmosphere, their stance elegant and statuesque—one leg in front, slightly bent—their carriage full of supple grace. When they lift the bugles to the level of their faces with one charming and confident motion, the instruments cast off the sun's reflections like golden glances. They remind one of the colored lithographs that the "Patriotic Union" affixed to every wall, inviting volunteers to join the revolutionary "National Defense" movement, and bearing the inscription from Aeschylus: *Ite paides Hellenon* (Forward, sons of Greece).

Suddenly there is a great murmuring in the assembled throng of soldiers, a swelling and turbulence as though in a sea just before high tide. All eyes turn toward one spot where a wide thoroughfare opens up instantaneously in the middle of the crowd.

"They're coming. . . , they're coming."

Two gray lorries are groaning, braying, and snorting along the narrow road at the field's edge, a road so white that it seems sprinkled with fine chalk. Soon they stop.

The division chaplain alights from the first, together with the condemned men and five gendarmes, two of whom are supporting a soldier firmly beneath the armpits. This man's head is hanging down in front and he is swaying to the left and right, his knees buckling, feet dragging along the ground. But the gendarmes, who are robust, well-built stalwarts in new uniforms, have a solid grip on him. A single question is on a thousand lips, a question that needs no answer:

"The man with typhoid—are they going to kill him after all, him as well?"

About fifteen armed soldiers jump down from the second lorry, accompanied by a sergeant and an officer. They assemble immediately into two columns. A few brief commands and they are behind the condemned, whom they follow step by step, advancing at an extremely slow pace. The prisoners' escort enters the field ever so slowly on account of the sick man. They are practically dragging him on his feet. At a point very close to me, the two gendarmes who are supporting him halt for a moment until they can transfer him to another pair. Then all the rest halt as well: the priest, the two remaining prisoners, the guard, and finally the firing squad. I can see the sick man's face now. It is on fire: swollen and red. His eyes are wide open and staring—two large greenish eyes with dark lashes. They are languid, expressionless, lost in the blur of fever. For a moment they fall on me by chance, but without seeing me. The sweat is dripping in large knots from his nose. . . . Now they have all started out again. He is hunched over and his body is pitched even further forward. His boots keep catching in the furrow left by the plough. The other two are marching behind their sick comrade, every so often casting fleeting glances at the crowd. They are pale. The priest walks next to them, mumbling the service for the dead between his teeth. This division chaplain, a huge athletic man from Samos, has the vulgar mug of a peasant, and cowled eyes whose pupils play inside a cluster of tiny red veinlets. He looks fat, dressed in khakis, because of his strong large-boned limbs and plump backside as big as a woman's. He has bulging, voluptuous lips. His tightly tied pigtail seems to be made of horsehair.

An oppressive silence extends everywhere as they pass. Our hearts are thumping beneath our tunics. When the procession reaches the foot of the mound there is the command to halt. The condemned are placed in a line, each one three strides from the next. The sick man cannot stand on his feet. He tries his best when they speak to him, shouting directly into his ear, but fails to manage. They sit him down, his knees spread wide, his hands dangling like oars. He is breathing very rapidly. The detachment is ordered to attention. The recorder of the court-martial, that good-looking masher of an adjutant, reads out the sentence amid absolute silence. He has on a shining, brand-new cap and all in all is svelte, polished, and dapper-fresh from the ironing board. A plump blond in a short pistachio-colored silk dress is standing behind him. She is his wife. I've been told that she loved him so much that she eloped with him. She's the first smart woman I've seen all this long long time—a true "lady" with blue eyes, who uses a fan. She is like an exotic fruit full of juice and encased in a silken rind. You feel like peeling her and then downing her in a single gulp. All the officers who have come out of the trenches have been behaving most obligingly toward the recorder of the court-martial—even his superiors, overlooking military rank. It is because of his beautiful wife.

The handsome adjutant finishes the document with the bravura that is his by right. After all, he is playing one of the leading parts in this ceremony. Rolling up the paper again, he takes two steps backward. Next, the condemned are asked if they have any requests, or if they desire to make a statement. The one with typhoid does not speak. Perhaps he has already spoken. His lips have been moving ever since he was placed on the ground, but without emitting any audible words. Raving deliriously, he has been staring with his large eyes at the people all around him. At one point he let his gaze come to rest on the firing squad and looked at them naïvely and stupidly, with an obedient expression that reminded me of a lamb I once saw garlanded with roses on the feast day of the Archangels Michael and Gabriel, just before they cut its throat. In the lamb's case, too, the priest had mumbled something first.

In the middle, next to the sick man, stands the young volunteer—the one who wanted to carry full mess tins home to his mother. He is a blond lad with delicate features and pale, thin lips. His chin is trembling, and he keeps scratching the palm of one hand with the fingernails of the other. When they ask him if he has any requests, his childish eyes flash with hope. Turning suddenly toward the officer of the detachment, who is stationed motionless at the edge of his platoon, he extends his hands and says:

"Do I have any requests? What . . . what could I possibly request, Sir?" (When he says "Sir" he snaps to attention from force of habit.) "I want . . . please . . . I beg of you . . . please, DON'T KILL ME!" Whereupon he immediately begins to cry, to whimper with uninterrupted sobs, convulsively, like an extremely unhappy infant.

The third one behaved in a manner as repulsive as it was ridiculous.

"Pardonnez-moi, do you mind if I smoke a cigarette?"

They gave him one. They struck a match for him. He lighted up, the cigarette trembling slightly in his hand. He drew in two large showy puffs. It was assuredly a scene conceived in advance. Next, he tossed the cigarette away and ground it into the soil with his boot—as though to extinguish it properly were an indispensable mark of good breeding. Then he spat next to it with boorish propriety (first covering his mouth with his full palm) and commenced to deliver an entire speech! By God, an honest-to-goodness effusion with all the imbecility and illiterate overworked *katharevousa* of official oratory: ". . . regarding which, honorable officers, . . . regarding which, dear comrades-in-arms . . ." He uttered a pile of nonsense about "eternal parting" and "heart-rending death, in regard to

> *What a season Charon chose*
> *to take me to my doom*
> *just when the earth grows green again,*
> *and mountains are in bloom.* "

Last of all, he requested that they write to his people to say that he had fallen "in battle, facing the eternal foe."

Was he an insensitive dolt incapable of considering the seriousness of his plight? Was he a mysterious Greek who performed his pranks even in front of the firing squad? Or was he perhaps a ludicrous yet admirable hero who dared to mock death right under its very nose? On the other hand, if he could display so much insensitivity—or pluck?—now that he was confronting certain death, how is it that not the slightest grain of either insensitivity or pluck had been available on that other occasion when he took off in the face of enemy shelling in order to hide in his dugout? These are puzzles that I have never been able to solve.

As soon as his oration was finished, the gendarmes began to cover the eyes of the three condemned, eyes that in a moment would be closed forever. The man with typhoid remained in a motionless stupor at first while they affixed the blindfold, but no sooner had this task been completed than he raised his hands slowly, pulled off the strip of cloth, which was bothering him, and smiled. The underaged one started to scream. It was necessary to tie his hands behind him. The "orator" signified his refusal to be blindfolded with an ugly grimace of the lips and eyebrows. He crossed his arms over his chest, spat onto the field next to his foot, and ground the saliva into the soil with his boot, displaying the same air of the well-bred rustic.

The officer raised his unsheathed sword. The blade remained vertical in the sunlight for a moment, adorned with *brilliants* and silver flashes. The men took aim; several of the barrels were quivering. The sword came swiftly down. The dry crack of the rifles thundered out like a single detonation. The condemned sank to the ground, covered with blood. One eye had spilled out onto the sick man's cheek; it slid peacefully toward the ground next to him. His panting breaths had stopped at last; his cap slipped gradually from his head until it fell. The young boy twitched convulsively, rolled about, clawed the soil. The sergeant finished him off with a *coup-de-grâce,* a pistol-shot in the temple at point blank range. The "orator" died instantaneously. He collapsed in a heap, making a half twist to the left.

At the same time that the detachment's salvo rang out, we heard a piercing screech from the throng of soldiers who were witnessing the execution. Someone had fallen down unconscious, and the men had formed a seething, gesticulating mass all around him. It was the old reservist from Salonika, the friend of the boy with the tight shoes. He was groaning on the ground, twitching and palpitating as though in an epileptic fit. A doctor removed a cork from a canteen and stuffed it between his teeth so that he would not bite off his tongue.

Suddenly the place was filled with great clatter; the detachment's volley seemed to have unlocked thousands of lips. The various groups of friends were all talking vigorously as they departed. Another detachment formed from all branches passed in front of the corpses in parade march. A squad of Engineers began hurriedly to dig three ditches next to the bodies. The corporal in charge stepped by accident in some blood and wiped his boot in the soil, grumbling.

Some of the Macedonian women from the village, their hands clasped as always over their wombs, came slowly up to the spot. Crossing themselves, they lighted three candles and affixed them to three stones. The flames were invisible in the strong sunlight. Then, swaying their heads left and right, they knelt and bewailed the three corpses with a strange, monotonous chant, each verse of which ended with a prolonged and strident "Vaiiii!"

When we left, the expression on every face was that of men who had just escaped some overwhelming danger.

40

The "Hellene"

*H*ere in this house where I am billeted, I have been toiling to explain to my hosts why the three soldiers of our division were shot. I've been struggling to justify the execution to them, but without any success.

Babo, Anjo's mother, said to me sternly: "First the enemy kill your boys, then your own officers do the same. Those officers: . . . they aren't Orthodox Christians!"

"Why, why did they shoot them?" asked Givezo, a tear quivering in each of her exquisite eyes. The way she posed the question, she seemed to be saying: Why did *you* shoot them?

"They were killed, Givezo, because they refused to fight. They went and hid themselves so that they wouldn't have to fight."

Anjo stood up, tall and white. She locked her hands beneath her ample bosom and said in her tranquil voice: "They were killed because they refused to kill! Gospode, may the curses of their mothers be on those officers!"

Inside me, my soul pronounced a spontaneous "Amen."

To tell the truth, these "exemplary" executions did produce the desired effect. 'The desertions ceased at a stroke. Between that time and now, only one man has been recorded as "missing." Does this mean that once you go away to fight you must accept war's special logic? Maybe. (War does have its own special logic, you know.) On the other hand, this unique desertion is extremely strange. The missing man is Sergeant Zafiriou. Have

I ever told you about him? Of all the career N.C.O.s in the regiment, he was the only one from Lesvos. The men regarded him with that secret contempt that all we new-fledged Greeks felt, in the years immediately following our liberation, for anyone who lived off public funds instead of his own labors. Such people were called "Hellenes" by the peasants. Zafiriou was a "Hellene," one of the exchequer's fatted calves. All the policemen, lawyers, officers and civil servants sent to us by mainland Greece after the annexation—these are "Hellenes." By means of this term, which they fill with sarcasm, our men indicate their disenchantment with the representatives of the State. But Zafiriou was a real stalwart and did not deserve this appellation. His only problems were a fierce, consuming chauvinism and the ambition to become an officer. His calling he loved fanatically. In the face of danger he was impertinent; he sought out wounds and glory by deliberate provocation. The whole time we were in the trenches he was always the first to insist on undertaking every hazardous mission. In the instructional sessions we had with him he used to say: "Cold, hunger, rain, and sickness exist only for civilians, for domestic types and stay-at-homes. The soldier writes them off. In fact, the only reason they exist for him is precisely so that he may write them off." And he would declare to us as well: "As long as even a single Greek remains enslaved, our ideal will be Sparta, not Athens. Greece must be respected by its friends and feared by its foes." And he would tell us, furthermore: "Justice holds a sword in her hand. If you take away the sword, the only thing left are her scales—and those you'll find in any greengrocer's. The same with Wisdom. Look at Athena. She is never without her armor." He believed all this, demanded it of his men, and applied it first and foremost to himself. Everyone feared this "Hellene"—and respected him.

Yet Zafiriou the model soldier, Zafiriou the stern nationalist, the N.C.O. so severe with his men and even severer with himself—this same Zafiriou had disappeared from the company less than a week after the execution. The captain, entirely baffled, was forced to fill out a "desertion slip" for him and to order an inquiry. This revealed that Sergeant Zafiriou had risen during the night, gone out of his tent, and never returned. The strangest thing of all was that he had left his arms, pack, and even his tunic behind him. He had departed in this shirtsleeves!

"There's not one chance in a million that he deserted," says my brother. "I'm afraid that some Serb or other intruder did away with him on the sly."

The captain found this supposition most convincing. Despite all the search and inquiry, however, not a single trace of Zafiriou has been discovered anywhere. Thus the bravest warrior of our regiment has been officially proclaimed a deserter.

41

Autumn Rains

*M*y time here passes tranquilly, filled with the delusion of peace, for there is nothing in Anjo's home to remind me of war's savagery. My leg is coming along splendidly, and I am able now to follow slowly behind the family on Sundays when they go out to the mountain to collect hazelnuts. The hazels are self-propagating in this area; there is a whole forest of them. Anyone who feels like it can go and pick to his heart's content. The village people take these excursions each Sunday. They do not regard this as work. For the unpracticed eye the hazelnuts are hard to discern because, wrapped in their green swaddling-bands, they have the same dull color as the tree's foliage. From a branch that I consider already picked, the women bring down whole fistfuls. Afterward, they spread the nuts out on platforms to dry in the sun. In this way they lay up provisions for the entire winter.

Today is Sunday again. But no one has gone to the hazel trees because it is raining. It has been raining since morning. All the people in the house—men and women alike—have gathered on the large verandah to watch the cascading torrent. The sky has descended, has settled over the yard until it touches the roof. All shapes, colors, and masses are obliterated in the blur, like paintings blanched by water. A sheet of rain is undulating in the atmosphere, and the warm soil—the rich Macedonian soil—is drinking the moisture, swallowing it insatiably. The water is so abundant, however, that the plain, for as far as the eye can see, looks like an enormous marsh.

The women sit with their hands clasped around their knees. They watch the rain, listen to it, and do not speak. But I am tired of staring so stupidly and for so many hours at the flooding of this inert landscape. My soul is glutted. This monotonous, changeless drumming has gradually filled me with melancholy, awakening in me the nostalgia that settled inside me earlier like a malady. Closing my eyes and blocking my ears, I try to hear the sounds of Lesvos's first autumn rains and to feel them refreshing my heart.

There, it rains and thunders boisterously for an hour or so, kicking up a terrible row. The soil exudes that provocative fragrance of its own: the perfume of a woman's armpit. You inhale deeply and insatiably with small repeated breaths. A watery shawl flutters over the red roof-tiles and each neighborhood fills with a joyful din. Girls caught in the street lift up their skirts with screeches, exposing their calves. Drain-pipes sing; tin roofs play piano. Afterwards, out peeps the sun all of a sudden from behind the clouds, rollicking with laughter. The trees glisten in the light, drip with freshness. And just see then what takes place in the harbor! Festively, the caiques begin to hoist all their wet sails, spreading them out to dry; the creaking tackle seems to emit tiny good-humored cries. You'd think that a great marine fête were being celebrated in the harbor. On the ships, the white topgallants—square banners of joy and peace—hang from glittering masts. The trees cradle their foliage happily, the roof-tiles turn even redder than before. Arrayed around the entire circumference of the horizon is a confraternity of tranquil, cottony clouds with frizzled polls. They are full of sunlight, and remind one of the "bright cloud" of the Ascension. Now that the squall has passed, all the snow-white angels have come out to seat themselves in a circle on heaven's blue benches in order to dry their long wet wings in the sun. Their garments are of light, their faces are white, their hair is silver.

Infinite kindness and sweetness pour out of the sky. The slender aspens, washed ever so clean inside their autumn foliage, stand up tall and straight in the pure air. They are white with golden leaves—like the large silver tapers of Eastertide when they have been lighted at the Resurrection and sustain at their tips the tiny flutter of a thousand red-gold flames. Hosanna! A mischievous, good-natured God looks down on all things from on high. He is entirely satisfied. Everything is dripping with "sweetness and joy."

Ah, the first rains of autumn on our island . . .

* * *

Anjo's daughters are struggling to attract my attention. They offer me an ear of freshly roasted corn, bringing it close to my mouth. It is fragrant and warm, but I nibble it only a little at one end. Anjo keeps regarding me nervously out of the corner of her eye.

"Leave the *ashker* alone," she says to the little girls. "His heart is sad."

The little ones stop their chatter and leave me, retreating one behind the other. As they go off they turn to give me a serious look: Their diminutive faces are smudged, as always, with roasted corn.

42

Asimakis Garufalis
the "Good-Looking Young Man"

*T*oday I took my walking stick and went as far as the tents of the Third Mountain Surgery. They stand just outside the village, only two hundred yards away. The doctor in charge was there with some medical attendants—from Mytilene, every one of them. Pandelidis, the doctor, is a reservist, a man with a heart of gold. We talked at length about our island; he feels the same nostalgia that I do. Most of his patients have scabies, a disease that was entirely unknown to the islanders previously but that has now become the most common malady in the division. Initially, our men caught it in the contaminated dugouts they inherited from the French and their blacks. Recently, however, everyone has been deliberately trying his hardest to become infected, as a way of escaping the trenches for as long as possible. An infected soldier becomes an invaluable asset to his friends, who go to the "scabies squad," ostensibly to visit him, and surreptitiously rub against his sores in order to catch the disease themselves. It wasn't long before this "squad" of the Third Mountain Surgery was promoted to a full company. When you consider that the incessant itch gnawing tirelessly away at these poor wretches prohibits them from enjoying a single wink of sleep throughout the night, their desperation the minute they learn that they are cured, or soon to be cured, sets you wondering. They scratch their few remaining sores then, and transmit the disease with their nails to the healthy parts of the body, especially to the joints. The doctor is aware of all this, but he feels more compassion than anger for these sly rascals because the treatment for scabies is a living torment. The patients are given frequent baths and their bodies are then rubbed with stiff brushes. Afterwards, their wounds are coated with mercury.

"The moral deterioration of men in wartime is frightful," the doctor told me. "Boys whom I knew to have the most splendid character in civilian life—I see them wallowing out here in the vilest degeneracy. The other day, no sooner had one of my patients been cured and given his discharge for the trenches, than he puts his palm over the muzzle of his Lebel and pulls the trigger. His whole hand, up to the metacarpus, was blown to a pulp."

"Do you have many fatalities, doctor?"

I asked this suddenly, having just seen two medical orderlies transporting a corpse on a stretcher. They were taking it away from the large rectangular tent of the surgery in order to deposit it inside an out-of-the-way conical tent whose designation was inscribed in black letters on a wooden signboard: MORGUE.

"We have our share," replied the doctor. "Mostly from abdominal complaints. The one you just saw is from your regiment. He died a minute ago. Dysentery. What do you expect? Vegetable fat and salted meat raise havoc with the system.

"Garufalis. See . . . : Asimakis Garufalis."

He was from our company and I knew him well—a middle-aged fellow as tiny as a thimble who came from a village on the flanks of Lesvos's Mount Olympus. Farmer, with a family to support. Leaving the doctor for a moment, I went to pay my last respects. Two stretchers gleamed whitely inside the conical tent. One was empty. Resting on the other were Garufalis's wretched mortal remains. I drew back the sheet that covered him from his head to his boots, and stood there, looking at his corpse.

It was with great difficulty that I brought to mind his former features in order to reconstruct the face that had been so drastically altered by the exhausting disease and by death's impassivity. The skin on the forehead displayed the yellowish transparency of wax paper. The large, thin nose protruded with frightening stiffness, all wrinkles and creases. It resembled a finger pointing insistently at the jaw. His mustache, reddened by smoking, hung down in an unnatural manner, and the cyanotic lower lip was pulled back at the left end by a yellow tooth that stuck out like a long, solitary insect. The scalp, visible beneath his sparse head of hair, seemed dirtier and paler than before, and the untrimmed nails extruded blackly from the stubby fingers of his curled-up hands. There is nothing more repulsive than a filthy cadaver. I covered him again with a strong feeling of nauseous horror.

Into my mind came a scene that I happened to witness once when we were together on march. We had halted at the outskirts of some village and had camped there for five days. Only on the first of these, however, had we been allowed to catch our breath and recover from our fatigue. That was a very special day: the first batch of mail from home was distributed. On the next morning the regiment ordered "precision drill" lest discipline begin to slacken and the men grow unruly and idle. The drillmaster for Garufalis's platoon was that cannibal, our sergeant-major.

"One! Left foot first and chest out, Garufalis," he kept barking hoarsely. But the more Garufalis heard him the more he slouched under the weight of his pack. The sergeant-major persisted in marching alongside him; Garufalis kept darting frightened sideways glances in his direction, and his left foot continued to step out on "two."

"I said your *left* foot on 'one,' you doddering old blockhead!" The drillmaster began fuming with rage. Garufalis's confusion increased. His ears blushed clear to the eyeballs. His vision blurred, and he staggered like a drunkard

"Swine! Your left on *one* I said, on one, you fucking idiot. On one! Oooone!"

In the end, foaming at the mouth, he ran forward, laid his huge claws on Garufalis's shoulder loops and started to shake him maniacally while the rest of the men continued on in their ranks of four.

He was given chores as a punishment—polishing the cook-pots—and then assigned to a fuzzy-cheeked infant of a lance-corporal, surely to humiliate him all the more. Garufalis had to keep marching, hup-two-three-four, all the while the rest of the men lay on the grass during our ten-minute breaks and watched, guffawing at this old gaffer being taught his first toddling steps by a juvenile draftee.

When the bugle signaled us to fall out, I discovered Garufalis collapsed in a heap behind a shrub with his gnarled hands locked around his knees and his head drooping so much, it seemed to be hanging from his neck as though he were drunk. I tapped him on the shoulder. Re gave a start, as though awakening from deep slumber.

"Never mind, never mind, old chap," I said to him. "Don't take it to heart. That's what the army is like. We've all had to bear it. . . . You've just got to concentrate a little when you march, so you can keep your wits about you."

He lifted his head and looked at me stupidly with those ugly, swollen eyes of his. Then, realizing that I had approached him solely out of genuine sympathy, he gave me a bitter smile. With clumsy movements of his jagged hand, which looked more like some agricultural implement, he slowly unbuttoned the upper pocket of his tunic and took out a cheap green envelope folded twice over. This he gave to me. A letter was inside.

"I received it yesterday," he said without looking at me. "It's from my wife. You know how to read. Read it."

The letter explained all too well why Garufalis was always so confused. It said: "First I hope that you are enjoying the best of health and second if you ask about our health we are enjoying good health. Dear Asimakis I inform you we sold Beauty when you wrote us from Mytilene-town but the money is all eaten up and now we're short of food. The other ox Blacky your *koumbaros* Thanassis wont let us sell it because he owns half. We haven't had bread from Arvanitas the baker for four days. Dear Asimakis don't be offended but the last time I went to get some on tick he winked at me and said come up first to the loft for a while to settle old debts and then you can buy on tick again, may god punish him! Didn't he pity a serviceman fighting for Christ and country and a mother with three children, saying such a thing, etc. I your wife Asimenia am writing you through the hand of niece Stavritsa and I embrace you."

* * *

That whole forgotten incident in its every detail came back into my mind with a clarity that was astonishing. I reflected on the extraordinary unhappiness that may be hiding beneath a corpse-sheet in a military hospital. A nightmarish sense of suffocation overcame me inside the canvas walls of this morgue whose air reeked of iodoform, and I turned to go out. But before I could stride through the triangular entranceway I froze stiff as a board. Coming straight in was the general, accompanied by his adjutant and our doctor. I backed out of their path and they entered. The adjutant placed himself in front of the door in a way that blocked it. Not daring to disturb him, I drew to one side. Balafaras, continually slapping his riding crop against his boots, began asking the doctor about the surgery, patients, and every which thing. The words issued from his mouth as plump as fritters, slowly and lazily, each in its own good time, with the crop beating out all the accents.

"Dysentery, eh?" (swish) "Ah, dysentery! Stomach and gut—they're the whole works, eh doctor!" (swish) "I'll never require your services, doctor!" (swish) "Sixty years old with a stomach that digests gravel!" (swish)

"Indeed, you have an exceedingly strong constitution, General."

(Confirmation:)

"Ex—c e e e e d—i i i i n n g—l y . . ."

(Pause.)

"Poor chap!" (swish) "Doctor, uncover his face!" (swish)

The doctor exposed the remains. Garufalis's ugly mug protruded horribly again with its grimace of death, the yellow tooth still biting the lip at the end.

"Poor chap!" (swish) "One more turned to dust!" (Air of confidential announcement:) "We all die sooner or later, doctor!" (swish)

"Sooner or later, General."

"He was a good-looking young man . . ."

(Pause.)

". . . a good-looking young man and a gallant warrior!" (swish)

(Pause.)

"Isn't that right, Adjutant?" (swish, swish)

(Heels clicking together, spurs clanging with fright.) "Yes, General. Yes, indeed!"

"Remember to have a lovely letter of notification composed for his family. And make all necessary arrangements for the War Cross to be sent to them as well." (swish) "The War Cross shall be bestowed instantaneously upon all the families of my heroes!" (swish! swish!)

(Spurs, heels, etc.) "Yes, General. Yes, indeed!"

43

How Zafiriou Died

*A*long with my rations today, Dimitratos brought me a piece of news from the company that has kept me in a state of turmoil ever since. From the disconnected fragments he let fly, I realized from the start that he had something to tell me. As soon as he had put down the mess tin, my wine, and the plate of meat (you see, we don't eat too badly here in the rest-camp), he emitted a hypocritical sigh:

"Ah, my friend, the world is full of surprises."

"What surprises, for instance?"

"Mmm, nothing. It's not the best of subjects for mealtime. Eat first; we'll have the leisure to talk afterwards. Ask the girl to make me a cup of coffee if you don't mind and give me your cigarettes to keep me busy in the meantime."

He dropped the bomb as soon as I had finished.

"They found Sergeant Zafiriou!"

"They caught him?"

"Heaven help us, no! First and foremost, he didn't have to be caught— he was absolutely stationary. Second, in the state he was in, no one had the nerve to set hands on him."

"So he's dead, is he? Get it over with; you're driving me crazy!"

"As you like. It's a rather . . . um . . . *filthy* story. He didn't come to a good end, this 'Hellene.' Have you ever considered the worst possible way a man could die? No? Well then, listen. You know we have a common latrine at the regimental encampment—a large ditch with some long, wide planks placed over it from one edge to the other, like bridges. The boys pull down their skivvies and squat there in rows with their left foot on one plank and their right on another. Groaning away, they evacuate their whole gut along with the salted Australian buffalo the French toss us to eat—you'd think we were wild beasts in a circus. When we pitched camp we found a French regiment cursing up hill and down dale as they pulled up stakes and put their kits together for up top—for the trenches. So we inherited some nice things from that regiment: its kitchens, artillery, a lumber dump, quite a few barrels of vegetable fat, a couple of sleeping-dens infected with scabies, and last but not least a colossal ditch like the one I was telling you about. Nearly full. . . . Well we, our bellies flat as tambourines from the rations in the line, no sooner do we pitch camp than we set the dixies bubbling and dive into the chow. So it didn't take us more than a day or two, praise the Lord, before we filled that ditch right up to the top with shit. Then comes an order: we were supposed to get a working party to remove the planks from the old ditch and throw them over the new one that had been dug alongside it. The same working party was to stuff the abandoned latrine solid with stones and dirt. Stones! That was fine in theory, but in practice they'd have to be hauled from a considerable distance in wheelbarrows, since Ordnance Stores wouldn't allot a single cart. So the men of the working party got going. They sprinkled the ditch with dirt only, and the hell with the rest.

"'Did you stuff it full?' they were asked when they returned.

"'Yes.'

"'Really full?'

"'Solid!'

"A lousy pack of lies. . . . Well, Zafiriou the 'Hellene' gets up one night to take a piss. Maybe he was a little tipsy—who knows? We'd had a ration of cognac distributed to us that evening. Maybe he was just groggy because his sleep had been interrupted. In any case, instead of going to the new latrine, he heads straight for the old one. This looked like firm ground because of the dirt they'd thrown over it. He makes a beeline for it with that regulation marching-step he used even for going to the jakes, and braaaaf! Down he goes, almost to the bottom. He fought down there, he struggled, tried to jump out, but no use. The poor devil just sank deeper and deeper until he suffocated and kicked the bucket. The doctor says he died from asphyxia. Your fine hero gave up the ghost gorged with shit."

"What you're doing is cheap and vulgar, Dimitratos."

"Take it easy, friend. What doesn't become cheap and vulgar as soon as you tell it the way it really is?"

"Zafiriou was a genuine hero. He proved it in the trenches. You should show some respect. . . ."

"A hero by pre-arrangement, just like all the others who make war their profession. And what about me? I'm a hero too, aren't I? I even have the War Cross, now that we're on the subject. But never mind; that's another story. . . . After all, as soon as we fished your genuine hero out of the latrine with a net, Balafaras of course must have sent one of those 'lovely letters' to Mytilene—typewrirten. You know, the ones the men have learned by heart, offering the parents 'congratulations [Is there any reason for congratulations that you know of?] for the glorious death of your son, who, having demonstrated incomparable gallantry worthy of the best Hellenic traditions, was killed on such-and-such a date, bravely fighting for Faith and Fatherland, against the foe.' As soon as you decide to tell the truth, all this becomes cheap and vulgar. Just imagine, for instance, if he'd written: 'Zafiriou died gallantly wrestling with allied Franco-hellenic shit. Unfortunately, he was unable to cry "Long live the Fatherland" at the moment of his glorious demise, because . . . er . . . he happened to have a mouthful'!"

44

The Parade

*I*t seems now that we shall have to leave this simple and kindly village that has given us rest for so many days—shall have to leave it forever. The bugles have sounded shrilly, repulsively. The general has determined once and for all to review his "lovely regiments" before we cram ourselves into the railway carriages that will dump us at the southern sector, together with a pile of other junk.

It was a gray, overcast afternoon, very humid and enervating. There seemed hardly enough air to allow a full breath, a state of suffocation intensified by the straps digging into our bellies and chests. The sky was a reflection of the land: the color of mud. Bowed under their full packs, the troops fell lazily into line, full of weary vexation.

> *Doughboys and their tools,*
> *Loaded down like mules.*

Our lungs, after growing moldy from the inert atmosphere of the dugout, had enjoyed so much pure, living air in this village. And now, after all that, here were our stalwarts marching as gloomily as a procession of consumptives. I had not seen the men of our entire division massed together like this for months, not since the time of our long marches up to the front before we buried ourselves in the tunneled earth. We were still healthy and red-cheeked then—truly the "lovely regiments." Our rifles were covered with osier-flowers, our bodies fragrant with the island's sea-salt and mastic. But now every man seemed to bear a mystic seal on his face and hands, the stamp of impending death. You could sense Charon following stealthily behind this multitude; you knew that this was the black cloud that had placed itself over the assembled companies. Beneath its shadow, every man strode laboriously.

I have noticed some strange wrinkles, chiefly around the eyes, on many faces of lads known to me previously—tiny wrinkles like tunnels left by woodworms. Certain faces have completely altered their former features. As for hands, without exception they have become ugly and—how shall I put it?—they seem so hunched over, so sad. A similar appearance must have been diffused over the hands, face, and eyes of Lazarus when they loosed him from the linen windings of the gravecloth after he was "called out of the tomb, having been dead four days."

As soon as the bugle ceased, the officers began to sound their whistles. More and more soldiers kept arriving in their patched greatcoats and frayed sleeves. The sluggards and whiners. The officers kept shouting at them, hurling insults, threatening. But we all understood perfectly that we were a flock of condemned good-for-nothings who in a short while would be underground again, like worms. Consequently, none of the indictments proclaimed by the threats and the piercing whistles had any significance in comparison with those terrible words whose horror was coated over our bodies, clothes, and inside our guts: "the trenches." We were returning to the trenches: this was the unbearable reality that filled the air and made it impossible for us to breathe.

A whole show had been arranged by the general so that this review, which was being staged chiefly for the sake of the two journalists who had been enjoying his hospitality for the last three days, might be more festive. These two, Kondelis and Gribis, had left the island to come here in search of sensation, notoriety, a fake "baptism of fire"—and subscribers. With them came Garifalou, the "national orator." Kondelis is a very well-known character—owner/editor of *Patriotic Voice* and a member of parliament. He writes the fiercest leaders about the war and sends copies *gratis* to each company so that the men will be "inspired with self-confidence." His son, who is studying political science abroad, mails home beautiful dispatches describing how the mustering of the Archipelago Division made such a good impression in Western Europe that they have already given us a partisan label: *l'armée vénizéliste*. All the establishment people, olive-oil merchants and notables on our island show utmost respect as they play backgammon with him and listen with gaping mouths to his political sermons. He has a chubby-faced little wife as plump as a pudding and as appetizing as a dumpling with whipped cream. At the carnival balls held at the Olive Oil Merchants' Club during Shrovetide, the French officers in the occupying forces christened her *la parisienne de Paris,* an event that *Patriotic Voice* did not neglect to include discreetly in its gossip column. The other one, Gribis, although a bigger rat than Kondelis, ends up almost likeable in comparison because his rattiness manifests itself openly, in a naïve kind of cynicism. Every time you turn around he is announcing the inauguration of a fresh newspaper and collecting subscriptions, only to halt publication after five or six issues. He has one great asset, however, which made him especially attractive to Balafaras the whole time the division remained on our island. This asset is his wife: Madame Aglao. You used to see her at the general's side more frequently than his adjutant. She is as airy and well packed as a good loaf of bread, this amazon, with globular breasts and well-nourished hindquarters that the general particularly fancied. As white and tall as a Hungarian mare, she matched Balafaras's gigantic figure splendidly, while that half-pint raisin of a man Gribis roamed around her foothills like a skinny little iota-subscript next to a capital omega. The general displayed an admirable simplicity in his relations with this lady. Once, an excursion was scheduled to the island's Mount Olympus—men only. Along went Gribis with a pocketful of carbonpaper-interleaved subscription forms and a camera slung over his shoulder. When the party reached a grove of wild chestnut trees with a spring nearby, they stopped and dined like gods. Balafaras drank native wine, wiped his upturned mustache majestically, and spread out his heavy-boned limbs this way and that upon the thick grass. Moved by the abundant good health he enjoys in advanced age, a health that he could feel tingling sweetly in his veins as he lay there surrounded by teeming nature in all its wantonness, he turned to Monsieur Gribis and burst into his famous lyrical ejaculation:

"Oh! Oh! This place, Apostolis my friend, is a veritable Olympus, a home fit for the immortals. What a shame that Madame Aglao is not here, too!"

This saying leaked out, went the rounds of the city, and was repeated by the town's dandies after every regalement: "If only Madame Aglao were here with us now, my dear friend Apostolis!"

Well, Gribis is getting ready now to bring out a six-page daily—quite an achievement for the provincial press. Its name: *The Seven Hills.* He has been after Balafaras for abundant details connected with the general's life in the trenches, and has already begun to write the description that will resound all the way to Athens. Its title: "The Dragon in His Lair." The general gave him a pile of photographs; he also obliged his officers to put themselves down as subscribers to *The Seven Hills.* One of these, in order to vent his spleen, inquired of Monsieur Gribis if he had in mind the *Horned* Gulf and the Golden *Horn* of Constantinople, the city of the seven hills, when he chose the name. Gribis did not neglect, while writing out a receipt, to express his admiration for the joke with hearty laughter:

"E x—c e l—l e n t, my good friend, e x—c e l—l e n t!"

Then, as we have said, there is Garifalou, the national orator. He has red hair, a red nose, red eyes, red necktie, and well-polished black boots. Starting out as a singer in operettas (in the chorus), he became successively a civil servant, the manager of a movie theater, a real estate agent specializing in the renting and selling of building lots, finally a middleman for off-the-peg German suits. Having failed successively in each of these pursuits, he was now attached to the Revolutionary Government and was going the rounds of the regiments in order to teach patriotism to front-line soldiers. What do you expect? A man has to make a living somehow, doesn't he?

As for Balafaras, what with one or the other of his two journalists, he has it made; he is clutching immortality firmly by the hair. He sees to it that he is continually photographed with them, and each time asks the division photographer if the negative will make a satisfactory plate for engraving.

By this time the commands for right and left dress had been given. This was reported to Balafaras, who ordered the regiments to be arranged in a square on the field where we had fallen in. He went and stood in the middle together with his visitors and the adjutant, Second Lieutenant "Pol'itis." That's how everyone pronounces the name, because when he speaks he sucks in his l's as though they were caramels. He is an effeminate rosy-cheeked boy, as delicate as porcelain, with pink hands and foppish high-society airs. Balafaras uses him as an interpreter to the French because he has spoken their language ever since the cradle.

They were joined in the middle, soon afterwards, by one more person.

This was Father Theodoros, the division chaplain—that gawking colossus with the plump red mug and huge distended lips. He goes the rounds of the companies in order to get pickled free of charge. Once we had to drag him out of the ditch where he was snoring away in an alcoholic stupor, having fallen off his horse, which was grazing peacefully nearby. (They say, moreover, that at night in his dugout he embraces his batman, a young volunteer with the fuzz still on his cheeks.) He was wearing a forage cap bearing a golden cross and the three stars of a captain. Today he was also wearing his stole over his khaki greatcoat. But most important of all: he was wearing, for the very first time, the War Cross, which he (together with the conductor of the military band) had received the previous week on the general's recommendation. The priest was awarded it because he showed Balafaras a time-bomb fragment that he found—so he said—in his cap on the day he went to the trench of a particular company to say prayers over the bodies of some machine-gunners who had been killed. But most of all he was decorated because each Sunday in his sermons at the encampment's outdoor services he speaks to the men about Balafaras's imposing glories. Indeed, it is his custom to take majestic phrases from the Old Testament and to recite them out of context, gesturing significantly in the direction of the general, who stands there proud as a peacock.

"And the prophet said: Gird thy sword upon thy thigh, O mighty one, and be strong!"

At the end of every service, Balafaras places an ostentatious kiss on the priest's hand, a massive thing as hairy as a bear's paw. He does the same, first rising with respect, whenever Father Theodoros enters his office. . . .

The bugles blared out the call for "attention"; the show was beginning. The general offered a few introductory remarks in his booming voice, selecting his words slowly (though he had no difficulty in finding them). It was a question of receiving salutations from our dearly beloved island before we went to the new sector. These salutations would be delivered to us by those two most estimable personages, etc., etc. In addition, we were to hear greetings from the nation, brought to us by national orator Garifalou of the shiny boots. Afterwards, a short requiem mass would be recited for our comrades whom we had left behind, stuffed beneath the ground in the sector we had been holding until now. Finally, there would be a "roll call of the dead," that customary event that nevertheless always sends such shivers down one's spine.

The first to speak, accordingly, was our parliamentary deputy: father of the son studying abroad, husband of *la Parisienne de Paris*. Employing the inflated *katharevousa* of the editorial page, he told us how happy he was to see us (ten thousand votes "at attention" is surely nothing to shake a stick at!) and said that he was bringing us a charge from our island: all of us who returned home must embark at no other place than Constantinople! Otherwise . . . we should not return at all. As for those of us who died, for them an imposing cenotaph would be built. This heroes' monument would be surmounted by a statue of Liberty and inscribed around the base with the names of the dead in letters of gold. Each man's village would be indicated as well.

Next to speak was the husband of Madame Aglao, Monsieur Gribis (or "Monsieur Aglao" as he was dubbed in a satirical ditty back home). As I was saying: He told us, this Monsieur Aglao, that he had come on behalf of the press with the mission of promulgating to the four corners of the earth the glory with which we had been crowned. He told us a thousand and one things about Balafaras, and afterwards assured us that *The Seven Hills* had assumed the responsibility of assigning us our proper place in the Greek tradition, putting us in the niche that we deserved, next to the warriors of Marathon and the Three Hundred of Thermopylae. This tradition was no laughing matter, etc., etc.

The next to have his number pop up was Garifalou, who proved the most interesting of the lot. He began to gesticulate, shout, twist about like an epileptic, leap into the air, to recite verses from Valaoritis, to shoot out punches in all directions. He wailed "eleleu! eleleu!" and pronounced the oath of the ancient ephebes: "I shall fight both alone and with many." What set me wondering most of all was how this joker had been able to get all worked up to such a degree so very suddenly, when just a moment earlier, before his turn had come, he had been standing so placid and well-behaved in his place.

After this, all the bugles blared out "Attention!" in unison. A sergeant began to read the roll call of the dead. He pronounced the name, village, and military rank of each, whereupon Pol'itis added the location where the man was killed or where he perished from illness or privation. All the while this was happening, Father Theodoros kept spluttering absolutions through his nose, the army presented arms, Gribis snapped photo after photo of the general, and the parliamentary deputy wiped his tear-stained spectacles with his handkerchief, overcome by emotion. But the hardest job of all was reserved for us. We silently cursed our late lamented comrades, who were causing us to stand at "present arms" for three-quarters of an hour by the clock. When "at ease" was commanded we all sighed with relief.

Next came Act Two.

The general and his party left the field, withdrawing to the far side of the carriageway at its edge. The band lined up next to them with the conductor in charge. Like Father Theodoros, he was wearing his War Cross, which he had received for composing three marches in Balafaras's honor. One of these, pillaged from "Sambre et Meuse," was especially dear to the general because in it the cymbals and bass drum boomed from start to finish. When Balafaras desired to specify this particular tune he would say: "Play us . . . hmm, what would be nice . . . play us that one . . . you know, the one with all the noise." This time, however, he designated "I enter the vineyard," that folk-melody from his own village, as the theme song of the parade. The maestro raised his baton and the band threw itself energetically into the job of beating out the song's meager and monotonous motif on the snare-drums, *sempre fortissimo*. The various units began to pass in front of the general in ranks of four, after which they headed in a direct line for the railroad station. Once there, they were to commence the loading operation. Each man pulling the next up in turn, they would clamber into the large freight cars whose engines were puffing away impatiently, as if eager to fill their iron bellies with the living men and beasts that they were about to swallow.

The sky pressed down upon us heavily. There was no rain, but tiny droplets filled the air and turned the ground into slippery mud that stuck in clods to our boot-soles. Some jagged, misshapen cloud-fragments were floating toward the south, where they hastily stuffed themselves behind a repulsive yellowish hillock like a filthy pile of "unserviceable raiment." We had grown unaccustomed to carrying full loads, and our packs, crammed now to overflowing with all our gear, were lacerating our shoulders and armpits with their straps. Our hands were numb from the "present arms." Our knees were warped out of shape by prolonged rigidity; we stomped up and down in order to unlock them. In this manner, our company awaited its turn to begin parading.

Standing at my right in the rank of four was Stefanou, a man of advanced years—he had served as a collector of duties on fish even under the Turks, before our island was liberated. This man was burdened with two daughters and a whole sheepfold of orphaned nephews and nieces, the children of his widowed sister. Taciturn, always engrossed in his misfortune, he spent all of his off-duty hours writing and rewriting letters and memoranda to Athens and to our island. The problem was that he had been pressed into service with gross injustice, solely because his age had been recorded erroneously in the records of the Recruiting Office. As you can well imagine, he sent memorandum after memorandum, letter after letter. But the result was zero, and in the meantime that huge mob in his house had to be content with eking out a miserable existence by means of credit and the extra allowances they received in fits and starts. Stefanou never told any of this to me, nor would he have revealed his troubles to anyone else. They were related to me by my brother, who, as his sergeant, saw to it that a report was submitted to the company.

Stefanou kept to himself, not mixing with anyone except to exchange the hackneyed phrases of one combatant to another. All alone, he was being devoured by the sorrowful chagrin that had dug deeper into his bony face than had all the misery of the trenches. His eyes seemed to gaze out at you from two deep wells. Once you had seen them you realized immediately that this man often wept in secret. Sometimes, when he forgot himself, his mind elsewhere, he would clasp his bony hands around his knees and then his grizzled mustache would begin to quiver. To quiver! It is my opinion that at such times he was perhaps weeping inwardly, within his soul. People can laugh inwardly; they can weep in this way, too.

"If only we could die, to escape this," I moaned, ready to drop from exhaustion. He turned and gazed at me sadly, from the depths of his tranquil eyes.

"First you need both the courage and the right; then you can do it," he said softly.

At that moment our platoon received the command of "attention," followed by "forward march." The ranks of four set out tiredly, but with a reasonably good pulse. When we arrived within the sonorous radius of the band, however, our legs came to life willy-nilly, and our hanging heads snapped erect. Unfortunately, just before the platoon reached the general's towering figure there was a small disturbance. Dindinis the buffoon, a half-mad zany who had a lifelong assignment to K.P. and whose rollicking spirits spread by contagion to the entire company, suddenly darted out from the rank and began to proceed forward with a strange dance-step, retaining the beat of the music:

> I enter the vineyard as mistress,
> but find there the owner, my wooer.

Our panic-stricken captain tried immediately to coax him back into line. But the general was even quicker to respond. He ordered the company to halt, signaled the music to stop, and (ostentatiously protracting his delivery as he always did when he thought he was creating history for his future biographers), declared:

"You! Come here! What's your name? (Take note, Adjutant.)"

"Panaïs Dindinis, son of Andonis and Pirmathoula, from Pirghi, General."

"Bravo! That's the kind of men I want! Men of Zalongo, every last one of them! Daaaaanciiing toooowaaaards theeeeir deeaaath! I grant this man a fortnight's home-leave. Adjutant, see that he departs at once! The company shall proceed. Forward, march!"

The band thundered out again, and our platoon started moving. Suddenly, when we had more-or-less reached the general's colossal bulk, I saw Stefanou slip out of our line to a position adjacent to the platoon and begin a dance just like Dindinis's, directly in front of Balafaras. It was such a tragic sight, this overaged doughboy leaping like a madman, laden with his full kit and his rifle! The bayonet slashed this way and that on the barrel as he twirled, and the marchers recoiled for fear of losing an eye. He danced on and on, gracelessly, stamping the earth as he advanced and singing in a monotone, along with the band:

> Tread the black grapes, kiss the fair girls . . .

On and on he danced, on and on he staggered—ugly, stooped, filthy, and loaded like a mule. At first I thought he had gone batty. Then I suddenly understood, and a lump formed in my heart. This middle-aged—almost elderly—man, so frightfully ridiculous as he cavorted like a buffoon or clown, possessed nevertheless two extremely deep and sorrowful eyes that turned every so often and stared at the general out of their deep wells, filled with anguish, entreaty, and timorous expectation. What was going to happen next?

The general split his sides with laughter, ho! ho! ho! and found himself faithfully supported in this merriment by his entire entourage. Then, shaking his finger playfully at Stefanou, he said in a tone of mock severity:

"Back into line, you antiquated old rascal! So you thought you'd put something over on me, did you!"

Stefanou returned to my side at a run, as red as fire, and resumed his place in the rank. Skipping twice to get back in step, he began to march again in the regulation manner, while the notes of the music rebounded like copper balls inside the steel forest formed by the bayonets. And in this marching posture, without losing step or one jot of the idiotic rigidity of parading, he suddenly began to weep, softly. His tears ran unchecked from the dark hollows of his eyes, dripping unwiped onto his cartridge belt from his grizzled mustache and the tip of his big nose. His extremely prominent Adam's apple juggled up and down with rapid, spasmodic jerks inside his narrow, wrinkled throat, as though someone were pulling at it through his mouth and struggling to tear it loose.

The column kept advancing through the mud. Nothing could be heard except the rhythmic tramping of our boots. No one had laughed; it was clear that everyone understood.

When we reached the bottom of the hillock the captain ordered "sling, ARMS!" and then "at ease, MARCH!"

Our pace slackened abruptly, but no one had any appetite for talk.

It began to rain. Hard. Right in our faces.

45

Mothers in Wartime

I am writing this manuscript for you inside a freight car, squashed between two sackfuls of bandoleers as hard as bricks. We have been traveling—the whole regiment—since afternoon, salted away like miserable sardines in these colossal green trunks that have chalked up outside with how many men or horses each is carrying. Why are we leaving? In order to reinforce some other sector of the front. Where our new grave will be or when we shall arrive there, nobody knows. And who cares about knowing? Here, there, or elsewhere—it all adds up to the same thing. Our stopping-point will always be the same: some trench or other where some dugout or other will bid us welcome and some "big boys" will turn our blood to ice. All trenches, dugouts, and shells are identical no matter what their location. As we jolt along we remain forever beneath death's irremovable shadow, that black cloud that is suspended continually above us, following the journey, the train, and the living souls within.

I am still extremely touched by the sadness displayed by those kindly village-folk as soon as they heard I was about to leave their region for ever. We received the news last night; it came like a box on the ears, awakening me in the nastiest manner from my seraphic dream. When I read my brother's note telling me to be at Company H.Q. at the crack of dawn because we were pulling up stakes, there must have been so much consternation visible on my face that everyone in the house gathered round me to learn what was going on. I told them the news. They stood there and stared at me for a moment, then began to ask me a thousand and one questions about the transfer. I of course did not know (nor did I wish to know) the answers. We all ate together, hastily, without appetite. Givezo avoided looking at me the whole time. Afterwards, Anjo lighted the large lantern they have for evening chores and began to go through all my shirts and underwear, setting aside the soiled items for the old grandmother, Babo, so that she could lather them up at once, in time for them to be dry by morning. Anjo herself, along with her two sisters-in-law and Givezo, began to darn my socks and to patch my other clothes. We were all sitting on the large open verandah. The night, full of joyful sorrow, was moonless, but a swarm of stars winked their little eyes at us through the plaits of red peppers suspended from the rafters to dry. Everywhere—in the gashed roofing above us; in the stables below, where the buffaloes were shifting about and snorting; in the whole of the plain invisible in the distance—all the crickets were singing their tender, doleful anthem that has neither beginning nor end.

I had seated myself off to one side in the dark, on a rudimentary stool, a circular slab sawn from the trunk of a thick chestnut tree and fixed to three legs whittled with a penknife. The women sat opposite me around the lampstand, mending my linen. As for the men, they smoked for a time, blowing through large holders to send the butts flying into their palms, then lay down on the carpet, dead with fatigue, and began to snore rhythmically the very instant they closed their eyes.

The women's faces were illuminated strangely by the lamplight—from below. Their hands worked away hurriedly, with careful, attentive fingers. Their talk was sparse and monosyllabic. Anjo, who never allowed her feelings to overflow the boundaries of a stern and dignified decorum, did begin a kind of conversation while she sewed, but one that was directed neither to her daughter nor the other women: it was more like a monologue, or else a colloquy between God, herself, and her sons, who were away at the front—who perhaps had already been killed and whose unmourned bones were bleaching away in some ravine.

"Ouh, lele! It was just like this, two summers ago, that I bundled up Giovan's clothes, and Petko's. They'd come from the lower field, from the river, and had just unhitched the wagon. Before they could even put a morsel of bread in their mouths, they were taken from me. And now this foreign gospodin delivered by God into our midst, he is leaving us too. *Zavali ashker,* poor little soldier-boy whose mother is sitting in front of her doorway now with idle hands, patiently awaiting his return. She wakes in sudden fear in the middle of the night and pricks up her ears. Was that the knocker of the front door she thought she had just heard? But it is not your sons, *zavali maiko;* no, my sister, it is not your sons! Ashker, you should take paper and pencil, you should take paper and pencil and write a letter to your sorrowing mother. Tell her, my child, that every mother sits in this same way, stunned and motionless; that we are all waiting with patient endurance for our sons who have been taken from us by war. And tell her, my child, that Anjo, the grieving mother of Giovan and Petko, attended to your clothes and packed them for you all freshly washed and clean and mended. Lele. And tell her to pray to God to send my boys back to me just as I am praying that He may send back her children to knock one day on her door. Because, Gospode, Anjo's heart is filled to the top with grief, is filled and cannot bear any more, lele, cannot bear any more. . . . "

Such, more or less, was the soliloquy voiced by Anjo as she mended my linen. The sound of her colorless, monotonous voice carried placidly into the night. The lamp with its dancing flames covered the walls with large shadows that skipped about and gesticulated vivaciously. The plain sent us its innumerable cricket-songs and the stars leaned over to signal to us between the peppers, winking their silvery eyes. Anjo's voice flowed impassively on, as though she were reciting things devoid of interest, passages taken from a prayerbook or some collection of saints' legends:

"And why should this terrible thing happen? You are living in peace and eating your God-given bread, all in accord with Christ's will, and one day misfortune comes and knocks at your door. Is it our own unknown sins, Gospode, or are we paying for the sins of our fathers? Glory be to Thee, O Lord. What can we know—we worms—about Thy designs? . . . Lele. . . . On which day will my fine lads come back to me as sound and handsome as the day I gave them up? When will they return and bring a smile again to my embittered lips? Ohh! Our visitor is going away again to fight. Zavali ashker! May Thy blessings follow him, Lord, and may he return to his home after Thy wrath has passed over Thy sinful world. May he return with his brother and may their mother welcome them joyfully, just as she welcomes the returning swallows; just as I too shall joyfully welcome my boys Petko and Giovan. . . . Lele. And may some other mother be caring for my two at this very hour just as I am caring for the foreign soldier who is going away, leaving us at the crack of dawn, like the swallows. . . ."

All the while Anjo spoke, her two sisters-in-law listened to her in silence, nodding their heads and sighing occasionally but never interrupting their work. I kept observing Givezo, who sat directly opposite me. She would raise her eyes from time to time—eyes made enormous by the lamp's penumbra—and would look about stealthily in the dark, turning (as though by chance) toward the corner where I was sitting. She struggled to see, but the light was in her eyes and she could not. Her childish bosom was convulsed by a storm that she fought obstinately to control. Every time her eyes commenced to brim with tears, her lashes fluttered ever so rapidly, like the wings of a dying moth, their shadows reaching all the way to her shapely eyebrows, which always contended with each other like two little black snakes when she was upset in this way. Her large mouth grew even more scarlet, and there was a quiver at the corner of her lips the whole time her mother spoke. Suddenly she flung down the shirt she was mending and fled at a run into her room, hiding her face in her arms.

Anjo halted her sewing for a moment. Slowly rotating her jaw, she glanced placidly toward the door that had closed behind the girl. She shook her head slightly, sighing. Then she bent over her work again. The other women followed her glance with theirs, without speaking.

A lump had formed in my throat; I was weeping inwardly, secretly, for my mother. Forcing my voice to remain steady, I said: "Maiko, you shouldn't tear your heart out with your own hands like this—it isn't right."

She neither raised her head nor answered. She simply said in the same colorless voice, as though reciting: "Zavali chupa . . . —poor girl."

I could hear Givezo's sobs in the darkness. I waited a long while, but she emerged again only after I had retired. I asked to be awakened betimes.

At the first lovely gleams of daybreak the following morning I jumped up in surprise. A shower of green hazelnuts thrown directly at my face had awakened me from the deep and uneasy slumber that had finally overcome me in the small hours. At the same time I saw Givezo's eyes peeking around the half-opened door, whereupon another fistful of hazelnuts flew directly at me. Her entire physiognomy was laughing because of my initial fright, her teeth gleaming in their whiteness like newly fallen hail. She closed the door again with a bang and fled, like some vision in a dream.

Dressing myself quickly, I went out into the yard where I found her waiting for me as usual with the woven towel thrown over her shoulder and the copper *briki* in her hand, ready to pour out water for me to wash up. But now she displayed not the slightest sign of playfulness or joy. On the contrary, she was extremely serious.

"Dobro outro, gospodine," she said, refusing to lift her eyes from the ground.

"Good morning, Givezo."

She maintained this silence and melancholy reserve while she poured for me. Then, attempting to lend a cheerful tone to her voice, she suddenly said:

"It seems you're going to leave us, gospodine. . . ."

Her voice trembled although she was struggling to hold it steady.

"Yes, Givezo, I am going to leave you."

Silence. Afterwards, again in a choked-up voice:

". . . You might be killed. . . ."

"'Every soldier takes that chance, Givezo."

"But *you*—you won't be killed, gospodine."

"Thank you, Givezo. That's the way I've planned it, too."

Another pause.

"Will you always remember us, wherever you are?"

"'I shall always remember you, all of you, wherever I am."

"Always? Always?"

"Always."

Then another pause, followed by a hesitant, almost fearful question:

"And Givezo . . . ? Will you remember Givezo, gospodine?"

"I shall remember her as a sister and bless her, until my dying day."

Pause. Then a sudden outburst.

"Don't leave, gospodine! Don't leave!"

I stared at her, astonished. Her voice was strange now; it had lost all its childishness and had become the heartbroken voice of a fully grown, wounded woman.

"Don't leave, gospodine. . . ."

She was crying tranquilly, without sobs, the tears flowing from her eyes and rolling slowly down her cheeks to the corners of her lips, where they quivered like leaves. I wanted to tell her that I understood, that no, it was impossible for me to feel anything for her except brotherly love and tender gratitude, that the kind of love she sought from me I had already bestowed elsewhere, very far away, beyond plains, mountains, and seas. I wanted to tell her that if I accepted from her a portion larger than I was now accepting, this would force me to steal from the meager hoard that belonged to Another—to Another who was burning feverishly in her solitude with a love as grave as an illness and as strong as death.

But Givezo had fled from my presence at a run, leaving the copper *briki* on the ground.

I never saw her again, not even when I bade farewell to all these goodly folk whose gracious home I was leaving forever (forever! forever!), a home that for so many days had provided a happy anchorage for the storm-lashed dinghy of my life. I even pretended not to notice her absence, because I saw that nobody was saying a word about her to me. Instead, I simply took Anjo's two little girls into my arms and covered their tiny faces with kisses and tears.

Anjo—tall, motionless and solemn—remained in the entranceway until I turned a corner and was lost to her maternal sight.

At the outskirts of the village, near a wine-shop, I heard shouts, running, a patrol. I approached. Giorghalas was walloping Jacob again. In another of his drunken fits he had chanced upon the Jew and was wiping up the ground with him.

"Why did you Jews crucify our Lord, you bloody pimp? Why did you crucify him? Why? . . ."

* * *

Now, squashed between two sackfuls of bandoleers inside this sealed, windowless wagon that took us on like a load of freight, I can hear the storm outside as it whips against the boards of one side-wall and the roof. I can hear the train's roar as it thrusts its iron chest through the thick mass of night lying on its tracks. Where is it taking us? We do not know; neither does it. Its destination, as well as ours, is known by someone else. The wheels call out with their iron pulse: "Further-on, further-on; further-on!"—an indeterminate answer that includes all places, all trenches, all positions. Even the grave. Even non-existence or eternal bliss. "Further-on, further-on!" But all of us sense something else as well: that shadow, the shadow of death that accompanies us extended over the top of the train. Death's cloud is racing along above the wagons without a sound, without the slightest noise, racing through the dark with identical swiftness.

A prayer as ardent as fire is rising into the rain and darkness from the purest corner of my soul. I am praying for the happiness of that kindly, simple peasant home that gave me repose and love so open-handedly. Oh, I wish there were a God in heaven, if only to hear my prayer. If there were, I would forgive Him all the miseries that so pitilessly (with His sufferance) lash mankind.

Everywhere around me my companions are smoking, spitting, farting, cursing, and snoring, each attempting to snuggle comfortably between the legs of the next. The train drags itself along, howling angrily in the night; the storm continues to lash the wagon with thousands of strokes—while I, who have neither belief nor hope, offer up cowardly prayers.

"God—please!—Giovan and Petko, of all the millions of enemy soldiers, please don't let them be killed!"

The wheels push through the viscous night, crying out more rapidly now: "Further-on . . . , further-on . . . , further-on . . ."

46

In the Mud

*H*ere we are again, rolling about in the hopper of the blood-red mill! We had escaped the millstone for a few days like so many wheat-grains caught in the crannies. But along came the miller's broom, swept us up afresh, and tossed us back into the hopper. We are in the trenches again, in the front line of a sector far more difficult and harsh than the one we left behind. We don't even have any mountains opposite us now to relieve our minds with their refreshing vegetation and the various movements of the enemy line. Nor do we have the ever-murmuring Dragor in the vicinity to make our souls weep with that inscrutable song of eternity and youthful derring-do that it hums in the blackness of night.

Everything here is stunted and oozing; everything crawls dankly along the ground. The gray hills squat like huge terrified tortoises that wish to burrow into the mud and hide. The draggle-tailed sky pulls its muddied backside through the soil; no, it is not the sky any longer, it is the sooty ceiling of a huge dugout continually dripping. The sun has failed to appear for an entire week. Yet you cannot say that rain has been falling. Rather, the rain-pregnant clouds, as sluggish as monsters in the final hours before parturition, have descended and seated themselves above us. We move and breathe inside a chaotic mass of water vapor that has rendered the air as murky as a steamed-over window-pane. "And the earth was without form and void, and a spirit moved over the deep." Sticking to everything like grease is a nauseating humidity that saturates our clothing, penetrates inside the collar and cuffs, and touches our bodies, covering them most unpleasantly with permanent goose-pimples. It drenches the soul as well, buries it beneath a delicate layer of lugubrious thoughts, as though beneath mildew. I still have not experienced the sensation of being dry for one whole hour at a time. The wetness is everywhere. A watery dust flies through the air and settles like sweat on our helmets. It infiltrates our hair, rusts our weapons, sits like hoar-frost on the woolen fibers of our khakis. It even penetrates the dugouts and saturates our blankets.

The trenches here are so extremely deep that you can stretch to your full height when you walk in them. Visible above you is nothing but a long narrow strip of sky. My dugout is solid, a spacious chamber constructed with obstinacy and patience three fathoms beneath the trench's deck. The oaken timbers— entire tree-trunks—line even the bulkheads. They support the crossbeams of the roof and are packed in so densely that each seems welded to the next. Seeing them hold up so many tons of soil and rocks above us, I caress their craggy bark upon which men of every race in the whole wide world have carved names and slogans with penknives or bayonets. I feel the protective presence of these trunks around me as though they were living creatures faithfully and heroically arching their strong backs in order to preserve me. It must have been from wood such as this that my ancestors chiseled their first idols. And it was from inside such an oak, a sacred oak, that the Dodonean oracle proclaimed its wishes and advice.

After the bright interval of Velušino and despite the fact that we are all experienced veterans with hides weathered by the hardships of the trenches, we seem to be starting life all over again from the beginning—a miserable, ugly existence fit for dogs. When we descended the muddy steps, the oppression of life underground tore at our hearts despite our familiarity with it— perhaps because of our familiarity. In each of us the old struggle began anew. Man resists with his full humanity for as long as he can; a desperate denial issues from all his senses, mental faculties and nerves. But this accomplishes nothing. The established order of things in the trenches is determined by certain blind and all-powerful laws that regulate subterranean existence during wartime. The prevailing element here is dirt. This has its own dark hue, its own smell, its own internal, well-organized life. And it follows its own special regimen, which is entirely different on the one hand from that which legislates life in the ocean and, on the other, from that which legislates life on the earth's surface and also in the air.

Yesterday as I was digging into the wall next to the sentry box in order to carve out a niche for hand grenades, my pick struck a long worm that had been dwelling unsuspectingly inside a clod of earth. The air suddenly encircling its naked body shocked it greatly. It was red and elastic. The blow cleaved it in two in the middle, making one half curl into a ball, bitten with sudden pain, while the other half halted its toilsome march and turned back the part that presumably is the head in order to comprehend what had happened to the rest of it. The wounded end dragged along cumbrously, swollen from the injury. The worm looked to the right, to the left, then began to advance with difficulty and to bury itself slowly in the soil's dark kingdom, having abandoned the other half of its body, which continued to writhe for a long while as it struggled to die.

I came to realize that here, beneath the surface, worms are the proprietors, the natural inhabitants, and that we humans are intruders violating their sanctuary. The worms themselves of course fail to recognize this. But when it comes to true self-knowledge, can human beings do any better?

What I sensed with ever-increasing clarity was that the worm constitutes the legitimate authority here and we the illegitimate. As intruders, we would eventually have to submit. . . . And so we did, once again. What else could we do? And now, just as before, we belong to that most improbable of communities, the commonwealth of underground creatures. We are citizens of the trenches. With each passing day, our environment overpowers and assimilates us all the more. The trenches are gradually digesting and liquefying us, as though they were a long, endless intestine. The dirt spreads its hue over our faces and hands, invades the sense of smell, becomes familiar to the touch. Then, little by little, it insinuates its stagnant breath into the human soul. Boredom—a formless, suffocating element, a grayish heap of combed-out cotton—arrives again and seats itself on top of our bodies and spirits. The mind, all embroiled within, begins to grow confused; it moans and writhes from asphyxia.

Nobody on the outside is aware of this agony. The struggle is unequal, unnatural. In the end you admit defeat arid surrender. Then comes the day when filth, lice, and weary disgust enter from all sides and pillage you. On that day the trench claims you as its own. The worm ceases to startle you or to be startled. The mouse enters your pack and gnaws at hard tack. You hear it beneath your cheek (because the pack serves as your pillow); you bang on the pack with your hand, not to kill the mouse but simply to drive it away so that you can enjoy a few winks of sleep.

The other night a lance-corporal from Lemnos emitted a furious yell that made all the other men in his dugout jump up and reach for their guns. It was nothing—just a mouse chewing at his big toe. Everyone was annoyed with him; they threw the blame on him for sleeping without his boots. On another night Fikos, the orderly, woke up with half of his hair shorn away. At first the men treated this as a nasty practical joke; afterwards they realized that his head had been shaved by mice because he had gone to sleep beneath the lamp. The margarine had dripped down from the wick and congealed in his hair. Ever since that night, he has slept wearing not only his forage cap, but also the helmet on top.

Your soul moves sluggishly in this inert, stagnant horror, like a tortoise in slime. Fatigue caused by idleness: this is the consumption that forces the soul to rot and disintegrate until finally it sinks into an unnatural lethargy. Nothing is of interest any longer. This situation very often begets madness, or distraught heroism. On the other hand, just as we begin to say "The soul is dead," a spark appears for a moment and suddenly shoots out of our lackluster eyes like a speeding arrow of light. This happens in the case of a detonation, or of an envelope from home that is being torn open with trembling fingers. Sometimes nothing more is required than some heartfelt words or an old folksong.

This is communication trench "Alpha bis." Across from us, very near, indeed just a pistol-shot away, is an ugly yellow hillock with some square patches on its ridge, most likely old meadows that are now uncultivated and neglected, ploughed only by shells. Yet they decorate this Bulgarian mound in a strange way and make its official name all the more appropriate.

"The Turtle," that fortress dense with machine-gun emplacements and strong bomb-proof shelters—this is the hill that our captain is pointing out to me now on the map of our sector.

The Turtle reposes peacefully in the mud, all hunched over and ugly beneath its mottled shell. It does not bother us, and we are under orders not to bother it. This peculiar armistice has already lasted two months. One night The Turtle woke up and tossed some five or six hundred rifle grenades at Alpha bis. A few men were killed; we buried them the same night in *boyau* no.4, out beyond the latrine. The ground there still gives way beneath one's boots, and every so often the sergeant-major orders soil to be thrown over the area to level off the surface, which continues to subside and become pitted. Our forces bombarded the enemy in reprisal. The heavy artillery batteries pounded the Turtle for three hours, isolating its garrison with a fire barrage so that no one could escape. And no one did.

After that slaughter, which proved fruitless because operations from now on will take place only when a push forward by the entire line is involved, a kind of peace was concluded between Alpha bis and the Turtle. Both sides have remained vigilant, cautious, and prepared, but neither bothers the other. We frequently see the Bulgarians assembling at mealtime. Their helmets are visible, and quite often we can even glimpse some darkish mess-tins in the distance.

My dugout is fully occupied now. Living there with me are three Tsesmelian fishermen, a truck driver from Mytilene, and a young university student who volunteered for service. I enjoy listening to the fishermen. They are all from the same village and have their private affairs that do not interest me, but I am delighted when they begin to talk about caiques, fish, and the sea. At such times I shut my eyes and discern passing before me in the darkness an endless succession of the Aegean's blue waves, together with gulls and sails. On and on they come, singing. And there goes a Tsesmelian trawler as well, with a painted mermaid on its prow and a cherry-colored sash beneath the gunwale.

One night the young university student began pounding his knees and weeping hysterically, his eyelids squeezed tightly shut. We hurried to his side to help him. Continually pounding his knees with a rhythmic beat, he repeated in a sobbing voice:

"Let something happen at last, let something happen at last, let something happen at last!"

Then he opened his eyes and stopped blubbering. But he continued to fix us with an abstracted gaze and to repeat as before, monotonously, though in a lower voice now:

"Let something happen at last, let something happen at last!"

When he ceased doing this as well and became completely silent, that was the worst of all. He refused to speak, to answer questions, to eat. They took him away to the hospital and he still has not returned. No one knows what became of this boy with the shaken mind.

His area, the spot in the corner where he curled up to sleep, remained vacant for a time. We used to turn and stare at it, our eyes converging on a tiny Madonna that he had glued to one of the timbers. We would look at each other, then turn away without exchanging a word. But recently they brought us someone else to take his place—a peasant who uses foul language, whines, and never stops smoking a loathsome brand of French tobacco. But he is tough and sure of himself when it comes to work.

It has been raining incessantly now for three days. The trench has become a channel in which the mud flows like must-jelly, squeezing into the dugouts and covering everything with filth. We have a never-ending job to keep things clean. Opposite us, the Turtle swims in its own yellow mud.

* * *

On our island, too, at this time of year—autumn—there is considerable rain. I remember the many occasions when we enjoyed those downpours together, standing behind the windows of your tidy little sitting room. You used to lean your cheek against the cool glass, and I would admire your sensitive, animated profile, so pure and delicate yet at the same time so solid, just like an ancient medallion. Outside, the down-sloping lane with its cobbles of bluish marble had turned instantaneously into a clattering brook carrying tin cans and other trash downstream. In the villages, where they still have flat roofs of packed soil, the "rolling" takes place during this season. The housewives climb up onto the roof as soon as the weather clears and with a good firm kick set going the marble roller (the "cylinder" as they call it) in order to pack down the soil and keep the roof from leaking. If you are inside at this time you become aware of a terrible racket coming through the ceiling. When I was tiny and heard the skies thundering away in wintertime, I used to ask Granny (trying to conceal my fright) what was happening to produce such a fracas. And she always explained with the air of someone possessing information of the most unimpeachable reliability:

"God, my child, is rolling the roof of heaven so it won't leak onto his head now that a storm is brewing."

47

"A Voice Has Been Silenced"

*D*o you remember Lilitta, the poor invalid confined to a trundle bed by that horrible disease of the spine? How beautiful she was—just like an angel. And how patiently she accepted her disability. She used to smile at us as though seeking our forgiveness. (Forgiveness for what, her beauty or her illness?) You adored her so much that you refused to leave her side to go to the mountains or the seashore with the other girls. Once you said to me, "I feel guilty just because I have a sound body and can walk and climb and dance." Tears were quivering in your eyes.

One winter evening we were posing riddles to keep her entertained. Cousin Angelica began this one: "A thing that sings at night . . . ," whereupon Lilitta, who had been listening rather absent-mindedly, interrupted her and announced triumphantly:

"A turtle!"

I remember how we all burst out laughing, how we roared until the tears flowed from our eyes—from Lilitta's first and foremost.

I wish I could be in the same cozy room right now, together with the whole of our little confraternity—you, Angelica, Marika, and of course our exquisite, cherubic Lilitta. If I were there, I would give her the most improbable justification for her answer. Yes, the thing that sings at night is indeed the Turtle! . . . But I had better start from the beginning. . . .

All of a sudden the weather became summerlike. We have no calendars here, and no one worries about dates. I suppose, however, that we must have been going through "Saint Demetrius's time" in late October: our Indian summer.

The night was dark with only a few stars in the sky, but the air had a pleasant feel, and some gentle gusts conveyed a lovely scent from the distance (where from, I wonder): something like the breath of flowers, a refined aroma as though from acacias, although this was hardly possible. As usual in our sector, there was not a single rocket, shell-burst, or machine-gun report. The Turtle, its insignificant hump submerged in the refreshing darkness, was not even visible.

How beautiful everything was! One by one, two by two, all those not on duty began to stick their noses out of the dugouts. Without talking or making the slightest sound, they climbed onto the parapet or stood on sandbags all in a row, and poked out their heads to look. Sighing, they inhaled the sweet night. Anyone who lighted a cigarette leaned over and smoked it inside his helmet or in the hole where the grenade launcher fastens to the barrel. Everyone was listening to those mysterious whisperings, those sounds that seem to come from distant foliage or from cascading waters and that the night transports to us from the sky, from seas, or from the far corners of the earth.

Suddenly in the midst of this tranquillity there came a song. It issued from the darkness, from nearby, directly across the way. It was the Turtle: singing!

At first the voices of two pipes leaped into the air. They mounted just so far on the scale of sounds, then halted and balanced timorously in mid-air as though wishing to find something to catch hold of. For a moment they fluttered like chicks setting out for the first time on new-fledged wings. Then, as though steady now in their flight, the two notes rose as a united pair, straight up and parallel. They seemed to be taking off for the stars, but this was not the case. Ceasing to climb further, they halted and there on high commenced to pursue one another playfully, full of svelte coquetry and pouting airs. The first tone wrapped itself around the other like a vine and was caressed in turn; then, after tracing out some undulating revolutions, it skipped back again to its starting place.

Ağ, aman aman, nar gibi,
nar gibi, memeleri kar gibi.

The voice was a deeply masculine one, as warm and tender as the voices of the pipes. These it allowed to fill one's heart for a time with their amorous play; then, after the atmosphere had become saturated with nightingales' sighs, it shot its own arrow into the pure air. Now the pipes were summoning the song, escorting it, or clearing a path while it undulated with triumphant freedom, full of passion and supplication:

> *Ah, aman aman, like pomegranates,*
> *like pomegranates are her breasts,*
> *and like snow.*

The masculine voice sang this song that clove our hearts in twain; then the two pipes took it up and sang it again. Embroidering it with poppies, they sang it still once more. Afterwards the virile voice joined in afresh, and all three, arm-in-arm, sang it together.

Coming as we did from Lesvos or Asia Minor, we were all able to understand the words more or less, and we repeated them over and over in our hearts. When the player finished and allowed the air to escape from his musical sack, a flock of wee sounds vented from the holes of the pipes and traveled as far as our lines. We had remained motionless within the magical spell that bound us to the parapet. The notes came right up to us, and then expired amid the blades of yellowed grass like lovesick butterflies.

We waited for the miracle to recommence, waited some more. . . . Nothing. That was all. One by one, two by two, the men retired to their burrows. Most did not speak; a few did, but in subdued tones.

When we had assembled again in the dugout and had carefully blocked its ingress with the canvas sheet so that no glimmer of light could escape outside, we ignited the four wicks in the margarine-filled box that served us as a lamp. Able now to see one another, we discovered that each man was squeezed into his corner with his knees up and his arms twisted pretzel-like around his shins. Escaping frequently from every eye was that spark that signifies the undying soul. The way the men were sighing, you would have thought they wanted to pick a fight with someone. That newcomer, the peasant, removed a pinch of execrable tobacco from his cartridge-pouch, rubbed it well in the hollow of his palm, and began to roll a cigarette. The others watched him. No sooner would he succeed in making the roll stick together at one end with his saliva than it would come unglued at the other. Finally he produced something like a badly stuffed sausage. His eyes enflamed, he knelt to light it at the lamp.

"Damn those Frenchmen," he grumbled maliciously; "the only thing you can do with this stuff is whittle pegs out of it."

As an answer, Fotolias, the fisherman, said:

"My god, how that bastard could sing! What feeling, eh? By Saint Nicholas, he almost had me blubbering."

And the moment he said this, his eyes did indeed brim with tears.

"See?"

The same thing happened on the following evening. Then nothing for two nights running. On the third: there he was again, the singer with his bagpipe! This was a joy that we all awaited anxiously. After the second time, the sergeant-major gave one of the patrols a piece of cardboard on which was written in large Roman characters: "Aşk olsun, meraklı kardaş!" (Bravo, virtuoso comrade!) Waiting until complete darkness had fallen, the patrol set out, went up to the Bulgarian barbed wire, and hung it there so that the enemy sentries might find it in the morning.

Each day, hoping that we would hear him again, we all waited impatiently for evening to come. And whenever he started up, we all felt happy —that is, happily sad.

The captain began to invite colleagues from other trenches to come and listen. The major arrived, and one night even the colonel picked himself up and came as well. On that night, however, the singer was not heard. But he sang again on the following evening, with the result that all of us, for yet one more time, were able to feel our stony hearts being softened by the gentle rainfall of kindness that drizzled down upon them.

One evening we received a strict set of commands. With the exception of those on duty, no one was to stick his nose out of the dugout. No one was to undo his cartridge pouches or garrison belt. Gas masks affixed to belts. Weapons in order, cartridges clean. Helmet and boots to be worn at all times. Guns between our legs when we slept.

No one found this surprising. It was not the first time we had received such commands for strict preparedness, nor the second. Every so often a Bulgarian deserter or our own reconnaissance brought us word of a surprise attack being planned across the way. Thus we slept with one eye open, in sitting posture leaning against our packs, the lamp extinguished. In this manner, we waited for the Turtle to sing.

It was a truly summer-like night as delicious as one could wish, with a sky outside all mauve and star-embroidered, like a vestment. As for rifle shots, grenades, machine-gunning—nothing. And then, in the midst of this serenity, there he was once more: the singer with his bagpipe!

The double melody welled up from the pipes as from a fountain with twin jets. Next came the deep voice, that male lovesick voice so desperately enamored.

"Listen!"

The men said this in a whisper. Then, guarding their silence, they uncovered the ingress by raising the canvas sheet, so that the words and music could enter.

But suddenly everyone stared agonizedly into the darkness. A terrific cannonade from a thousand mouths had opened up all at once. It came from our side, from the French batteries that were covering us from the ravine. The low hills behind us howled and shook; the air rasped as shells ripped it in two. An innumerable pack of wild beasts passed darkly across the sky in a thick invisible swarm and bore directly down upon the singing Turtle. All sounds coalesced; whizzes and bangs became the incessant multisonous thunder of a heaven transformed into a torrent rushing clangorously in mid-air. You seemed to be locked inside a bronze drum being pounded on all sides by iron cudgels.

This lasted a short while, scarcely half an hour. Then the din subsided. The cannons fell silent on both sides and hand grenades could be heard bursting in the distance, together with seething fusillades. But what dominated everything was the cackling of the machine-guns. These are the most chilling of all because they operate with the imperturbable rhythm of mechanized slaughter.

I never heard any further details about that night. Nor did anything significant happen on the succeeding days we had Alpha bis in our keep. The only exception was the constant illumination we saw around the Turtle's base on the first few nights. The Bulgarian sentries, still jumpy, kept sending up flares every time they heard the slightest noise. Then this stopped too.

But the song? Gone. Never heard again. The song across the way has been killed, dear Lilitta; the Turtle sings no more. We went out to the parapet so many times. Whenever the constellations began to sail over the trenches and the nocturnal weather was perfumed with kindness, we all lined up and waited. We conversed with each other in hushed tones as though in church, and waited. But we never heard the song again. . . . I am thinking now of that young university student pounding his fists rhythmically on his knees:

"Let something happen at last, let something happen at last!"

I am speaking to him in my thoughts:

"Something has happened, dear comrade. Yes, something has happened at last."

"What?" his innocent eyes inquire.

"A voice has been silenced . . ."

48

The Two Heroes

I debated a great deal before deciding to write to you about what happened to me the other night. I feel splattered with filth from head to toe. I am covered with shame and disgust, wrapped in it as in the mud that has remained caked upon my clothes for so many days. If it were a question of sending these notebooks to you now, immediately, I never would have included the part I am writing at present. But I have no idea when this war will end (will it ever end?!) or how many of these installments I shall eventually "liquidate." It might even enter my mind sometime to tear up the whole lot, or to heave them into some old abandoned dugout as a legacy for the wild beasts that will one day claim our shelter as their den. These blasted papers have begun to take up too much room in my pack. Maybe I shall even roll them up and stuff them inside the casing of a .15 shell, inscribing on the bronze with a nail, in great big striking letters: "The true story of a soldier." Because sometime, surely sometime, this evil crisis that the conscience of humanity is experiencing will dwindle away— this crisis that leads those who have seen war to produce counterfeit versions of it in various genres of printed matter, out of fear, fanaticism, or vainglorious conceit. When the end does come, perhaps at that time— sometime—the voice of a plain soldier will emerge into the light of day, a voice that will possess the courage to tell the whole truth without fear of court-martial or defamation, because it will be the voice of a corpse. The truth about war harms many people—all sorts of merchants, speculators, and "professional heroes" (as Dimitratos likes to call them). It is incredible, for example, what happens with awards for valor. All those various colored ribbons you see so many soldiers pin on their tunics: surely they make a ludicrous impression on any well-balanced man. Just think—each of those ribbons cries out on behalf of its bearer: "I am brave; I am really and truly ferocious." Tell me, can a serious person walk around with labels like that on his tunic? But you must possess close, first-hand experience of this improbable life so full of despicable baseness and pseudo-chivalry if you want to see what role this dumb-show plays in a multitude of fine upstanding men—grown-up, settled characters with a whole armful of mustache beneath their noses. They forge documents and are court-martialed; they become flatterers, liars, footstools for their superiors, all in order to win one more such infantile gimcrack. Military society is an alien, incredible world that lives and operates according to its own values, its own fantastic illusions. It is these that govern existence here in the trenches, govern it with the power of a biological law.

Take Lance-corporal Dimitratos for example—Dimitratos, George, son of Antipas, who came to us from the Serres Division and was attached to our company. He sticks close to me all the time, and is a never-ending source of revelation. Well, everyone stares goggle-eyed at Dimitratos because he has the War Cross. To be sure, this character is a first-class rascal, maybe rotten to the core as well, or really loose in his rocker. Nevertheless I like the tough cynicism he employs as a means of confronting life. Sometimes I suspect him of being a sentimentalist in disguise. There are even times when I envy him, because I realize that he possesses a tremendous power that protects him like a cuirass in the face of every unexpected or unforeseen contretemps. I am sure that he has lived through years of great misfortune. He has led me to understand this many times, without ever really elaborating. The details, I suppose, must be very humiliating. But these years have filled him with a first-class hatred and have infused in him an absolute disbelief. Indeed, to tell the truth, a thoroughgoing disbelief the likes of this is well worth the effort. After all, it is one way of escaping moral angst. I would say that an absolute disbelief weighs equally in the scales with a genuine belief.

He is a family man with three sons. Once he wrote his wife the following letter:

"Dear wife: Reservists with four or more children are exempted from trench duty. The first thing you've got to understand is that the trenches are a filthy business surpassing all other filthy businesses. Next, you've got to see about bringing the number of my children up to the required level as quickly as possible. From where I am, don't expect me to send you regular shipments of food for our family. On the other hand, with three kids it's impossible for you to go out and work. You're not at all stale yet, you know, and sooner or later how can you help but succumb, poor girl, and set up shop somewhere or other, eh? But this in itself, you understand, doesn't save me from the 'big boys.' Conclusion: Since the law is so indisputably clear on this point, take heed of what I'm telling you and see that you make me a fourth without delay. I'd rather be a cuckolded volunteer than an involuntary corpse. You go and ask Apostolis the butcher, on my behalf, to help you get yourself knocked up in accordance with that majestic clause 'concerning reservists with four or more dependent offspring, said reservists having been called to active duty in the armed forces. . . .' If Apostolis chances to make things difficult for you—which I scarcely imagine will be the case—you tell him that I once offered him a similar service, without his permission. (It's something I'm confessing to him for the first time.) If he wants to know more, let him go and ask Marigula."

Why did he write this letter? Why did he send it through the military post? Was it to stretch his cynicism to the breaking point? To get out of serving by being thrown in the guardhouse? A mystery. The Censors' Office returned it to the regiment. The regiment called him to defend himself. Dimitratos appeared at the hearing with his War Cross pinned proudly to his tunic. The colonel, who was breathing fire and fury, brandishing the letter in his hand, took one look at the Cross hanging on Dimitratos's chest, and simmered down. He himself still had not won it. All his indignant wrath turned to milk and honey. Dimitratos came back to us with a full pardon and a flattering citation in the Order of the Day, mentioning the War Cross, "which adorns the breast of the aforementioned heroic lance-corporal."

Dimitratos returned to the dugout bursting with laughter. Appropriating half of my cigarettes in the most natural manner and depositing them in his aluminum tobacco tin, he began to deride the colonel mercilessly. Finally he drew a little box out of his pocket and, winking his eye at me, removed the Cross with its ribbon and clasp. Dancing it about playfully in his palm, he said:

"If you give me your word, your word of honor (you of course believe in honor, don't you?), and if you promise me that what I say will remain strictly between the two of us, I will tell you the story of my Cross. Because I'm sick and tired of guffawing about it all to myself, like some madman. O.K.? You're going to burst a gut laughing. Only remember what we said: not a soul must know; mum's the word. You see, I still need this thingumajig for the time being. It's an absolute necessity these days!"

"I give you my word of honor that everything you say will remain strictly between the two of us."

"One more thing. For a whole week you'll make me a donation of all the cognac or bread you have to spare."

"Agreed. . . . Keep in mind, however, that I've already read the story of your decoration as related in the official copy of your regiment's Order of the Day. If I am not mistaken, you deposited this with our company on the morning you joined its forces. That's right, isn't it?"

He rubbed his palms together with glee.

"But that is precisely what's so entertaining. The story I'm about to tell you is the reverse side of the coin."

So he set about relating to me how he won his Cross.

The Bulgarians had attempted an assault in his sector. But the plans had been betrayed to our side in sufficient time by some deserters, enabling the Serres Division to prepare a gala reception for the enemy. They waited for them in the trenches, allowed them to come close, then suddenly let loose a concentrated barrage, a veritable storm of machine-guns, rifle fire, and hand-grenades. They literally mowed them down. When the enemy turned tail, our side launched a counter-attack and began to pursue them hard on their heels. Among the dead was an officer, a German all decked out in a really natty uniform. Dimitratos drew up alongside him, searched him through and through, cleaned out his pockets. When he had terminated this "delousing" (that is what we call it in our trench-language) and was about to leave him, his eye caught something shiny inside the corpse's half-opened mouth.

Dimitratos spread the lips apart with his finger and discovered a whole row of gold teeth. These he wiggled, but they refused to come out. Then he drove the sharp end of his bayonet into the gum to act as a wedge, and began to pound the other end with his canteen in order to dislodge the gold. Well, in the midst of this undertaking he was spotted by a liaison lieutenant who was crawling around on his belly. The lieutenant asked him what he was doing. Dimitratos—caught with his pants down—was at a loss what to say. He just kept waving the empty canteen in bewilderment. (He had managed to lay down the bayonet in good time, but was still cradling the German's head in his arm.) The lieutenant made note of his name and hurried away. When the battle was over he reported the incident to the regiment as he had understood it—whereupon Dimitratos, who had expected to be court-martialed "for despoliation of a corpse," received instead his lance-corporal's stripe and also the War Cross, "for the genuinely Hellenic chivalry that he demonstrated, attempting by means of the contents of his canteen to revive, during the foe's retreat and upon the open battlefield, a wounded enemy officer, and embellishing this deed by means of uncommon modesty in his efforts to conceal this noble and heroic activity from the liaison officer who was interrogating him."

This, then, was the reverse side of the coin: the true history of the decoration and half-stripe by which my worthy comrade and colleague Dimitratos, George, son of Antipas was—and still is—honored . . . .

Here I've sat and recounted so very much about Dimitratos, without uttering a word so far about myself—that is, about what I had intended to write when I started today's manuscript. I believe that my pencil is roaming inside other people's stories on purpose, hoping to give the slip to the incident that I originally set out to expound. But let's proceed. Unless I tell you all about it, my swelling heart will never find relief.

To come to the point: This morning I was recommended for a second stripe and guaranteed the War Cross! In the whole company there is only one other man who has it; from now on Dimitratos and I are mates. The recommendation is already in. This important fact was made known to me through the company's Order of the Day, and my poor captain imagined he was endowing me with the whole wide world when he announced it. He turned red as a beet with pleasure and started biting his mustache and smiling, full of pride. He was so extraordinarily happy, I decided not to deprive him of his illusions.

To make a long story short, here is how this strange business happened: The night before last I was patrol leader from one to three a. m. It was so dark, you couldn't see the nose in front of your face. We kept slipping on the damp soil, we tumbled headlong into ditches and tripped on rough ground—all without breathing a single word. Sprains and deep lacerations are of no account when you are patrolling on a pitch-dark night outside your own barbed wire. On the contrary, it is crucially important that you manage to gulp down every cry of pain. When you slip, you are well advised to protect not your head, but the scabbard of your bayonet and the bolt of your gun, either of which might betray you by striking a stone and hence making a noise. The slightest little thump, you understand, is all it takes to reveal you to the Bulgarian hunters who are crawling along on their bellies in the thick darkness and trying to ambush you. The sky was like the soot-covered lid of a cook-pot; you could feel it touching your helmet. It took me great pains to keep the patrol together; I had to struggle at this with all my might. Though we were almost touching noses, one man could not make out the next. As a recognition signal to prevent us from losing each other, I had assigned them three light taps with the fingernail upon the cartridge belt. Every so often I would stop, tap out the signal, and wait to hear it repeated in the darkness, as many times as there were men in the patrol. It took considerable effort just to move forward. Our boots stuck to the ground, or slipped. The mud, mixed with bits of hay, loaded itself by the kilo onto our soles, the weight often becoming so considerable that we had to drive our rifle-butts into the soil in order to pull loose our unbudgeable feet.

Whenever a rocket soared, we halted and stretched out prone in the mud. The illumination blazed with a dull, pearly hue in the mold-encrusted darkness, then branched into long pale fingers of light that penetrated the mist and caused the shrubs to cast slowly swaying shadows. It was as though a soot-covered lantern were wandering noiselessly in mid-air or proceeding at a slow, melancholic pace through an enormous low-ceilinged cellar full of many years' accumulation of mold and dampness.

This is what it's like out in the open between the two lines when the humid night is as oozy as cuttlefish ink, when the murk is so thick that you have to push it away with your chest, and you are on patrol from one in the morning until three. Your heart is in your mouth as you crawl along in this cellar that you know is inhabited by slippery scorpions lying in wait with raised stingers, and by huge spiders suspended in invisible webs, like knots of green poison. Little by little a mute dread penetrates your heart; icy needles graze their points against your shivering bones. You stir inside this death-cellar as in a nightmare. Your eyes are tightly bound with the black blindfold of darkness and you grope your way haphazardly, playing a tragic game of blind-man's-buff. (Who are you trying to catch? Death?) The bottom of your boot acquires something like its own sense of touch. You advance your foot with deliberate precaution, ever so slowly—you might be stepping over a void. Trembling lest you lost your orientation, which would mean certain death or capture, you move forward blindly. You perk up your ears (and your eyes as well, though it makes not the slightest difference whether they are opened or closed). Your whole being becomes an auditory receptor as you toil to detect each and every sound: a rustle, a footstep, the stirring of a blade of grass. If someone could observe your eyes, he would see them distended with fright, filled with darkness and anguish, staring without discerning. A wild boar suddenly scrapes against the entanglements at some point; they jangle, and your heart skips a beat. Your senses detect sounds that emanate from your imagination. The rockets' glare pours into your veins, congealing your blood. Your hand moves of its own accord and fingers your bayonet, which is ready to pierce someone's breast or to plunge into someone's belly, and your palm rests on the heavy sack of hand grenades that continually presses down upon your stomach. From head to toe you are covered with mud. Your tongue can taste it between your teeth; you feel it glued to your entire face like a mask. You are prepared to be mercilessly killed by some stranger or to slaughter him yourself the moment his bulk emerges from the darkness and butts against you, despite the fact that the two of you have never met, have never seen one another long enough to develop a mutual hatred, man for man.

Suddenly a twig snaps; a foot stumbles; one of your comrades rolls to the ground; a breechblock becomes disengaged and falls open with a dry crack. This makes the ensuing silence all the more desperate and intense.

You are surrounded by a black chaos, a mute sea devoid of waves or voices. You sense that something terrible is going to happen, and then your heart begins to throb beneath your greatcoat, your finger binds itself nervously to the little ring of the hand-grenade, your fist clenches your rifle. You wait, saying to yourself: "Please God, whatever is going to happen, let it happen and be done with, so that this torture may cease." But the torture endures for hours on end, hours whose savagery you will never again experience as long as you live.

All things, however, draw to a close, even the hours of patrol-duty. It became necessary for us to return to the trench so that I could submit my report. We started back. We must have been no more than about twenty meters from our lines when, out of the absolute silence came the sharp, whining call of an owl. My men halted automatically, though I had given no command.

Soon there was another call, this time further away:

"Cou-cou-va-ou!"

I tapped our signal on my cartridge belt and it was returned to me in the darkness by all my comrades. The entire patrol was near me. I commanded one of the men to go to the ingress of the barbed wire and act as guide for the patrol-leader who was to replace us; also to tell the sentries nearby to be sure to send up a flare at the first report of a rifle. I had the men lie down parallel to the line of the trench, distancing them one from the next in such a manner that no unknown person could pass between any two of them without betraying his presence. Then I lay down myself.

I was certain, as were all the rest, that these "owls" were Bulgarians communicating with one another. It was not the first time they had used the call of a night bird as a signal. Suddenly, at this point, my mind began to work clearly and intensely in the strangest of ways. It was as though someone else were intoning his opinions and commands into my ear and I were obediently listening to them, fully prepared to act in accordance with them in every respect. The first owl, the voice told me, was the Bulgarian infantryman who had scented our patrol. He had been following close behind us and had notified his comrades the moment he perceived that the time had come for a change and we were withdrawing. They, in turn, had replied in the owl's voice, "Fine, here we come." The conclusion drawn by this stranger whispering in my ear was as follows (the speaker was the patrol-leader in me, the corporal, the helmsman):

"The darkness is such that if you ambush them, your own men might kill each other. If you inform your artillery to fire at this ground that is so close to your own lines, once more you will only hurt yourselves. Let them come close, therefore, and then make a spot decision what to do, depending on their numbers. If they are few, capture some or kill them with your bayonets while they are scattered, one by one, separately. If they are the first to attack, let the nearby sentries light a rocket so that you can see where to fire and to toss your grenades."

This is what the stranger, the patrol-leader, whispered into my ear. Apart from him now, nothing else existed.

Soon a gentle drizzle began, a rain so fine that the drops made no sound as they hit the soil. They were just freezing pins pecking at our hides and stinging our cheeks and hands. My brain, working with a cold and well-ordered clarity, was taking into account even the most infinitesimal of probabilities and was examining every possible situation. Now that I am writing all this down, the thing that especially impresses me is this: How could the "human being" inside me have disappeared so completely, leaving only the patrol leader and warrior behind?

I have no idea how much time we spent waiting in this way. I could hear my heartbeats as though they were outside my coat. The rain continued to fall upon me, silently. . . . Then I became aware of a rustling, as though someone were dragging a bundle of clothes with utmost care. Stopping, then starting again, it moved toward me, coming closer and closer. It was something that kept hesitating, taking care, listening—after which it continued to advance. When it couldn't have been more than six meters away, I tapped out the three beats with my fingernail, just loudly enough so that the man or "thing" that was coming could hear. It stopped instantly and did not reply. Clearly then, this was an enemy. It stayed in place for a long time, without moving, so long that I began to wonder if I had made a mistake. Certainly not! Soon it started to crawl again, with increased caution. It moved with such extreme slowness that doubtlessly no one beside myself could hear the muffled stirring. Nevertheless, I felt over the whole surface of my body that "he" was drawing closer; my very skin was able now to feel—"hearingly." My pounding heartbeats seemed to resound throughout my entire body, down to the tips of my extremities. So loud and ubiquitous were they as they rang in my ears, I was afraid that "he" might hear them, too. Yet this did not prevent me from registering every motion he made, even the tiniest alteration of position.

At this point I was nothing but an intricate super-sensitive ear planted in the mud like a colossal mushroom—an ear listening in fright, a heart thrusting punches into my chest, a hand clenching the naked steel of my bayonet. "He" was directly next to me now. As he slid along, the edge of his trench coat grazed my boot for an instant and then withdrew at once, abruptly. Horror raced like an electric current from my foot to the very top of my head, beneath my helmet. The moment "he" recoiled from the touch of my boot, in that same moment I drove the point of my bayonet into his dark bulk. All this happened in the selfsame instant, simultaneously, and in a manner completely automatic. I plunged it in again, and again, four times in all, until I heard a raucous gurgle, as from muddy water sluicing from a narrow gate and seething with foam. You can never imagine how easily a bayonet enters human flesh; it might just as well be piercing a sackful of yogurt. I found a little resistance only the third time, the blade entering askew. Seeing that "he" was completely inert now, I felt a chill clutch at my heart. I had to lock my jaws together to stifle the huge cry that was emerging from my breast. Afterwards came a flash and the curt thud of a rifle; then other bullets whizzed by, though I did not hear the reports. A grenade burst with a heavy roar, a piece of its shrapnel passing "ffrrrn" right next to my ear. At this same time the rocket was glaring overhead and I saw four shadows racing toward the Bulgarian lines. Several of my men rushed after them, but I called them back. We returned to the trench with the dead man's body and with one prisoner who had been wounded. Their identification-tags and whatever papers they had on them were duly examined. When I saw that neither of them was called Petko or Giovan, despite the commonness of those names, a whole mountain was lifted from my chest.

It was following all this that the recommendation went in for me to receive a sergeant's chevron and the War Cross. The company's Order of the Day described me as "a model of cool-headed valor and the very pattern, so rarely found, of heroic leadership." All because I had tremblingly stabbed a man in the dark, fearing that he might stab me first. I feel so terribly debased in front of myself. I think that if I had a mirror, I would not dare to look myself straight in the eye.

After we returned I felt a sudden and generalized collapse of both mind and body. It was an absolute fatigue that extended all the way to my viscera, a cowardly, impotent rage and at the same time an unflagging need for sleep—for a long, deep and endless sleep into which I could plunge as into a bottomless sea of gray cotton. But this redemptive sleep refused to come. I felt an invincible urge to rise in order to go and see "my" corpse at close range—to keep looking at him until I came to know him and had my fill. Yet I lacked the courage to face his body. I was obsessed with an *idée fixe:* "That corpse is my work!" Right now I am waiting for the moment when I shall be all alone in the dugout; I am waiting in other words for the opportunity to cry. But this in itself is something that terrifies me, because it is a sign of decadence. I do not even have sufficient pluck to weep openly in front of the others, much less to throw away the gory chevron and the medal. People keep congratulating me from dawn to dusk, and despite everything I am able to smile and say "Thank you" with that false modesty displayed by heroes when they recount their exploits in major newspapers of nation-wide circulation—the only difference being that when I am asked to describe my adventures I say nothing, for this is beyond my strength. And everyone interprets my silence as modesty! Meanwhile, I am a Dimitratos Number Two. The insignia of bravery that we now possess in common unite us just as the common skin unites Siamese twins—except that he is able to find deliverance through cynicism.

There are times when my suffering makes me wish to summon death as my redeemer. There are hours when I implore God to protect my mind from the madness that encompasses me on every side. I have already experienced this in a small way. Last night I managed to sleep five whole hours before I was awakened by a terrible nightmare. I had seen a madman in my dream. He was all alone in a huge square, advancing with the rigid posture and creeping pace of soldiers at a state funeral. Wearing a black uniform of mourning so tight and well fitting that it looked ridiculous, he kept advancing all by himself. Following him at a distance of about fifty paces, however, was a large crowd of civilians all proceeding at the same pace as the madman, rigorously maintaining their distance from him. No one spoke; yet all knew that they were following the lunatic. Whenever he started, so did they, always with the same solemn pace. I was among them, and I was trembling lest they realize that the person marching in front, the madman, was myself. Then suddenly they all disappeared and I remained the only one following him. I was very close to him now, directly behind his back. He stopped. I heard him laugh; it was a subdued laugh that had no end.

"Turn around and let me see you," I said. "I know who you are. You are Gighandis. Turn!"

The madman turned, but he had his open palm over his face.

"Uncover your face," I implored. "I know that you are Gighandis."

I went closer. And it was only then that I saw the translucent gleam of his palm in the light, as though his hand were made of pink cigarette paper. I could discern the veins inside it, and the circulating blood. And, between the veins, I distinis face. It was my own. . . .

Do you deny that dreams, too, can be real experiences?

49

Sacrifices to the Sun

I still cannot believe the miracle we experienced yesterday: the sun came out at two in the afternoon and stayed out until a quarter to four! After not seeing it for so many days, I had begun to think that it would never show itself again. It must have forsaken us, I said to myself; it must have sunk behind the humid soot that grazes all day long on the muddy hills. "And he turned his face from us, and we became like them that go down into the pit." But no, it was God's will that he should settle his golden glance upon us yet once more. He had appeared, and his light had penetrated our rancid souls to their depths. It was a smile of hope. In our dugout we charged forward in astonishment and wedged our filthy muzzles into the small oblong entranceway. All we could see was the opposite wall of the trench and a long ribbon of sky. But what did that matter? The muddy ditch in which we lived was filled with sunlight. Golden, precious sunlight! It flowed from the parapets, filled all the crannies, dyed the timbers aureate. Even an empty tin can thrown up on the sandbags scintillated now as though made of sterling silver. Turning, I looked at my comrades one by one: at their bushy faces that had been so horribly transfigured by life underground. But now, sitting deeply within the pitted sockets of each of these faces was a pair of fervid brown eyes overflowing with light and ecstatic wonderment. They were the poor, deprived eyes of Lesvos insatiably drinking in the sunshine.

No one spoke. But my brother, who was biting one end of his mustache, exclaimed in amazement:

"Jeeeesus!"

An absolute silence— a placidity—reigned everywhere; not a soul was in sight. You said to yourself, My goodness, this war is not real, it is just a horrible dream, a dark nightmare full of imaginary anxieties and terror. I have half a mind to pick up and leave this worm-eaten tomb that oozes with liquid putrefaction, with the fetor of human remains, and that is consuming my youth. I shall go out into the sun. I shall head for Mytilene-town in order to bathe, shave, change, and dedicate myself once more to the joys of life, creativity, and love. . . .

Just as I was thinking all this, gggrrann! an explosion. Close; very close. The shell must have burst inside our trench. We herded back in a turmoil, back into the darkness of our lair.

My brother wagered that it was a torpedo. Its peculiar whistle had been characteristically brief. Once ignited, the discussion flared up, each man parading his technical knowledge of the subject. At the same time we heard something floundering about outside, accompanied by the sound of a scabbard scraping against the walls. Fikos, the orderly, was running through the trench in a terrified daze. He leaned into the entrance, his face buried inside an oversized helmet, and spewed out at us in a choked-up voice, precipitously:

"To the captain's, quick! Men have been killed!"

Then he continued to run, crouching as low as possible.

"Oh no!" we all cried in agony.

I tightened the chinstrap on my helmet and flew outside. Crouching wherever the trench was deep enough, crawling like a tortoise in the places where the walls became lower, I pushed forward and turned all the familiar corners, my face besplattered with mud. The entire trench was deserted except for the sentries, who squatted in their boxes without moving or speaking, and stared at their appointed sectors. They resembled bales of muddied rags, or rubbish thrown down in a heap. Following the explosion's clatter, the silence that reigned had become even more intense. It was almost tyrannical, that "vociferous" silence, as one was tempted to call it. The moment I squeezed into the dugout that served as Company H.Q., I found myself instantaneously surrounded by all the horror that had taken place. The air still reeked of gunpowder. Two stretcher-bearers and the company's medical aide were struggling by hook or by crook to help the four who had been hit. The captain had been wounded slightly in the shoulder. He was lying on his bed, his eyes swollen and inflamed from the explosion. His greatest pain was in the knee, which had been banged by a stone. Second Lieutenant Apostolou, a strapping fellow as huge as an ancient *kouros*, had been killed. A tiny steel fragment no bigger than a chickpea was all that hit him, but it chanced to lodge directly in his heart. There he was, stretched out in the entranceway, gigantic and clean, without a single spot of blood on him, seemingly without even a wound. The other two were Quartermaster-sergeant Perdikis and his assistant, Corporal Ioannou. Three of Perdikis's fingers had been sliced off as he was writing. They had been flung onto the ground and were still there, looking like three yellow caterpillars with crushed heads. The sergeant, half-wedged beneath the captain's bed, was emitting tiny moans, his body twitching frequently with powerful shudders, his wide-open eyes pinned on the oozing dressing that covered his hand. The one who was truly in bad shape was Ioannou. His right leg had been completely severed at the thigh as though by a single chop from a dull axe. His left arm, crushed above the elbow, was held to the shoulder by a few ragged slivers of flesh. Drunk with pain, he lay on his back screeching while the attendants fought to stanch the flow of blood.

"Where is the battalion doctor?" I asked, running to the telephone. But the captain, without ceasing to rub his knee, stopped me short.

''The fucking thing doesn't work," he said with a grimace of pain.

"Let me run then . . ."

"Sit down," he murmured wearily. "I've already sent a messenger."

Ioannou's screams continued, loud and monotonous. Despite all the agonized efforts of the attendant, the blood gushed uninterruptedly from his truncated limbs, soaking the ground. The shrieks he emitted were prolonged and piercing, like those of a woman in the pangs of childbirth. Taking a wet cloth, I went up to him and wiped his forehead, which was covered with large knots of sweat. He stretched his gaze above the spectacles which hung from his ears, and looked at me with unspeakable pain, his childish blue eyes full of tears.

"Save me . . . the doctor . . . where is the doctor . . ."

"Courage," I told him. "It's nothing. . . . Stop carrying on like that."

Aside from these imbecilities, I had no idea what to say as I watched his poor life run from his gashed limbs in a red stream. The flow from the arm had stopped, in a manner of speaking. But that horrible hatchet-wound at the thigh was an incessant, silent fountain of blood. You realized that it would not be stanched until his life was stanched as well.

"Ohhh, forget about my leg!" he shrieked. "Here ... here's the trouble!" Shifting his eyes, he indicated his left arm.

I gave the attendants a quizzical look. Didn't he care, then, about his leg? With vigorous nods they signaled me not to speak. I understood. The poor man was not even aware that he had lost one of his extremities, that it had been lopped off of him, pruned like the branch of a tree. He did not know that his body had been mutilated. I turned and my horrified eyes encountered the severed limb. The foot lay on the ground where it had been thrown, near the narrow passage by the entranceway. The end that had received the blow was still resting on top of the open ledger that contained the quartermaster's accounts. The final drops from its empty veins were draining onto the large bloodstained pages. I looked at this wretched leg that had long since died. Swaddled in its blue puttees, shod with the large boot whose lacing consisted of telephone wire, it lay there like a separate corpse, like a slaughtered child. I went over and discreetly covered it with a burlap sack, one of those spread along the narrow passage so that all who entered could wipe their feet.

"The doctor . . . where is the doctor . . ."

The pitch of his screams grew gradually lower and his voice weaker and weaker until he was emitting something like the bleats of a lamb: "Mehh! Mehh!" Life continued to drain from the mangled flesh. His lips lost more and more of their color; his eyes moved with difficulty. Finally his voice turned into a subdued but incessant complaint, like one long monotonous sob:

"Mother . . . mother . . ."

Soon this ceased to be audible even though a slight quivering continued on his lips, which were now as white as bleached cotton. Suddenly he opened his eyes wide and focused them on a canteen that was hanging above him on the wall of the dugout. For a moment a frown settled on his

forehead: a small vertical fold between eyebrows that had been pulled together by perplexity. It was as though high above him on the wall, directly
over the canteen, something extremely remarkable was happening, something that required great concentration if he were to understand it. Then
the fold dissolved little by little like a departing worry, the chest fell in
with a deep sigh, and became still. His body went limp as a rag, instantly.
The aide clasped his one remaining pulse, then let the hand fall.

"Gone to his Maker . . . ," he said softly, scratching his ear.

One of the litter-bearers rose to his knees, then stood up entirely. He
went to the severed leg and picked it up. Grasping it like an infant (by now
he could perform such tasks with complete nonchalance) he brought it
next to the mutilated body and set it down. In the very center of the wound,
surrounded by tatters of flesh and trouser-cloth, the marrow hung out of
the smashed bone like a huge and corpulent red-white worm.

"All over with?" asked the captain weakly, in a voice that betrayed a
certain impatience.

"May he rest in peace, Sir."

"Well then, move! Carry Perdikis to the station. On the double!"

"And what about you, Sir?"

"It's nothing. I can be treated here."

The bearers placed the quartermaster-sergeant on a stretcher and lifted
him. The captain instructed them to take along all his things as well. When
they had gone, the medical aid—a filthy brute from the Ionian Islands—
turned his sharp nose toward me while he was redoing the captain's im-
promptu dressings and suddenly said in his lilting accent:

"Oops! The sergeant forgot to take along some of his things."

"What things?"

"Oh, nothing very important, of course, my good friend. Just . . . just
. . . those three fingers!"

"Devil!" whined the captain.

The aide picked the fingers up one by one with a piece of cotton and
placed them near Ioannou, whose congealed glance was still fixed on the
canteen hanging from the wall. The lashes of the lifeless eyes were bathed
in tears, and the horn-rimmed spectacles were leaning askew, having
worked loose on the right-hand side. I reached out in order to replace the

temple-piece behind his ear, but at the same moment realized with astonishment how senseless this act of solicitude was, and drew back my hand. As though a pair of glasses hanging awry could ever have bothered him now!

A large golden-fly (how did it appear so soon?) came through the sunlit ingress throwing out yellowish-green flashes as it reflected the light. Settling upon the captain's helmet, which was hanging from a peg next to me, it surveyed this ground from all angles, thoroughly. Then, using the helmet as a vantage point, it swept its gaze round the dugout like a prospective tenant inspecting new quarters just prior to occupying them. Extremely pleased with the inspection, it rubbed its little forelegs together and tsooup! suddenly perched like a heavy glob on Ioannou's waxen forehead. Then it rubbed its forelegs together once more and immediately ran with rapid little steps to the bridge of the dead man's nose, whence it hurriedly thrust its sharp proboscis into his eye, the left eye, in the very corner, next to the nose. I quickly chased it away. Then I lowered the corpse's tear-coated lids with the tips of my fingers. Orderlies came and arranged the two bodies side by side. The second lieutenant they placed upon his camp bed, Ioannou upon the ground, with a clean sheet of canvas underneath. Then they covered them completely, head and all, using a blanket for each. Soon the doctor arrived, along with the major and other officers of our company. They all spoke in hushed voices; and they all clasped the captain's hand.

Suddenly the sun disappeared—it seemed to have been engulfed—and a vigorous rain began to lash the trench with maniacal fury.

The captain shook my hand before I left for my dugout. He told me to join him that evening for a cup of tea.

I went at nightfall. I found a crowd of others there besides our bedridden captain. There was a Frenchman named Desroux who was a second lieutenant in the Engineers and inspector-of-works for our battalion's entire sector, the two other second lieutenants in our company—a pair of vulgar insignificant characters—and Sergeant Dalas, a misshapen gawk who smoked incessantly (thanks to packs donated by the company's non-smokers) and could not stomach any of the enlisted men who happened to have an education. As soon as I entered I felt my face caressed by a pleasant warmth mixed with cigarette smoke and the strong odor of freshly spilled blood. The ingress was carefully blocked off with a double layer of hanging canvas. A lighted acetylene lamp with two burners stood on the wooden table, in the middle of which was a gaping triangular hole produced by the same steel fragment that had scythed off the quartermaster's fingers. In one corner of the table a large patch that had been stained by blood gleamed whitely now, having been freshly sandpapered. Orderlies had scraped away the blood-soaked soil on the floor with a shovel. Remaining as mementos for the company were nothing but the mess-ledger with its gory pages, a blood-soaked pile of playing cards, and some pieces of the murderous torpedo. All these mementos had been neatly arranged in the corner cupboard.

Like the others, I seated myself on one of those huge sheet-iron reels of telephone wire that serve so splendidly here as stools. A large kettle was boiling on an improvised trivet placed over an iron container. This held a sizeable chunk of solidified alcohol whose blue flames were poking over the top. Everyone was noisily sipping hot tea out of aluminum cups that the captain's servant kept refilling. In addition, a large tin of biscuits, the captain's sugar bowl, and finally a bottle of English rum were at the group's disposal. The men helped themselves to the last at frequent intervals, pouring the rum into their tea. This sanguinary soirée was really very melancholy at the same time that it was so very pleasant. The captain had begun to relate how the catastrophe had happened. He did this leisurely, screwing up his face with pain from time to time and interrupting his account in order to shift the position of his swollen knee.

Yes, it had been a torpedo after all. Desroux, who had examined the fragments, gave us details about the missile's weight and brand. This was the first time such a type had been fired on this front. It was of the "roaming" variety—that is, launched without any objective at all, the dugout not being visible to the enemy's observation post—; the kind "that is dispatched unaddressed but that always arrives by registered mail," as the men like to say. So, it must have been fired in this haphazard manner, just because some artillery gunner across the way suddenly had a brainstorm. Or perhaps they were testing some new "launching tube." It burst precisely in front of the dugout's entrance, at lintel-height.

They had dragged the table in front of the ingress in order to enjoy the sunlight, the suggestion originating with the late-lamented Apostolou— "Why not bring the table over there, Captain, so we can recuperate a bit in the sun?" The two of them had been playing slapjack while the quartermaster-sergeant and his assistant entered dates in the fair copy of the mess-ledger. Apostolou was recounting a bad dream he had had that morning. It seems that peace had been concluded. The whole regiment came out into the open, climbed onto the parapets, and began to cheer. Down below, far in the distance, a black ship flying all its colors appeared out of the plain. It seemed to be coming toward them, sailing on dry land, its whistles tooting, smoke pouring from its funnels. Its deck was crowded with sailors who all stood at rigid, strained attention, their peculiarly austere faces staring "strongly" (as Apostolou put it), their arms folded tightly over their chests. Passing between the bare, eroded hills, the ship kept climbing up and up until it stopped directly in front of the trench, near the dugout. . . .

The captain sighed. "The longing for sunlight: that is what did us in," he concluded.

We all turned to gaze once more at the two covered corpses: two victims offered as sacrifices to the sun. The flames of the lamp flared up and subsided, making the shadows on the remains shift in such a manner that one could almost imagine the dead men wrestling beneath their blankets in a struggle to draw the coverings away from their faces. Thus it suddenly occurred to me that Ioannou was still wearing his large round spectacles askew over his lifeless eyes. I remembered one day when I had found him asleep with the glasses on his nose.

"You there!" I said, nudging him on the shoulder. "So you wear them even in your sleep, eh?"

He awoke with a start, spread wide his childlike eyes, and said to me with that kindly, beatific smile of his:

"Why of course! All the better to see my dreams with, my dear!"

We continued to drink tea with rum and to smoke the captain's cigarettes. The sense of grief and affliction seemed to flee this underground morgue more and more, as though gradually driven outside by the acetylene's abundant white glow and the ever-increasing jollity and liveliness of the group's voices. All the misfortunes and horrors of that massacre were slipping past the canvas curtains that covered the oblong entrance, slipping past and moving outside toward the cold, muddy trench with its disemboweled sandbags, then proceeding toward the murky hills that were being stung by the freezing rain and stabbed by the north wind. It was almost enjoyable to feel ourselves healthy and warm, our stomachs full, a cup of boiled tea fortified with rum beneath our noses, and a lovely luxury-brand cigarette between our lips. We knew all too well that it was cold and rainy outside and that a savage manhunt was taking place in the mud between the two lines, with the opposing patrols lying in wait for one another. And here, stretched out at our side, were two dead comrades, one of whom had just now sprinkled all his frothing blood onto the soil, twitching like a slaughtered lamb. Whereas we . . .

To be sure, these thoughts were not engendered in us in such a completely clear and shamelessly naked form. Nevertheless I know very well that they—more than the captain's rum and his excellent cigarettes—were responsible for the intoxication that was gradually taking us unawares.

The captain asked me if he were right in supposing that Ioannou and I came from the same village. Yes, we hailed from the identical place on the foothills of Mount Lepetimnos. He had been married; newly married in fact. To the daughter of a priest. Recently he had told me that his wife wrote to inform him that in a few days he would become a father. At this point the sergeant-major removed a package from Ioannou's cupboard. It was done up in brown paper and contained the effects found upon the dead man. The company was going to send them to his home. The sergeant-major unwrapped the package slowly and drew out a cheap cardboard wallet with two compartments.

"Look, here's a picture of his wife," he said.

The photograph was sharp and clear, though quite worn at the edges. Hanging down from a little hole in which a golden eyelet had been fixed was a plait of glossy hair bound tightly with a thin blue ribbon. It was the color of ripe chestnuts. This conjugal keepsake passed from hand to hand, each of us retaining and fingering it for a considerable time, without speaking. One of our second lieutenants—a man with frizzy negroid hair, minuscule eyes, and thick blackish lips—kept devouring the photograph with his gaze. Then he deeply inhaled the plait's aroma and said with a sigh:

"A beautiful dish, by God! A first class dumpling!"

The Frenchman confirmed this in his stumbling Greek:

"She is *très chic*, much pretty, *oui*, much pretty."

I looked at her in my turn.

Yes, there she was: Amersuda, the priest's youngest daughter, with her ebony eyes, ribbon-straight brows, impish little laugh and those splendid breasts burgeoning there so high, so defined one from the other as they pressed unrestrainably against the thin blouse—two juicy, infinitely desirable fruits swelling as though in the offer of love. All of this was very keenly depicted on this photograph that smiled, moreover, with a strange and inexplicable coquetry. It was smiling now, at this very hour, here in this dugout whose floor—just think!—had only a few hours ago been scraped of the dirt that had turned to mud as it soaked up Ioannou's hot blood. That hair had brought its feminine fragrance *here*! Here, into this accursed cave that stank of cigarettes, iodoform, rum, burnt alcohol, and whiffs of Ioannou's blood. As for him, he was lying over there on the ground upon a canvas sheet, his right leg hacked from the thigh as though by a single stroke from an unhoned axe. It was severed, and it sat there beneath the blanket completely detached and separate from the rest of the body, turned in an unnatural direction. It sat there like a dead child, lay swaddled in its blue puttees, wearing a boot. High up at the thigh was a frightful red-black wound; and the marrow hung out amid the gory shreds of the tattered trousers, like the carcass of a corpulent pinkish-white worm.

Yet the girl: she continued to smile sweetly on her photograph, as from behind a windowpane. She continued to smile amorously and happily at all of us; to laugh at those half-drunk hooligans who were stripping her naked with their eyes; to laugh at the Frenchman and the gawky sergeant-major. Poor sweet thing, she was completely ignorant of what we knew, and her two breasts stood there swelling and erect, as in the offer of love. . . .

While he . . .

Of all the men in the company, he was the most courteous, goodhearted, and obliging. In these traits he stood second to none. If he happened to encounter someone else in the narrow trench he would glue himself to the muddy wall like a decal in order to allow the other sufficient room to pass. And he was never missing that tiny smile that sparkled in his blue eyes without interruption even during this recent time when the wretched conditions of underground life had raised our irascibility to such a pitch that we quarreled with one another for no reason at all and came to blows, full of somber hatred.

Once, while Ioannou was busy preparing the company files to be loaded—it was on one of the long marches—a muleteer guided his animal too close to him and the beast trampled his toenails, very seriously. Ioannou let out a loud scream of pain and sat down on the ground. The captain, enraged at the careless muleteer, was ready to pulverize him for good, whereupon Ioannou jumped up immediately and started to laugh, assuring the captain that it was nothing at all; Thus the muleteer escaped a beating, but Ioannou limped surreptitiously on a march that lasted four days, four entire days of torture.

"He had a stout heart, that boy," said the captain. "One day I watched him from the Artillery's observation post as he crossed the 'fox's saddle' with the Order of the Day under his arm." (The "fox's saddle" is the name we have given to an exposed pass between two hills. The Bulgarians keep pounding it with shells; not even a cat can get through. But Ioannou had to cross it every day to go to the Regiment and copy out the Order.) "Well, one morning I was observing him through my binoculars," continued the captain, "and I was all awonder at the stout heart concealed inside that girlish character. The Bulgarians could see him no matter how fast he ran. And they started after him, whizz-bang! whizz-bang! one on top of the other, without losing a minute. Well, you should have seen him, lads—how he fell flat on his face at every whistle and waited for the shell to burst so he could get up and begin to run again, all hunched over. You'd have thought he was on maneuvers, going through dummy fire."

Everyone turned and cast a respectful glance at the blanket that covered the corpse. The thought passed through my mind that lying underneath this cover was his waxen face with its white lips and closed eyes; it also occurred to me that he was still wearing his eyeglasses askew, hanging off to one side. ("All the better to see my dreams with, my dear!")

Subsequently, I don't know how the conversation spun itself out in this way, but after going from subject to subject they finally settled upon . . . corns!

"That's a problem affecting big brass and civilians," said the sergeant-major, dipping his biscuit (as well as the fingers that held it) into his tea. "We ordinary soldiers have the best cure for corns: a pair of boots, because you can do an about-face inside them and they don't even change direction."

The Frenchman then told us with great gusto that he had been suffering from a corn for four years. Yes, by God, four whole years, and things had reached such a pass that he had a mind to . . . to . . . get married in order to put an end to his troubles! What? Get married? Surely Lieutenant Desroux must be pickled!

"*Non, non,* me *non* peekled, *sapristi.*" Whereupon he told us the whole story. It seems that Desroux had once been walking absentmindedly along a boulevard. Suddenly: ouch! A girl was next to him, and he had accidentally stepped on her corn. The little thing turned ashen with pain. As for Desroux: a thousand pardons and out goes his arm for the girl to lean on. Well, she leaned, . . . and she's been leaning ever since, with no sign of packing off. Nor does Desroux have any appetite for unloading her. Indeed, he is so head over heels in love that he is trying to arrange for her to come to Salonika so that he can marry her "eeef ze goud Dieu want me eez —how you say?—'pale and hardy.'"

"Hale!" they corrected him, all shouting at once and guffawing. And they explained the difference.

"Me understood, me understood. Eef on eez pale *non* eez hale. Eef *on* eez hale *non* eez pale. *C'est* ça. Zees beezeness *non* want pale, want hale, *n'est-ce pas?*"

And so the conversation fell into its usual rut—women!

When we talk about women here in the trenches, what fervor we display! Good grief, it is almost maniacal! And when we do not talk about women we think about them with a morbid, feverish intensity. When we go to sleep in our burrows, all worked up and at the same time exhausted by fatigue and boredom, we dream of them and stretch out our hands to them in prayerful supplication. For us, to be concerned about women is to be smoking hashish. In our tired minds we passionately clear the dust from former memories, lineaments, motions, and then re-engrave them through our imaginations. Everyone here speaks about Woman with such ferocious adoration. Oh, where is She, cruel goddess of lust, that we may worship Her with ecstatic rites? Where is She that She may grind Her rosy heel into the napes of millions of bemuddied warriors who will then bellow like happy beasts beneath the voluptuous debasement? Where is She that hungry poignards may flash for Her sake in the deep damp hollows where entire flocks of males are huddled together? They drag themselves about in the filthy darkness, inebriated with their own ruttish fetor. And they rave away in a delirium, rave about Her in this place that is beneath the shadow of death, long to tear Her limb from limb in an erotic frenzy, like jackals, to rub their famished snouts between Her legs, and lap up Her rosy, female blood.

The moment the group started to "talk dirty," an excited flush invaded every face. A savage vehemence displayed itself in the movements of all who were present, and in their tone of voice.

The sergeant-major began to gesticulate like an epileptic. An anecdote from 1912, from the Balkan Wars:

". . . so I kick open the door and go in. A *hanum*, white as milk. Tits like plump quinces. A bit of all right. She understood straight off. *Buyurun, çavuş, buyurun* . . .—welcome, sergeant, come right in . . ."

The rotund, stumpy officer with the negroid hair and thick lips wanted to propose a toast. He raised his cup high in the air and cleared his throat:

"Ladies and gentlemen! I drink to the health of all beautiful women of both hemispheres. And I drink to the health of both hemispheres of all beautiful women!"

He surveyed each of us one by one with his tiny eyes to see if we had appreciated his cleverness sufficiently. Unfortunately no one was paying attention. In the end, extremely pleased with himself, he laughed at his own joke, joined only by the sergeant-major, who added a small, obligatory snigger—out of obedience to a superior, you might say—revealing as he did so a line of yellowish teeth suspended between the handlebars of his mustache. The officer expressed his gratitude with several appreciative glances. After this, his colleague, the other second lieutenant, brought out the fact that this toast was not his—no, by God!—that without the slightest doubt he had heard it from someone else or read it somewhere.

"By the crown I wear . . . !" protested thick-lips out of habit, forgetting that he no longer wore a crown on his cap.

"If our late comrade heard you swear like that, you wouldn't get along very well with him," said the captain seriously, casting a prolonged glance at the remains of Apostolou, who had been a fanatic republican.

The Frenchman sang a canzonetta full of obscene *double-entendres.* The rest accompanied him by tapping out the beat with their cups:

"Saloniki - niki - niki!"

What a rumpus! It appeared that the whole lot of us had become drunk; yes, the whole lot of us were soused.

As I was thinking this, we heard footsteps in the ingress and boots stamping on the ground to dislodge the mud that was caked on their soles. A finger tapped discreetly on the hanging canvas.

"Come in."

Four bearers entered, with two stretchers. They had been sent to remove the dead. Our conversation ceased abruptly. A slight disturbance occurred when they tried to lift Apostolou's large body, because his shattered arm slid off the stretcher and dangled over the side, whereupon various fluids began immediately to drain, tsiourrr, from the sleeve onto the dirt floor, leaving a damp stain there. The longer the liquids flowed the larger grew the stain. We all maintained our silence while we watched it swell. Then, turning our heads, we shifted our gaze elsewhere on account of Apostolou's leg, which had eluded the stretcher and fallen onto the floor with a hollow thud. Taking four safety pins, the litter-bearers toiled to secure it firmly beneath the tunic, since the remaining portion of the trouser-leg was nothing but a damp rag all in shreds and tatters. Thus the boot of the severed limb reached only to the knee of the other leg; it was twisted outwards, moreover, as though the ankle had been severely sprained. By all accounts Ioannou should have been suffering unspeakable torture to have it in such an unnatural position, yet his face appeared entirely placid in the white light and his eyeglasses sparkled as though casting glances at us. One of the bearers adjusted the right temple, which had fallen off the ear. Strange how everyone seemed to be worried about this. The sergeant-major recommended, for what it was worth, that they also secure the crushed arm with pins if they did not want it to drop off along the way; also that they put the quartermaster's three fingers in Apostolou's pocket. He might find them somewhat superfluous on the Day of Judgment, but no matter—he would need them for thumbing his nose at Lady Luck with all the more digits.

Now it was the swarthy officer's turn to smile at the sergeant-major for his cleverness. *Touché.*"

I said good night and made off toward my dugout. Dripping on all sides was a chilling, humid darkness. The thick, damp night filled the trench, seated itself in sovereignty upon the mud. You felt that you were cleaving it in two as you walked, were thrusting it aside in order to pass. Muddy clods fell from the walls in great chunks because of my fumblings. They were pieces of darkness that worked loose lump by lump and fell, making a "plash" in the water that lined the bottom of the trench. I found only two of my companions snoring away when I reached the dugout; the others were on duty. In the container holding the margarine the flame was sputtering on its wick. We hang this container on telephone wire from the end of a bayonet driven into a ceiling-beam, so that the mice cannot get at it. If the sleepers had not been snoring, you would have taken them for corpses illuminated by an improvised funeral-lamp.

One of the men was rudely and prematurely roused by my entrance. Mumbling through the sheepskins he had wrapped around his head, he told me that a lot of water and mud had leaked in through the ingress. "There, in your cranny, he said. "Watch out."

Then he began to scratch himself somewhere, hard. I heard his nails moving rapidly over his hairy hide. When slumber overcame him again, he was still grumbling and scratching away, in his sleep.

Feeling the captain's rum throb at my temples, I snuggled into my things in one corner. Then, closing my eyes, I meditated on the extraordinary ease and simplicity with which one becomes a corpse. Take Apostolou for example. A tiny bit of steel no bigger than a pea, and youth, ideas, ardor, strength, dreams, motion had all run out, tssrrrr, through the teeniest little hole, a hole like the eye of a darning-needle, just an insignificant fissure in the skin.

My meditations continued in a peculiar vein.

If it is true that nothing in nature ceases to exist but only changes form, then into what new forms do you suppose all the unspent powers of that gigantic youth have been transformed—the powers that would have become actions if that tiny fissure in the skin had not intervened?

Then came a feverish current of thoughts, one pursuing the next. Apostolou was a handsome, healthy man, I said to myself. He was full of ideals, knowledge, volition. This was how nature had created him: an elect creature whose soul had flared up with enthusiasm for great flights. Yet along came an ever-so-small piece of steel, and that superb creation was metamorphosed into a corpse. And what is a corpse? Just a lump of mindless dough that has already begun to turn gluey. Yes, just so much rancid jelly.

But wait . . . Nature seizes the materials straightway and begins to distribute them liberally, transubstantiating them in the process. A sizable portion of his heart (the heart of big-hearted Apostolou) it donates to a yellow root that crawls along like a snake, burrows into the soil, and proceeds toward the bowels of the earth. No one observes this slender reptile as it struggles to stay alive, nourish itself, and expand. No one even knows of its existence. As for the root, however, it sticks faithfully to its task, moving continually further down. It is a strong herbaceous worm fighting to thread its way like an elastic band through a pair of underpants, in order to girdle the earth. The wild root bumps against a stone that blocks its path. It is troubled displeased perplexed as it halts in the subterranean darkness. Hmmmm, this rock seems to be hard all over, it says thoughtfully.

The wild root has no eyes; it is blind. Yet it does have innumerable little hands and feet, also millions of tiny herbaceous tongues that explore, eat, and suck. The verdant reptile wishes to find its path. It waits. Years—whole centuries—go by and it waits in the darkness, lies there vigilantly, in ambush. It does not sleep; it does nothing but search and grope. Some fearsome and indomitable Force is prodding it to advance. Forward! Frenzied effort: that is its anguish, the tragedy that no one apprehends or observes. Suddenly an uneasiness disturbs the wild root, a hope sends shudders throughout its body. One of those hairlike appendages that serve simultaneously as legs, mouths, and antennae buries itself into a very fine, imperceptibly narrow fissure in the rock: No one knows how this fissure chanced to spread in the heart of the rock. No. one knows—except the worm.

"Now that's more like it!" it says. All of the herbaceous reptile's power converges now upon that one spot. It has to squeeze into that rock no matter what the cost, has to pierce the stone's heart though no one knows why. For this, however, it requires strength; food, chemical nutrients. And it is at this precise juncture that the Force that looks after all these strange and frightening needs tosses Apostolou's flesh to the wild root. Here: eat! It tosses the black eyes that brimmed with dreams and glistened with life's teeming vitality; it tosses the brain that was so full of light and lucid cerebration; and it tosses the chamber that pounded his chest with its fist and said: "The Whole of Greece is contained herein: such is the greatness of the human heart."

It seems, however, that taking precedence over all these in God's sight is the need for a wild root to grow strong so that it may slide into the secret core of a stone there in the bowels of the earth, for a purpose that no one has ever discovered . . . . So you think you can find it, do you? Well then, go ahead and try! . . .

The captain's English rum kept hammering at my temples, engendering still further thoughts.

Ioannou and Apostolou were alive for barely twenty-five years, I said to myself. They will remain dead for all the rest, all the infinite years of eternity. In short, this is their permanent, immutable condition. The other twenty-five years, those of their "life," were twenty-five droplets in a deluge of time so huge that it will suffice to drown all worlds, stars, and universes in the silence of death, with still another infinite span of time left over to spare. Hence something completely tragic is going on, and right now I am about to be driven out of my senses by the following quandary: Why do we fail to grant this fact the attention it deserves?

My thoughts continued:

Beneath the hide of each of us lies a corpse. It sits there patiently in dignified silence, awaiting the opportunity to appear robed in that royal imperturbability that characterizes all things eternal. In our few "living" years we involve this corpse in a surfeit of harassing confusions. We drag it up and down, left and right. But the corpse holds its tongue. Who cares (it must be thinking); if I'm up I'm up, down I'm down. This annoying roll and pitch is destined to end very shortly . . . .

I recalled that the late lamented Apostolou had the revolting habit of cracking his knuckles. Every two seconds: cric-cric-cric. Maybe it was his bony skeleton sending out word of its existence from inside: "Present!" A strange business . . . I certainly must be good and drunk to lie here like this and think up such nonsense. Yet . . . Here is still another strange idea. See what you can make of this: If the quartermaster-sergeant were able to attend Ioannou's funeral, in a certain sense he would be attending his own funeral as well. This would make him the first man ever to participate in his own obsequies, because the quartermaster's three fingers must still be sitting curled up in Ioannou's pocket, severed at their roots. One of them, I remembered well, had an ink-blotch on the second joint, where it held the pen. Two of the nails were stained orange from smoking . . . .

A mouse has started to munch hard tack inside my haversack.

Let him munch as long as he likes. I say; and I hope he gets good and sick of it!

50

Coup de Main

*T*his is precisely how it happened.

All the N.C.O.s were summoned to Company H.Q. There, on the table, the captain spread out a plan of the trench directly across from us, and also produced a whole packet of photographs taken by aerial reconnaissance. These showed the entire enemy sector. He pointed out the lines of barbed wire, marked the weakest points and the ingresses, even indicated to us the enemy dugouts, offices, telephone locations and known machine-gun emplacements—all of which had been designated with elaborate detail. This was the first time I had been exposed to such intricate and pedantically conscientious workmanship on the part of our Intelligence and its technical adjuncts. God only knows how many human lives those documents had cost. Afterwards, the captain took a red pencil and drew demarcations that isolated for us one part of the trench in question. This part was a bulge in the Bulgarian line; it protruded on the map and stuck out toward our forces like a mocking tongue. Next, he explained that our company had been entrusted by the regiment with the task of launching a *coup de main* against this objective. Thirty resolute men were required, and the purpose was to bring back captives and whatever records could be seized—because these were required by Intelligence, whatever the cost. The captain looked each of us straight in the eye, and said:

"I need two sergeants for this mission. Volunteers. It's going to be dangerous; I won't hide that from you. The detachment will have to cut its way through three rows of barbed wire before reaching the objective. It will then take the trench by surprise and pillage it. All those who know in your hearts that you wish to bring honor to the company, take one step forward."

The moment he concluded these words, my brother snapped to attention and darted forward. Clicking his heels together vigorously and raising his hand to his helmet, he said in his firm bass voice:

"At your command, Captain!"

Standing behind him as I was, I could see his back towering in front of me. He was uncommonly tall and well built, his broad shoulders and athletic physique strongly highlighted by the acetylene lamp burning in front of him. My heart constricted with pain. After a moment's hesitation, two others stepped forward at precisely the same instant, as though prodded by the identical stimulus. The captain chose my brother and one of the others. After we had left he kept these two behind along with the officer who was going to command the mission, so that he could brief them in greater detail and have them draw up the list of thirty, choosing the best men in the company.

Numbed by an imprecise, generalized fear, I waited in my dugout. Three days earlier I had dreamed that one of my teeth had fallen out. I paid no attention to the dream at the time; but now—the moment I saw my brother offer himself for tonight's adventure—it hammered itself back into my consciousness. (I behave like a superstitious grandmother every now and then.)

He returned an hour or so later. He was lively, but also a trifle nervous.

"You've been waiting for me, I see," he said in a tone that he tried to make as natural as possible, whereupon he proceeded to whistle with counterfeit nonchalance the whole time he prepared his kit: gun, bandages, and so on. He showed me a short, wide dagger with a good healthy blade and a wooden hilt. I had never seen it before. "We call this a trench dagger," he said. "One like this will be taken by every man. They're in case of engagements inside the trench, when fixed bayonets can't be used because it's too narrow. Not bad for a weapon, eh?"

I kept watching him, without responding to this palaver. He spoke rapidly never looking at me directly. Eventually, however, he was obliged to return my gaze, which had been following him pertinaciously. He looked me straight in the eye then, almost aggressively.

"Why did you do it?" I asked. "You might—"

He had been holding the swab that he used for cleaning the bore of his rifle. Tossing this onto the ground in a rage, he interrupted me:

"Yes, I might . . . So what!"

I looked at him, shrugged my shoulders:

". . . Forget it."

He went on with his preparations, but he stopped the whistling now, and did not jabber any longer.

After that we did not exchange a single word. When the time arrived for the detachment to leave, however—at the very last moment, just before he vaulted over the parapet—he suddenly threw his left arm around me and kissed me firmly in the darkness, so firmly that his helmet hurt my cheek. Then they departed, jumping out one after the other. No one spoke. There was just the noise of the equipment clanking faintly behind them for a few moments. I noticed that the last one to leave the trench crossed himself hastily in the darkness. In a short while not a sound could be heard. One by one the men were swallowed by the night. I remained staring out at the murk. No one stood near me any longer (even though the trench was full); my soul was wrapped in solitude, an unpleasant and chilling void. Lifting my eyes, I saw Jupiter shining brightly and vivaciously, practically palpitating with brilliance. How beautiful it was: just as in our childhood years when I used to point it out to him as it appeared amidst the olive branches on Sentry Hill. But my brother was never a great one for understanding the stars or loving them. (A pain in my cheek. Yes. Caused by his helmet. I stroked the spot.) . . . I became aware of someone next to me, telling me something. I had only just begun to hear him. He was talking about the thirty men.

"First," he said, "they'll cut their way through the entanglements with their shears, through three rows of wire, and the enemy won't even catch wind of them. Next, they'll kill the sentries without a sound, or capture them, and jump into the trench. The minute they've done that they'll ignite a green flare as a signal and then our artillery will let loose a terrific barrage that will cut the trench off from any reinforcement."

"Yes," I replied, "it might work out something like that."

Overhead, the stars were twinkling. Everyone was arrayed on the parapet, all eyes staring into the darkness. A dry, frigid wind from the north numbed our feet, sent stabs of pain into our ears. Each man, in his mind, was following our comrades, and each kept whispering his thoughts as his aching eyes struggled to pierce the night.

"They must be at the battered mulberry by now."

"Now? Surely they've already reached the 'white ground'—except if they scented some patrol and are lying low in the ravine."

"Not a single Bulgarian flare. The job seems to be going well."

"They're taking too long."

"You forgot the wire-cutting. That's where all the skill comes in. And all the danger, too."

They were talking now about my brother. My heart began to beat faster.

"Don't worry: Sergeant Kostoulas is with them. He's a crackerjack with the shears."

"Better'n a London tailor! I remember him one night in the other sector when—"

A grenade opposite. Our hearts froze. Everyone drew back with a start and fell silent. Then—vrrrrr—rifles, followed at once by a machine gun. At first only a single one, rattling away slowly, leisurely, with reports like a hammer nailing down sheathing to a roof: tap . . . tap . . . tap. Repeated hand grenades bursting in the distance amidst the fusillade. Illuminating rockets, brilliantly white—one, two, three, five, ten—shooting up from all parts of the Bulgarian trench and converging on the same spot. The Turtle remained silent. Asleep? Anything but. It opened one eye—an electric searchlight—and then closed it again, slowly. Other machine guns joined in during the interval. They swept bullets in every direction, firing rapidly now. It seemed that all the tardy ones that hadn't managed earlier were now suddenly in a great hurry to fire: a multitude of sewing machines stitching away. (At shrouds?) But no green rocket . . . nothing green.

"What happened to the signal? I don't see the signal. *Nobody* sees the signal!"

I raced to the captain. My hands were trembling, and so were my knees. I grasped his coat-sleeve.

"Sir," I said, "still no green rocket! What's the matter with our artillery? Our men are being hit over there."

The captain did not answer me. He was on the telephone, boiling with rage, practically breaking the instrument in two.

"Damn you, what's wrong with our batteries, what are they doing! All my men are going to be killed on me over there, and your cannons are asleep! What? . . . What'd you say?" (Drrring, drrring, drring.) "Hello? Hello? . . . Waiting for the signal? What goddamn signal do you expect at this point? Start the barrage at once! The barrage! . . . Hello? . . . The ba-RRAAGE! That's right! . . . What? . . . Who'll be responsible? Shit! Me, me!"

The barrage commenced. Shells passed high overhead, whole jolly flocks of them hurrying along without a break: a river of steel pouring through the cold air and heading across the way. They flew sang raced, those shells, yet it seemed to me that they were taking far too long to arrive. Faster! Faster! All the cannons together were uttering a single indivisible, incessant bellow. Hills trembled, hearts trembled, the air throbbed. Across the way, the detonations tied the cape-like bulge of the Bulgarian line inside their fiery semicircle: a half moon of flame and lightning. The fray, however, did not cease. Rifles still seethed even though the fusillade was no longer audible in the pandemonium caused by the bombardment. Nor was the Bulgarian artillery tardy in joining the dance. Scattered shells began to arrive now from the opposite lines, seeking out our batteries in a groping and haphazard way. The detonations resounded behind our lines like great cauldrons released high above the stony earth and crashing down onto the rocks.

The captain came into the trench to issue commands, a harsh and bitter expression on his face.

"Return to your dugouts—everyone! I want only the sentries in the trench."

"Sir, will you allow me to stay?"

No answer.

I stayed.

An entire hour; one interminable hour. Gradually, the cannonade grew less on both sides and ceased. Then the rifle shots died out little by little as well. Detonations from a grenade or two, here and there. Over opposite: nothing but flares, flares, and more flares. Holiday illuminations, one would have thought. A veritable sprouting of luminescent flowers, the thin red stems rising from the earth without cease: spreading their petals, withering, then blossoming once more. And that single machine gun that continued to fire away absentmindedly: it was the same that had begun ahead of the others, drawling out its remaining belts of ammunition now in its turn, finishing everything it had neglected to fire because of its sluggishness while the others reeled out their cartridges. Tap . . . tap . . . tap. The sound resembled a hammer patiently driving nails into a large wooden crate. (Into a coffin?)

Suddenly: a noise in the darkness. Coming closer and closer. Very near now, just outside our trench. Stifled groans, equipment clanking, many feet close together, stamping heavily. Then a protracted groan—"ehhhh . . . ehhhh"—like a sheep's bleating. Shadows passed by; shadows crawled rolled or jumped into the trench.

"This way! This way!"

A voice splitting with rage:

"What happened to the goddamned signalers and the green flare?"

A voice shattered with fatigue:

"I have the honor to inform you, Captain, that the signalers were killed by the Bulgarian sentries' very first grenade. The enemy had received word; our attack was expected."

I pushed my way past a lieutenant, tramped over someone else, flattened myself against the wall, was flattened against the wall.

"Kostoulas? Sergeant Kostoulas?" I was practically screaming.

"All right, quiet down," answered a testy voice emerging from underground. It came from behind a square patch of light through which hastily moving shadows passed at frequent intervals. "In here," said the voice, "Kostoulas is here. We brought him . . . "

They brought him? Brought him! These words I pronounced to myself, struggling to understand their meaning, as though hearing them for the very first time. Pushing people out of the way with my elbows and begging everyone's pardon, I advanced toward the square of underground brightness. My ears kept snatching the rag-ends of meaningless phrases:

"Over there! Look, over there . . ."

". . . the bastards! the bastards! . . ."

"... split his skull with the grenade discharger ..."

The large bunker. A veritable gallery. Wounded men everywhere. Medical aides with stretchers that they folded, unfolded, loaded, lifted, carried away.

"Careful there, careful! He's also got a broken spine." ...

"You, in front! Hold on tight!" .

"I'll shoot you! Louse! Patsy!"

"... they won't cut it off, will they, doc?" ...

My brother. My brother with clothes pulled back, pale chest exposed— lighted with barbarous clarity by the acetylene lamp; A delicate red ribbon trickled down between his nipples and disappeared at the waist. He was lying on a stretcher and a physician, a second lieutenant, was wrapping entire packages of dressings around his neck, winding the gauze beneath the armpits and then around the neck again. Each layer turned red before the next was applied. He carried out this procedure with assured motions, as though producing a work of art.

"My brother? Doctor, my brother?"

He glanced at me hastily, raising his eyes, then devoted himself once more to the bandaging. He was clasping a safety pin between his lips. Speaking through his teeth and wrapping the bandages all the while, he replied:

"Your brother? This fine chap your brother? Well ... I'd say he's mighty lucky, your brother. Shot clear through the neck. Just a hair's-breadth more toward the carotid and the projectile would have slaughtered him like a lamb. There's still a chance of infection, but that's all. If nothing develops, the sergeant will be back with his platoon in a month or two."

My brother raised his eyelashes little by little and searched wearily about, trying to spot me. He lay absolutely motionless, the only movement being in the irises of the eyes—his whole life had concentrated itself there. I moved into the light directly in front of him and he saw me, gazed at me with a long glance that touched, that kissed. Afterwards, he smiled at me as well, but only with his eyes. Then he closed them again. The physician secured the bandages with his safety pin and instructed the stretcher-bearers: "As soon as you arrive be sure they give him a tetanus shot."

They covered his shoulders thoroughly and began to take him away on the stretcher, one lifting in front, the other in back.

"Did you hear?" I asked one of the bearers in a pleading voice. He was fat and ruddy. Tugging timorously at his sleeve, I reminded him: "As soon as you arrive be sure they give him a tetanus shot . . . . You won't forget, will you?"

He eyed me angrily (my brother is big and heavy).

"All right, all right for god's sake!" And he moved toward the exit.

I remained there mutely for a moment as though struck dumb, then hastened to look for my captain. I found him at the back of the gallery; he was standing in the half-darkness, looming over some soldiers who were stretched out on the ground all in a row.

"Sir, pardon . . ."

Without turning to look at me:

"What do you want?"

"Please, Sir, may I follow the bearers who carried off my brother?"

"What for? I need you here. You're taking over his platoon—starting now!"

"Captain, Sir . . ."

Suddenly he spun half around and said in a harsh tone:

"All right, then, have a look!"

Removing a flashlight from his coat pocket, he pressed the button and cast the luminous disc upon the soldiers who were lying on the ground. He paraded the light over every face, each in its turn, and allowed the radiant circle to remain for a moment on each, apparently to add stress for my benefit.

On the ground lay five men with motionless faces and halfopened sightless eyes. One of the faces was missing its entire lower jaw; the light came to rest on the teeth of the upper jaw. Another had its right eye open, as though winking slyly. The features of still another were youthful, clean-shaven, immaculate, with lips resolutely closed and eyes wide open, their lashes dense and long.

The flashlight penetrated deeply, cruelly, into all those eyes. It pierced them, yet no one was disturbed, no one blinked his lids.

51

The Deserters

*E*arly this morning a group of Bulgarian deserters was delivered to us—
one sergeant-major and seven men: an entire patrol. They had suddenly turned up in front of our company's sector, just as a little glimmer of
blue was invading the sky and you could begin to distinguish a human
form from a bush They surrendered to the two sentries on duty at the post
furthest from the trench. Why they didn't collide with our final patrol is a
mystery. Placing their weapons on the ground, they undid their cartridge
belts, even took off their tunics. Then they raised their hands high and
shouted to our men to capture them. Their sergeant-major had a white
handkerchief tied to a stick that he held up in the air the whole time. Our
sentries took handkerchiefs, waistbands, whatever they could find, and
blindfolded them, then led them to the trench. They walked so slowly,
groping their way forward, that daybreak was well advanced before they
arrived.

It was the hour when our men had just returned from their patrols and
various work-assignments. No sooner had the news spread than they all
popped out of their dugouts, every one of them, to watch the strange procession as it headed toward Company H. Q.

The deserters proceeded in single file. As is always the case when blindfolded people have to walk, they were hunched over and stumbling. Their
feet tested the ground at every step. They held their arms out in front of
them to help negotiate bends in the trench and avoid collisions. Our men

conversed among themselves in hushed tones, their faces thoughtful but undemonstrative. Suddenly one of the deserters tripped over a spade that had been left in the middle of the trench. He fell flat on his face; the others behind him halted, frightened. Their shoulders, which had nothing but a shirt for covering and were shivering, rose up as though trying to conceal their heads from some blow that might come from an unknown direction. The man who fell did not utter a sound. One of our corporals darted forward and helped him onto his feet, then gave him an encouraging pat on the back. The prisoner was a tall, extremely skinny man who wore a yellow shirt. The black waistband bound over his eyes covered his entire scalp, like a turban. His palms were exceedingly broad, his arms disproportionately long. They hung down like paddles. He smiled when he had been placed on his feet again, revealing a row of yellow teeth. Blood was trickling from one nostril; he kept wiping it off his chin, smiling continually.

When he crashed to the ground, one of our men had laughed out loud —"haw haw haw"— and had shouted the call of a farmer starting up his oxen: "heee-aaa!" This was Mitreli, the jaundiced little hunchback. He had been sauntering behind the procession, his hands thrust into his trouser pockets. The others who were watching turned and looked at him reprovingly. A strapping fellow from Ayiassos, a muleteer with colossal fists, placed his finger on Mitreli's hump and pushed—you'd have thought he was driving a stake into it. Lowering over him with sparks in his eyes, he barked forcefully and significantly: "You! Don't laugh!" whereupon Mitreli shrank into his hump, like a snail into its shell.

After the initial interrogation the prisoners were apportioned to the various dugouts, for hospitality as well as surveillance. So long as they stayed inside our underground chambers their blindfolds could be removed. They were to be our visitors until nightfall, after which they would be transferred to regimental headquarters.

The one brought to my dugout was the sergeant-major, Anthony Petrov by name. He was absolutely delighted to be out of the war and even more delighted to find himself here with us since we all know Turkish after a fashion. So did he; thus we communicated splendidly.

All his belongings had been returned to him, except weapons. Judging from the stale chunk of hardtack discovered in his pack, these men were

STRATIS MYRIVILIS

starving over there. The bread was dark, almost blue, and full of rye as well as dirt. We gave him something from our rations; we brewed him some tea. For dunking we offered him half a loaf of our own bread: oven-fresh, and ever so light and fluffy. He devoured it to the last crumb, the joy of eating spread across the whole of his broad face. He was a burly, well-built man of about forty, with a blond mustache. Our ministrations touched him deeply and he strove to demonstrate his gratitude in every way possible. With men on all sides asking him two or three entirely different questions at the same time, he could scarcely get the answers out fast enough. He told us about his family. Back home he had fields full of roses: he manufactured attar of roses. What do you think of that! Attar of roses! This elicited barrels of laughter from our Lesvians and Anatolians, leaving him most perplexed. You see, our olive growers and wheat farmers failed to understand how anyone could make a living out of roses. But when Petrov told them the prices fetched by rose oil their jaws dropped. Now his wife was working the rose fields by herself, looking out to make ends meet and trying to manage the best she could, between the fields and the babies—three of them. As for managing: don't ask—it was enough to make a man weep. The blockade pinched the area severely; the Germans carted away the entire wheat-harvest to the very last grain. His family was starving. In addition, it was a bad year for roses: they had a blight that covered them with a cottony substance. In any case, there wasn't any demand for the product despite its scarcity. One calamity on top of another. But no matter—let be, let be. Petrov accepted it all, did not begrudge his fate. What could you expect—it was wartime. But that Liuba should go hungry. . .

Liuba!

She was his youngest, the last child, a little girl only three years old. And for two whole years he hadn't seen her. "Iki sene bitti." All his thoughts were on Liuba. Liuba had a headful of golden curls. Liuba wanted daddy to send her a whole sackful of rusks because she was hungry. Liuba told mommy it was high time her curls were cut. She didn't want dresses any more; she wanted to wear trousers like her brothers, to become a boy just like them. Because she thought that all little children wore dresses and were called girls when they were very very tiny but that as soon as they grew up a bit they were given trousers, had their hair cut, and in this way

308

were turned into boys. Ha ha! Hee hee! Liuba this, Liuba that. Most important of all, she was cross-eyed in one of her little eyes (they're dark blue) and this explained why she was more delectable than the others, why Petrov loved her the most of all—more than his wife even, and more than his two boys. Because she was cross-eyed in one eye.

Before long we all knew Liuba inside out, as though we had brought her up right here in this chamber. Petrov reached into his kit and removed a small package done up in yellowish wax paper. He undid the wrappings and brought out triumphantly: a bonnet!

"It's Liuba's," he informed us. He passed it to each man in turn, following it and caressing it with his blue-eyed gaze as it went from hand to hand. He asked if any of us was married. We told him we were all single.

'Agh, you can't understand, you can't understand," he sighed.

Petrov deserted chiefly because of Liuba. He didn't want to die. He would crush rocks for the French and English until the war ended; and he would find some way to send a little money to his wife now and then. He was strong, healthy—he could work no matter where he was. This war would end sooner or later, no doubt of that. Then, if they didn't let him return home in peace, he would arrange for his family to come to him. He was sick and tired of fighting. He'd been in the Balkan Wars, too; from 1912 until now his family had known him only as a visitor. He possessed two wounds from Greek Mannlichers. Received at Kilkish. One in the shoulder and one in the chest. "İşte!" He pulled open his shirt and showed us the scars.

"You see? That was a war, a really bad war."

"But that means we've met previously," I said to him. "I have two Bulgarian machine-gun bullets in my leg." (I showed him the wounds.) "İşte!"

"They weren't from me," he replied with a thunderous guffaw. "I was never a machine-gunner."

Together, we reminisced about that terrible battle, recalling all the events as though they had happened just an hour ago. Three days and nights of uninterrupted massacre and struggle. The Bulgarians granted us the victory at the price of seven thousand of our men killed or wounded. First, they caught us out in the open on a plain and slaughtered us. A plain covered with wheat; a whole sea of ripe grain. The crops caught fire in the end and our wounded were burned alive. The red-black flames danced upon the wheat, leapt and raced like waves. The grain crackled, then lay down flat. And the whole plain howled. The earth itself uttered howls of pain—it was the wounded, howling as they roasted alive. Then came our turn. We plunged into the flames like madmen, into the uproar of the shell-bursts. In we plunged like drunken madmen, armed with nothing but our bayonets. The Bulgarians kept discharging their rifles from the trenches until the very end, until we extracted them from those ditches with our bayonets. Like ripping baked snails out of their shells with a fork!

Anthony Petrov remembered all this extremely well. He kept clapping his hands upon his knees every few moments and exclaiming "Allah! Allah!" with relief.

He said that he would prefer to lay down his head and have his throat cut like a lamb, rather than have to go out again and fight. It is clear that this Bulgarian veteran "has seen war." And he has seen it with the eyes of tiny Liuba, one of which (they are dark blue) is slightly crossed, making her all the more delectable.

He was asked to explain how he and his mates had managed to fly the coop over there. Ah, they'd been thinking of it for ages. When they finally made up their minds, they set themselves up as a patrol.

Then: "Bizim tellerde sizin tellere"—"from our barbed wire to your barbed wire . . ." (this. is the phrase that invariably begins accounts of desertion).

Many of our neighbors, men from Aivaly and Adramyttion who knew Turkish, began to slip one by one into our dugout. They wanted to hear the adventure directly from Petrov's lips. And Petrov, not the least bit loath or fatigued, began it all over again and repeated it—recited it by rote now—for each and every newcomer. He repeated it from the very beginning, his blue eyes laughing happily:

"Bizim tellerden sizin tellere."

52

Alimberis Conquers His
Fear of Shells

*F*or the past two weeks they've been preparing us for the great undertaking. Our entire division, reinforced by two non-divisional regiments of reservists, is going to charge the enemy in order to capture one of
their large fortified garrisons The organization needed for this colossal
slaughter—needed until the very moment we receive the signal for it to
begin—is proceeding with a system so scientifically refined, down to its
last insignificant detail, that it boggles the mind. Every conquest of the
human brain in engineering, the sciences, psychology, even in art, has
become an instrument to aid, as much as it can, the complete extermina-
tion of the human beings across the way, men who are lying in wait just as
we are, wrapped in their mud.

Satanic engines, murderous vapors enclosed in tubes and shells: they
poison the air, expunge the vision from one's eyes, raise suppurated pus-
tules on the lungs. Flame that lays waste whatever it finds before it except
tanned leather. Flame that re-ignites automatically by itself after it has been
dipped in water and drawn out again into the air. Short, plump torpedoes
pregnant with terrible explosive matter. A smaller type that we launch in a
kind of tiny trench mortar, using compressed air instead of gunpowder
and wick. Incendiary bombs that spill thousands of burning grains out of
their bellies when they burst, grains that hop about on their own like devils and can therefore kindle a great number of fires. Thermite bombs capable of developing sufficient heat to melt the breech and barrel of a large-

bore cannon, fusing them into a doughish lump of undifferentiated metal. (Once we ignited one inside a steel helmet, which melted and turned to ash in a minute, as though made of cardboard.) Complicated pumps whose nozzles sprinkle fire and death. Masks resembling those worn by sponge-divers. Straps, rubber belts, respirators, chemical apparatuses, electronic mechanisms with microphones that overhear secrets and betray them. Magnificent flares that will ignite like multicolored constellations over thousands of innocent men when they are writhing on the ground, their lungs smashed and their living intestines wriggling between blood-stained clots of mud like flayed serpents.

But of all these repulsive inventions, the one that sends the ugliest chill up my spine is the trench knife. This simple, plain knife with its wide blade is used by the "liquidators": soldiers who stay behind in a conquered trench in order to "mop it up" while the "waves" of the assault move forward. What this means is that they slaughter all of the enemy who have remained hidden in dark corners or in the abandoned dugouts, whether from fear or cunning—slaughter them coolly and deliberately, by hand, at close range, like lambs. These liquidators or "mop-up men" (doesn't their ironic name remind you of municipal street-cleaners or of peaceful bank-clerks?) must put every last one of the laggards to the knife, one by one. If you want to "cleanse" a dugout you start by tossing in a couple of hand grenades, or you spray it with the flame-thrower. If you have a gas bomb on you, so much the better. This is the burning of the hornet's nest. You heave one inside and all who are hiding there dart through the entrance, stumbling from suffocation and inflamed eyes. The liquidators are waiting for them outside. They slaughter them and then proceed to the next dug-out.

All this is being instructed by means of lectures, illustrations, realistic mock-ups, and very enlightening theory.

Last night the captain gathered the whole company together in the large anti-bombardment bunker. He told us that he didn't want a single coward to be found among our ranks during the attack. One and one only, he said, was enough to spread panic, causing the failure of an operation and the useless deaths of countless comrades. This we all found very reasonable in every respect. Afterwards, however, he rested his eyes on us and, smiling in a kindly manner, issued a request. If there was anyone among us who knew himself to be "faint-hearted," would he please not hesitate to say so frankly. What mattered was that he declare himself *now*.

This made all of us feel rather strange. The great bunker where we had assembled is a complete gallery burrowed six meters beneath the surface. We gather here whenever the enemy begins an all-out bombardment, because the other dugouts cannot withstand the "big boys" for very long whereas this place is an. entire fortress. The timbers lining its walls and roof are whole tree-trunks, its ingress a veritable labyrinth; there is a layer of soil five meters thick above it, and armor plating inside. Big as it is, however, it holds all two hundred of us only with difficulty. Whenever we remain inside for more than a few hours at a time, the air grows noxious. If the sentries at the door had allowed it, many would have slipped outside during the bombardments to fill their lungs with "clean," cool air, at the risk of losing their lives. . . .

The atmosphere this time was just the same, gathered as we were once more in the great bunker, the cannons howling across the way. During a long interval we did not talk; we just listened to the bursting shells as they barked in the air. The captain's voice had sounded so calm amid all this uproar in the background that it made one feel almost safe just to be near him. With that ingratiating smile on his rosy lips, he promenaded his gaze upon us and waited to discover whether or not there really was a "faint-hearted" man in our company.

We all understood perfectly well, yet no one possessed the courage to open his heart and utter the truth. Looking straight ahead because of our embarrassment yet filled with a certain curiosity, we waited. As soon as the slightest murmur or noise was heard, however, we turned with a mass movement and searched about in order to discover who was ready to confess his "faint-heartedness." The unshaven faces gleamed as white as plaster beneath the illumination of the acetylene lamp, a secret fever burning in their sunken eyes. I felt an inner urge to push my way through the crowd and station myself at the captain's side so that I could face all of my comrades and say to them: "Listen, every one of you—does this mean that there isn't a single brave man among us? We're two hundred strong here. The captain is looking for one coward; I'm looking for one man of courage—a man brave enough to confess that he is afraid to die. Nobody? Well then, every last one of us is faint-hearted; we're a lot of cowardly and good-for-nothing liars."

At the same time, however, I felt that not even I myself possessed such inner courage. Indeed, I wouldn't have been at all surprised if my lips were being sealed by the War Cross, my tongue being tied in knots by my second stripe.

Meanwhile, a voice did speak out. It came from the rear of the gallery during those difficult moments we were all experiencing.

"Sir, if you please . . ."

A rustling, a stirring. The mass of soldiers squeezed itself together even tighter than before and opened an aisle down which came a short private with curly hair and squarish shoulders. Vasilios Athanasios Alimberis. Speaking slowly, and searching for the proper expressions, he made the following declaration:

"I respectfully inform you, Captain, that I am faint-hearted, and I earnestly request that I may be left behind when the attack takes place."

"Do you mean to say you're afraid?"

The captain asked this in a tone of near-astonishment, as though actually insulted that such a declaration should be heard in his company. Alimberis answered, more boldly now, a confessional tone entering his heavy, boorish speech:

"That's what I mean, Captain. Yes, afraid. I'm a carpenter, just a simple carpenter, you understand. I'm still single, because I have my old mother and four sisters to support—a hopeless business to be sure. I haven't even been able to marry off the oldest yet. They sold our little farm, the only thing our father left us when he died, and for the time being they're eating up the proceeds. I've got them on my mind day and night; I can't think of anything else. Tell me, what will become of five women with no means of support, if the war lasts much longer? . . . In my whole life I've never quarreled with a single soul. I don't have the courage to kill. Every time I hear a shell, I feel like I'm giving up the ghost. I shiver; you'd think I was freezing. I might faint at the sight of blood. But work—nothing but the best. Give me all you like; I'm at your service, with pleasure! I can run a lathe. Hand me some wood and I'll turn you out the most ingenious things you've ever seen, absolutely first class. . . . Please forgive me, Captain, for making bold to tell you all this. You see, I've spoken as in the confessional. We all know you to be a man of good heart. That's why I said to myself, Let's tell him the whole truth, seeing that he's ordered us to, and he'll forgive me."

Vasilis Athanasios Alimberis spoke these words and then fell silent. He had remained at rigid attention the whole time, motionless except for his fluttering eyelids. Behind his coarse pronunciation I felt that I heard the muted, tender tones of another voice that had died. Yes, what I heard was the painful lamentation of Gighandis—the only difference being that he, lacking Alimberis's extreme simplicity and possessing an ego whose multifarious weaknesses had been cultivated to an incredible degree, would never have yielded up the unpardonable truth about himself to so many people.

No one knew what would happen next. Alimberis remained at attention. His innocent eyes, fixed directly upon the captain, were awaiting some response that assuredly would be crucial for his life. All the rest of us were awaiting that response, too, since very likely it would have repercussions for others as well. Outside, the cannonade was still bellowing away maniacally. The captain grimaced, deep in thought. His hands were behind his back and he was thinking—but he certainly was not thinking pleasant thoughts. Ugly wrinkles creased his ruddy features and a flash of harsh cruelty passed across his eyes as he slowly lifted his gaze from Alimberis's feet and paraded it gradually up his entire body until it halted inside the carpenter's eyes. This stare into the eyes lasted just a moment. Then the captain smiled courteously (Alimberis returned the smile, mirror-like), motioned the soldier to stand at ease, and commanded:

"Sergeant Pavlelis!"

"Here, Captain."

"You will accompany the second patrol when it leaves. You will take four men from your platoon and convey Private Alimberis through the exit *boyau* to the second row of barbed wire. There you will bind him to the steel post that stands to the right of the entanglement's ingress, where he shall remain—in order to grow accustomed to shellfire—until I send someone to bring him back." (Then, as though by way of explanation:)

"It's just a question of habituation, this. Getting it out of one's system, that's all. Then you're not afraid any more."

The captain's very first words had turned Alimberis pale as wax. Now he held out his hands and cast terrified glances first at the captain, then at Sergeant Pavlelis, after which he began to stammer rapidly and in great confusion, his eyes filled with tears:

"You couldn't do that, Captain, Sir . . . I respectfully inform you . . . no, you wouldn't do that to me, Sir . . . you'll take pity . . ."

"But it's not anything you need be frightened about, as you seem to think," said the captain. "You won't get the slightest scratch, I assure you. The place is hidden behind some bushes, quite aside from the fact that our friends happen to be pounding us on the left flank just now. I'm trying to help you get it out of your system, don't you see? Tomorrow, never fear, you'll come back to us a real champ. Greece has lots of good carpenters. Well, now they've all got to become good soldiers. . . . And there's no call, if you please, for sniveling and tears. Men at war, Private Alimberis, do not cry!"

Alimberis wiped his eyes with his huge hands and answered:

"I'm crying for myself, Captain, and I'm crying for five women, too. . ."

Late that night, Sergeant Pavielis presented himself at the captain's dugout, his hand raised in salute.

"Your orders have been carried out, Sir."

"My orders?"

"Concerning Private Alimberis. We bound him to the post at the ingress to the second row of barbed wire, just as you commanded."

"How did he behave? Did he offer any resistance?"

"None at all. He just kept pleading with us, blubbering away. He said he'd die if we left him alone out there in the darkness with all those rockets. I felt sorry for him, to tell you the truth. Every shell that passes overhead makes him jump clear out of his skin."

* **

Who knows what tragedy unfolded out there at the ingress to the second row of barbed wire, during the night. The darkness was so thick, probably even God himself was unable to witness it.

316

Two men went out at dawn to bring Alimberis back. They found him completely calm. His arms, bound at the elbows behind the post, were bloody from the rope and the barbed wire. He was leaning back against the post, his head resting on his left shoulder. When they released him he sat down on the ground and studied his hands, first the palms, then the backs. Next, he commenced to cut off his buttons one by one and to pull out the threads ever so slowly with his fingernails, whistling softly all the while. He performed this task with the utmost care. The soldiers, who still had not understood, kept telling him: "Let's get a move on before daylight comes and you get us in trouble. You can do your mending in your dugout. Looks like they've really made a man out of you at last."

Alimberis seemed not to hear. Bending down in the half-darkness, they saw him close at hand, clearly, and only then did they understand. They grasped him beneath the armpits. With one in front dragging and the other in back pushing, they got him into the exit *boyau* and brought him from there to the trench. He whistled the whole way. Afterwards, he continued to whistle, always unraveling his clothes. When he finally gave this up his lips remained puckered in the same position, as though still whistling. Today, he was sent to the hospital. To arrive there you have to negotiate an exposed pass, a section that the enemy bombards if even so much as an ant attempts to cross it. With great difficulty they got him to crouch over and make a run for it. The shells that raced shrieking over his head were unable to instill either fear or interest into his tormented spirit, which had already died. It had been taken out there to the exit at the second row of barbed wire one terrible night during the bombardment, and killed. Why? Because he had dared to let this spirit reveal its true condition.

I feel no love for my captain any longer. I can only pity him—or can I?

53

The Jack-of-All-Trades

Yesterday, an unusual scandal involving the entire regiment broke out in our company. Since then, we've been talking about nothing else.

They discovered that my friend Dimitratos has been concocting sick and crippled soldiers in our trench. The man who betrayed him was Batalis, a middle-aged private who paid Dimitratos twenty drachmas—not to mention a pair of new socks, 100% wool, and a cigarette lighter—to fabricate a pain in the eyes that would confine him to hospital for a month or two, thus giving him a respite from trench-duty. Dimitratos succeeded so magnificently well that he completely destroyed the sight of both eyes. When the doctor informed Batalis that his chances of ever seeing again were nil, the poor man started screaming in desperation. He tried to get hold of his gun in order to kill himself, and he began to curse Dimitratos for maiming him. In the inquiry that followed, the Regiment examined the particularly high incidence of ill health that has been observed in our company and the ones near to us. A whole pile of strange tales came out into the open.

When we first arrived here I proposed to Dimitratos that he make himself at home in my dugout, but he did not accept. Instead, he chose to roost next door, all by himself, in a cramped and inconvenient nest into which he had to wedge himself like a bat. I see now that he had his reasons. The lieutenant conducting the inquiry took away his kit unexpectedly, and also searched this lair of his. Discovered inside was a whole collection of "tools of the trade." You see, throbbing eyes were not the only things Dimitratos concocted. In the other sector he had collected an herb which, when rubbed between the fingers or in the joints, caused spots to erupt that were indistinguishable from those caused by scabies. Soldiers removed to the hospital because ostensibly they had the symptoms of scabies, brought along a sufficient supply of this plant. No sooner did the spots begin to disappear from their bodies than they rubbed themselves again with the scabies-herb, whereupon the treatment commenced all over again from the beginning—far away from the shooting. Even a syringe had been discovered in Dimitratos's kit. This he employed to inject fuel oil into the thigh-muscle. In a few days a terrible inflammation would begin, followed by an open wound giving off pus and putrescent flesh. But this was not all. He also had a kind of sulfur-cigarette that caused chronic coughing complete with râles and crepitations. With these cigarettes a liberal smoker could turn himself into a "consumptive" with no effort at all; but, by the same token, he could secure permission to return home. In addition to this, Dimitratos fabricated sudden rises in temperature, recurrent low-grade fevers, and various kinds of other illnesses. The men called him "Jack-of-all-trades," and no one ratted on him. All this is coming to light only now, detail by detail; the file of documents in the case is piling up and swelling. The accused—a whole mess of them, with Dimitratos heading the lot—will be court—martialed, and the universal prediction is that he'll be shot. As for the Jack-of-all-trade's customers, testimony has shown them to be spread throughout the entire regiment. Also noted was a sudden increase in business commencing on the very day the division began to contemplate its great assault and to prepare for it.

Drawing Dimitratos aside, I asked him if all this were true.

He shot a blob of snot onto the ground with much noise, rubbed his mustache between his fingers, and said to me with a shrug of the shoulders:

"So it seems . . ."

"What are you going to do about it?"

"Going to do about it? If they jail me before the attack, I escape certain death. They'll take me into custody and keep me there—if I'm lucky—until the end of the war. Meals, a bed, and to hell with you suckers."

"Supposing they interpret your activities as 'fomenting and instigating desertion'?"

"Death and cashiering! . . . Big deal! The minute the attack starts, there'll be thousands of similar executions without benefit of court-martial—as sure as we're standing here looking at each other. . . . Come on, give me that pack of cigarettes."

He lit up, puffed out a mouthful of smoke, and scratched his beard with all five fingernails.

"Let's be entirely straight with each other, Dimitratos. Tell me frankly: Haven't you ever been bothered by the moral implications of this 'trade' you've been practicing? Your work has put rifles out of action. Greek rifles. See what I mean?"

"The fact of the matter is, I don't see any 'moral implications' whatsoever. We're fighting because we have to; we have no choice. The Bulgarians aren't after us; neither are the Germans. But behind our lines the court-martial is in session. That's why we're fighting. As for my 'trade': I rescued various people from the trenches, from this hell, and I sent regular remittances to my poor wife and my kids to keep them from starving. That —*that!*—is my 'trade.' My kids!" (His heavy eyebrows quivered with irritation, his eyes stared glassily, like those of a vulture when its nest is being despoiled. He repeated with a sudden outburst of rage:) "My kids! . . . As for all the rest: you know where it goes? . . . Right here!"

Raising his hand with the fingers joined, he placed it unambiguously in his crotch.

54

Gas

*F*rom all appearances they've caught wind across the way of the great undertaking that we are organizing in our front lines and in the supply stations behind us. For three days now, enemy planes have been operating over our positions with admirable bravery and daring. In all the raids the sky fills with little cotton-like clouds that sprout everywhere and follow behind each enemy aircraft like a flock of lambs. These are the shells from our anti-aircraft batteries bursting high in the blue sky. Occasionally, one of the metallic war-birds is brought down. Three mornings ago a lone German bomber engaged seven allied fighters above our lines. It escaped intact after downing an English plane, which fell from the top of the sky, howling as it descended (as though in pain) and trailing a comet of pitch-black smoke behind it. The pilot's body worked loose and fell straight downward like some kind of black thing, whereas the airplane kept burning and weeping until it crashed a mile away. On another day two German planes came and trained their sights on a huge observation-balloon that hovered in the air like a colossal yellow kidney, permanently moored to a small humpish mountain. A bullet found it, igniting the hydrogen inside, and the observer who was in its basket plunged to the ground out of a majestic fire whose flaming tongue licked the heavens, fluttered for a moment like a sheet of gold, and then abruptly died out. The observer was a young French major. He lived for a short time, and with his last breaths he begged his Command to tell his brother, who was serving in France, not to remain in the forces any longer but to go and stay with their mother. Of her four sons, this brother was the only one left.

* * *

The offensive is now the one great topic of conversation in the trenches. Apparently the hour is approaching. And apparently the enemy are fully expecting us. These last few days their artillery batteries have been literally maniacal in their attempt to eradicate our trenches—especially in the mornings, when the whole universe seems to be falling apart. The men have come to display a melancholy fatalism when they discuss the impending events. Everyone knows that he is bound to play a part, like it or not.

Two days ago, at dawn, the Bulgarians started bombarding us with time-fire projectiles and asphyxiant gas, combined. It was our first opportunity to experience the latter weapon in actual use. True, we had heard of it previously as a kind of legend, thanks to the theoretical lectures delivered to us before we buried ourselves in the trenches. Since then, our gas masks had been an almost senseless luxury, indeed a troublesome one, since their containers, suspended awkwardly from our belts at the end of a cord, bang relentlessly against our thighs and make noise as they strike our rifles.

About a dozen friends were gathered in my dugout telling stories when the initial gas bombs landed, making a special type of hollow sound. We took them at first for common shells that had plunged into some boggish area and failed to explode. Several of the men even shouted out the customary mock—"New fuse needed! Take aim, boys!"—and then returned to their storytelling as if nothing had happened.

Afterwards we caught a whiff of some scent in the air. It was an extremely light and pleasant aroma resembling bitter almond. The concentration soon increased, however, and before long the air was acrid, pungently sour, poisoned. In an instant the trench hummed with sudden stirrings. A pandemonium of cries, the stupefied confusion of shrieks and commands.

"Gas! Gas!" shouted the N.C.O.s maniacally. "Masks everyone! Your masks!"

But practically none of us had his mask ready to hand. Those who chanced to be visiting in someone else's dugout at that moment, far from their kits, had an especially bad time of it. What followed was a tragedy of mass confusion. Most of the men attempted to flee my dugout. It's a deep one, you see, and thus more and more of the gas—which is heavier than air—kept settling inside and filling it. But how could anyone stick even his nose out into the trench? It was guaranteed suicide. The sky out there was raining lead and steel, the time fuses just waiting for each man to scamper out of his dugout so that they could smash him head-on; the "bonbonnières" were bursting at a fixed height over our lines and scattering a thick hail of lead upon anyone who dared emerge. So all the men retreated back into the shelter. Climbing over one another like drunkards or lunatics, they dug their fists into eyes that were smarting horribly and flooding with tears as though sprinkled with red pepper. Their noses and mouths (which were locked tight) they thrust so deeply beneath blankets that they were in danger of suffocating. A painful clawing in the throat and nose made everyone bellow with a harsh cough while the mud-covered hands kept furiously rubbing enflamed eyes. It was a sight whose unspeakable bestiality I could never have imagined before I actually saw it. In my own case, I had managed to find my mask in time, searching blindly with eyes squeezed tight. Soon, I was staring through its clouded lenses, overcome by the unheard-of horror and listening to the agony of my tormented comrades all of whom were rolling about in one frenzied mass of pale, blinded, mud-besplattered humanity, rolling about and bellowing as though in the last throes of rabies. Howling, they bit into their greatcoats and blankets. Their heads groped about and knocked against each other inside this skein of tangled bodies, like the heads of newly born puppies when their eyes are still sealed and they search in chaos, using the sensitivity to touch possessed by their naked snouts. I was glued against the shelter's partition-wall pressing my palms tightly against the mask and overcome to such a degree by fear and pain that I could give no assistance whatsoever to anyone. If an enemy soldier had entered our dugout at that point, one single enemy soldier, he would have been able to polish us all off without the slightest difficulty. We would have sat there and allowed him to slaughter us just as we were, with our blinded eyes, powerless to defend our lives, and weeping like little girls. Several might even have thanked him profusely for delivering them from this torment.

Fortunately, it did not last very long. Even better, a furious wind began to blow immediately afterward, a wind that went right inside us, reviving us as it raced refreshingly through our flaming lungs like a fountain of life. It rinsed the infection out of the trench's air and carried away the lethal vapor. Places where the gas bombs exploded are still unapproachable. Most of the shells, however, we buried. To fumigate the dugouts we burned solidified alcohol inside them.

Although the horror did not last very long, hordes of men were sent to the hospitals: blinded, vomiting, coughing until racked with convulsions, grimacing horribly and spitting blood, viscera festering, eyes swollen shut: pasted together by yellowish discharges and resembling two wounds beginning to scab. In our trench six men died, among them George Dimitratos, who suffocated within ten minutes. When I went to see him I failed to recognize him at first. His face was bloated, his lips so swollen that the hairs of his mustache were standing erect, like porcupine quills. He seemed to be holding a mouthful of water between his distended cheeks, prior to spitting it out at us in jest. In short, the Jack-of-all-trades will not be court-martialed after all. Nor shall we hear him ever again telling any of those cynical jokes of his. May God have pity on his children, so that he may repose in eternal peace. Amen.

The rest of us have acquired an uninterrupted watering of the eyes as our souvenir from this bombardment. Strong light irritates us now and we seek out dim corners like people infected with rabies. In addition, there have been repercussions in our stomachs, which balk at accepting nourishment. The chief sentiment that this weapon has left in us is rage—an impotent rage for having undergone humiliation, and especially a humiliation caused by such an unmanly means of waging war. All such means are so contrary to the traditions of Greek gallantry that they are almost incomprehensible to us. The men have been going into the trench and spitting toward the Bulgarian line.

"Cheats! Frauds! Charlatans! . . . Phthou!"

55

Waiting for a Quarter Past Two - I

*T*he great moment has finally arrived; the stupendous blow is scheduled for tonight. Warfare, this time, will involve all the multifarious
ingredients of battle. The strike will stretch over an area measured in square
kilometers, entire divisions will come to blows, huge distances will be covered. The complete fortified unit to our right must be wrested from the hands
of the Germano-Bulgarian garrison. Apparently their whole line in the Balkan sector depends on this fortification, and we are going to take it from
them—since it has to be taken. This is what you see, what you read, on
every face. It seems to be a sort of solution, and into this general solution
each man drags his own personal problem to solve that, too. The word that
is going the rounds is "offensive." They pronounce this word in hushed tones,
as though confidentially; they utter it with sarcasm accompanied by significant winks; they hurl it forth with stubborn resolution, though in relation to
whom no one can tell. Teeth clench, molars strain behind sunken cheeks:

"We'll have it out in the offensive!"

It is definitely scheduled for tonight at a quarter past two. "Two-six-
teen" is the exact order. Captains keep verifying the correct time by telephone. Although the hour is still far away, everyone with a wristwatch
lifts his arm repeatedly, looks at the dial, and keeps staring at it in each
instance for a considerable time, as though filled with anguished curiosity
to follow those tiny hands that are parading along time's road with such
minuscule steps each one of which brings us that much closer to the cru-

cial moment. People feel a certain kind of impatience regarding even the most terrible things. We all seem drained of energy—all except the captain. He is everywhere at once, anticipating the slightest eventuality, concerned about everything down to the minutest detail. He comes to each one of us and for each man he has a friendly word that eases the spirit and steels the heart.

Our artillery commenced to rake the enemy trenches an hour ago. One thousand and fifty cannons pounding away without interruption. It's amazing, almost unbearable. Without respite or pause. And this is quite aside from the "trench engines." What possibly can remain in the face of this wrath? A soldier's flesh is as soft as dough. One meager little sliver from a hand grenade is sufficient to slash through it (and every hand grenade bursts into a hundred slivers). The belly especially is so very soft and unprotected. And every wound in the guts brings a certain, slow, and painful death.

How huge, potent and merciless—how incredibly numerous—are the mechanisms that warfare opposes to the soldier's body! When will someone make this simple fact enter public consciousness: that tonight at a quarter past two it will not be a question of thirty thousand Greeks fighting thirty thousand Germans and Bulgarians, but rather sixty thousand tender human bodies fighting countless mechanisms of steel. These are the actual antagonists: men on one side, machines on the other. And victory will go to the machines. Machines do not suffer, do not love; they lack imagination. And they have no notion whatever of how joyful it is to be alive or how sweet and comforting is the sun.

"It" will take place tonight, two hours and sixteen minutes past midnight, and no one can alter that fact, not even God. Our one thousand and fifty cannons are already "preparing" the assault, which means that one thousand and fifty shells are digging into the enemy trenches every second in search of human flesh. And over there an equal number are awaiting their turn. Perched in their hideaways behind foliage and netting, they remain silent, awaiting a word, a signal, before they reply.

The whole world trembles and roars without cease. The sky trembles; the air trembles. I have to relight my candle continually because the pressure keeps extinguishing it. Whenever a "big boy" explodes nearby, I feel a pain in my stomach as though someone were suddenly punching me there with his fist. The air has filled with unheard-of sounds, as if some huge monster as shapeless and outspread as rain had saturated the atmosphere with its sensitive being and as if some titan were torturing it mercilessly—harpooning it with flaming tridents—whereupon the monster rolls up and contracts, howls, wails with countless mouths, bellows, threatens, and whiningly complains. . . . No, it's not that either: it's the whole of creation groaning, whistling, cursing. Every cave has become a croaking mouth, every ravine has spread wide its bare craggy jaws and is rumbling with intolerable pain. A divine whip lashes creation on this chilly night, a drizzle of sleet wets down its naked back. The whip whistles and falls; it wraps itself around the living earth, around its hindquarters, incising bloody furrows there. And the earth bolts forward in an attempt to snap the chains of the law that keeps it yoked to its rotation, as to a capstan. Goaded by terror's mad folly, it lunges in an effort to escape, its crust wrinkling and shuddering like living skin. It struggles to plunge over the brink into oblivion, seeks the most out-of-the-way corner where it can drag itself, quivering like a whipped hound. Large invisible bodies race in packs through the flaming darkness, trailing frenzied shrieks behind them. Opposite us a volcano with a thousand craters is erupting. Red flames and green flames vault from the earth's surface to lick night's face while our searchlights spill torrents of harsh light into the Bulgarian trenches. . . .

And here I sit, writing to you!

Whom else do I have? Whom else can I communicate with at such a time? Others here in this large gallery are doing the same. Still others are praying. Hesitant to do it openly in front of the rest, they are off to one side, sitting there without talking or moving. But you see their lips, and understand. One is reading the psalms of David. If anyone decides to speak, he moves close to his auditor and talks in near-whispers as though imparting secrets, while the other watches his lips. They are like two deaf-mutes. Everyone's face is sallow: as yellow as a fisherman's slicker. Now that night has fallen, the enemy have begun to batter us with their heavy pieces. Two of these always provoke especial fear among the men, who can recognize them from the distinctive sound that their shells make. It is said that they fire from very far away, from the rear of the enemy line, and are so enormous that they move on railroad tracks. They are called "Adam" and "Eve";

I don't know why. According to our captain, they are naval cannons removed from large battleships. Every time one of their shells explodes near our roof, the entire gallery is jolted, timbers and all; the beams creak; soil and small rocks fall through the cracks. At such moments the men stop writing, whispering, praying. Raising their heads, they look anxiously at the ceiling, then at each other, then resume what they were doing. The one reading the psalms crosses himself each time.

Since yesterday we have all been outfitted like store-window mannequins—everything brand new, from our boots right up to the blue bandanna around our necks. This apparently happens prior to every large operation in order to prevent wounds from becoming infected because of dirty clothes coming in contact with an open gash or tatters being swept into the guts along with a shell-fragment. It is extremely irritating to contemplate such things, yet I am delighted to feel fresh, clean underwear and linen next to my skin. This enlivens even our morale, especially mine, since I have always felt that the tiniest blemish on my clothes projects itself inward onto my soul. The men, however, have treated the matter with their customary sarcasm. The term they use for the new outfit is a gloomy one: "the shroud." Even the quartermaster-sergeant in charge of distribution found himself obliged to employ this same appellation:

"Come here, you. Check to see if anything is missing. Have you got your entire shroud?"

I should add that we received communion before the shrouding. Balafaras, when all is said and done, is a religious type. The division chaplain has been attending to this business for quite a few days now. "The servant of Christ . . . partakes of the body and blood . . ." Just to see his kisser makes me want to puke. When he came to us he recited the prayers mechanically, chatted simultaneously with the captain from time to time, and shoved in the spoon. What kind of God is this that accepts Priest Theodoros as His mediator enabling Him to commune with our souls, which are like frightened angels flapping their wings?

Truly, it seems that everyone here has set himself the identical task: to reconcile us to the fact that we are about to die. The colonel invited his officers to dinner and they called it the Last Supper. This may sound Spartan, but to me it smells a lot like second-rate histrionics. One of the reservist officers, a journalist in civilian life, took to his typewriter and distributed the following announcement:

STUPENDOUS MASKED BALL
Invitation

Madame Homeland, well-known in Balkan social circles and much esteemed by all, will be hostess at a garden party tomorrow to be given on Hill 908 at 2:16 in the morning. A *bal masqué* will take place. Muster *en garçons*. Ladies not admitted, except Red Cross nurses, who will be received . . . at the conclusion of the festivities.

Music: international jazz; one thousand fifty instruments.

Dress: campaign uniforms never worn before. Vizards available at the Health-and-Sanitation Warehouse.

Gourmet buffet: Nightingales and big boys will be served. Liqueurs: *Liquids enflammés.* Refreshing carbonated beverages: *Gaz asphyxiants* and *gaz lacrymogènes.* Fish: torpedoes and anything else caught by the barbed wire net. Silverware: trench knives; forks courtesy of the German Flying Corps. Pure silk napkins cut from the parachutes of illuminating rockets.

Special attractions: Majestic pyrotechnic display, flares of all colors and to suit every taste. Most unusual cotillions, marvelously picturesque. Aerial acrobatic exercises. Among the numbers: the man who walks without a head; the man who runs without legs; the man who is vaporized; the man who eats flames and swallows swords.

Distributed as souvenirs will be bonbonnières model F-1, as well as some with silverplated almonds (trademark: "time-fuse").

The final event: a *lanciers* (translation: bayonet-bearers) danced with very original steps. Equally original will be the appearance of the dancers. After the festivities are concluded, a special mopping-up squad, the liquidators, will undertake to make things tidy, removing all leftovers.

Entrance: free, obligatory. For those invited but failing to honor the festivities with their presence, "death and cashiering." For all the rest, only the first.

The initial toast will be offered by Priest Theodoros, who will elevate the Host.

Come, one and all.

Fun! Fun! Fun!

This parody made the rounds, passing from hand to hand. Everyone who read it—and there were many—found it most entertaining. And everyone laughed. But with a strange kind of laugh. This must have been the "sardonic laughter" of the ancient Greeks, something that our headmaster at school, Anagnostou, tried so very hard to make us understand.

* * *

Meanwhile, the hands on all our watches have been advancing. They have marched over the minutes with their tiny steps; the minutes have become hours; sooner or later—sometime tonight—they will indicate the great instant: 2:16. For how many of us will this be the fated hour? For how many of the enemy? No one knows. Nor do the loved ones—mothers, children, wives, sisters, fiancées—know that death lies in wait tonight outside of thousands of homes. These homes are peaceful, with hearth-fires burning in the grate and everyone asleep, or waiting for the letter carrier to deliver a blue postcard from the front, one of those with the evzone and the short imprinted message that brings relief for a few days and enables one's legs to stretch out comfortably beneath the counterpane: "Postal Zone 999. I am fine. With best wishes. . ." Meanwhile, none of these homes suspects that Death is prowling outside the door holding his scythe and waiting. As soon as the fated hour is struck—sixteen minutes past two o'clock by the watch at headquarters—he will lift his black hand and then the knockers will be heard banging on doors in the depths of night, thousands of knockers on thousands of closed doors. Knock-knock! This time it will not be the rural postman delivering the blue birds of Postal Zone 999.

They speak of a mysterious prescience granted to those about to die. I haven't experienced anything of the sort. I have never considered myself one of warfare's predestined victims. Even when I emerged from the battles of 1912–1913, even then I never felt surprised to be alive. I simply cannot believe that it is possible for me to cease (forever! forever!) to write, swim, sing, run, love, suffer, and hate. Even in my blackest hours there are times when I feel like shrieking out loud, so intense is the wave of joy that covers me and sweeps me along, lifting me to life's crest.

To the left, beyond our barbed-wire entanglements and across from the very end of the trench which our company occupies, is a very large and shallow grave. Frenchmen, Bulgarians and Germans—indiscriminately—are given perfunctory burial there. Every two or three days we send out a working party, after it gets good and dark, to cover the corpses with soil, but every morning the Bulgarian artillery fires, disinters them, and the place stinks. The wind, when it blows from that quarter, comes to us like poison, penetrates even to the stomach, and causes the men to vomit. It takes only the first few shells to make half-disintegrated hands protrude from the soil, hands as wizened as the dead branches of a fig tree. They spread their fingers toward heaven in an obscene gesture of derision, or brandish their black fists against our sentries. A certain head keeps protruding as well. It has no hair on half the skull, and its rotted eyes distend downward on the cheeks as though they had wept not tears but their own eyeballs. Then there's that young German, a mere boy—most likely he was a student still in the gymnasium. He continues to wear his helmet with the chin-strap tightly buckled. This fellow sticks out his head and stares at our trench with motionless concentration. The men in the working party say that he is still extremely handsome even in his present discouraging state. . . . There is also a leg shod in a boot. Completely unmanageable. No matter how deeply the men bury it, it refuses to stay entirely covered. If a shell falls anywhere nearby, that leg with its boot gives a kick and sticks out again right up to the knee. Twice already, our patrols have hung pieces of paper on the barbed wire in order to inform the Bulgarians not to fire there. But they've continued just as before. Well, despite all the times I've gone to the sentry-post and observed this spectacle, I have never brought myself to admit that my own leg or hand might some day be found in that sorry state. I think that those who are condemned—"predestined"—to die bear some kind of secret stamp, like the red cross marked on the foreheads of paschal lambs. I've been turning to observe the companions all around me as they move or sit still; I want to discover which faces carry this hidden paschal stamp. Every so often I find it on various men, or so I think, and then I go up to these unfortunates, give them some insignificant little thing —a cigarette or a piece of chocolate—as a token gift, and try to be tender with them, especially if I ever happened to exchange harsh words with them in the past.

331

Quite a few, tonight, are drafting letters of "eternal farewell." Most of these men probably don't believe a word of what they're writing. Nevertheless, several have already handed over sundry rings and family mementos to the division paymaster for safekeeping. Among those praying is a fellow from Ayiassos who's been a seminarian at the Rizarios School. He has already consumed all the reserve rations in his pack in order to make room for a bulky Old Testament bound in leather. Now he's taken to praying out loud, in a manner that I find positively exasperating. You'd think he was talking on the telephone with God, the latter holding the receiver somewhere and listening attentively to his gab. I've never been able to understand why words seem to be so obligatory when one is confronting the Lord. This seminarian has a pair of monstrous lips, and teeth as big as pickaxes. Gighandis once said of him: "Strange, to have the biggest lips in the world, yet not big enough to cover your teeth!" Every time he interrupts his prayer for a moment, he turns like the Righteous Pharisee and looks all around him. I imagine that these are the moments when he listens to God replying over the telephone. His lips meet for an instant in a well intentioned effort to join over the teeth. But then, unfortunately, they part again. There is "a great gulf fixed" between them.

I have never prayed in the critical moments of my life, having never felt the need. I find soliloquies distasteful, especially in tragedies.

56

Waiting for a Quarter Past Two - II

I've been listening to two comrades who are sitting close to one another and conversing in subdued tones. They are near me; every now and then my ear catches a few words. One of them is a fisherman. He speaks with long pauses, rubbing his palm against his forehead. The subject is his boat:

"I hauled her under cover, into the shack. Sotiris said I should leave her for him and he'd operate her on a partnership basis, but I refused. He's a good fellow, Sotiris, and I like him—but not the type you can rely on. Too much of a scatterbrain. And a bit of a smuggler as well. Last year they caught him fishing in Turkish waters. He lost his nets and his boat."

The other listens, nodding his head and smoking.

"Heh. . ."

"Yes indeed, I really love my 'Pipina,' I really do. What a strong hull! From the Plomarion yards. By any chance do you know Zisis the ship-wright there? No? Well, he made my 'Pipina' with his own hands. A good clean job; work of a master craftsman. He's old now but not giving up, not him. The craft has been going to the dogs lately . . ."

"That's right," says the other; "it's been going to the dogs."

"The 'Pipina' is yellow, sulfur-yellow. With a cherry-red band beneath her gunwale. Keel and hull are red as fire."

"Heh . . ."

"She might warp, being out of the water for such a long time. Do you think so?" . . .

He is worried that his boat might warp! Here he squats in the anti-bombardment shelter talking softly amid the din of cannon fire and looking up to calculate the strength of the gallery's timbered ribs every time "Adam" or "Eve" is heard. The minute-hand advances constantly, moves closer and closer to a quarter past two, and this man talks about his boat back home in Mytilene, worried that she might warp!

Next comes the friend's turn. He continues to sigh frequently:

"Heh . . ."

"No cigarettes, do you hear!" commands the sergeant-major in a huff.

The friend moistens his fingers with saliva, extinguishes his cigarette, and places the butt carefully in his cap.

"Heh . . . He's our oldest. I left him on his second birthday, on the very day. What a little scamp he is! One day his mother hears him crying. She'd given him a cup of milk and some rusks to soak in it. 'What're you crying about?' she asks him; 'Give me more milk,' says Tatos. 'More milk? When I just now filled your cup? Have you drunk all of it already?' '*I* didn't drink it,' whimpers Tatos, the rusk did!' Heh . . . You see what a little rascal he is?"

A whistling sound reaches us from a distance and slowly slashes the air as though cleaving through water. We all recognize it as "Adam" again. Conversation ceases; everyone raises his eyes. The whistling comes closer, flies over our line . . . , and soon we hear the detonation far in the rear. Then everyone takes a deep breath and resumes what he was doing.

I am near you now; I've been near you all these many hours, without interruption. I've been on our island. It is summertime there (oh, it is always summertime on Lesvos). It is a summer night with a full moon, and I am walking back to my house. The whole city is asleep: roads, buildings, trees in the public gardens, boats in the harbor, waves on the seashore. My steps awaken slumbering echoes in the deserted lanes. In their sleep, the locked buildings hear me as I pass. Once, on such a night, I encountered a drunkard singing at the top of his lungs:

> *I cocked my fez askew*
> *And ran to my love . . .*

"He's singing it for me, the old reprobate," I said to myself. I went up to him—he was beneath a street-lamp—and greeted him cordially: "Good evening, friend."

Inclining his head to one side and squinting his eyes together, he tried his best to see me. I lit a cigarette for myself as a pretext for offering one to him as well. This I did. He took it and groped to find his mouth.

"Well, what do you know!" he stammered. "First time in history! . . . Yes, the mayor finally managed . . . to turn on the street lights . . . like a decent fellow. Now the streets are bright and a man can see where he's stepping."

"It's not the street lights," I remonstrated; "it's the full moon."

"Fiddlesticks! Are you blind, my boy? It's the street lights, the street lights."

His voice was full of protest; he was visibly offended.

"Yes, you're right ; it's the street lights. What came over the mayor?"

"Are you joking?" He laughed with satisfaction.

I left him. Far in the distance I could still hear his song:

> *I cocked my fez askew*
> *And ran to my love . . .*

And now I can hear it again, just as I can hear my footsteps in the deserted city. My heart beats with such joy that I feel like singing, and I repeat the drunkard's verses—but to myself, silently, because I do not wish to provoke the police. "Singing and musical instruments are prohibited on public thoroughfares after 11 p.m." It is so wonderfully easy to be law-abiding when you are happy. So I sing at full voice, but only in my mind. I encounter the night-patrolman, pass him by, and smile to myself as I notice him remain where he is, completely unaware that I am transgressing the law . . . inwardly.

Here is Madame Therapeia's house. The old crone! She thinks she can hide the coffee-colored blotches all over her skin by plastering them with powder. Her husband Pandelis is terrified of her, she's so sly and conniving. As for him, he's a lazy, sluggish type, a genius at failure. And not too bright either. He has an alembic, and he drives himself batty from sun-up to sun-down boiling fragrant herbs in the hope of producing "perfume."

All he produces, of course, is a kind of juice the color of mud. When Madame Therapeia berates him he attempts to justify himself:

"I'm only trying to earn a living, Therapeia, my dear," he says cringingly, almost with whimpers, and using puristic forms because Madame is a schoolteacher's daughter and favors *katharévousa.*

Their house is an old one. Above the front door are two circular fanlights with frosted panes. As I said, it's getting well on in years: a house with bifocal spectacles on its nose.

Next door we have Trachanas's ancient shambles, a hunched-over ruin that has been given two crutch-like props to lean on, so it won't fall down. The public tap outside drips continually, the water gurgling in its stone trough. Trachanas's huge old barn of a house, poor thing, seems to be suffering from senile incontinence. . . .

Here is your door. Four stone steps; bronze knocker. You are asleep, I'm sure. I daren't knock. I don't want you to learn about this sleepless night whose draperies are being slashed by invisible polished objects. I don't want you to hear its agonized screams or to know anything whatsoever about the division's minute hands as they advance toward sixteen past the hour of two. I shall simply bid you "Good night." Good night to your chestnut eyes, your hair, your smile. Good night to your dear little hands that are reposed and asleep. . . . I continue on my way, leave the streets with their houses, cross the breakwater, and promenade along the shore. The moon has strewn a golden carpet upon the waters, a carpet that extends all the way from our island to the Anatolian mainland. Who will walk this golden path? The Fykiotrypa Rock looks out to the open sea, the moonlight silvering its hump. It still resembles a colossal frog, one of those monsters engendered by nature in primeval times, when the earth was one huge swamp. It emerged then from the slime, belched an extraordinary croak at the full moon, and was immediately turned to stone. Now its back supports the lighthouse and the keeper's small white cottage. If this monster ever decided to come back to life again, it would have to shift its shoulders only the tiniest bit and the lighthouse-keeper, his wife Asimenia, and their three children would find themselves suddenly dumped into the sea. . . . Towering nearby is the shadowy bulk of the old fortress, drawn with black crayon upon the midnight-blue silk of the sky, and beautifully festooned with battlements. Tonight a fishing boat is "herding" at its foot. It disappears into the shadows for an instant, then emerges again into the moonlight. The fishermen beat their bare heels rhythmically against the boards of the prow and at the same time slap the water with their oars. This frightens the fish and "herds" them into the nets. Dou-doup! Dou-doup! The thumps reverberate against the footings of the fortress's towers (the stones are covered with seaweedy hair), then expire and drop into the water—like mats thrown down upon the sea's surface. Picking up a stone, I fling it with all my might, far away, down into the water. There is a pause; then the sea answers me from far below: Klouap!

Zmbrannn!

An explosion. Very near. Too near for the shell's whistle to have been heard in advance. People are shouting at the ingress to the gallery:

"Out of the way! Make room! We're bringing him down."

The men abandon whatever they have been doing and everyone turns to look in that direction. The duty-sergeant, switching on his flashlight, shines it toward the staircase that leads into our shelter. Two men are descending. They had been on duty above. With their rifles slung across their chests they are carrying a casualty, one by the feet and the other beneath the armpits. First to come into the light are the legs of the soldier who is lifting in front; next come the wounded man's boots. He is one of our sentries. They take off his helmet, unbuckle his belt, open the trench-coat. He is lying on a stretcher now, next to the table with the acetylene lamp. His trousers and the front of his tunic are soaked in blood, his puttees dripping in it. As they begin to remove his waist-sash he lets out a shriek whose pitch gradually descends:

"Eeeeeeaaaa!"

I bend over him—it is Jacob. He emits rapid gasps as the medical aide, prepares cotton, gauze-pads, dressings. They lower his trousers, a difficult job. The projectile was large. It shredded the clothes and drew the tatters with it into the wound, mingling them with his intestines. It is a deep, black wound. The guts are hanging out, clotted fluids raining onto his testicles. While they are trying to reach the doctor on the telephone because the aide doesn't know what to do, Jacob suddenly spreads his eyes extraordinarily wide and bites his lower lip, making an ugly grimace. Then, little by little, the spasm relaxes. The eyelashes, which are extremely blond, remain motionless around the coffee-colored, beadlike irises, and the right hand, which has been clasped around the stretcher pole, releases its grip and hangs limply over the side, touching the floor.

His ugly face is lime-white beneath the harsh illumination. Now that he has lost his hectic flush, he bears no resemblance whatsoever to the living Jacob.

The quartermaster-sergeant empties his pockets of their belongings (before the stretcher-bearers have a chance to "de-louse" him). In this way, everything will be sent home to his people in due course. There is a tiny gold watch on his wrist. This, when removed, continues to tick unconcernedly in the captain's palm. It gives rise to a peculiar sensation, this watch that persists in telling time so diligently and impassively even now, when Jacob is outside of time. For whom, then, is it ticking? . . . A large soldier pushes his way through the crowd, goes to the remains, and stands there, gazing down at them. He is portly as well as tall, with cowled eyes and hairy skin. He keeps wiping his dripping nose with the back of his hand, from which one finger is missing. It is Giorghalas. His eyes are red, his fierce mustache quivering. Suddenly he collapses in a heap next to the stretcher, sobbing. The tears trickle through his beard as he rests his hands on the dead man's chest and groans:

"Forgive me, forgive me. My friend! My comrade! And may God forgive you. . . . Forgive me, forgive me. My friend! My comrade!"

It is an extremely ridiculous spectacle (yet my eyes are filling with tears). The men look at each other, without comment.

Approaching, the captain reaches down in order to pull him to his feet. But when he catches the first whiff of him he draws back in disgust.

"Who the hell gave him something to drink again today?" he demands of the duty-sergeant. "The dirty bastard, he's pickled!"

57

Waiting for a Quarter
Past Two - III

I remember your little cousin Angelica, who used to spend evenings with us as "chaperon." (In other words, she was sent to keep watch over us and prevent us from being alone with each other—seeing that we were engaged!) But Angelica was the most accommodating of chaperons. How wonderfully adept she was at not seeing! At such times her sparkling eyes became even more beautiful than before. . . . I want now to induce her to repeat that story about your singing teacher, the blind one who always flirted with you, settling himself in comfortably for the entire afternoon and showing no sign of leaving although he was paid only for a one-hour lesson. Our dear Lilitta would scatter some salt behind the door, even deposit some in his hat, but all to no avail. The exorcism had no power whatsoever over Monsieur Tsamis. Angelica is going to recount the story now. First she counterfeits his blindness by squinting her eyes and raising her brows; then she recites in a cloying tone:

"Mademoiselle, I cannot see you, but this does not bother me in the least. Your voice, when you speak, enables me to apprehend you in all your beauty." (Sigh.) "Oh, Mademoiselle, if only I could accompany you for the rest of your life!"

This is the high point of Angelica's recitation, and she pauses (in vain) to hear me convulsed with laughter. Failure! She opens her perplexed eyes, lowers her brows, and catches us red-handed as we gaze at each other, smiling and blissful, outside of space and time. Only then does she realize that she had been performing her parody the whole time without an audience. Losing her temper, she refuses to repeat for us the imitation of Monsieur Tsamis when he found Lilitta's salt in his hat.

"Just imagine, Mademoiselle, salt in my hat. Hee-hee-hee. Isn't that *marvelous*?"

Everything was *marvelous* for poor Monsieur Tsamis, except when it was *très chic*—a term used above all for things pertaining to himself: his romantic compositions for guitar, his suit, his shirt.

"Look at my necktie, Mademoiselle. Isn't it *marvelous*?"

He undid it and then tied it again unaided to show that vision for him was superfluous. He came close to arousing genuine sympathy when he did this, and especially when, with his astonishing sense of touch, he managed to make the little green flower come out precisely at the knot.

"Look, if you please. This little flower is *très chic*, is it not?"

And he would smile complacently, eyebrows raised and chin protruding, as is common among the blind.

One night when you and some others took him rowing, he propped his guitar between his knees, lifted his poor eyes toward the sky, and asked suddenly:

"This little moon tonight is *très chic*, is it not, Mademoiselle? Tell me, don't you agree? It is *très chic*, no?"

The only trouble was that the moon happened to be located precisely in the opposite part of the sky. . . .

So Angelica, having lost her temper, refuses to tell us any more anecdotes. She just tosses her head sulkily in that way she has of making her "unmanageable" hair fall back over her shoulders, and declares to you in severe tones:

"I'm not the dupe; you are. But it's my own fault if I've stayed here talking with you all this time as though I didn't know that when the two of you are together, everyone else around you might just as well be part of the upholstery. On the other hand, if you only realized how hilarious it is to watch two lovers in the pose of Eros and Psyche . . ."

"Oh, Angelica, dear cousin Angelica, stop trying so hard to be a stinker. Remember that one day you'll fall in love, too."

"That's another matter," Angelica says curtly, her eyes filling with dreams. Then, turning to me: "It's your turn now. Come tell us a story until you . . . leave. Whatever you want, as long as it's not nauseatingly sentimental. Tell us something strange, but true. I'm just wild about strange tales."

Bless us! Angelica wants a strange tale. Her eyes are opened wide with anticipation; they look like speckled artificial flowers. What am I supposed to tell her now? Should I recall this war and recount a dream I had one day (we sleep during daytime only, in the war), a dream whose dark and obscure symbolism weighs on me at this very moment, as I write?

Well, listen to it, then, cousin Angelica.

It was the eve of the assault. I was up all night in charge of a working party consisting of fifteen soldiers. Our assignment was to activate the hand grenades. This job is done as follows: The F-1's come in packing cases, a separate box for the iron "pomegranate" whose markings make it resemble a turtle's carapace, and a separate box for the percussion-caps. The iron pomegranate has to be filled with a damp, yellowish explosive that is something like the dry rot that falls from worm-eaten beams. This is mixed with castor oil. We call it "cheddite." It is unbelievably strong, but it cannot be detonated with a lighted match, or with pounding. It ignites only when a percussion cap containing fulminate of mercury explodes in its proximity.

Now for how the grenades are activated: With your left hand you grab a "pomegranate" filled with cheddite. Through the opening you plunge a long narrow stick resembling a penholder, to make a little nest for the percussion cap. The fulminate, you see, cannot encounter the slightest resistance or be constricted in any way, because the tiniest amount of friction sets it off. Next, you remove the little stick, release it, and with the same hand, the right one, grasp the cap. This you screw down until it sits in firmly. That's the long and short of it. It's a simple enough business, but one that requires the most scholastic attentiveness—no daydreaming on the job! Well, this was the task I supervised that entire night When we finished, dawn had already come; I lay down and dropped into a sleep so deep, it was like a fainting-spell.

Then I had a dream. I found myself in the other sector, on the hill we held opposite the Peristeri ridges. The sun was out, the weather gorgeous, and we were sunbathing on a titanic boulder that stuck its thick, mottled nape out over the brink of the gorge. We called it the Fykiotrypa Rock because it closely resembled the one back home. There were about a dozen of us—N.C.O.s and men—sitting on top of it as though the war did not exist and no danger were involved in being there in open view, exposed in broad daylight—noontime—directly across from the Dove. Sweet perfumes came from the cedars; the distant forests murmured like the sea; the Dragor raced frothily at the bottom of the ravine, beneath our hanging legs. It was from here that the white mist began to rise every morning. What appeared at first was a cloudlet of blanched cotton, a lamb (you might say) that had tumbled down the slopes of Peristeri in order to drink in the stream. Gradually that cloud grew more and more bloated, distending its alabaster belly until it filled the gorge. It transformed itself then into a spotlessly white flood tide rising constantly and covering hills and trees with its milky froth until the Dove, encircled, turned into a green island floating on a sea of foam—a sea whose surface glittered from the frolicking sunlight striking it.

This is the spectacle that re-appeared to me in my dream. I saw the haze beneath our feet rising as usual from the foot of the Fykiotrypa so thickly that you felt you could lie down on top of it and roll upon its outspread surface—the only difference being that this time the pure-white flood inundated the uppermost slopes as well, cowled the peaks, and extended ever-outward until it reached the furthest horizons, leaving our boulder completely isolated in its midst and us divorced from the rest of the world, like shipwrecked sailors on a desert isle. Then the sun began to decline toward the west. Brilliant yellow, like a golden baking-pan, it declined until it sank, swallowed by the pearly froth. Nothing remained in the air but a pale and diffuse glow that phosphoresced so intensely that you had to strain your eyes to see through its glare.

Suddenly we felt ourselves wrapped in absolute silence. It was something we became aware of abruptly, as though experiencing a sudden shudder. This remained the most significant event for quite some time. Then, ever so slowly, an infinitesimal something no larger than a trifling semicolon began to pulsate in the atmosphere, growing bigger and more vigorous as it advanced. What could it be? In any case, it had become an agony for us. It was like an expectation that spilled out over everything, came from everywhere, and each moment grew more unbearable. "It's something," I said to myself, "something that will give rise to something else that never happened before. It is a womb from which something will be born—and this accounts for all the anguish that is multiplying everywhere around me." These thoughts were accompanied by a revolting vexation, a constriction attacking my lungs, and I turned (always in the dream) to question my comrades with my eyes. I turned to the right, turned to the left. No one. The rock seemed to have opened up and swallowed them. A sudden fear pinched my heart. Here I was, alone and desolate, deserted and unprotected.

"They went away and abandoned me!" I gasped with indignation. But I voiced this complaint inwardly, to myself, because every sound, even a whisper, was intolerable there.

The way they had all vanished from my side—without the slightest murmur being audible—was the most terrifying part of all, and I dared not contemplate how it happened. Afterwards, the anxious expectations of what *would come to pass* grew denser and still more vigorous in the air; the *hour of birth* seemed everywhere present. It seemed impossible that such forces could move and circulate in a silence so absolute. Nevertheless, a deep entreaty had begun to issue from all directions: "Oh, whatever it is, let it happen and be done with. We cannot stand this any longer." I even raised my eyes aloft to the (completely starless) heavens in search of a little hope. It was then that I noticed an ash-colored cloud at the zenith. This cloud was of medium size and did not display any remarkable characteristics; nevertheless I had an instantaneous feeling that all my attention should be riveted there. There! In addition, some all-inclusive sense was informing me that the whole of creation had already concentrated its attention there, upon that cloud. The oceans, forests, and volcanoes, the atmosphere swaddling the earth, the grubs that had suddenly halted their activity beneath the bark of trees, the birds—all, all—felt that now, there, in that little ash-colored cloud, lay every possible hope of their expectation being fulfilled.

Suddenly my heart and pulse began to thump rapidly. Echoing my own, the all-embracing pulse of life in its entirety commenced to beat hurriedly and impatiently. Something had germinated up there: something had suspended itself from the sky's umbilicus—a living, mobile thing that was descending quickly and relentlessly, with serpentine movements. It did not take long for me to realize that it was a colossal octopus that kept its oval body firmly positioned somewhere aloft while with unimaginable velocity it lowered its constantly elongating tentacles toward the earth. These monstrous extremities writhed in all directions, swollen with a supernatural force that kept visibly entering the slimy red-black skin and filling it to the breaking point. They groped in the void like blind dragons, these tentacles with their opening and closing suckers; they nimbly rose and descended in the air, coiled and uncoiled in their search for a place where, catching hold of something, they might pacify their wrath. I struggled to run, flee, escape the terrifying sight, but my body was rooted to the boulder as though turned to lead. I strained to cry out, to utter a shout and thereby drain myself of the terror that was filling me. Although I opened my mouth, no voice emerged—or perhaps it emerged and I did not hear it. Thus I remained there trembling from dread while the tentacles descended hastily and relentlessly, making far-reaching , violent gesticulations in the silent air.

In an instant they reached the mist's upper surface. As they touched the snow-white sea with their tips, each in turn reacted convulsively, as though this contact were activating a subcutaneous spasm at that spot and sending it along the tentacles' entire length. Then, all together, they suddenly dived into the milky mist with gleeful impetuosity and were ingested. Now they extended the entire distance from heaven to earth; it was evident as well that they were laboring stealthily on the bed of this misty sea, beneath the surface. They must have been uprooting trees, lashing the hills, dislodging boulders, sweeping away the houses of deserted Magarova, the town between the lines. "What terrible things must be happening down there," I kept thinking, "yet not a sound of the disaster—nothing—can be heard." But then the realization flashed through my mind that lying beneath this thick sea of mist were the endless hedgerows of barbed wire, the dugouts, tents, bivouacs, and rest camps, the trench-lines that divided people from people . . . , and millions of soldiers—Greeks, Frenchmen, Turks, Germans, Bulgarians, Russians, enslaved colonials—: all beneath this misty lid, this mass of soundproof cotton. Suddenly the nature of this silence, the immaculate guilt-ridden muteness that covered the *activity* taking place beneath the surface, became clear to me. The tentacles were bundling together thousands of men like sheafs of grain—thousands of men, trees, entanglements, cannons, innocent animals—and were crushing them in their tight embrace, reducing them to a pulpish, muddy dough, and then breaking up the resulting clods and scattering them into the ravines. With insatiable fury the tentacles coiled and uncoiled, tightened and went lax, flayed and lashed, sucked and shattered. Then I flung my tormented attention deep into the silence's immaculate guilt, down to the bottom like a fish-line, and struggled to hear. A crevice seemed to open in the frothy surface, a fissure seemed to appear in the thick cream. I heard hollow, suffocated voices ascending from that sea floor and coming toward me. They rose from far far away and were muffled, passing as they did through cotton, through dream. There were violent drubbings accompanied by entreaties: a comprehensive wail from countless pain-rent shrieks; there were curses, raucous moans, snorts and bellows from a mass of beasts and men incapable of comprehending why they were being killed. All these doomed voices twined together into a prolonged howl that congealed the blood in one's veins. Sometimes they subsided momentarily from exhaustion, but then regained their former pitch, harsher than ever; sometimes they rose up to me in unison with an incantatory rhythm, as though all the doomed had coalesced their shrieks and gasps upon the same syllables of the dirge. Distinguishable among the voices were the cries of women, the whimpering entreaties of small children.

Angelica, cousin Angelica, I see that your sparkling eyes are damp. Well, you wanted something strange, didn't you? Strange, and true?

* * *

I'll have to stop now for today because my captain is calling me by name, telling me to arm myself and take up my position. The minute-hands are advancing unremittingly upon thousands of watches, and thousands of eyes are focused upon their merciless progress. In half an hour they will point to sixteen minutes past two o'clock, whereupon thirty thousand soldiers will leap out of the trenches, completely vulnerable beneath the frenzied machines that will be strewing their path with fire and steel. A cord in the soul is stretching, stretching. . . . Listen, then, while there is still time. Not too long ago a young private entered my dugout to deliver a telephone message. The sergeant-major told him to wait. In the meantime, until he received his next command, he struck up a conversation with a fellow villager whom he found in the dugout, telling him that at dawn, while he was on sentry-duty, a small bird had alighted on the barbed wire and begun to sing. The song did not last very long. The bird chirped just three or four times, then flew away.

"It was a 'drover'; I recognized it by its call," said the young private, laughing with pleasure. "Imagine!"

He imitated the bird's whistle and laughed again. The one listening to him, an older man with wrinkled brow, glanced at him and nodded his head gravely:

"Ehh, must have been a drover."

This episode made an equally profound impression on me. The story of the "drover" that alighted on the barbed wire and sang there keeps recurring in my thoughts, because I sense how touching it is and how universally significant. Strange how all things have taken on a new look of late, as though all were revealing their true features to us for the first time and inviting us to recognize them. Rifles, my comrades' faces, the barbed wire, the trench, various sounds—all have become so clear now, so distinct and palpable. It's almost as though a foreign substance had coated their surfaces, rendering all lines and colors more elemental. Yet at the same time everything has acquired symbolic extension to the most improbable degree. Lips form peculiar smiles that evoke no corresponding smile in the eyes. The latter are peculiar, too, because some foreign person seems to be standing behind their lenses and attentively spying on you. An essential significance lies hidden within every object, shape and gesture. Words no longer expose their meanings nakedly; they are hard almonds, sealed and intact, and must be cracked open if a person wishes to find their kernel—or break his teeth (I'm not sure which).

I am terrified. I keep this terror hidden, however, in the depths of my heart. On the other hand, I know full well that my actions—whether for good or ill—will not be inferior to the actions of my comrades. I shall fight with my heart in my mouth. I shall lash out blindly and be opposed by men who lash out just as blindly. Once more I shall become the infantry sergeant with his share of responsibility and his national traditions to uphold. We clasp our cigarettes now between trembling fingers. Yet in spite of this, one thing is certain: we shall come out on top. Tomorrow morning I shall be continuing this manuscript inside *their* stronghold, not ours. Of this I am certain, and so are all the others—I see it in their eyes. It's something we Greeks call *filótimo*—"self-respect"—a force whose enormous strength has never been sufficiently appreciated. Like the philosopher's stone, *filótimo* transubstantiates baser metals into gold. It alchemizes souls, spurring men to perform signs and wonders wholly and simply to avoid appearing more mangy than the company barber or that motley crew of foreigners who are fighting at our side and observing us through their binoculars. In my own case, this means that I still have not become sufficiently courageous vis-à-vis my true self, which stands next to me in the ranks: a cunning, vigilant, and mocking enemy (a real *ronió* as we say in Lesvos). But I find this hardly surprising.

Well, until tomorrow, then, my dearest. Until tomorrow, goodbye.

(The manuscripts of Sergeant Kostoulas end here.)

ΤΕΛΟΣ ΚΑΙ ΤΩ͵ ΘΕΩ͵ Η ΔΟΞΑ

Maps

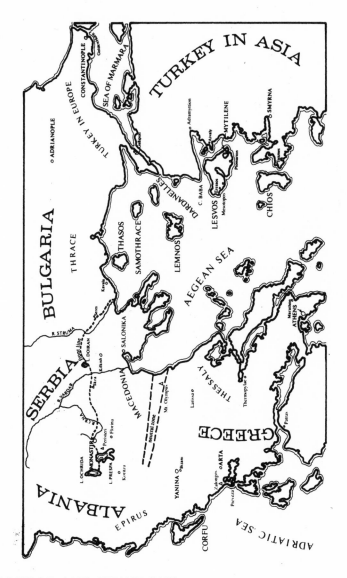

GREECE AND ENVIRONS

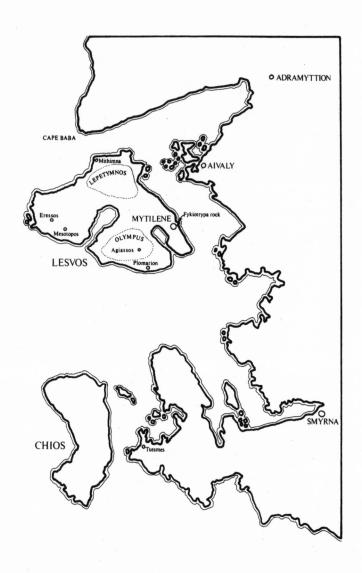

MYTILENE (detail)

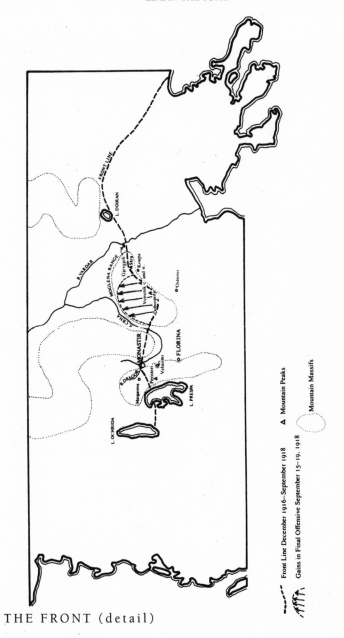

THE FRONT (detail)